"Every faggot's got the sweetness. It's just a matter of time."

–from *Massage* by Henry Flesh

"A major new literary voice from Manhattan."

–*Christopher Street*

"Henry Flesh writes like his own name: sensuously and sensitively, with an eye and a voice attuned to matters both demonic and angelic. *Massage*, also like its name, is a novel that will caress and stimulate."

–Janice Eidus
author of *The Celibacy Club*

"Written with impressive authority, *Massage*, Henry Flesh's debut novel, is the work of a perceptive and mature artist."

–Jaime Manrique
author of *Twilight at the Equator* and
Latin Moon in Manhattan

It is the mid-'90s, a time when the "sweetness" of AIDS lies across Manhattan like "a nebulous gloom…a deep distress." Randy, an erotic masseur, becomes involved with a client, Graham Mason, a famous writer dying of AIDS. Their sadomasochistic trysts soon become much more than business: Graham searches for his long-dead lover in the angelic face of Randy, and for the lost pleasure-world of the '60s and '70s–while Randy discovers in Graham the powerful image of the Midwestern businessman who seduced him as a child.

HENRY FLESH

Massage

AKASHIC BOOKS

NEW YORK

Published by Akashic Books
© 1999 Henry Flesh

Cover photo by Sheila Rock
Author photo by Mick Rock
Design and layout by Fritz Michaud

ISBN: 1-888451-06-8
Library of Congress Catalog Card Number: 98-74034

AKASHIC BOOKS
PO BOX 1456
NEW YORK, NY 10009
email: Akashic7@aol.com

In Memory of
Fred Einhorn

October 5, 1956-July 26, 1993

ACKNOWLEDGMENTS

I would like to express my gratitude to the following at Akashic Books: my publishers, Johnny Temple and Mark Sullivan, for their unflagging support and generosity; my editor, Gabrielle Danchick, for her insights and sensitivity; Fritz Michaud, the book's designer; and Kara Gilmour and Johanna Ingalls for their editorial assistance. Also, for their invaluable help and encouragement, I would like to thank my agent, Harold Schmidt, as well as Paul Calderon, Joe Cummins, Jill DeVries, Janice Eidus, John Greer, Kevin Heisler, Kaylie Jones, Kate Christensen Lewis, Wendy Lochner, Jaime Manrique, Tim McLoughlin, Glenda Pleasants, Mick Rock, Sheila Rock, Lena Ross, Thaddeus Rutkowski, Anna Shapiro, Janyce Stefan-Cole, Liz Szabla, Steve Turtell, Kathleen Warnock, and John Wynne.

PART ONE

I

Randy's new client—Graham Mason, the novelist—lived on the top floor of a renovated brownstone in the West Village. It was a beautiful old building on Perry Street, in an area Randy knew very well. This was, in fact, his favorite part of the city, and he often walked down its tree-lined streets, imagining life in the apartments he passed.

The Village Randy loved was not the Village he saw in the tourist traps on MacDougal Street. And it didn't exist near Sheridan Square, in the noisy, crowded gay bars on Christopher. He was not even taken in by the legends surrounding the Village's past, for he suspected the Bohemia of the fifties had been as grubby and shabby as the life he now saw in his own neighborhood on the Lower East Side.

The Village Randy loved could be glimpsed in certain small cafés, where he sat quietly for hours on rainy afternoons. Classical music played softly as fashionably dressed men and women ate delicate, foreign pastries while sipping cappuccino. Their conversations were muted, their laughter subdued. Waiters drifted effortlessly between tables, stopping to chat amiably with the patrons they knew. Although the atmosphere was relaxed and the attitudes informal, these tiny places felt immense to Randy, and the words he overheard seemed important and deep. He liked to bask in this ambience, soaking in the auras of the successful artists and writers, the designers and gallery owners who inhabited this world.

Graham Mason was one of them. Randy's lover, Jake, had told Randy all about him. According to Jake, Mason was one of the more famous living writers and an icon in the gay community. Critics had called his first book, *Dinner at Dawn,* a "pivotal work of the 1960s." Since then, he had written four novels and three collections of short stories, although he'd published nothing in over a decade. Even so, Jake said, Mason was still widely read and discussed, and his reputation seemed firm.

Jake had set up this appointment; he was always the one who found work for Randy. But Mason was not typical of the clients Jake procured, the businessmen from out of town, sales reps from the Midwest and small-time executives. Most of them seemed commonplace to Randy; Graham Mason, on the other hand, was a celebrity.

Randy was a nude masseur who gave his clients a hand job at the end of the massage. He was not, however, "full service," for he never had sex with these men. Still, the release he provided seemed to satisfy them, and there were many Randy visited regularly. Some out-of-towners called him every time they came to the city.

In the past, he had seen a few minor actors and the occasional politician. And a few months before he had entertained Jackson Reeves, the choreographer of a prestigious Southern dance company. But none of them had been as important in his field as Graham Mason. The prospect now of meeting this great man was intimidating.

"Don't be an ass," Jake said as he and Randy ate dinner that evening, just before Randy's appointment with Mason. "You hadn't even heard of him until a few days ago."

"Right, I've never read his books. What'll I say?"

"Just be friendly and pleasant. I mean, you can manage *that,* can't you?" Jake took a sip of beer. "Christ, I should have told you he was a plumber from Des Moines!"

Randy glanced at him. "You're making it worse."

Jake sighed, then leaned over and took Randy's hand. "Look, you've done this a million times before. He'll melt as soon as he sees you. They always do."

Randy said nothing more. He finished his dinner and left, going west to Perry Street. When he reached Mason's brownstone, he walked around the block two times before finally mounting the steps to the front door. Then he rang Mason's buzzer.

A few seconds later, a voice came over the intercom: "Who's there?"

"Jason," Randy answered. "Jake's friend."

The door opened immediately.

Graham Mason was tall and thin, with receding brown hair, craggy skin, and bad teeth. When he greeted Randy at the door, he was wearing a navy-blue bathrobe and brown-leather slippers; both articles of clothing looked expensive. He appeared to be in his mid-forties, although it was difficult to determine his exact age. Randy sensed an authority to his presence that helped negate the less appealing aspects of his appearance; despite his physical flaws, he was almost attractive.

Graham shook Randy's hand indifferently, then stood back, gazing at him for several moments. "I thought your name was Randy," he said, sneering slightly. "At least that's what Jake said it was."

Taken aback, Randy did not know what to say. Jake rarely made this mistake.

"Do you always lie to your customers?" Graham stared at Randy, his eyes sharp and piercing.

"Sorry," Randy said uneasily. "My clients usually call me Jason."

"*I* prefer Randy." Graham cupped a hand under his chin, studying Randy once again. "Still," he said after a moment, "deceit can be charming."

The telephone rang. "Come in," Graham said, for they were still standing in the doorway. Randy walked in. The phone continued to ring. "I'll be right back." Graham left the room through a door to his right.

Alone, Randy stood in what was apparently the living room, a large, sparsely furnished space, with many books on tall shelves lined up against three walls. The fourth wall was behind a long, black-leather couch, and hanging on it was a group of paintings, several smaller ones surrounding a huge portrait of Madonna. Her hair was very blond and her lips scarlet, and she was smiling slyly, white teeth glistening, grasping in her right hand a long knife with a golden handle. She held the sharp blade to her lips, making it look as if she were about to place the tip in her mouth. Bright red letters formed a halo around her head; "Turn the Beat Around, Motherfucker!" they read.

Randy moved closer, examining the smaller paintings. There were two pieces of graffiti art and several abstract works; none held his interest. But he was struck by a black-and-white sketch of a handsome young man dressed in a turtleneck sweater and jeans. Although he knew little about art, he had taken an art-appreciation course one summer. He noticed that this drawing had been signed by David Hockney.

"Tell the cunt to piss off!" Graham screamed into the phone in the next room. "Fuck, it's 1994!"

Startled by Graham's voice, Randy moved back and stared at Madonna. He had been feeling queasy all evening, and this garish painting only heightened his discomfort. It had an unsettling quality that belied its pop veneer.

"Do you like it?" Graham asked. He had finished his telephone conversation, returned unnoticed to the living room, and was standing directly behind Randy.

Randy could only nod his head, surprised as he was by Graham's sudden proximity.

"It's by Denise Lamour," Graham explained. "Fierce little Negress. And a ferocious dyke." He looked up at Madonna. "Denise loves blondes."

Randy tried to think of something to say, hoping to hide the uneasiness he was feeling. He remembered the drawing of the young man and pointed to it. "That's a Hockney, right?"

Graham looked annoyed. "Yes," he said quickly.

"Who is it?"

Graham glared at Randy. "It's a friend," he snapped. He started to say something else, but stopped. An awkward silence lasted several moments.

"So where would you like your massage?" Randy asked at last. He was determined to take control of this situation, something he tried to do when working.

"In the bedroom, I suppose." Graham seemed to have recovered his equilibrium. He looked at Randy, then glanced at the black-leather couch. "Or maybe it would be nice to feel leather against my skin. Where do you do most of your customers?"

"On a bed. But it's up to you. You're the client."

"Let's go with the leather."

"Okay." Randy sat on the couch and untied his shoes. Graham stood a few feet from him, staring. "You can get undressed as well," Randy said.

"I want to watch you." Graham spoke softly, almost gently. But

4

his voice had an insinuating tone that was disconcerting. Randy felt as if he were already naked, stripped by this writer, this celebrity he had just met. He took off his shoes, then his socks.

"Do it slowly," Graham commanded. "And stand up."

Randy obeyed. He rose, unzipped his pants, and removed them, then stood before Graham in his underwear and shirt.

"Stop for a minute," Graham ordered.

Randy remained immobile as Graham's eyes perused his body. He felt uncomfortable, still queasy, yet also a bit excited, even aroused—sensations he rarely experienced in these situations anymore.

"Take off your shirt."

Randy did as he was told. He stood still once again, wearing only his briefs.

"Nice," Graham remarked.

Both his discomfort and his excitement deepening, Randy said nothing as Graham examined him.

A few moments later, Graham spoke: "You can take off your shorts now."

Randy again complied. When he was naked, he remained standing, waiting for Graham to undress, too. But Graham only continued to stare, gazing at Randy in a detached, rather abstract fashion. Randy felt invaded—a not entirely unpleasant feeling, he realized. He glanced at Graham, and their eyes met. For an instant Graham looked alarmed, as if he saw something in Randy he had not noticed before. But his alarm seemed to pass quickly: When he spoke again, he was calm. "I think I'm ready for my massage," he announced. He left the room and returned with a bottle of oil. "It's jasmine," he said. He set the bottle on a table next to the couch, then quickly removed his bathrobe.

Randy looked at Graham's body, which appeared even thinner now that it was unclothed. His skin was very pale, almost completely hairless, and his ribs showed clearly beneath the surface. Randy noticed that his penis was extraordinarily large; he kept his eyes fixed on it.

Graham lay face down on the couch. Randy squatted over him, straddling Graham's sides with his feet. He started with the shoulders, rubbing oil into the skin. The muscles felt very tense. Randy poured more oil onto Graham's back, massaging down toward the buttocks.

"You seem experienced," Graham observed.

"I've been doing this for a while."

"Is that *all* you do?"

Randy stopped for a moment, then continued massaging Graham's lower back. "I'm an actor," he said, ignoring the more lascivious implications in Graham's question.

"Oh, really?" Again Graham's tone was mocking. "And is Jake your agent?"

Randy stopped once more. "Why would you think that?" he asked, disconcerted.

"Well, he seems to have his fingers in a lot of pies." Graham gave an obscene lilt to these words. "And he *did* arrange this meeting."

Randy moved back and kneaded Graham's buttocks. "That's different."

"I see."

Randy's hands went down between Graham's legs, and he briefly massaged the back of his scrotum. Then he stood and began working on his calves.

"Jake's your lover, I suppose." Graham spoke as if he already knew the answer.

"That's right."

"He's a lot older than you."

"He's forty, and I'm twenty-eight."

"Yes." Graham paused. "And *he* fucks *you*."

Somewhat jarred, Randy started massaging Graham's feet.

"I'm sure you're used to people assuming that," Graham continued. "You must know your ass was made to be fucked."

Randy said nothing as he rubbed oil between Graham's toes.

"Do you and Jake ever go to clubs?"

"Sometimes, yes."

"I mean the heavy ones: leather, whips and chains, that sort of thing."

"That's not my scene."

"Oh, no?" Graham seemed amazed. "How do you know? You should go to one with Jake sometime. You could get fucked by every

6

man in the place while he watches you. I bet you both would enjoy that."

Although Randy thought he had not found this idea appealing, he started to get an erection. He let go of Graham's foot, which he had finished massaging. "Let me work on your other side," he said.

Graham turned over. His penis was also erect. Randy sat on top of him, so that their penises were touching, and rubbed oil onto Graham's chest.

"Cut the crap." Graham moved Randy's hand down to their cocks.

Randy put oil on their penises and rubbed them together. His own dick felt puny when pressed against Graham's. He looked up at the painting of Madonna; she seemed to be watching them. Then he looked down at Graham, whose eyes were closed. Behind Graham—on the table, beside the bottle of massage oil—was a photograph Randy had not seen before, a picture of a bronzed young man in a bathing suit. He was, Randy realized, the same person Hockney had drawn. Randy stared at the photograph as he jerked the two of them off. Graham moaned and came. Randy continued to masturbate, but could not come. He eventually stopped. "That was hot," he said.

"Uh-huh," Graham murmured.

Randy noticed that Graham looked tired and drawn, as if all his energy had been expended when he ejaculated. "Do you have a towel?" Randy asked.

Graham stood and, grinning faintly, replied, "Why don't you lick it up?" Then he left the room. He returned a few moments later, wiping himself with a small blue hand towel. In his other hand he carried a glass of water and a prescription pill bottle. He sat on the couch and passed the towel to Randy. "Shit," he said as he opened the bottle, "I've got to go to this thing for Dakota Montoya."

"Thing?" Randy asked, wiping his groin. The name "Dakota Montoya" sounded familiar, but he was not sure where he had heard it.

"His fucking book party!" Graham grimaced. "I'm exhausted. But I *have* to make an appearance." He removed a triangular orange pill from the bottle and washed it down with water. "Would you like one?" he asked, handing the bottle and water to Randy.

The label read "dexedrine." Randy hesitated. He finally took out a pill and swallowed it, hoping the drug would relieve some of the uneasiness he was feeling.

"All those dreary faggots and their books!" Graham exclaimed.

"Why do you have to go?"

Graham looked at him incredulously. "Don't be stupid. You do know, don't you, that I've got a book coming out in six months or so?"

Randy said nothing.

"Of course, everyone thinks *that's* a joke. They don't think I write anymore." Graham chuckled. "Actually, there's a rumor that I'm dead."

Randy found his underwear lying on the floor. He pulled them on as he said, "I've written a few stories."

Graham frowned. "How unfortunate for you." His eyes did not leave Randy's face.

Randy paused, then went on: "Maybe I can show you one sometime."

Graham continued to stare at him. He placed his right hand inside Randy's briefs and squeezed his penis. "That'll cost you," he said, smiling.

"Sure." Randy smiled, too. He finished dressing.

"I suppose I owe you something," Graham offered. Just then the telephone rang. Graham put on his robe and went to the next room to answer it.

Randy walked to a book shelf. The titles there were eclectic, arranged alphabetically by author and including everything from ancient Greek philosophy to Victorian pornography. He searched under "Mason" and found a paperback edition of *Summer Swan,* one of Graham's novels. He opened the book and began reading:

> *Your room is heavy, dense. You can feel him everywhere: in the rumpled sheets, where you left him an hour ago; in the vase of flowers, which he arranged for you this afternoon. It was warm, but now it is cool. You look around. The emptiness you witness lets you know you are alone.*

He heard Graham's voice in the next room: "Don't worry, Dakota, I'll be there!" As he slammed down the phone, he muttered to himself, "Stupid cunt!"

8

Randy quickly put the book in his back pocket, then turned to face Graham as he re-entered the room.

"Fuck that psychotic queen!" Graham said. "She wants me there *now!*" He handed Randy one hundred dollars and led him to the door. "I don't mean to rush you, but I really must get dressed."

Randy, disoriented, hesitated before saying, "That's all right. It was nice meeting you."

Graham put a hand on Randy's shoulder and looked at him. "I like you. I'll call Jake and set up another appointment." He opened the door. "Bring me something you wrote."

Nodding, Randy shook Graham's hand. "Thanks. I'll see you later."

He left the apartment, and Graham closed the door behind him.

II

Randy walked home, thinking about Graham Mason and their hour together. Graham was the most successful—the most famous—person Randy had ever met. Indeed, he had never known an actual celebrity before. The fact that he had not until recently even heard of this writer was unimportant. His fame was now fixed in Randy's mind, as indelible a trait as his craggy skin or his receding hairline.

But their meeting had been disconcerting to Randy, for he preferred calling the shots in his interactions with clients. The men Jake procured were usually awed, grateful to be in the presence of a good-looking young man with a tight body. Randy knew how to handle them most of the time.

Yet Graham had managed to seize control from the start of their session. Randy's subsequent arousal was unusual, too, as was how close he and Graham had come to having real sex. This surprised him, for he did not consider himself a prostitute. He was a masseur whose services included a sexual release; he felt the distinction important. But this time he had almost crossed the boundary.

Randy remembered his first few years in New York, when, frustrated by his lack of success as an actor and tired of waiting on tables, he had worked intermittently as an escort for an agency. The experience was not a pleasant one; he disliked being obliged to have sex with many of the men he met. While working for the agency, he drank heavily and occasionally snorted heroin. At that time, too, he once tried committing suicide, although he was halfhearted in his endeavor, and the twenty aspirin he swallowed only made him ill.

Shortly after this attempt, he met Jake, who was then himself a nude masseur. Jake had a long list of regular, dependable clients, and he sometimes needed help meeting all their needs. Randy stopped working for the agency and, at Jake's insistence, discontinued any use of heroin. Then he started giving massages for Jake. It was certainly easier; often the client only wanted to talk. These sessions took less than an hour, and they paid well. Randy was able to sleep late, work out at his gym several times a week, and go to an audition every once in a while.

Jake now spent his time finding work for Randy. Because his connections helped, he shared in Randy's proceeds. He had stopped giving massages himself after clients started asking for a younger man, someone with an easy manner, smooth skin, and a handsome, pleasant face. Randy fit the bill perfectly.

Randy was a natural; men similar to these clients had been attracted to him for as long as he could remember. His first sexual encounter had been with an older man, his father's employer, Russell Hewitt. Since that time, he had known many men like Mr. Hewitt.

But his own recent history had not led Randy to expect the confusion his hour with Graham had induced. Then, too, he had always thought he was reasonably happy with Jake. Yet his composure was ruffled now, which disturbed him. Complicating things further was the imprudent lie he had told during this session. The lie that troubled him was not his use of a false name. And it was not his saying he was twenty-eight, when he was actually thirty-two. These types of prevarications were common in Randy's profession. It was another fabrication that concerned him: He had claimed to be a writer, but he had not written anything since he was eighteen.

He had started writing shortly after he began seeing Mr. Hewitt. It helped him ignore his widowed father and the Midwestern town they lived in. He found he could forget for hours at a time his father's drinking binges and the beatings he received when his father was drunk. Both his writing and Mr. Hewitt gave him a glimpse into another kind of existence, a world on a higher plane than the one he had known until then.

He moved to New York when he was eighteen, just after his relationship with Mr. Hewitt ended. His new life in the city left him little time for reflection, and soon he stopped writing. But he never abandoned his literary ambitions completely, and he always told himself he would some day write again.

Until tonight he had kept such thoughts to himself. After he blurted out the lie about his stories to Graham, he had been surprised when Graham called his bluff. Now, as Randy had nothing to show him, he could only hope that Graham would not remember discussing this subject at all.

Randy's confusion was augmented by the dexedrine he had taken, and he felt its full effect as he walked down Avenue A toward his apartment. Unfortunately, he found the clarity it was giving him unwelcome at this time: A huge, bloated man, dressed in filthy clothes and drinking from a bottle of Colt 45, was harassing him by screaming, "Suck my dick, pretty boy, eat my asshole, faggot!" He followed Randy for two blocks, shouting obscenities and occasionally sticking his hands down his pants. When Randy reached his building on East 4th Street, he ran in, relieved, and bolted up the stairs.

Inside their small apartment, Jake was smoking a joint and watching *Rivera Live*. The air was dense with marijuana smoke, and clothes were scattered everywhere. Randy stepped over a pile of dirty shirts and kissed Jake on the cheek.

"How's m'baby?" Jake said, greeting him. He pronounced "my baby" as one word, running the syllables together in a manner Randy sometimes found endearing. "You want some?" Jake asked, passing the joint to Randy.

Although Randy usually disliked pot, he smoked it now, hoping it would soften the effects of the dexedrine. After taking several hits, he handed the joint back to Jake.

"And how was Graham?" Jake took another toke and stared at the television screen.

"Interesting," Randy replied, his mind racing over the events of the evening. "But a real bitch."

Jake laughed. "He's got a big shlong, though, doesn't he?"

"How do you know?"

"Come off it! He was my client years ago."

"I should have known." Randy was always amazed by the number of people Jake knew and awed by the information he could come up with about each of them.

They watched *Rivera Live* for a few minutes. Then Jake turned to Randy and asked, "Did Graham mention Dennis?"

"Dennis?"

"Dennis Crawley, Graham's lover. He's dead now."

Randy remembered the Hockney drawing and the photograph of the man in the bathing suit. "The only people he talked about were Denise Lamour and Dakota Montoya."

"Oh, those tired old fucks!" Jake inhaled on the joint and looked back at the television screen. Then he asked once more, "So he didn't say anything about Dennis?"

"Nothing at all."

"I'm surprised." Jake put out the joint and lit a cigarette, then smoked for a few minutes in silence. "I still can't believe you'd never heard of Graham before," he finally said. "Or Dennis Crawley either. Sometimes, sweetheart, your ignorance is as stunning as your ass."

Randy wavered before speaking. "I'm an actor, remember?" he snapped. "I don't know much about trendy writers."

"I'll say. I mean, Graham and Dennis were *the* literary poster boys for years."

"Shit, it's not like they were movie stars or anything."

Jake looked at Randy in disbelief. "But they were *everywhere*: clubs, openings, in *Interview,* at the White House." He spoke quickly, enthusiastically. "They used to hang around people like Warhol and Keith Haring. You know the types. Dennis was beautiful, and Graham was…well, he was Graham."

Randy felt embarrassed by his own ignorance. He had often heard about the circles Jake mentioned, but was fuzzy about individual names. "So Dennis was a writer," he said.

"Yeah, Graham's protégé. And a vampire, if you listen to some people."

Randy was puzzled. "What do you mean?"

"Well, I told you, didn't I, that Graham hasn't written anything in years?"

"He's got a new book coming out." Randy felt like a child proudly telling his father about a lesson he had learned in school.

Jake looked surprised. "Graham told you that?"

"Yeah."

Jake inhaled on his cigarette. "That's news. He certainly didn't write anything when he was with Dennis. I think he stopped when they met."

"Why?"

"Who knows? Love? Drugs?" Jake shrugged. "All I know is that Dennis started writing as soon as Graham stopped. A book every year or so until he died. Even when he was sick he was churning them out. That's when some people began calling him a vampire, like he had sucked up all of Graham's talent. Of course, everyone else thought it was Graham who was doing the actual writing." He stopped, as if he were considering this idea. "But that's a load of crap; Graham was too stoned in those days."

Randy listened to Jake, his concentration honed by the dexedrine, so that each word seemed to reverberate brilliantly. "Was Graham jealous? I mean, he wasn't writing anything, and Dennis was doing so much."

"He didn't act jealous, just high." Jake laughed. "I think he was thrilled to be hanging around with this handsome young celebrity."

Randy thought again about the Hockney drawing. "When did Dennis die?"

Jake hesitated. "Around three years ago, I think. Something like that. I remember Graham disappeared right after the funeral. He may have been sick himself; I know he's been in the hospital a few times." He extinguished his cigarette. "Actually, he just started going out again recently. I hadn't spoken to him in years until the other day." He paused. "Someone had told him about you."

"Me?" Randy felt vaguely alarmed. "Who was it?"

"Jackson Reeves."

Randy remembered the Southern choreographer he had massaged. "What did he tell Graham?"

Jake did not respond at first. Then he glanced at Randy and smiled. "He said you reminded him of Dennis."

Startled, Randy turned away from Jake and stared at the television screen, trying to pay attention as Geraldo Rivera interviewed Jodie Foster. But he was unable to understand their words, for their faces seemed unnaturally sharp. Still, their voices soothed him, and he soon felt a million miles away.

Five minutes later, he wondered why he had been so upset. He watched *Rivera* for a few more minutes, then stood and stretched. "I don't know how you can look at this shit," he said to Jake.

Jake turned off the TV and stood, too, placing his arm over Randy's shoulder. "Sweetheart, you're right. Rivera's an asshole. Let's go to bed."

They walked to the bedroom and undressed. Randy got into bed, then looked on as Jake, naked, lit another joint and sat beside him. As Jake smoked, Randy studied the tattoo on his right arm, a crude drawing of a broken heart impaled by a knife. Randy remembered how aroused he had been the first time he'd seen it. But now that Jake's body was completely familiar to him, he rarely noticed it. Tonight, as he stared at this tattoo, he felt a hint of that earlier longing. This feeling passed quickly, swept away by a new wave of images, memories provoked by the dexedrine and by his activities that night.

When Jake finished the joint, he lay next to Randy and stroked his leg. "I made an appointment for you tomorrow. You're meeting George O'Hara."

Randy nodded, remembering a fat, obnoxious sales rep he had seen several weeks before. "What time?"

"Two. You're meeting him at his hotel." Jake moved his hand up Randy's thigh to his groin and played with his penis.

Randy lay still. Jake climbed on top of him, rubbing his penis against Randy's. This force helped stop the rush of Randy's thoughts, and he found himself responding to Jake's touch. He threw his arms around Jake's neck, caressing and kissing him, feeling a momentary lightness in his own body, so that it seemed as if he were floating

14

above the bed. Then his memories of Graham returned, and his responses dimmed. As Jake fucked him, Randy managed to follow the movements, while his mind remained elsewhere.

After several minutes, Jake groaned and ejaculated, then rolled over. "You weren't exactly enthusiastic," he remarked.

"Sorry. I guess I'm tired."

"Well, do you mind if I turn out the light?"

"Go ahead."

Jake kissed him on the cheek and soon fell asleep.

Randy lay quietly in the dark, listening to Jake breathe. He realized he would be awake for hours, that the dexedrine he had taken was strong. His mind was racing, and he thought again about Graham, Dennis Crawley, Graham's art collection and books. Then, unexpectedly, this reverie was usurped by memories of Mr. Hewitt.

Randy pictured him sitting on a leather chair in his living room, a drink in one hand, his many antique books on the tall shelves behind him. He saw the room's dark oak walls, and recalled its subdued, slightly sinister lighting. These images stayed with him, and he grew uneasy. He could almost hear Mr. Hewitt's voice, softly calling his name: "Randy, come here."

He shot upright, then dressed and quickly walked to the next room.

He found *Summer Swan,* the book he had stolen from Graham, and leafed through it. "You retain your customary silence as you watch him," he read, "and you refuse to comment on his actions or on your own discomfort. Your anger remains hidden, impenetrable, although you feel it feeds his fascination with you."

Randy stopped reading, his recollections making it impossible for him to concentrate. He remembered being ten years old and meeting Mr. Hewitt for the first time: He and his father had run into him at the supermarket while shopping one Saturday afternoon. He recalled the intense looks Mr. Hewitt had given him, the fear he had felt, his father's words afterward. Then he found a piece of paper and a pen and started jotting these memories down.

At first he found it strange to be writing again after such a long time. But as he lost himself in his words, a sense of familiarity came over him, and he worked as if in a trance.

After filling up several pages with his early impressions of Mr.

Hewitt, he wrote about a conversation he'd had with his father the day after that initial meeting:

> *"Mr. Hewitt thinks you're a bright boy," Dad said to me. He was drinking beer and watching a football game on TV.*
> *"Oh, yeah?" I couldn't figure this out. I mean, why should some rich guy care about a kid like me? Besides, I'd been so nervous when I met him, I'd acted like an asshole.*
> *"He says he wants to see you again. I'm going to take you up to his house tomorrow night."*
> *"Shit, Dad!"*
> *"Be nice to him," Dad said sternly. "He's my boss. Do what he says. He can help me a lot."*
> *"Do I really have to go?"*
> *Dad glared at me. "You'll go if you know what's good for you."*

Randy stopped writing. He wanted a cigarette, though he had given up smoking a few months before. He walked to the bedroom, where he found an unopened pack of Merits on the table beside the bed. He took it with him back to the next room and smoked two cigarettes before picking up his pen. He then continued writing:

> *Dad dropped me off at Mr. Hewitt's the next night. He lived in this big white house on top of a hill where all the rich people in town lived. It was an awesome place, with pillars and stuff. I'd never been in a house like that before. I mean, I'd only seen them on TV or in the movies.*
> *Mr. Hewitt came to the door with a drink in his hand and told me to come in. There was this marble hallway and a big carpeted staircase and antique furniture everywhere. We went into this huge room with a color TV in it and leather books in these shelves on all of the walls. Mrs. Hewitt was away and they didn't have any kids and no one else was around, so we were alone.*
> *Mr. Hewitt started asking about my family, saying what a great guy my dad was and everything. Then we went outside. He showed me his swimming pool and tennis court, and took me to this stable where he kept three horses. I didn't say much the whole time.*
> *When we got back inside, he asked me if I wanted a drink. I was just*

ten, so I'd never had hard liquor before, just some sips of my father's beer. I wanted to be cool, though, so I asked for a scotch. That's what Mr. Hewitt was having. I drank it real fast, even though it tasted pretty terrible. Mr. Hewitt just sat there watching me. When I was finished, he offered me another one.

I was feeling a little weird by that time, but it was the first time I'd ever been drunk so I thought that was the way I was supposed to feel. I said okay, I'd have another one. Mr. Hewitt went to the bar and poured more scotch into our glasses. Then he stood real still for a minute. He had his back to me, and I couldn't see what he was doing. His hands were down in front of him, and I started to feel kind of freaked. When he turned around, he had this strange smile on his face.

He held up a glass of scotch and said, "Why don't you come over and get your drink?"

I looked down and saw his dick hanging out of his pants. It was real big, much bigger than my dad's, and I couldn't stop looking at it.

"Don't be frightened," he said. "I just want to be your friend. Come here."

I was pretty scared, but I walked over anyway. He gave me the scotch, and I took a sip. Then he took my hand and put it on his cock. It was real hard, and he started moving it around.

"Why don't you kiss it?" he asked. He put his hand on top of my head and pushed me down to my knees. He held me there as he shoved his dick into my mouth.

"Jesus Christ!" he said. "Watch out for the teeth!"

He started moaning and stuff, saying, "Shit!" and "Great!" over and over. Once I stopped for a second, but he just pulled me back and said, "Keep going." After a while I started to space out. I just remember his dick sometimes made me gag.

He kept it up for a real long time, and I wondered if he was ever going to stop. When he got all stiff and jerky, I tried to pull away. He wouldn't let me move though, he just kept holding my head. When he came in my mouth, I thought I was going to puke, but he held me close, and I had to swallow everything.

Finally he patted me on the head and said, "That was good." Then he told me to get up and finish my drink.

I did what he said. After the second scotch, I guess I must have been *feeling pretty mellow. It was late though, and Mr. Hewitt said he'd drive me home. I said that I'd walk, so he said okay. When I left, he gave me twenty dollars.*

"Come back next week," he said. "I'll talk to your father."

I said goodbye and ran all the way home.

Randy put down his pen and lit another cigarette, then sat quietly, reading what he had written. Suddenly he thought about Ellen, a psychiatric social worker he had seen for a few months after his suicide attempt, when the hospital that had treated him had directed him to her. She was the last person with whom he had discussed Mr. Hewitt. He recalled those discussions, which had seemed at the time pointless and redundant, but which were in their own way as disturbing to him as some earlier inquiries she had made as to why he sometimes failed to practice safe sex and refused to be tested for HIV.

Ellen asked him for specifics whenever they talked about his past affairs. After several sessions, he told her about Mr. Hewitt: their weekly meetings, the money he was given after each visit, the trips they took together.

"We'd go to places like New York City, California, his house in Canada," he informed her. "Once we even flew down to Nassau for the weekend."

"And what was that like?" Ellen gazed at him kindly, her limpid blue eyes making Randy feel awkward.

"It was great," he replied after a moment's hesitation. "I mean, I'd never seen anything like Nassau before. All those rich people, gambling and stuff. And we stayed in this neat hotel. It seemed like something out of a movie."

"But what were you *feeling* then?"

Randy found this question odd, so he said nothing and peered out the window.

Ellen paused, then asked, "What did the other people in town think about this?"

Randy was puzzled: "What do you mean?"

"Well, didn't they find it unusual that this older man was taking such an interest in you? Didn't they question his motives?"

Randy laughed. "Shit, he owned the whole town! They didn't question anything he did. And if they did think something was weird, they kept it to themselves. Besides, they probably thought he was doing me a favor. You know, with my dad being such a drunk and everything."

"What about your friends? Did they ever tease you about him?"

"Not that I know of. Anyway, I didn't have any friends."

"None at all?"

"I kept pretty much to myself."

Ellen then asked how he had felt while seeing this older man, if he had ever loved Mr. Hewitt. Randy did not know what to say; he could only remember being overwhelmed, awed by Mr. Hewitt's wealth, which contrasted so completely with his own blue-collar surroundings. He told Ellen that love had nothing to do with it, that they were both just using each other. Mr. Hewitt had this thing for very young boys, he explained, while he himself only wanted to get away from his father, whom he had hated for as long as he could remember.

"What was the first thing you remember your father doing that made you hate him?" Ellen inquired.

Randy looked at her blankly, baffled by her question. Hating his father had always been easy, he said. His earliest memory of him was that of a sinister being, a dark, brooding presence that had eclipsed any recollection he had of his mother, who had died when he was two. Everything his father did in the ensuing years only reinforced the impressions he had retained from his childhood.

In a later session, he told Ellen a bit more about his father. Still, she continued to probe, wanting to know Randy's feelings about the things he revealed: How had he reacted to the drinking and the beatings, his father's moodiness, the abuse? What had he felt when he saw that his father had been made a foreman at Mr. Hewitt's factory, just after Randy's seduction? And what had he thought when he heard that his father was getting a generous bonus every month, payments he received regularly during the years Randy was seeing Mr. Hewitt? Was Randy aware then that his father had essentially acted as a pimp?

Randy nodded.

"Well, how did you *feel?*" she asked. "*What* did you feel?"

Randy stared at her, then admitted that he really didn't know.

"You must have felt *something*," she exclaimed. "Your father more or less sold you as a prostitute!"

Randy laughed uneasily. "That was probably the best thing he ever did for me."

Although Ellen said she found this response inappropriate, Randy insisted he had told the truth. When his father dropped him off at Mr. Hewitt's that first evening, he had opened up a whole new world for his son, enabling Randy to escape from what had been until then a dreary and unpleasant life. Randy's experiences with Mr. Hewitt seemed to expand his horizons in every way, inspiring him to invent elaborate and fantastic tales, stories about fabulously rich and famous personalities, which he would write down and then act out for himself in his bedroom. He decided he was going to become either a novelist or an actor. And, after seeing the outside world with Mr. Hewitt, he hoped he could some day leave the Midwest forever.

Randy told Ellen how, as a teenager, he started making plans to get out of town. By then his relations with Mr. Hewitt were cooling off, and they were seeing much less of each other. Randy spent more time away from home, driving around the countryside by himself, sometimes visiting the only gay bar in a nearby city, where he picked up men who occasionally gave him money.

After Randy turned eighteen, Mr. Hewitt did not seem interested in him at all anymore. Eventually, when Mr. Hewitt began seeing the ten-year-old son of another employee, he severed all ties with Randy.

Ellen hesitated after he told her this story, appearing to Randy uncomfortable. "Were there any other boys he saw that you know of?" she asked gently.

Randy shrugged. "What difference does it make? It's all in the past."

Ellen hesitated again. "Well, what about you? Didn't you feel used? Weren't you hurt?"

Randy frowned; he just didn't know.

"But you must have felt *something* when Mr. Hewitt abandoned you."

"Abandoned me?" Randy paused. "I guess you could call it that. But I moved to New York right after we broke up. I was ready to get out."

Ellen sighed. "What about Mr. Hewitt? Have you seen him since you left?"

"No, I've never gone back. He and my dad could both be dead now; I wouldn't know."

There was a long silence. Ellen gazed at Randy, and he shifted in his chair, looking down at the floor. For an instant he felt a twinge of something he barely remembered, an emotion he recalled from a long time before. He managed to hold it in check, and the session soon ended. But after that visit, he called Ellen and canceled all further appointments.

Now Randy, chain-smoking, once again felt that emotion he had experienced in Ellen's office. He extinguished a cigarette and immediately lit another one, then picked up his pen and resumed writing. He worked all night, putting his memories down on paper. When he was done, the sun was coming up and he was exhausted. He reached for a Merit, but he had finished the pack. Unable to smoke, he stared at the wall in front of him.

He did not move for several minutes. Then he started to cry, placing his hands over his face and emitting quick little gasps as he sobbed. He kept this up for an hour, until Jake, looking tired, walked into the room.

"What's the matter with m'baby?" Jake asked uneasily.

Randy looked at him, then stood and rushed into his arms. He put his head on Jake's chest and continued sobbing.

"Sweetheart," Jake said, patting Randy on the back, "don't be silly. Come to bed."

He led Randy to their bedroom, then tucked him under the covers and searched for his cigarettes. "Did you smoke the whole pack?" he asked when he realized the Merits were gone.

Randy nodded.

"Jesus!" Jake exclaimed. He got into bed and stretched. "Try to sleep. You've got an appointment at two."

Randy curled up in Jake's arms, stifling his tears and trying to feel safe. He lay awake for another hour, the remnants of the dexedrine running through his brain.

When he finally slept, he dreamed about riding in a car with Mr.

Hewitt, cruising over hills in the Midwestern countryside, speeding down back roads past green pastures and rows of corn. Mr. Hewitt was driving while fondling Randy. Suddenly he lost control of the car. They veered off the road, whizzing over a field toward a hidden precipice and a steep drop into the ocean. "We're not going to make it," Mr. Hewitt said. "I can't stop the car." They plunged over the cliff, and he looked at Randy, smiling. Randy gazed back at him; the face he saw was Graham's. As the car sank into the ocean, Randy knew they were doomed.

III

Randy was forty-five minutes late for his appointment with George O'Hara. The sales rep seemed annoyed when Randy arrived at the hotel, but he regained his good humor as Randy undressed.

"Long night, huh?" George asked with a wink and a leer.

"What's it to you?" Randy gibed, laughing. He slowly peeled off his briefs.

George said nothing. Keeping his eyes on Randy, he removed his own clothes and waddled to the bed.

Although it was cool outside, George sweated profusely. Randy thought he was even fatter than he remembered, and he found the hair on his back repellent. During the massage, George babbled inanely about his wife and twin daughters. Still, he came quickly when Randy jerked him off and tipped well, so Randy was out on the street again in less than an hour.

Jake had booked Randy heavily for the next few days, and Randy saw a succession of unappealing clients. Many were not nearly as compliant as George O'Hara. One drunk man was especially annoying, insisting it was his right to fuck Randy.

"I'm a masseur," Randy said. "I don't sell my body."

"That's a crock of shit!" The client grabbed Randy's ass.

Randy left. Back at his apartment, he made Jake promise never to book him with that client again.

A week went by, and Randy heard nothing from Graham. He read *Summer Swan*, but found it slow and boring. Although he was impressed by what he thought were the book's literary qualities, he was relieved when he put it down.

He went back to his own writing. This was difficult without the aid of Graham's dexedrine, so he asked Jake where he could get some. "What do you want that shit for?" Jake asked.

"I'm trying to write," Randy answered, embarrassed.

Jake laughed, and Randy did not press the matter further.

In the next few days, he managed to complete thirty pages. When he was finished, he was happy with his work and anxious to show it to Graham. But as more days passed and a call did not come, Randy began to think that he would never hear from him again.

Two weeks after his first appointment with Graham, when Randy came home from his gym, Jake looked up from the television screen.

"Graham Mason called," he said, sounding pleased. "He wants to see you tomorrow night."

"Really?" Randy asked enthusiastically. "What time?"

"Eight." Jake stared at Randy. "You sound awfully eager."

"He said he'd look at my writing," Randy quickly replied.

"Oh, right." Jake laughed, then went back to the television set.

Later that night, Randy read what he had written, making many changes and typing everything up. He worked until two in the morning, then got into bed. Although he was exhausted, he did not fall asleep until dawn.

The following evening he went west to Graham's brownstone. Once again he walked around the block a few times before ringing the buzzer. This time, when Graham asked who it was, Randy gave his real name.

As he climbed the stairs to Graham's apartment, he was surprised to hear loud music floating down from the top floor. When he got there, he saw that Graham's door was ajar. After knocking three times and getting no response, he walked in falteringly.

Inside he saw Graham, once again dressed in his navy-blue bathrobe and brown-leather slippers, taking a sip from a half-empty glass, then placing it on a table and dancing wildly to the music playing. "Baby, baby," a woman sang, "give me some, give me some." Graham twirled around clumsily, perilously flapping his long, thin arms, not acknowledging Randy's presence or even appearing to notice he was there. Randy looked on, amazed, his eyes darting from Graham's frantic movements to the portrait of Madonna, then back to Graham. He remained still, clutching the envelope containing his manuscript.

As soon as the song ended, Graham stopped dancing. He picked up his glass and took a sip, then turned to Randy. "Sorry," he said, "I was just reliving my youth." His voice did not reveal any sign of inebriation; it was level and cool, just as it had been the first time Randy had met him. "Would you like a drink?"

Randy looked at the glass in Graham's hand. "What are you having?"

"Why, gin, of course." Graham seemed surprised that Randy did not know.

"I'll have some of that."

"Fine. Take a seat."

Still holding his manuscript, Randy sat on the edge of the black-leather couch. Graham left the room, then returned a few moments later with two full glasses of gin and the bottle of dexedrine. He gave one of the glasses to Randy and sat next to him, briefly touching his leg. After he removed his hand, he unscrewed the cap from the bottle and took out two pills.

"Do you want one?" He passed a dexedrine to Randy. "I need something myself. I've been feeling ill for the past week. Some wretched flu." He gazed at Randy, half smiling. "That's why I didn't call you until yesterday. I'm fine now, but I do want to be aware of everything that happens tonight."

Randy took the pill and swallowed it. "Thanks," he said, and gulped his gin. His drink was strong, not diluted at all, but he was relieved to have it, since he was feeling as queasy as he had the first night he had been here.

Graham looked at the envelope in Randy's hand. "What's that?"

Randy wavered, then said, "A story I wrote."

"Story?" Graham seemed confused at first. Then he laughed. "Oh, one of your stories. Of course."

"You said you wanted to read it."

"Right. And I will." He took the envelope from Randy. "Do you want me to read it now or after the massage?"

"Whenever you want."

Graham hesitated, then opened the envelope and removed the manuscript. "I think I'll look at it now. Save the best for last. And I'd like the pills to take effect before we get into anything else." He read the title. "Mr. Hewitt," he murmured. "Interesting."

Gripping his gin, Randy remained perched on the edge of the couch as Graham read his work. Occasionally Graham chuckled, and Randy would look at him, wondering what had prompted this reaction. Then he would glance away at the bookshelves, hoping to find titles he recognized or ones he might want to read.

Soon he felt the dexedrine kick in. High, he finished his drink.

Graham looked up from the manuscript. "Would you like some more gin?"

Randy nodded.

Graham went to the kitchen and refilled their glasses, then returned and continued reading.

It took him forty-five minutes to get through the thirty pages Randy had written. When he was finished, he put the manuscript aside on the table by the couch, just next to the photograph of Dennis. He turned to Randy and stared at him, saying nothing at first. Randy shifted uneasily.

"This isn't a story," Graham said abruptly. "It's not fiction at all. You've written a memoir."

Randy did not respond.

"Still, it's interesting. It rambles, and you break every rule in the book, yet there's something about it…." He paused, then went on: "You're rather emotionless about some pretty peculiar things. I like that." He took a sip of his drink. "I'm not saying it's actually *good*. Far from it. Just interesting."

Randy wanted a cigarette, though he'd not had one since the night he began writing his story.

"This Hewitt," Graham asked, "the man who took your cherry: You really haven't seen him since you moved to New York?"

"No."

"Or your father either?"

"I don't want to see either of them."

"I can't imagine why." Graham smirked. "Hewitt's probably plugging some five-year-old's ass right now."

Randy swallowed the rest of his gin, then grasped his glass tightly with both hands.

"What was it like getting fucked when you were ten? I mean, he *did* fuck you then, didn't he?"

Randy looked at the floor, then back up at Graham. "We didn't do anything like that at first."

"Oh, you mean he had to break you in?"

Randy raised his glass to his lips, then remembered it was empty.

"I'd imagine you'd have to be at least eleven to take a grown man's cock," Graham said softly. "But I'm sure Hewitt prepared you for that." He smiled. "What I really like about your memoir," he went on, chuckling, "is the fact that it turned me on. I *must* go to the Midwest sometime. I mean, only twenty dollars for a blow job and from a luscious ten-year-old kid at that!"

Randy gripped his empty glass.

Graham laughed. "I hope you're not offended. It's just that you're so much fun to tease." He noticed the empty glass in Randy's hand. "It looks like you need another refill." He took the glass from Randy and walked to the next room.

Alone, Randy realized he was already drunk. He stood and stared at the Hockney on the wall, drawn in by Dennis Crawley's face and by everything he had heard about him. He wondered what it was like being dead, if there was an afterlife, if in fact Dennis was at the moment floating through this apartment, watching him. He had a fleeting stab of envy, a longing for the detachment and the safety that he imagined the dead possessed. Closing his eyes, he became a spirit, the ghost of Dennis, hovering above the room, gliding in space, flowing out the open window to the cool November air.

A voice cut into his thoughts: "Come and get your drink."

Randy turned around. Graham was standing in the doorway, two fresh drinks in his hands, his bathrobe opened to reveal his enormous penis, jutting out, erect.

"Have one for Daddy," Graham said.

Randy remained where he was, his eyes fixed on Graham's dick.

"I said come here."

Randy did not move.

Graham walked to him and, placing his hands firmly on his shoulders, forced him to the floor. Randy, on his knees, faced Graham's cock. He put it in his mouth.

"Good boy." Graham patted the top of Randy's head.

Randy was now aware of nothing except the force of Graham's movements. He dimly perceived being led to the bedroom and undressed. Soon he was lying on a bed, and Graham was licking his body, moving his tongue down Randy's chest to his groin. Randy's perceptions faded for a few seconds. Coming back, he felt as if he were watching himself as he lifted his pelvis from the bed, savagely forcing his cock into Graham's mouth.

Graham, choking, sat up and looked at Randy. "Stupid cunt!" he screamed, slapping Randy's face. "That's for all the shit I put up with from you!"

Randy froze. Graham grabbed his legs and pushed them straight back over his head, so that Randy's ass was raised toward Graham. Graham leaned over and stuck his tongue into Randy's asshole, rimming it, then pulled away.

"I'd like to get some rope," he said, "and tie you up, just like you are now." He used three fingers to massage Randy's anus. "Then I'd like to ram my fist up your hole." He pushed his three fingers further in.

Randy listened to someone say, "Why don't you just shut up and fuck me?" Then he realized he had spoken these words himself.

Graham slapped him again and cried, "I want you wet and dripping, like a woman. You've got to beg for it, then I'll fuck you." He inserted a fourth finger. "When I'm through, I'll make you lick the shit off my dick."

"Go ahead," Randy heard himself say, "do it, cocksucker!"

Graham slapped him once more, then started fucking him.

Randy felt himself responding to Graham's thrusts, lifting his ass so that it could take all of Graham's cock. He shoved Graham over onto his back and sat on top of his groin, twisting Graham's nipples as he moved up and down, riding the penis, strangling it with his asshole. He caught his own scent, the smell of his shit, as he continued to move rapidly, violently. Finally, in a sudden, almost miraculous spurt, he ejaculated on Graham's chest. Moaning, Graham came as well, his semen dripping out of Randy and forming a puddle on the sheets.

Afterward, Randy lay on his stomach, not moving at all. Several minutes later, the dexedrine overcame the effects of the alcohol, and he stirred.

Graham, lying next to him, massaged his ass, then slapped it. "You must let me whip you sometime. I'd love to see red welts on your skin." When Randy did not reply, Graham laughed and slapped him again. Leaning over, he whispered in Randy's ear, "Our games are always fun, aren't they, baby?"

Randy looked at the clock on the bedside table. It was after midnight.

"I've got to go," he said. "Jake will be worried."

"Fuck Jake. I wouldn't even think about him if I were you." Graham paused, then added, "But if you must go, I won't hold you back."

Randy got out of bed and dressed quickly.

Graham put on his robe. He found his wallet and gave Randy one hundred dollars.

"Thanks," Randy said as he pocketed the bills.

At the door, Graham put his hand on Randy's thigh. "I'll talk to Jake and have him send you here in a couple of days."

Randy left the apartment and ran down the stairs. When he was on the street, he hailed a taxi.

IV

The next morning Randy had only a vague memory of going to bed. He assumed Jake had been sleeping when he came in, because he could recall no conversation. He was lying under the covers now, a blanket drawn to his chin, with Jake snoring heavily next to him. The clock by the bed said 8:30. Randy knew he had not slept, but he had no idea what had happened in the hours that had passed since he'd arrived home.

All his memories from the night before were spotty. He remembered Graham reading his story, then, later, he himself catching a cab outside Graham's building. But when he thought about the time in between—the "massage"—a dreamlike haze cloaked his mind, and his impressions—somewhat disturbing, yet strangely thrilling—were muted by a hellish headache.

He felt heavy and thick, at the same time almost giddy. He could not budge and wondered if he was coming down with Graham's "wretched flu." That would be fine, he decided; he had no intention of getting out of bed for a very long time.

He perceived Jake moving, turning over and running a hand across his leg, but he did not respond. He heard Jake get up and walk to the kitchen. Then he smelled coffee brewing and listened to the babble of the morning television programs. After that, he was aware of nothing for some time, until, suddenly, he saw Jake standing over him, holding a cup of coffee.

"Are you gonna stay in bed all day?" Jake asked. "It's one o'clock."

Randy studied Jake, who looked for a moment like a stranger. "I'm sick," he replied, closing his eyes.

He heard Jake leave the room. Then a song drifted up from a radio on the street, an upbeat tune he had heard many times before: "You've come at last. This feels so right. You don't know, you just can't. Oh, no!"

Slowly, images from the night before came back to Randy, startling him with their intensity. He felt the sting of a hand slapping him and heard Graham screaming, "Stupid cunt!" between blows. He remembered Graham's cock pushing into his asshole and the trickle of semen dripping down his legs. He opened his eyes, but the memories persisted, so he closed them again. He lay still, then masturbated. After he came, he fell into a deep sleep.

He dreamed he was with Graham, walking through a field near Mr. Hewitt's house. The grounds of the estate were overrun by a dense forest of twisted trees and by a moist fungus that emitted horrid, noxious fumes. Randy and Graham walked hand in hand over a path partially obscured by snaky black roots. As they turned a corner, a thick fog engulfed them, and they could no longer see anything. Frightened, Randy squeezed Graham's hand. Then, as suddenly as it had appeared, the fog lifted, and Ellen, Randy's old social worker, was standing before them.

"What are you feeling, Randy?" she asked. "Who is this man?" Randy stared into Ellen's clear, blue eyes.

"It's not safe," Ellen continued. "Go home."

Randy let go of Graham's hand and ran back over the path, pushing aside branches and tall, brambly weeds. He came to a clearing, where he saw Mr. Hewitt's house, bright sunshine streaming down upon it. He cupped a hand over his eyes, shading them from the sun, then saw his father and Mr. Hewitt standing on the front porch, each holding a glass of gin.

"Welcome back," his father said.

"Yes," Mr. Hewitt added, "come and join us."

Randy walked toward them. As he moved, the glare of the sunlight intensified and he stopped, turning away.

"I said come here." It was Mr. Hewitt.

Looking back at the house, Randy saw that it was in flames. Laughter floated up from the porch. As the heat from the fire seared his skin, he felt himself melting and cried out in pain. Then, with a start, he awoke.

Jake, carrying a dinner tray, was standing before him. "What's wrong with m'baby?" he asked, placing the tray on the bed. "Are you all right?"

"I'm burning up," Randy murmured.

"Well, try to eat. This chicken soup should help."

Randy ate the soup listlessly, only finishing half of the bowl. When he was done, Jake took his temperature.

"No fever," Jake informed him. "Let's see how you feel in the morning."

For the next few days, Randy drifted in and out of sleep, having strange dreams he could never remember. After four days in bed, he felt somewhat better, but he neglected to tell this to Jake.

Jake had already lost his patience. "What the hell's the matter?" he asked, sitting beside Randy on the bed. "You don't have a fever. There's not a fucking thing wrong with you. So why're you lying here like a slug?"

"Leave me alone," Randy cried. "I've got to rest."

"You're as bad as you were when we met," Jake observed. "I'm getting tired of making excuses every time a client calls."

Randy sat up slightly. "Who called?"

"Oh, I don't know. George O'Hara, Albert Meyers, a friend of Jackson Reeves. A couple of others, I guess."

"What about Graham?"

Jake stared at Randy. "No, I haven't heard anything from him." He hesitated. "Did something happen there the other night?"

Randy stared back. "Yeah, I caught this fucking flu from him."

Jake stood. "Well, get over it, sweetheart. I can't keep sending clients to Haircut forever."

"Oh, shit, has he shown up again?"

"Yes. He's coming here in half an hour."

"Fuck!"

"Well, someone has to fill in for you."

"Right." Randy closed his eyes, trying to fall asleep.

But as soon as Jake left, he reopened them. The news of Haircut's imminent arrival annoyed him, and he found it impossible to relax. Totally awake, he lay still, brooding.

Haircut was an old acquaintance of Jake's, a person Randy had never been particularly close to or fond of, but someone Jake had known casually for over fifteen years. He was thirty-five years old, tall, thin, and rather gawky, with long, shaggy, blond hair that he was continually trying to tame by switching frequently from one trendy hairstyle to another, always with disastrous results. This succession of unflattering haircuts led to his nickname, which everyone, even his clients, now used, few being aware that his real name was Doug.

Haircut was a full-service prostitute who advertised regularly in several widely distributed newspapers and magazines. His ad read "$40 Quick Lunch," which meant he could be had for forty dollars between the hours of eleven in the morning and three in the afternoon. At other times, he charged fifty, less than half the price of the average whore, but then Haircut, not being particularly attractive, knew he was not worth the normal fee. His enthusiasm and willingness to do anything, however, almost compensated for his less-than-adequate appearance, and he never said "no" to anyone. He would fuck, get fucked, suck, or get sucked, even participate in the heavier bondage-and-discipline scenes, all for forty or fifty bucks. For an extra ten, he'd dispense with a condom. He often saw seven or more clients a day, since his services were a bargain that many could not resist.

Haircut was usually strapped for cash, for he had incurred many debts while addicted to cocaine. He had snorted daily for years, until the membranes of his nose gave out and his septum had to be replaced by one made of plastic. Although he had cut back on his use of coke, he still did it quite often. He liked pot, too, and drank wine ravenously.

Sometimes, when he was drunk, he removed his plastic septum and poked a chopstick through the cavity where the septum had been, until the chopstick came out on the other side. Jake had taken photographs of him performing this trick, which invariably amused friends at parties.

Haircut's desperation ensured that he could be counted on to fill in for Randy whenever such a need arose. Often Jake and Randy would not see him for months; then he would show up unexpectedly, looking for work or hoping Jake might offer him some pot or wine. Randy tried to be polite whenever Haircut was around, although his presence made him uncomfortable. Still, Randy put up with him, knowing he amused Jake and hoping he himself would never be so reckless as to allow himself to fall into Haircut's unfortunate position.

Now, though, Randy was in no mood to see him. He sat up in bed, his irritation having obliterated any remaining symptoms of his illness. Then, when he heard the buzzer, he lay down again, grateful that he could use his sickness as an excuse and thus avoid contact with Haircut today.

He tried to ignore the conversation that ensued after Haircut arrived. But five minutes later, roused by laughter, he sat up once more.

"That's the answer!" he heard Haircut shriek. "He can afford it."

Although Randy was unable to make out Jake's response to this remark, Haircut's subsequent cackling retort came through loud and clear: "Graham Mason! What a hoot!"

Intrigued, Randy got out of bed and put on his clothes, then walked to the next room.

"Sweetheart, you're alive!" Jake cried, greeting Randy.

Haircut, holding a glass of white wine, looked up. "We were just talking about Mr. Mason," he said, crossing his legs as he studied Randy.

"I heard," Randy replied, sitting on the couch next to Jake.

"I understand you're *very* close to him now," Haircut continued. "Tell me, have you gotten a taste of his big shlong yet?"

Jake smiled, placing an arm on Randy's shoulder. "Randy's not interested in *that*. He's a masseur, after all." His voice had a smug tone that irritated Randy.

"Oh, right." Haircut smiled. "Even so, Randy, if you need me to take care of him for you, I'll be glad to help."

"I think I'll be all right." Randy noticed Jake's Merits on the table beside the couch. Desperate for a cigarette, he removed one from the pack.

"I thought you'd given up," Jake laughed.

Randy took a deep drag. "I guess I'm just bored. Being in bed and everything."

Haircut leaned toward him. "Graham's got you all hot and bothered, huh?"

"No. Why would you think that?"

"Come off it, I've been around."

"We know," Jake said. "You tell us that all the time."

Ignoring Jake, Haircut took a sip of his wine, then addressed Randy: "Don't let Graham get away with any shit. You're the one with the young flesh."

"He's just another client. I meet new ones all the time."

"Sure, stockbrokers and salesmen, big fucking deal! But Graham Mason! With him, anything is possible."

Randy stared at Haircut. "What are you trying to say?"

"I'm saying...." Haircut paused, as if the answer to Randy's question was obvious. He took another sip of wine, then went on: "Look at Dennis Crawley. He was just some pretty-boy faggot until Graham came along, about as much of a writer as you are. But Graham took care of him real good. I mean, he *made* him. When you get your hooks into someone like Graham, the world is yours."

Jake frowned. "You're so full of shit. You don't know what the fuck you're talking about."

"Oh, yeah?" Haircut's voice turned shrill. "Listen, I've got about a dozen men in the palm of my hand right now. Real high queens. They'd do anything for me. Jeez, just the other day, one of them gave me a Hermés scarf."

Jake laughed. "Well, smell you!"

"No, really! Now he's talking about setting me up in this penthouse on Park Avenue. He says he wants to keep me near him. I'm gonna kiss the East Village's ass goodbye forever."

"I've heard *that* before," Jake observed.

"Oh, fuck off! Why don't you make yourself useful and get me some more wine."

Jake stood, taking Haircut's glass. "I suppose you want a joint, too."

Haircut beamed. "I think that's the answer!"

As soon as Jake left the room, Haircut turned to Randy. "Listen, you've gotta get everything you can while Graham's still around. I mean, you don't meet tricks like *him* every day."

Randy ground out his cigarette. "You're making this all into too big a deal."

"I don't think so. Remember: You've got the power. Use it."

Jake returned with the wine, then rolled a joint. Randy took a few tokes, which he immediately regretted. Uneasy, he said nothing as Jake and Haircut discussed a new club in Chelsea. Soon their persistent chatter made him so uncomfortable that he announced he was tired and went back to bed. Jake and Haircut continued conversing loudly, but Randy managed to ignore them and fall asleep.

He slept until eleven the next morning and awoke feeling remarkably refreshed. He felt so good that he wondered how he ever could have allowed himself to become as morose as he'd been the past few days.

Jake noticed Randy's improvement and demanded that he dress and take a taxi to a midtown hotel.

"Tom Reynolds wants to see you at one," Jake said. "It has to be you. Haircut got too fucked up last night. Besides, sweetheart, you seem okay now."

Randy arrived at the hotel on time. Tom Reynolds was impotent and only wanted a massage. When it was over, he gave Randy a fifty-dollar tip, which Randy welcomed after his four days in bed. As he left the hotel, he walked away jauntily, relieved that he seemed to have recovered from his illness at last.

The next day, a cold snap descended on the city, and the temperature fell below freezing for the first time that fall. The sky was overcast, gray and gloomy, and Randy, depressed, stayed inside. He had nothing to do, so he looked for the story he had written, thinking he might work on it some more. Then he remembered he had left it at Graham's. For two days, he had given little thought to Graham Mason. He realized it had been almost a week since that evening, and he had not heard from him. He wondered if he should be grateful, if he really wanted to participate in another intense session. Yet he felt disappointed, and whenever the phone rang, hoped it was Graham.

But as more days passed, he resumed his usual activities—seeing clients, going to the gym, watching television with Jake—and stopped thinking much about Graham. Late one night, he attempted to write another story, but lost interest after half an hour and went to bed.

A week later it was Thanksgiving, and Jake invited Haircut to dinner. Randy had decided to prepare it this year, though, not being much of a cook, he had never before attempted such an elaborate feast. But Jake had recently bought a microwave oven, and Randy thought it would be simple to roast the turkey in it. Unfortunately, the bird cooked unevenly, drying out inside while remaining too rare on top. The gravy was canned and the mashed potatoes packaged, and the meal was a total loss.

"I guess m'baby's not Martha Stewart," Jake said when he saw the meal spread out on the kitchen table.

"No," Haircut agreed. "His talents obviously lie elsewhere."

Still, food was not the most important part of the evening's entertainment. Haircut had started drinking several hours before his arrival and was already drunk. As the night progressed, the three of them drank lots of wine and snorted many lines of cocaine, and most of what Randy had prepared remained untouched.

When Randy and Jake went to bed at four, Haircut stripped off his clothes, hoping to join them.

"Come on," he slurred, "a threesome's the answer!"

"Fuck off, Haircut!" Jake pushed him away.

Haircut fell off the bed onto the floor. "You don't know what you're missing," he moaned. Then he turned over onto his side and passed out.

Laughing, Jake switched off the light. Both he and Randy fell asleep instantly.

At ten the next morning, Randy was awakened by the phone. He ignored it for a minute, thinking Jake would pick it up. But when the ringing continued, he grabbed the receiver.

"Yeah?" he said.

There was no response at first. Finally: "It's Graham."

"Graham Mason?" The voice sounded strange to Randy, not like Graham's at all, It was softer, almost wispy, and had a distant quality, as if Graham were calling from another city. "Are you in New York?"

"Of course. I've been sick." Again there was silence. At last Graham continued: "Can I see you tonight?"

Randy clenched the receiver. He had a bad hangover and was unsure how he would feel that evening. Still, he thought he could recover if he slept for the rest of the day. "How about eight?"

"Perfect." Graham started to say something else, but stopped to chuckle. Sounding more like himself, he said, "I'll see you later, baby. Be good."

Randy hung up, wondering if he had made a mistake. He considered calling back to cancel, but he was exhausted and instead fell asleep.

v

Randy awoke with a start at 5:30 in the afternoon, alarmed by a dream he'd had about Dennis Crawley, the specifics of which he could not remember. The sun was setting, and his bedroom was only dimly lit by twilight. For an instant he sensed a hazy presence in the room, as if the Dennis of his dream were lingering by the foot of his bed. He shut his eyes and visualized the Hockney portrait, that simple, black-and-white sketch of the beautiful dead man. Dennis isn't here, he thought; he's at Graham's. But he was unable to shake the feeling that Dennis was near him. He opened his eyes and decided that his mind, still under the influence of his dream, was playing tricks on him. He closed his eyes once more and imagined he was pulling the phantom Dennis toward him, allowing it to envelop him. He waited a few minutes, then reopened his eyes and turned on the light. His hangover was gone, and he now felt nearly himself.

Jake seemed happy when Randy told him Graham had called that morning. "I think he likes you a lot," he said. "See if you can get him to tip you this time."

Randy nodded. "I'll do what I can."

Haircut was sleeping on the floor of the bedroom, not having budged since he'd passed out the night before. Randy put a cover over his naked body, then showered and dressed. Later, when he left the apartment, Haircut was still inert.

As he walked toward the West Village, he noticed Christmas displays in the windows of the stores on 8th Street, and saw that holiday decorations had cropped up everywhere, seemingly overnight. The street was bustling with shoppers, festive strollers, and drunken revelers, and this frantic activity disquieted him. His discomfort intensified as he drew closer to his destination. At Sheridan Square, he bought a pack of Merits. By the time he reached Graham's building on Perry Street, he had smoked three of them.

He hesitated before ringing the buzzer, then waited an inordinately long time for a response. As he stood there, he could hear in the distance the soft, saccharine sound of a particularly grating Christmas carol. Impatient, he pushed the buzzer again. At last, Graham clicked him in.

Inside, he thought about his last session with Graham, when he had been greeted by music booming down from the top floor. Now there was only silence. He climbed the stairs cautiously, acutely aware of the creaking floorboards, almost regretting the fact that he had not canceled this appointment and stayed home.

At the top of the stairs he saw Graham, dressed in his bathrobe and slippers, standing in the hallway by the door to his apartment.

He appeared very frail, even thinner than the last time. But his eyes were still sharp and intense; Randy found the contrast intimidating. "You're early," Graham said.

Randy looked at his watch; it was 7:55. "Sorry about that." Graham stared at him. "Never mind. Come in."

They stepped into the apartment, which was much darker this evening, the only light coming from a small lamp on the table near the leather couch, just next to the photo of Dennis. Randy glanced at the portrait of Madonna, which seemed more sinister in the half-light of the room.

"Sit down." Graham motioned toward the couch.

Randy did as he was told.

"I suppose you want a drink. Gin, isn't it?"

"Whatever you're having."

Graham shrugged. "In that case, you'll have nothing." He cleared his throat. "You see, I'm being very good. Doctor's orders."

"You're still not feeling well?"

"I've been better. But it's not necessary to follow my lead." Graham produced a half-smile. "In fact, I think you should drink twice as much tonight. It'll give me a vicarious thrill."

"All right. I'll have some gin."

When Graham left the room, Randy lit a cigarette. He searched for an ashtray, but could not find one. Growing increasingly anxious, he cupped the used match in his hand, then stood to look at Hockney's sketch of Dennis. The drawing disturbed him, and he returned to the couch.

Graham came back carrying a tall glass of gin and the bottle of dexedrine. "I didn't know you smoked," he remarked.

Randy looked up. "Sorry. I gave up for a while, but I guess I've started again. I couldn't find an ashtray."

"I've got one somewhere," Graham mumbled. "But no one's smoked here in years."

"I can put it out if you want."

"No, no." He studied Randy. "Actually, it's rather charming. Another vicarious pleasure for me. But I still think it's a filthy habit. Thank God I never took it up." He passed the gin and the glass to Randy, then left the room once more.

Randy sipped his drink and smoked his cigarette, examining the bottle of dexedrine, wondering if he wanted to get high. He decided the drug might ease his discomfort, and he unscrewed the cap. After hesitating a few seconds, he took out a pill and washed it down with gin.

Graham returned with an ashtray and sat next to Randy, gazing at him briefly before looking away. Randy extinguished his cigarette and lit another. Neither said anything for a few moments.

Graham broke the silence: "God, I hate this fucking season."

"You mean Christmas?" Randy gulped his drink. "I know what you mean. It's crazy outside."

"Bloody lunatics!" Graham paused, smiling slightly before going on. "So many people seem to kick at this time of year. That doesn't surprise me at all."

Randy stared at him. "I hadn't noticed that."

"Well, they do. Just this morning Dakota Montoya called to tell me about another one. A rather dreary editor named Charles Lawrence. Pathetic little man. No social skills whatsoever. But I've been depressed all day. That's why I wanted to see you; I thought it would cheer me up."

"Did you know him well?"

Ignoring Randy's question, Graham asked, *"You* have social skills, don't you? I should think they would be absolutely necessary in your profession."

Randy took another gulp of his drink.

"I can't stand people who don't have any. My friends may be avaricious, backbiting cunts, but they do know how to work a room."

Randy looked at the floor, then up at Graham. "I'd like to meet them sometime."

Graham frowned. "Why in the world would you want to do that?"

"They sound interesting."

"But they'd tear you apart!" Graham exclaimed. "Five minutes with them and you'd long for the warm, sheltering embrace of Mr. Hewitt."

Randy ground out his cigarette, then gulped the rest of his drink.

"Speaking of which," Graham went on, "are you through with your memoirs yet? You know, don't you, that you left the first installment here?"

Randy nodded.

"I was rather charmed by it, if you recall. Have you written any more?"

Randy turned the empty glass in his hand. "I haven't had time."

"Pity. That means we'll have to start the massage without any foreplay."

"Now?" Randy thought that he felt a slight rush from the dexedrine.

"Of course. That's the reason you're here, isn't it? Why don't you get undressed?"

Randy wavered, reluctant to begin a possibly intense session so soon after he had arrived. He placed his glass on the table next to the couch and leaned over to untie his shoes.

Graham stood. "I'll get you another drink. But I want to see you stark naked when I return." He picked up Randy's glass and walked out.

Randy removed his shoes and socks, then stared at his bare feet, thinking about how, at the age of eight, he had cut his foot on a piece of glass while wading in a shallow pond one summer afternoon. When he returned home, crying and bleeding, his father, furious, beat him, screaming, "I can't believe the shit you get into!"

Afterward, Randy soaked his foot in a tub of warm water, relieved that the beating was over, finding the warmth of the water comforting, the combination of his relief and this warmth pleasantly sensuous. Later, in bed before going to sleep, he masturbated, imagining as he did that he was swimming naked in a painfully hot pool.

As he remembered this, Randy felt the arousal he had experienced then. He remained still, seduced by his memory, unwilling to move.

His thoughts were interrupted when Graham returned with a fresh glass of gin. "I believe I told you to undress."

Randy looked up, but said nothing.

Graham passed the drink to him. "Not that it really matters. I'm sure I'll be useless as far as sex goes tonight. But a little voyeurism is always nice." He took off his robe. "Come on, let's get started."

Randy gazed at Graham's nude body, observing that his penis

looked preternaturally large when displayed against the frail backdrop of his emaciation. The contrast seemed grotesque, yet Randy felt strangely stimulated.

"What are you waiting for?" Graham demanded. "We haven't got all night."

Randy swallowed some gin, then placed his drink on the table and stood. Graham lay face down on the couch. Randy stripped off the rest of his clothes and sat next to him.

"Where's the oil?" Randy asked.

"Oh, I'm afraid it's all gone. Some little whore I saw a few weeks ago was an absolute glutton with it."

"Little whore?" Randy picked up his glass.

"Why, yes. Some piece of trash an agency sent me. I saw him just after our last session." Graham laughed. "His asshole was like the Holland Tunnel. The next day I got sick. Somehow I blamed him for everything." He looked up at Randy, leering. "Don't worry, baby, you're much better than that. I'll think twice before I cheat on you again. Just give me a good massage, okay?"

Randy gulped some gin, then sat on top of Graham's buttocks and massaged his shoulders and back. They did not speak again until Randy came to a particularly knotty muscle.

"Stop," Graham said. "Right there."

Randy kneaded the muscle and asked, "You mean here?"

Graham emitted a soft moan, letting Randy know he should continue.

When he had finished the lower back, Randy stood and worked on Graham's feet and legs. Then he moved up to his buttocks, sliding his hands down between his legs and playing with his scrotum. As he squeezed Graham's balls, Randy started to get an erection.

Graham groaned.

"Why don't you turn over?" Randy suggested.

"Must I?"

"I want to do your other side."

Somewhat reluctantly, Graham rolled onto his back. Fully erect now, Randy sat on top of Graham's flaccid penis. He massaged his chest, then leaned over and sucked his nipples.

"Stop it!" Graham cried irritably.

Randy stood, looking down at Graham's limp cock. He fell to his knees and took hold of it, massaging it gently. It remained flaccid. He lowered his head and put the penis in his mouth, concentrating on the tip at first, then moving up and down over the shaft. Nothing changed.

After several minutes, Graham laughed and said, "You remind me of a boy I once had in Tangier."

Randy looked up, letting the penis drop. "Tangier?"

"In Morocco. You know, North Africa."

Randy hesitated, then put the penis back in his mouth.

Graham sat up and placed his hands on Randy's head, pulling him away. "No, baby, I'm not in the mood."

Still erect, Randy got off his knees and sat on the couch. Graham put a hand on Randy's groin and tweaked his erection. "There'll be other times," he said. "Daddy's been sick." He removed his hand and put on his robe.

Randy picked up his drink, waited a few moments, then found his pack of Merits and lit a cigarette. Graham watched him as he smoked. Disconcerted by the silence, Randy asked, "So when were you in Morocco?"

Graham gazed at Randy, his face suddenly imbued with an expression that appeared almost eager. "Why do you want to know?"

"Well, I've always wanted to go there. I've never been to Europe."

Graham chuckled. "I thought I told you that Morocco was in North Africa."

"Well, you know…." Randy blushed. "It's just that I haven't been out of the States much. I mean, there was that trip to Nassau with Mr. Hewitt." He paused, then quickly added, "And once we went to his summer house in Canada."

Graham gaped at him in astonishment. "Oh, you missed a lot! I lived in London for years, back in the late sixties and early seventies. I used to fly down to Tangier all the time."

"What was it like? You know: London, Morocco, the sixties?"

About to respond, Graham eyed the glass in Randy's hand; it was nearly empty. "Let me freshen your drink. When I get back, I'll tell you everything."

Randy passed his glass to him, then waited for his return, finishing his cigarette and lighting another. The uneasiness he had been feeling all evening subsided slightly, replaced by a desire to find out more about Graham's life. He had always been fascinated by the sixties, by the stories he had heard and by the things he had read. He wished he had been older then, that he could have experienced something other than the world he knew, a world that seemed depleted, as if its energy had peaked and waned before he'd had a chance to participate in anything. Graham Mason, he suspected, had been in the thick of things. And, more importantly, Graham had lived during an era when being at the epicenter of activity really mattered.

Graham came back with the gin, then sat next to Randy and talked about his travels, his years in London and Morocco. He had been in his twenties at the time.

"It was a magical period for me," he began. "For the world, actually. The sixties were fabulous. And London was the place to be."

"I always heard it was San Francisco."

"Oh, please, all those hippies with their love beads! Give me a break! London was much more glamorous. That was long before Maggie Thatcher had her way and turned it into another wretched den of yuppies." He beamed. "Of course, I was on top of the world then myself. I'd just published *Dinner at Dawn* and was getting my first taste of fame. It was all very heady."

"It sounds so great!"

Nearly hypnotized, Randy listened as Graham spoke for over an hour.

He described his life in London, talking first about his flat in Belgravia, the most fashionable part of the city. It was given to him, gratis, by a wealthy patron of the arts, a brittle, hard-drinking heiress, who only required that he attend her weekly literary soirées, lengthy, pretentious affairs that bored him immensely—even when they produced excellent connections. But those evenings were not all *that* painful for him. And once he got through them he was free.

He wore velvet pants and kept his hair long, having it touched up once a week at an expensive salon in the West End. He accrued a large network of friends, clever, pretty people, artists and fashion designers, drunken aristocrats and assorted arrivistes, all of whose lives revolved around the cafés and boutiques that had cropped up along the King's Road. He smoked hashish the European way, mixed with tobacco in long, fat joints. He drank French wine at lunch and tripped in Holland Park, hallucinating wildly while watching the peacocks that roamed freely over the lawns. He attended elegant drag balls held in barges docked on the Thames and participated in elaborate orgies during weekends at country estates. He sucked off strangers in various parks throughout the city and had an affair with his drug dealer Nicholas, a silent, elfin boy with long, pristine fingers and large, doe-like eyes, who sold acid at his parents' house near Regents Park. The year before Graham met him, Nicholas had played a small but important role in a film by Federico Fellini. In the months after the film's premiere, he acquired two skittish Afghans and a taste for bondage and heroin.

And then there were the trips south, Graham's excursions along the "hippie trail," which took him to the Balearic Islands off the coast of Spain, where he caroused in the bars of Ibiza and sunned on the beaches of Formentera. But his travels ultimately led to Morocco, to the port of Tangier and inland, down to the Sahara Desert and the market city of Marrakech. Graham kept a house in Essaouira on the southern coast, a blindingly white town surrounded by a turreted medieval fort. It was there that he did his writing.

He had a Moroccan lover, Ahmed, who cooked succulent stews called tagines and played Beatles songs badly on the guitar. Graham helped Ahmed learn English; Ahmed taught Graham to ride a camel. They smoked hash daily, took long walks in the morning on Essaouira's endless sandy beach, then napped in hammocks every afternoon. In the evening, after dinner, Ahmed sipped mint tea as Graham worked.

Their affair lasted three years, ending when Ahmed moved to Marrakech and married. They stayed in touch and saw each other regularly, until Ahmed died of typhus in 1973. Immediately following Ahmed's death, Graham moved back to the States. "I couldn't stay over there anymore," he said. "It seemed haunted." Wherever he went after that, things never seemed the same.

Now, Graham concluded, he realized how happy he had been at

that time. "Today everything is just fucked. It's all turned to shit." Frowning, he turned away from Randy and was silent.

Randy, stoned on the dexedrine but mellow from the gin, absorbed Graham's words, thrilled by everything he had heard. These stories fascinated him, and he felt a surprising tenderness for this man who had just shared them with him. He held onto this feeling, longing to augment it, to heighten the empathy he was experiencing.

He finished his drink and lit a cigarette, waiting a moment before asking, "So when did Dennis come into the picture?"

Graham looked back at him, then froze, his face revealing nothing for what Randy perceived to be an eternity. He drew in his breath, glaring at Randy with fiery eyes. "What exactly do you know about Dennis?"

Randy clutched his empty glass, unable to respond.

Graham twisted his mouth up, sneering. "Actually, it's inconceivable that *you* could know anything. The very idea is absurd." He leaned closer to Randy, lowering his voice. "You see, Dennis was never very big on sleaze. That seems to be *my* unfortunate predilection."

Randy drew on his cigarette, then stammered, "I…I'm sorry. I really am."

Moving back, Graham turned away again.

Randy raised his empty glass to his lips, then set it on the table. He extinguished his cigarette and, moving slowly, lowered his head onto Graham's lap, parting the robe slightly, gently placing a hand on Graham's penis, and easing his mouth over the shaft. He stopped and looked up, saying almost inaudibly, "I didn't mean to be a naughty boy."

Graham's right hand shot out, pushing Randy away, then slapping his face, striking him with a heavy, resounding blow that hurled him against the back of the couch. He lowered his hand and stared at Randy, smiling slightly now. "You're just a silly little slut, aren't you?"

Stunned and shaking, Randy gasped for air, then fell across Graham's lap, crying.

Graham said nothing initially, allowing Randy to sob unhindered for several minutes. Then he placed a hand on Randy's head and, tentatively, ran his fingers through his hair. "Baby," he whispered. "My sweet baby boy. Daddy's here."

Randy rested on Graham's lap, still crying softly. Graham continued stroking his hair.

Suddenly the dexedrine overcame Randy's inertia, and he bolted up. "I've got to go."

Jarred, Graham stared at him. He finally raised his arms and stretched. "Yes, yes, we know," he yawned, "Jake will be worried."

As Randy dressed, Graham slapped his ass playfully, then stepped into the next room and returned with one hundred dollars. He gave the money to Randy and walked him to the door.

"I'll call soon," Graham said as they parted. He leaned over and pecked Randy's cheek. "By the way, do you want your memoir back?"

Randy shook his head.

Graham appeared surprised. "How very odd. Well, at any rate, when you come back, I want to read some more."

"I...I'll do my best," Randy stammered.

Disoriented, he hurried home.

Haircut was with Jake when Randy entered the apartment. Both were drunk, stretched out on the floor and smoking a joint, a jug of white wine between them.

"Sweetheart!" cried Jake.

"Yes, indeed, it's Sweetheart!" Haircut shrieked. "Why don't you join us—that is, if you can sit down after seeing Mr. Mason."

Randy peered at them. "I'm pretty tired. I think I'm gonna go to bed."

Jake tottered up and lurched over to Randy, throwing his arms around him and kissing him on the mouth. "Oh, stay with us for a while. I'm so happy to see m'baby!"

Randy pulled away. "I'm exhausted."

"Yes," Haircut said, "big Graham's worn Jake's little sweetheart out."

"Graham's been sick," Randy told him.

"Again?" asked Jake.

"He's better, but he's still not himself."

Haircut took a swig of wine. "It's the sweetness. Dennis had it; he's dead. Now Graham's got it, too."

Randy was alarmed by the direction the conversation was taking. He focused on Haircut's head, observing that he had bleached his hair again.

"Every faggot's got the sweetness," Haircut continued. "It's just a matter of time."

"I don't want to talk about it," Randy murmured. He started walking toward the bedroom.

Jake grabbed Randy's arm. "Where are you going?"

"Please. I'm tired."

"Let him go," Haircut said. "Sweetheart needs his rest. Why don't you roll me another joint? I mean, that's the answer, isn't it?"

"Oh, all right," Jake relented.

In bed, Randy lay awake for more than two hours, listening as Jake and Haircut's laughter seeped in through the walls. Eventually their voices seemed to dim, and he drifted off.

He dreamed he was inside Graham's house on the Moroccan shore, its interior looking exactly like the apartment on Perry Street. As he stood by the doorway, he watched Graham fuck Dennis on the couch, then slap him repeatedly and beat him with a thick leather belt. When Graham was finished, he wrapped his hands around Dennis's neck and strangled him. Dead, Dennis rose, and Graham struck him once more, this time with a whip. "Sweet baby," Graham cried, stabbing Dennis in the chest with a knife. "Sweet, sweet baby, bleed for me!" Feeling the blade enter his own heart, Randy stirred.

It was dawn. Jake, naked and smelling of wine, was crawling into bed.

Still half asleep, Randy grabbed Jake's penis. "Fuck me," he whispered. "I want to be nasty."

Jake laughed. "What's this? M'baby's horny?"

"Just do it!"

"I'm drunk, sweetheart. It's late."

"Please!"

Jake played with Randy's asshole, then, despite his inebriation, obliged. When it was over, he passed out. Another hour passed before Randy fell asleep again, but this time he slept for the rest of the day.

VI

Randy spent the next five days in a haze, feeling much of the time as if he were only partially awake. At first he thought he was suffering from a relapse of the illness he'd had a few weeks earlier and that he would once again be forced to stay in bed. But his symptoms never progressed that far, and he was able to keep all the appointments Jake had scheduled. Even so, he was troubled by a persistent discomfort, an obscure anxiety and dissatisfaction that seemed to ooze out of him and permeate all he saw.

As he walked through his days—apathetically taking care of his clients, watching television, performing sets on the weights at his gym—he found himself thinking about Graham's tales of the sixties. Those stories made his own life seem bleak in comparison, and he became obsessed by them. He liked to envision a much younger Graham, a dandy dressed in velvet pants strolling on a trendy London street, his long hair flowing down the back of a brightly flowered shirt. Then he pictured himself strolling there as well, living a fabulous adventure. After indulging in such fantasies, he returned to the present with a sense of regret, a bit depressed, but resigned to the fact that he would never know a time as exciting or appealing as that period Graham remembered so vividly.

Sometimes, when he was in bed and half asleep, he was struck by his memory of the way Graham had looked while reminiscing about those days. Although Randy hadn't registered it then, Graham seemed at the time younger, almost robust, healthy again. In retrospect, the contrast with Graham's usual pallor had been startling, particularly when, after Graham finished speaking, his face resumed its usual countenance and his familiar frailty became more apparent. Whenever Randy thought of this contrast now, he also recalled Haircut's talk of the sweetness. He'd tried to deny it to himself in the past, but it had become increasingly obvious to him that Graham was very sick. For once, he knew, Haircut had been telling the truth: Like so many others, Graham was dying.

Randy had long ago stopped counting acquaintances who'd disappeared. Doing this was fairly easy: Not having many friends, he had never witnessed anyone's disintegration. But he'd grown used to presuming that those he no longer saw were sick or dead. The sweetness even seemed to have an odd logic to it, albeit a logic that he intuited but did not completely understand. He realized, however, that it connected with the despair he felt whenever he compared the bleakness he witnessed around him with the seemingly magical era that Graham had described. Death appeared to suit today's world.

This omnipresence of death brought with it new rules and codes of behavior, guidelines and strictures that Randy refused to observe at all times. He found these restrictions grating; often they reminded him of his father's decrees and of the punishments he'd received if he disobeyed them. He liked to think that he'd left such constraints behind in the Midwest, that he was now free to do as he liked, to ignore anything he found suffocating, to be, if he wished, a "naughty boy." Besides, he wondered, did he really want to experience old age, to become senile while lingering in the muck he saw? Graham was right: Everything *was* fucked; things *had* turned to shit. The world had become a very unpleasant place. Randy could not see the point in taking excessive precautions in order to prolong an existence in such a shithole.

Still, he found the signs of imminent death in Graham unsettling; he knew the risks he himself had taken. And yet there was also something comforting, even reassuring in these signs, an indication that all things *did* come to an end, that life really was finite.

He remembered talking with Ellen shortly after he began seeing her, when she'd questioned him about his suicide attempt.

"Did you really want to die?" she had asked, peering straight at him, her eyes kind but piercing.

Randy looked away for a second, then stared back at her and said, "I guess I didn't want to die. It's just that I didn't want to live anymore."

After he said this, he was surprised by his words. Yet he knew today that he'd been telling the truth.

He found himself drawn to Graham, to the fame and the glamour, the power and the acclaim. But the strongest pull came from his knowledge that it would all end soon, that Graham would not go out anonymously, but instead would die in a blaze of glory, an icon in an increasingly grim world.

On the first of December, Graham called Randy at five in the afternoon.

"Listen, baby," he said, "you hate Christmas as much as I do. I'm still not feeling well, and I can't do that much. I want to spend a lot of time with you this month. Every night, actually. You've got to keep me amused."

Randy felt a familiar unease creep up on him. He paused, then lit a cigarette. "I'll have to talk to Jake," he answered. "You know, to see what we can do about my other clients."

Graham laughed. "I'm sure something can be arranged. I'll pay you very well: your usual fee, plus a little something extra. A Christmas bonus just for you."

Randy hesitated again, then asked, "Can I call you tomorrow? I've got to find out what Jake says."

"If you insist. But I won't let you disappoint me."

Randy waited until later that night to tell Jake about the proposed arrangement.

"Shit, we're going to be raking it in, sweetheart," Jake exclaimed excitedly. "I want you to make Graham *very* happy. Haircut will take care of the others. There'll be no problem there."

As Jake expected, Haircut welcomed this opportunity to expand his business. "That's *definitely* the answer!" he cried. "What a Merry Christmas this'll be!"

Randy was not so effusive. The money Graham had promised him would, of course, be welcome. He also saw this as an opportunity to discover more about Graham and his world. But he was uncomfortable with—and a bit frightened by—the idea of his spending so much time with someone who provoked such unpredictable reactions in him whenever they were together. He was not sure he wanted to spend every night in this manner.

Despite these qualms, he made the first of what became daily excursions to Perry Street the following evening. He established a pattern, arriving there at eight and staying until two or three in the morning. After overcoming his initial uneasiness, he realized that he was actually enjoying himself immensely. In fact, this was becoming the best December he could remember.

Graham was amazing, unlike anyone Randy had ever before met, and Randy was thrilled that such a prominent man wanted to spend so much time with him. Besides, he and Jake rarely made plans for the holidays, and it was great having something to do for a change. Then, too, Graham gave him at least one hundred and fifty dollars at the end of each visit, often more. Randy was making more money than he had ever earned in his life.

Unlike their earlier encounters, these sessions with Graham were relatively uneventful. Always dressed in his bathrobe and slippers, Graham was full of stories about the fabulous things he had done in the past. He told Randy about legendary clubs and restaurants, gallery openings and book parties, film screenings and Broadway premieres. Stoned on Graham's dexedrine and drinking his gin, Randy listened eagerly as Graham gossiped about celebrities: Andy Warhol, Dakota Montoya, Keith Haring, Denise Lamour, and dozens of others, all of whom he appeared to have known intimately at one time or another.

But when he wasn't gossiping, Graham seemed subdued, much quieter than he had been the first times Randy had seen him. He continued to abstain from the gin and the pills, although he insisted on Randy's getting high. Sometimes, between anecdotes, he gazed at Randy in a peculiar, almost melancholy way, which made Randy uncomfortable. Fortunately, Graham would soon look away, remaining silent or, perhaps, relating another story about an escapade from his past.

The massages, too, were less intense, commencing around midnight and lasting for about an hour. If Randy tried to recreate the intimacy they had experienced during their first two sessions—by, for instance, massaging Graham's penis or taking the flaccid shaft in his mouth—Graham did not respond. Randy's attempts at initiating sex only seemed to irritate him.

Although he tried to hide it, Randy was disappointed whenever Graham failed to react, for many of the things they'd done together had made him feel deliciously naughty. One morning, just before falling asleep, he realized that, in his more intense encounters with Graham, he had felt like a child—albeit a child totally unlike the one he had actually been. This little boy—the one he became sometimes with Graham—would have pissed on Mr. Hewitt's carpets and smashed his antiques. He knew that if he'd ever really allowed himself to behave in this way, he would have been punished. Still, he felt, any punishment given in response to such a joyful crime would have been easy to take.

He longed to abandon himself to Graham once again, to experience even more freedom than he had before. But as his attempts at arousing Graham no longer worked, he learned to concentrate on the massage and cease any other endeavors.

After these sessions, when Randy returned to his apartment in the middle of the night, Haircut was usually with Jake. Ever since the two of them had gone into business together, they were practically inseparable. If Haircut was not seeing a client, he and Jake would go to clubs, crash Christmas parties they had heard about, or just stay in, watching television, drinking wine, smoking pot, and doing the occasional line of coke.

Haircut was relentless in his efforts to give Randy advice and to elicit from him information about Graham.

"So what was the big man up to?" he'd ask when he saw Randy.

"He was pretty quiet again." Randy would say or something similar, never offering anything more.

"Pity. But you still hold all the cards. Let him think you're his lover. He's practically treating you like one anyway. What harm can it do, right? He's not gonna be around forever. If you play things right, you could end up on top."

Randy always had to drink a few beers in order to come down from the dexedrine he had taken at Graham's. As the sun came up, he'd go to bed.

His schedule became a nocturnal one, and he ceased all the activities he had previously pursued during the day. He even stopped going to the gym, deciding to exercise at home instead. Having cleared his agenda, he slept most of the time.

Jake, too, fell into this pattern. Now the only time they spent alone with each other was when they had breakfast in the early evening. By seven-thirty, Randy was out of the apartment, heading west toward Graham's.

The almost-soothing monotony of this routine was broken on Christmas Eve, when Graham phoned Randy at noon, awakening him.

"Baby," he said, sounding better than he had in weeks, "I've been so boring lately. I need a change. Denise Lamour is giving a party tonight, and I'm going to go. I'm sure it'll be wild."

Disappointed, Randy asked, "You want to cancel our session?"

"Don't be *stupid*! I want to see you *afterwards*. I'll definitely be in the mood then. It'll be just like old times, I promise." Graham chortled. "Don't come until two, though. We'll toast in Christmas together."

Excited, Randy hung up. He got out of bed and smoked several cigarettes. As he smoked, he found himself anticipating that evening, wondering if Graham were indeed better, if things would now be as they'd been before. After an hour, he returned to bed and masturbated. He then drifted off and slept until nine.

When he awoke, he found Jake and Haircut smoking a joint in the kitchen.

"You're late!" Jake cried. "I've been trying to wake you up for two hours! Aren't you going to Graham's?"

Haircut leered at Randy. "Yes, what about Mr. Mason?"

Randy laughed. "He's at Denise Lamour's. I'm gonna see him later."

Haircut sucked on the joint. "Oh, *really*? Well, you seem awfully chipper."

Jake took the joint from Haircut and turned to Randy. "You should make him give you something extra tonight. I mean, sweetheart, it's Christmas Eve and everything."

"Don't worry," Randy replied, "everything'll be fine."

At midnight, Jake and Haircut left the apartment, having decided that they wanted to check out a new club on Avenue D. Randy drank two beers, then left the apartment himself.

The streets were quiet that night; most people, Randy assumed, had chosen to celebrate Christmas Eve with relatives and friends.

Despite the calm, he felt a vague anxiety creeping up on him as he drew further west, an apprehension similar to the uneasiness he had experienced just before his first few sessions with Graham. Near Sheridan Square, he stopped at a bar and ordered a gin and tonic. He finished the drink quickly, then hurried to Perry Street.

When he reached Graham's brownstone, he was amazed to find Graham sitting on the stoop outside, wearing a tuxedo and holding a champagne glass. Randy realized this was the first time he had seen him dressed in anything besides his bathrobe. The formal clothes he wore made him appear distinguished.

"You're late!" Graham rose.

"Am I?" Randy looked at his watch. It was precisely two.

"I've been dying to see you." Graham kissed Randy on the cheek and pinched his buttocks. "Come in, baby. Let's get started."

Inside, Randy sat on the leather couch. Graham immediately handed him a glass of champagne and a dexedrine. "Drink up, I'm way ahead of you," he said, then swallowed a dexedrine himself.

Randy could see by the bright lights in the apartment that Graham was flushed, apparently very drunk. He drank half of the champagne in his glass and took the pill. "So how was the party?"

"Divine." Graham placed a hand on Randy's lap and squeezed his upper thigh. "I was, of course, the star."

Randy gulped the rest of his champagne. "They must have been pretty worried about you."

"Well, yes. They made such a fuss, it was embarrassing." Graham laughed. "That cunt Dakota couldn't stand the fact that I was getting all the attention. He kept making these absurd, sloppy passes at practically every man there." He refilled Randy's glass, then his own. "Really, it was like old times, the seventies *redux*. Everyone looked gorgeous, fabulous! I even danced for a while. I haven't done that in years."

Randy took a sip of his champagne. "I wish I'd been there."

"Well, maybe some day I'll let you come to an event with me." Again squeezing Randy's thigh, Graham winked at him. "But you have to be very, very good."

Randy felt himself getting an erection. "I'll do my best."

Graham tightened his grip on Randy's thigh and stared directly at him. "You know, all the excitement tonight really titillated me. I suspected it would. That's why I wanted you here when I got back."

Feeling giddy from the champagne, Randy moved his right hand onto Graham's groin and started to unzip his pants. Graham turned away and retrieved a magazine from the table next to the couch. It was, Randy noticed, a pornographic pictorial entitled *Teenage Butt Juice.*

"I left the party early," Graham said. "For some reason, I was really anxious to see you. But then, of course, you little shit, you weren't here. I was irritated by that and bored, too, so I started digging through my old pornography collection. A lot of it was pure garbage, but I did find this one from the seventies." He held up *Teenage Butt Juice.* "It was one of my favorites."

Graham passed the magazine to Randy, who leafed through it, studying its many photographs of nude teenage boys. Some of the models were on their knees, their pimply buttocks pointed toward the camera, others lying on their backs, their legs raised and spread-eagled. Each boy offered an almost-proctological view of his anus.

Randy did not know how he was meant to respond. "This old porno's pretty interesting," he said.

"Interesting?" The pitch of Graham's voice grew higher. "Baby, it's much more than that! I suspect in the future *Teenage Butt Juice* will survive as a monument to our time, a beacon of light from an obscene age."

Randy decided that Graham was even more intoxicated than he had suspected. He found this focus on the magazine disconcerting.

"I mean, look at these." Graham leaned over Randy and turned the pages to a spread in the middle. "Masterpieces, all of them! My own work is nothing!"

Randy gazed at four photographs of a youth named Jamie Gilmour, a light-haired, blue-eyed, tanned adolescent, who, the text claimed, was a surfer from California. Jamie's poses were similar to those of the others, for he, too, provided a number of tantalizing views of his opened anus. But he was much more attractive than most porno models, which was, Randy assumed, the reason Graham found his posturing so piquant. Yet there was something else about him that was intriguing: After studying the photographs for a minute, he realized that Jamie resembled Dennis Crawley. Startled, he glanced up at Graham. "They're nice," he said hesitantly.

"Nice?" Graham grabbed the magazine from Randy. "I think they're sublime!"

Growing more uncomfortable, Randy lit a cigarette. Graham was silent, lost in the magazine. Randy sipped his champagne.

Graham finally looked up. "I had a brilliant idea earlier."

"Oh, yeah?" Randy hoped they could move away from Jamie Gilmour; his resemblance to Dennis was too strange.

"Yes." Graham peered at Randy. "I'd like you to recreate one of these photographs for me."

"What?"

"I want you to take off your clothes and pose for me. You're going to be Jamie Gilmour tonight."

Randy looked downward, then back up at Graham. "I was sort of hoping we could get into something else."

Graham smiled, squeezing Randy's leg. "Baby, you do remember, don't you, that I'm in charge here? I'm paying for your time, after all. You've got to do what *I* want."

Embarrassed, Randy muttered, "I'm sorry," and, extinguishing his cigarette, stood. He took off his boots.

Graham slapped him on the ass. "Good boy!"

Randy undressed. When he was naked, he stood before Graham, unsure how he was supposed to proceed. Graham only gazed at him.

"So what do you want me to do now?" Randy asked.

Graham glanced at the magazine, which he still held. Then, looking up, he said, "I told you: You're going to pose like Jamie Gilmour."

Randy winced. "Can I have some more champagne?"

Graham laughed. "You can't drink and pose at the same time!" He shoved the magazine at Randy. "Now, which one do you want to do?"

Randy studied the photographs, struck once more by Jamie's resemblance to Dennis. He wondered if they had been the same person, if Dennis had been a porno model, a prostitute, someone from the gutter whom Graham had taken under his wing. This did not seem entirely improbable. He focused on a shot in which Jamie was on his knees, his buttocks facing the camera, his cheeks spread, his crack opened. He was gazing back over his shoulder toward the camera, smiling at the photographer. Randy found himself smiling as well. This is definitely Dennis, he thought. He looked up at Graham and said, "I'll do this one."

"Go ahead."

Randy pointed toward the floor in front of the couch. "Right here?"

"That's right."

He dropped to his knees, his hands in front of him, arching his back so that his buttocks were raised. "Is this okay?"

Graham poured himself another glass of champagne. "It's perfect."

Randy did not move. He hoped this would lead to something else, that Graham would overcome his recent resistance to sex.

But Graham only sat on the couch, staring at the magazine, then looking down at Randy. He spoke just once, when he asked Randy to turn to the left. Randy obeyed. After that, Graham was silent.

As he posed, Randy looked around the room, at the bookshelves and the portrait of Madonna, settling on the Hockney sketch of Dennis. He took this in, then closed his eyes.

Everything from his past, everything familiar to him, floated away, leaving him feeling empty, depleted—a condition he found oddly pleasant. Soon he was not even aware that Graham was near him. Instead, he felt another presence, a spirit in the air. He took this spirit in and, for a moment, thought he had become someone else.

Then he heard Graham stand and come toward him. He sensed him leaning over and peering at his anus, examining it.

"Baby," Graham whispered, shoving two fingers into the opening, turning them brusquely inside. "You always liked this, didn't you, baby? It's been a long time."

Randy shifted his buttocks up, allowing the fingers to slide further in.

"I've missed you." Graham's voice was soft and distant.

"But I've been here all the time." Randy tightened his muscles, squeezing Graham's fingers. "Come on, fuck me!"

Graham stopped moving. "What did you say?"

Randy opened his eyes and looked at him. "Don't you want to?"

Graham frowned and, as abruptly as he had started, pulled his fingers out, wiping them on Randy's thigh. "Get dressed," he said. He turned away and sat on the couch.

In a daze, Randy got off his knees and crouched on the floor. "What's wrong?" he asked, shaky.

Graham glared at him. "I told you to put your clothes on."

Randy rose. "Don't you want me to do another pose or something?"

"Just leave me alone."

Randy started to say something else, but stopped himself. He found his clothes.

When Randy finished dressing, Graham pulled his wallet from the inside pocket of his jacket. "Here," he said, handing Randy two hundred dollars. "Now get out."

Although Randy did not know what he had done wrong, he felt guilty. "Please," he asked, upset yet stimulated, "let me stay. I'll do anything you want me to."

Graham sighed. "No," he said firmly. But then, his tone softening, he added, "I'll talk to you later."

Bewildered but reassured by Graham's last words, Randy pocketed the money. He put on his coat and slowly walked to the front door. As he left, he looked back at Graham and said, "Merry Christmas."

Graham did not answer.

Later, in bed, Randy had a dream about being with Dennis, retaining afterward a vivid image of the two of them naked and tied to a tree, their hands bound together, the bark cutting into their backs. In the distance, Ellen watched them. Randy then saw that it was he himself, not Dennis, who resembled Jamie Gilmour. He awoke screaming.

"Christ," Jake exclaimed, roused by Randy's cries, "you aren't going to start that again, are you? Grow up!" He rolled away and slept once more.

Randy lay next to him, quivering. He managed to fall back asleep after an hour, but his sleep was fitful. To his relief, he had no more dreams.

VII

At six the next evening, Christmas Day, a phone call from Graham woke Randy.

"I'm sick again!" Graham snarled. "I really overdid it last night. I hope I wasn't too much for you."

"That's okay," Randy said groggily.

"It's fucking annoying, I have to be so careful. Now I won't be able to see you for a few days."

Randy lit a cigarette, trying to stay awake.

"I'll pay you for your time anyway," Graham continued. "But while you're free, I want you to start working on your memoirs again. That episode with Hewitt really whetted my appetite. I can read what you've written the next time you're here."

After Randy hung up, he was relieved that Graham had phoned, yet grateful that he would have a break from their daily contact. Graham's behavior the night before had left him feeling drained. A lot of people do weird things when they're drunk, he told himself.

But it was more than Graham's behavior that had disturbed him, though he could not understand the precise cause of his confusion. He thought about Dennis, then recalled Jamie. The resemblance *had* been peculiar. Even so, thinking about it, he decided they could not possibly have been the same person. The same type, yes. *Graham's type.* The thing is, he thought, I'm Graham's type as well.

He remembered how he had felt while posing for Graham, when, for a few seconds, he'd sensed that he had become someone else. The sensation he'd had then frightened him now, particularly the pleasurable emptiness he'd experienced just before taking in that other identity. It was almost as if he were dead. Graham's rejection of him afterward only reinforced this feeling: Naked, he had felt like a carcass. And, although Graham's subsequent actions upset and humiliated him, he had, underneath it all, liked the fact that he was getting what he was sure he deserved.

It was startling to see this here in bed, half asleep as he was. He didn't want to let it get to him, to brood and make himself ill again. Besides, wasn't seeing the truth supposed to bring with it freedom?

Wasn't it even possible for him to use this self-knowledge, to be free all the time?

Then, remembering Graham's request to read more of his memoirs, he wondered how free he could be. He preferred leaving some things alone. Why couldn't Graham be satisfied with that one story about Mr. Hewitt? It was bad enough that he'd had to go over his past with Ellen; he didn't want to have to wade through it all again.

He decided that he wouldn't worry about this today. He was going to have some time on his own for a change. He could relax; he'd think about his memoirs later.

Haircut arrived at nine, drunk. He had stayed up all night and then spent the day at a sex club on 14th Street.

"It was so sleazy!" he enthused to Randy and Jake. "You should have been there. I was a *star*. Everyone was standing around watching me get porked by this *gorgeous* sailor from Rio."

Jake was not amused. "Shit, Haircut, you really fucked up this time. You were supposed to see Jackson Reeves at six. I bet he's pissed!"

Momentarily confused, Haircut recovered rapidly. "I totally forgot. I mean, it's *Christmas*. I'll make it up to you tomorrow, I promise. Why don't you pour me some wine and light a joint. That's the answer, right?"

Jake sighed. "You're such an asshole!" He brought out the pot and opened a bottle of Almaden, saying as he did, "You owe me one, remember."

"Jeez, of course!"

They ordered food from a Chinese restaurant. Haircut passed out before it arrived. He snored heavily as Jake and Randy ate dinner, and continued sleeping, not moving, as they watched television.

At five, just before going to bed, Jake looked down at Haircut, lying clothed but uncovered near the couch in the living room.

"What a mess!" he remarked. "If m'baby ever gets like that, I'll divorce him."

Randy laughed. "I wouldn't blame you."

Although Haircut was meant to see Wayne Lewis, another client, at eight the following night, he was still sleeping at seven. Jake asked Randy to take Haircut's place.

"Just this once, sweetheart. I'll talk to Haircut. He can't keep fucking up like this."

Not willing to argue, Randy grudgingly agreed.

When he arrived at the hotel suite, he discovered that Wayne Lewis had expected a full-service escort.

"You've got the wrong person," he protested when Wayne asked for a blow job. "I'm just a masseur."

Wayne was not pleased. "I'm not going to give you a hundred bucks for a lousy massage. No way!"

Randy was reluctant to move beyond the services he normally provided; oral sex was definitely not a part of his repertoire. But then he'd crossed that boundary—and others—in his sessions with Graham. Besides, Wayne Lewis was sort of attractive. Relenting, he got on his knees and did as Wayne requested.

When he arrived home, Haircut apologized effusively. "Today was not the answer," he declared. "It won't happen again, though. Really, I promise."

Randy remained annoyed and did not speak to Haircut for the rest of the night.

Several days passed, and Graham did not call. Haircut had by now recovered from his Christmas binge, and was once again able to fulfill his obligations to Jake. As Randy had nothing to do, he considered working on his memoirs, but could never quite muster the necessary enthusiasm; the prospect of sleeping or watching television was more enticing. Then, too, he felt he needed dexedrine to write. Since he'd stopped seeing Graham, his energy level had been considerably lower.

The afternoon before New Year's Eve, a messenger arrived with an envelope from Graham. Inside was a check for $1,500.00 and a note:

Happy New Year, baby! Recovery is slow, but I want to see you soon anyway. Things have been too boring. Give my regards to Hewitt. Kisses, G.

Even though he was thrilled by the size of the check, Randy felt apprehensive, reminded as he was of Graham's desire to read his as-yet-unwritten work. He considered starting on it immediately, but Haircut had another idea.

"Let's go to the party at The Scrotum!" he exclaimed, excited by the news of Graham's check. "The Bloody Tampons are playing. And everyone says Madonna's gonna show up. I'll make myself look really fierce. She's bound to notice me then."

Randy groaned as he heard Haircut's plan, not wanting to spend New Year's Eve at The Scrotum—even if it was, as Haircut explained, "the coolest place around," and even if this party would be, as was rumored, a major, A-list event. He didn't relish the idea of spending the night in a crowded bar full of posing club kids, listening to the Bloody Tampons, a heavy-metal band comprised of four tall, hairy transvestites.

Jake, on the other hand, was enthusiastic. "Come on, sweetheart, it'll be good for m'baby to get out for a change."

"Yeah," Haircut agreed, "get a life, sweetheart!"

"Well…" Randy began.

Jake pulled a prescription pill bottle from his shirt pocket. "Maybe this'll change your mind."

Randy took the bottle from him. It contained several kinds of pills, including a few that were triangular and orange, which he knew were dexedrine. "Where'd you get them?"

Jake smiled. "I thought m'baby'd like a New Year's treat."

Haircut stared at the bottle in Randy's palm. "I don't know about m'baby, but I'll have one."

Randy took out two dexedrine and handed one to Haircut, then swallowed the second. Although he still did not want to go to The Scrotum, he gave in, insisting he wasn't going to make a big deal out of the evening, dress up or do anything like that.

Jake told him they could wear their standard T-shirts and jeans.

"You two can wear whatever you want," Haircut said. "I'm going home to douche!"

He returned at eleven, very high and heavily made up, dressed in a black rubber shirt, black-velvet biker shorts, and black combat boots, his purple Hermés scarf and an ornate crucifix around his neck. In the few hours that had passed since he'd left the apartment, he had gotten a Caesar cut and dyed his hair jet-black.

"Happy New Year!" he shrieked. "Won't Madonna love it?" Randy found the outfit ridiculous and laughed.

"She'll certainly notice you," Jake remarked.

The three of them had some wine, then walked to The Scrotum, which was five blocks away.

When they arrived at the club, there was an unruly mob gathered on the sidewalk outside, everyone vying for the attention of the person at the door, a surly, muscular woman with short, spiky black hair and enormous breasts.

"Forget it!" Randy muttered, eyeing the crowd. "Let's just go home and watch Dick Clark."

"Are you kidding?" Haircut looked at Randy as if he were crazy, then screamed, "We're on the list! We're on the list!" until he saw an acquaintance who was about to be admitted.

"Oliver!" he cried, running forward. Jake and Randy followed.

Oliver didn't recognize Haircut. "Excuse me?" he asked, scowling at the three of them before letting his eyes rest briefly on Randy. "There must be some mistake." He had an English accent, which Randy thought pompous.

"Come on, we met at that new place—you know, The Citadel— a few weeks ago," Haircut said. "You remember, don't you? I was wearing chartreuse shorts."

Before Oliver could reply, the woman at the door bellowed, "Are you going in or what?"

Oliver dashed for the door. Haircut, Jake, and Randy tagged along. Once inside, they left Oliver and wandered off on their own. The club was packed and unbearably stuffy, with many in the crowd milling around the long bar. At first they stood on the edge of the dance floor, watching the ecstatic dancers, most waving their arms in the air, some rolling their hips against their partners, others thrashing about alone, staring into space. The lights were flashing on and off as a techno mix blasted out of the loudspeakers.

Haircut saw another acquaintance on the other side of the room, a muscular black man dressed in a leather jock strap and knee-high boots.

"There's Calvin," he said. "He's always got coke." He ran off.

Randy and Jake said nothing, watching Haircut in the distance as he embraced Calvin, then darted to the bathroom with him.

As Haircut disappeared, Jake asked Randy, "Would you like a drink?"

"Yeah, gin." The music drowned out Randy's words.

"What?"

"Gin!" Randy screamed. "With some ice!"

Jake bolted to the bar, leaving Randy alone, hemmed in by the crowd, the speed he had taken cascading through him. Although he felt uncomfortable, he tried to admire the dancers' movements and absorb their apparent exuberance. Many of them had taken off their shirts, and he could smell amyl nitrate. Everyone appeared to be enjoying themselves and seemed amazingly free. He remembered thinking about freedom a few days before, and thought that perhaps he should try to join in. But after a few minutes, he realized this was not possible for him; the abandonment he was witnessing felt threatening.

He noticed several men watching him and was careful to avert his eyes, to avoid giving any indication that he was interested in them. He stared straight ahead, wondering why Jake was taking so long.

The music stopped, and the countdown to the new year began. Nearly everyone in the club converged on the dance floor, and Randy found it impossible to move. Then, when the deejay announced that it was midnight, the crowd went wild, surging forward, screaming madly, kissing each other passionately. Thousands of small styrofoam balls, colored in Day-Glo shades of green, pink, and orange, rained down from the ceiling, barraging the mob. An immense, red-faced skinhead in a leather jacket descended on Randy, sticking his tongue in his mouth and groping him. Randy pulled away, sweating and breathing heavily, searching for Jake. He craned his neck, scanning the room, and observed Haircut standing by the wall near the door to the bathroom, his biker shorts pulled down to his knees. Calvin was shoving an orange styrofoam ball up his ass.

"Sweetheart!"

Randy saw Jake pushing through the crowd, carrying a glass of gin and a can of Budweiser. After what appeared to be a great deal of effort, he reached Randy.

"Sorry I kept you waiting," he shouted. "I ran into Adrian Peterson. He's been telling me about this amazing trip he took to Puerto Rico. Here." He passed the glass to Randy. "I'm going back to him now. I want to hear what he has to say about the clubs in San Juan."

"Don't go," Randy implored. "It's New Year's Eve!"

Jake threw his arms around Randy and kissed him on the mouth. "Sweetheart, I'm sorry! Happy New Year!" He drew away. "Really though, I have to go. Adrian was in the middle of his story. I'll be right back." He hurried off.

Again alone, Randy took a few gulps of his drink, then looked toward the bar and saw Jake conversing with Adrian Peterson, a trim, pretty, blond man in his early twenties, dressed in a tight black T-shirt and a ripped pair of jeans. Randy knew Jake had had a fling with him six months before. Fuck them both, he thought, and turned away.

He noticed a tall, dark-haired man standing nearby, staring at him, and realized it was Oliver, who was, he saw now, very handsome. In the crush of their entering the club, this had not been evident to him. He returned Oliver's gaze, then looked downward.

The taped music stopped, and after an effusive introduction by the club's owner and much applause from the audience, the Bloody Tampons appeared on the stage above the dance floor. Relieved to have this distraction, Randy watched them perform.

The show was a disaster. Sabrina, the lead singer, seemed confused and stoned. He wobbled around awkwardly in his high heels and forgot most of the lyrics to his songs. The audience grew restless and jeered.

"Show us your cock, bitch," a drunk near the front screamed during the band's heavy-metal rendition of "The Love Theme from *Mahogany.*"

Sabrina stopped singing and glowered at the heckler. Turning haughtily, he lifted the skirt of his long red evening dress, pulled out his penis, and pissed on the stage. The show ended precipitately.

The crowd began to hiss, but when the disc jockey started to play a new mix, they responded to it and rushed onto the dance floor.

Randy saw Oliver dancing with Adrian Peterson.

"Sweetheart, I'm back!" Surprising Randy, Jake shoved a fresh glass of gin at him. "I bought you another drink. I didn't mean to leave m'baby alone."

"I see Adrian's busy now," Randy observed, an edge to his tone.

"Please! We were just talking!"

An old seventies disco hit could be heard through the mix blaring out of the speakers.

"Come on, let's dance," Jake cried. "You remember this song, don't you?"

It was "Ring My Bell," which had been playing the night Randy and Jake met. They had been at a bar called Mike's, and the song had been old even then. Randy had found Jake incredibly sexy, assertive and seemingly in control of everything. He was smitten. After dancing to this tune, they went home together. Fed up with his work at the agency and desperate for a change, he moved into Jake's apartment a week later.

Shit, Randy thought, that was a long time ago.

"Ring My Bell" was supplanted by a discordant blend of unrecognizable songs.

"I just want to get out of here," Randy said.

"But it's New Year's Eve!" Jake hugged Randy. "M'baby's not having a good time?" He released himself and looked out at the dancers. "See, *everyone's* here. Why, there's Dakota Montoya and Denise Lamour."

He pointed at a couple standing a few yards away in a corner. Both appeared to be reviewing in a critical fashion the activity on the dance floor. Intrigued, Randy studied them.

Dakota was around forty years old, short, pockmarked, and extremely homely, with thinning brown hair and mean, lively eyes. He was dressed in a blue blazer and an opened shirt, an ascot looped under his nonexistent chin.

Denise looked a little younger than Dakota, although her attire made it almost impossible to ascertain her precise age. She, too, was short, but with long electric-orange hair that jutted out wildly from her head, giving her a stature she would not otherwise have possessed. She was black and exceedingly fat, dwarfing Dakota, and wore a tight, purple sequined dress and huge, round tortoiseshell glasses. Every once in a while she turned from her observation of the dancers and whispered something in Dakota's ear. Then they both laughed heartily.

"Let's go talk to Dakota," Jake suggested.

"Do you know him?" Randy was reluctant to move; Dakota and Denise seemed even more forbidding in person than he had imagined them to be when he'd heard Graham talking about them.

Jake smiled. "Dakota's an old client of mine. From a while ago, when I was working."

"Right." Randy didn't budge.

"Come on, sweetheart! M'baby needs to get around more." Grabbing Randy's arm, Jake pulled him away.

"Dakota!" he shouted, striding toward Dakota and Denise, Randy at his side.

Dakota stared at him icily, then, seeing Randy, offered an almost-imperceptible smile.

Denise continued to peer at the dancers, not acknowledging either of them.

"You remember me, don't you?" Jake inquired. "It's been a long time."

"Yes," Dakota agreed. "You've aged a lot." He looked at Randy, again smiling slightly. "And who is your friend?"

"This is Randy. He knows Graham."

"Graham Mason?" Dakota appeared incredulous.

"I introduced them."

Randy noticed that Jake seemed proud of this. Feeling self-conscious, he lit a cigarette.

Dakota regarded Randy, his expression puckish. Grinning mischievously, he exclaimed, "Ah, yes!" He turned to Denise. "Did you hear that? I believe this is Graham's young friend."

Denise looked away from the dance floor at Dakota. "What's that?"

"Graham Mason. You remember him talking about that boy he's been seeing, don't you? The masseur?"

Randy swilled his drink. His stomach was churning.

Denise gazed impassively at Randy and Jake, then back at Dakota. "I don't know what you're talking about."

Dakota looked exasperated. "Don't be a silly pussy! You know: Mr. Hewitt!"

Randy's pulse quickened. He gulped the rest of his gin.

Jake remained silent, clearly baffled.

Denise giggled. "Oh, right. But I didn't know Graham was still seeing him. I thought that was last month." Her tortoiseshell glasses had fallen to the end of her nose and were resting there precariously.

Dakota turned to Randy. "I understand you started early."

Randy tightened his grip on his empty glass. He felt nauseous and unpleasantly high.

Denise giggled once more. "I know what it's like, honey," she told Randy. "I lost my cherry at nine."

Jake smiled uneasily. "What are you all talking about?"

Dakota ignored Jake. His eyes darted up and down Randy's body. "I think there's a lot you and I could discuss," he said to him.

Randy looked away, wanting to flee.

Just then Haircut, emerging from the crowd on the dance floor, rushed up to Jake.

"Have you seen Madonna?" he asked, speaking rapidly and slurring his words. "I've been looking everywhere for her."

Denise's eyes lit up. "Madonna?"

Dakota glanced at Haircut, sneering. "Are you talking about la Ciccone? I believe she's in Aspen tonight."

Haircut was shattered. "But everyone said she was going to be *here*."

"They always say that," Jake snapped, visibly embarrassed.

Randy clung to his glass, more desperate than ever to get away.

Looking bored, Dakota turned to Denise. "I think it's time for us to circulate, don't you?"

"Sure, babe. We don't want to grow any roots here."

Jake stood still, staring disconsolately at Dakota and Denise.

Dakota spoke to Randy: "I'll see you very soon, I'm sure."

"Right." Randy nearly sighed with relief now that the two of them were leaving.

"Give me a call," Jake said to Dakota.

Dakota nodded, then, Denise at his side, walked away.

As soon as they had gone, Jake pounced on Haircut. "Christ, I can't take you anywhere! You're so fucking rude sometimes."

Bewildered, Haircut said nothing, his mouth wide open.
Jake turned to Randy. "Dakota seemed to like *you* a lot, though.
I hope he calls." He paused, then inquired, "But what was all that
about Mr. Hewitt? Who the hell is *he?*"
Randy blanched. "Can we leave soon? It's really hot in here."
"Please!" Haircut piped in, recovering from Jake's reproach. "The
party's just starting. And Calvin's got the best coke tonight!"
Jake swerved toward him. "Can you get me some? It's the least
you can do after your fuck-up with Dakota."
"I still don't know what you mean," Haircut sniffed. "But
Calvin's got a huge stash tucked away in his boots. He's over there
by the men's room. Let's go talk to him."
Jake looked at Randy. "You want to come?"
Randy shook his head. "You won't be long, will you? I really want
to go."
Jake squeezed his arm. "I promise, sweetheart. I'll be right back."
Relinquishing his hold on Randy, he and Haircut headed into the
crowd.

Randy watched them leave, wanting another drink, still stunned
that Dakota and Denise knew about Mr. Hewitt. He felt a contained fury within himself, an anger he'd not noticed while in their
presence, intimidated as he'd been. He tried to push his anger away,
but was only partially successful. He couldn't understand why
Graham had betrayed his confidence.

He knew that he'd never asked Graham to keep what he'd written
about Mr. Hewitt a secret, but he'd assumed it was one. Ellen was
the only other person to whom he'd ever confided this. Jake never
showed much interest in his past, and Randy never volunteered anything. He felt it better not to.

He suspected he shouldn't be angry with anyone except himself,
that it was his own fault for sharing this information. In the end, it
had only led to Graham's wanting to hear more. He didn't know
why he'd done such a foolish thing; he supposed he'd been trying to
impress Graham, make himself appear more interesting than he felt
himself to be. And it had worked, too, he thought.

He wondered if he should be grateful that Graham *had* told everything to Dakota and Denise. They were, after all, the sort of friends

he'd always imagined himself having since he'd been in New York—although he could never relax once he came into contact with such personalities. People like Dakota and Denise appeared glamorous from afar, but he felt inhibited near them. Even Graham still scared him sometimes.

Be that as it may, Dakota and Denise had seemed interested in him, which was flattering. Yet their attitude toward his history, their amusement, was unsettling; it was not what he would have expected.

Still feeling a glimmer of anger, he looked toward the dance floor and saw that it was becoming more and more packed. Glancing in the direction of the men's room, he noticed Adrian Peterson standing with Jake, Haircut, and Calvin. Suddenly much hotter and very thirsty, he moved toward the bar.

As he pushed through the crowd, someone tapped his shoulder. He swirled around. Oliver stood before him, a drink in his right hand, grinning self-confidently.

"Hello," Oliver said. His English accent sounder even thicker to Randy than it had.

"Oh, hi." Randy stood still, feeling awkward, trying to think of something to say, acutely aware of how handsome Oliver was.

"I see you got rid of your sleazy friends." Oliver held up his glass. "Cheers to you."

Randy clutched his empty glass, flushing. "I was just going to the bar."

"I'll come with you." Oliver winked at him. "I'm sure you won't mind."

"Great." Randy was surprised at how eager he sounded.

They walked in silence to the bar, where they found two just-vacated stools. Randy ordered gin. When it arrived, Oliver asked, "So tell me, are you a model?"

Randy grabbed his drink. "Why would you think that?"

"Well, you know, someone who looks likes you. Then you're an actor?"

"No."

Oliver smiled. "A waiter?"

Randy shook his head.

Oliver's smile grew wider. "You're not a model, you're not an actor, you're not a waiter. And such a gorgeous kid! I guess you must be a prostitute." He chuckled at his joke.

Randy took a large swig of gin.

"Just kidding, of course." Raising his glass to his lips, Oliver grazed Randy's arm with his hand. "So then, what *do* you do?"

"I'm a writer," Randy answered quickly.

"Fiction?"

"Yeah."

"I should have known. I saw you talking to Dakota just now." Oliver took a cigarette from his pack and offered one to Randy, then lit it for him when he accepted. "I'm an artist myself. A sculptor. Not that it matters. But you Americans always want to know everyone's profession." He stared at Randy. "Me, I just want you to suck my willy."

Startled by the abruptness of this, Randy stared back at Oliver, thinking he resembled a beautiful, aristocratic lizard. He felt like a fly under his gaze. He looked over Oliver's shoulder, and saw Jake and Adrian walking toward the dance floor. He returned to Oliver. "Willy?" he asked, although he knew what Oliver had meant.

"Cock. Dick." Oliver exhaled a cloud of smoke. "I want you to give me a blow job." He placed a hand on Randy's groin and, smiling, caressed the denim above his penis. "Come on, let's go somewhere."

Responding to Oliver's touch, Randy moved closer to him, allowing their legs to rest together, wondering if he should proceed. There was Jake to consider. But then, although they didn't talk about it, he and Jake had never been monogamous. He turned and saw Jake dancing with Adrian. Feeling some of the anger that had cropped up earlier, he tried to suppress it. He looked back at Oliver and asked, "Where should we go?"

Still smiling, Oliver finished his drink. "It's a large club."

At that moment the deejay's voice boomed out of the loudspeaker, announcing a special, previously unpublicized guest appearance by Melissa Livingstone. Audibly excited, the crowd swarmed toward the stage.

"Oh God, Melissa!" Oliver exclaimed. "How dreary! I saw that tired cunt at The Kitchen last summer. What a sophomoric, histrionic hack!"

"Oh, yeah?" Randy took a drag on his cigarette. "Who is she?"

Oliver gaped at him. "You've never heard of Melissa Livingstone? I can't believe it."

Embarrassed, Randy said nothing.

"She was all over the news a few years ago. Some stiffs in Congress seemed to think her act was obscene. There was this absurd little uproar, and then her NEA grant was rescinded."

"But what does she do?"

Oliver laughed. "Oh, she just gets up on stage, naked, talking about being ten years old and getting buggered by her mother's second husband. Of course, while she's doing that, she's beating herself with a riding crop."

Randy felt the way he had the last time he'd heard about a particularly vicious crime in his neighborhood. "But why? What's the point?"

"God knows. You Yanks always seem to be moaning about something." Oliver took a drag on his cigarette and blew out a smoke ring. "I know if *I'd* been fucked like that when I was a kid, I'd just shut up about it."

"Yeah." Randy felt queasy. He had no desire to see Melissa Livingstone's act or hear her story. He looked up and saw that the area around the bar had cleared out. Practically everyone had moved closer to the stage, leaving Randy and Oliver alone with just a few other stragglers.

Oliver also noticed the bar's relative desolation. "I guess we're in the minority," he said gleefully. "I bet the loo is empty now, too."

Randy finished the dregs of his drink, then, feeling the effects of the alcohol, glanced toward the stage and saw Jake with Adrian in the midst of the crowd. He turned back to Oliver, conscious of their legs pressing against each other. He extinguished his cigarette and stood. "You want to go there?"

Oliver grinned. "Let's." He stood as well.

As Oliver had predicted, the men's room was nearly deserted. A man was pissing at the urinal, two others preening before the mirror, the first combing his hair, the second examining his nostrils. All the toilet stalls were empty. Randy and Oliver slipped into one and closed the door behind them.

Inside, Randy kneeled on the floor, pinning Oliver against a stall wall.

"Thank God for Melissa Livingstone," Oliver said.

"Yeah." Randy unzipped Oliver's pants and clutched his penis. He took it in his mouth and shut his eyes.

He could feel the dexedrine he'd taken, the wine he'd had before he left his apartment, the gin he'd consumed at the club. His high seemed for the moment perfect; tonight, he felt, he'd achieved the right mix.

The three other occupants of the room left one by one. Soothed, then almost hypnotized by the rhythm of his movements, Randy concentrated on Oliver's shaft.

His trance was broken when two other men entered the room.

"Come on, Calvin," a voice said, "let me have one more line."

"Shit," Randy whispered, pulling away from Oliver's groin, "it's Haircut!"

Oliver glanced down at him. "Haircut?"

"Shhh!" Randy put a finger to his mouth. "I don't want him to see me."

"Oh, Christ!" Oliver tried to pull Randy back. "Let's just carry on, okay?"

"Wait!" Resisting Oliver, Randy looked out through the crack in the stall's door.

Calvin stood before the urinal, pissing, his jock strap pulled down, as Haircut gesticulated beside him.

"It's because of Madonna," Haircut was saying. "I want to be really together when she arrives."

Calvin pulled up his jock strap and moved away from the urinal. "No way. You and your friends have been like fucking vacuum cleaners all night. And don't even think about Madonna. She's not gonna show."

"Please," Haircut begged, "just another toot."

Pressed against the stall's wall, Oliver was losing his patience. "Look, if we're not going to get it on, I want to go."

Randy put a hand on his arm. "Just a minute. They'll be gone soon."

73

Oliver sighed. "You American queens are so fucking neurotic."

Randy looked through the crack again.

Calvin was washing his hands in the sink. "Forget it, Haircut. I've given you enough. Just fucking leave me alone, why don't you?" He turned off the faucet and began drying his hands under a blower.

Haircut, indignant, said nothing for several seconds. At last, raising his voice to a shrill pitch, he cried, "I don't believe you! You've fucked me twice tonight, I've sucked your cock, I've done whatever the fuck you wanted. And now you're acting like a cheap nigger."

Randy pulled away from the crack. "Shit," he mumbled, "what's he doing?"

Oliver moved from the wall. "Have you had enough? Let's get out of here."

Randy held Oliver back. "Not yet!" He peered through the crack.

Calvin stood before Haircut, glaring at him, his muscles glistening under the fluorescent lights. "What did you say?" He gripped Haircut's arm. "What was that, faggot?"

Haircut glared back at him, then assumed a haughty, defiant tone. "I said you're a cheap nigger. A big-dicked, ass-licking, cock-sucking coke coon."

Calvin pulled his arm up, releasing his grip on Haircut, and after pausing for only a moment, slammed his fist into Haircut's face, knocking him against the sink and onto the floor.

His nose bleeding and visibly broken, Haircut covered his head. "Cheap nigger!" he shrieked. "Cocksucker!"

Calvin kicked him repeatedly, concentrating on his chest, stomach, and groin. Haircut screamed each time Calvin's boot came down.

Oliver pushed Randy aside and threw open the stall's door, shouting, "I've had enough!" He stomped from the room.

Randy remained on the floor behind the open door, transfixed by the spectacle before him, barely conscious of Haircut's screams.

Two men entered the room.

"She's such a joke," one of them laughed. Seeing the fracas he stopped. "What the fuck...?"

Infuriated by this intrusion, Calvin kicked Haircut one last time. "Faggot!" he yelled, then fled.

The two men watched Calvin leave, hesitating, as if deciding whether or not to pursue him. Finally, looking at Haircut, they hurried to him.

"Are you all right, man?" one asked.

Haircut clutched his stomach. "Motherfucker!" he moaned. A trace of blood trickled from a corner of his mouth.

Still on his knees in the stall, Randy took in the scene before him, dazed.

"Shit," the second man exclaimed, "he's really fucked up." He turned to his friend. "What should we do? We can't leave him alone."

The first one noticed Randy in the open stall. "Hey, man, what're you doing in there? Why don't you go get some help?"

Randy looked up. The man's words had not registered. "What?"

"You heard me. This guy needs help."

Randy tried to fathom everything that was happening. "Right," he muttered. He stood. Moving slowly, he approached Haircut, then leaned over him, riveted by his blood. "I'll get Jake," he said. "He'll know what to do."

"Cocksucking nigger," Haircut groaned.

The first man sat on the sink and lit a cigarette. "Hurry up, for Christ's sake!"

Randy managed to run from the room.

He stopped by the bar and let his eyes adjust to the dim light. For a second he wondered why this area was so deserted. Observing the mob on the dance floor, everyone unusually quiet, seemingly engrossed, he remembered Melissa Livingstone. Moving in that direction, he joined them.

He pushed through the throng toward the front of the room, peering at the rapt faces, searching for Jake. Jake was nowhere to be found. Looking ahead at the stage, he became aware of a nude woman standing before the audience, holding a black-leather riding crop in her right hand, her arms and shoulders streaked with bloody welts.

"So, Uncle Russell," the woman screamed, striking her left thigh with the riding crop, "is this the way you like Mommy's sweet baby girl?" She paused for just an instant. Then, howling, she beat her thigh over and over. The audience gasped.

Horrified, Randy froze. Although he wanted to, he could not turn away.

Melissa stopped beating her thigh and lifted the riding crop above her head. "What's it like having a ten-year-old twat, Uncle Russell? Isn't it the best snatch you ever had? And don't I suck your cock real good, Uncle Russell? You taught me how to do it, after all." She lowered the riding crop and whipped her already-bloodied thigh, giving it several vicious whacks. "You don't need Mommy at all, Uncle Russell. You've got your own little baby whore. I'm here when you get back from the golf course, when you've had your Scotch and joked with the boys. I'm here in my bed, where you can snuggle up next to me. Now I'm waiting, Uncle Russell, I'm waiting for *you*. You see I've learned, after everything you've shown me, that the world is your oyster and I'm the pearl."

Breathless, she stopped. Emitting an ear-shattering shriek, she whipped her other thigh.

Randy closed his eyes and had a vision of Mr. Hewitt sitting on the side of a bed. He was naked, his skin pale, for it was still early summer, his belly protruding, fleshy despite his golf and his tennis. Randy, twelve years old then, was lying beside him, his nude, newly pubescent body uncovered. Mr. Hewitt gazed down on it and stroked the light fuzz that had recently grown around Randy's penis. "Well, boy," he said, "it looks like you're getting a beard." He cupped his hands behind Randy's head and, grasping it tightly, pulled him toward his groin. "Kiss it," he whispered. "Just kiss it." Randy opened his jaws as wide as he could and, as Mr. Hewitt pushed at the back of his head, took the penis in his mouth. He gagged and pulled away. Mr. Hewitt increased the pressure on his head. Randy took the penis again. He choked.

Gasping, he opened his eyes. Melissa Livingstone, expertly wielding the riding crop, was furiously beating her thighs. Thin lines of blood ran down her legs. "Motherfucker! Motherfucker!" she screamed. "You're a motherfucker, Uncle Russell, and you know it. But it doesn't matter. This little girl loves her big, bad step-daddy!"

Randy felt as if he couldn't breathe. He shoved through the mob and, forgetting all about Jake and Haircut, headed toward the front door. At the edge of the crowd, he noticed Calvin in a dark corner, his jock strap pulled down, Dakota Montoya on his knees in front of him, sucking him off. Denise was beside them, inhaling fumes from a popper and giggling.

Randy continued past the bar to the entryway, his heart pumping wildly. Outside, he took long breaths of cold air. He remained there for a few minutes, sweating. When his heart started to calm down, he put his hands in his pockets and rushed home.

VIII

The apartment was empty. Instead of trying to sleep, Randy sat in the living room, switched on the television set, and turned the dial until he found a station that was not broadcasting any New Year's Eve festivities. He watched a biker movie from the sixties, something with Nancy Sinatra and Peter Fonda. Although the film made no sense to him, he was drawn to its gaudy images. They seemed to have a clarity and vividness that was distracting. He kept his eyes on the screen, hoping to erase from his mind any memories of The Scrotum or of what had happened there.

But he could not forget Dakota and Denise, their strange demeanor and odd laughter. He thought about Adrian Peterson prowling around the club and dancing with Jake; himself in the men's room with Oliver; the scene that ensued between Haircut and Calvin. At last he saw Melissa Livingstone—her riding crop, her bloodied thighs—and then, just for a second, Mr. Hewitt. He was standing on the front porch of his summer home in Canada, smoking a Kent, his lips curled up in a thin smile. Randy forced himself to concentrate on the television again, to become immersed in the old images, the absurd, hypnotic scenes of Nancy Sinatra and Peter Fonda riding their motorcycles across a glorious California landscape.

When the film was over, he undressed, got into bed, and lay there, unable to sleep. He remained in bed for hours, willing his mind blank, unconscious of the passage of time.

At four that afternoon, Jake returned, jarring Randy out of his trance.

"I don't want to hear a word from you," Jake said as he entered the bedroom. "Not a peep." Weaving unsteadily, he removed his boots and lay down beside Randy. "We went for a walk. That's it. We were talking."

Randy stared at Jake. A strong smell of alcohol permeated the room.

"What are you looking at me like that for?" Jake leaned over on his elbow and glared back at Randy. "Nothing happened."

"I'm not saying anything. I was sleeping."

"Well, good." Jake kissed Randy on the cheek and lay down again. "I want m'baby to forget about it, okay?" He closed his eyes and fell asleep.

Randy lay still, attempting to ignore Jake's heavy snoring. He knew Jake was lying. Things like this had happened before, and he was sure they would happen again. He'd had his own little flings. He recalled Oliver, but forced that memory to pass.

As soon as Oliver's image disappeared, he again became conscious of Jake's snoring, of his leg pressing against his side. Its touch infuriated him, and he rolled away to the other side of the bed, resisting an impulse to muzzle Jake's mouth with a pillow. He remained awake. Jake's snores pummeled his brain.

Jake's snoring subsided, and Randy's anger, too, abated. He became aware of a familiar despondency rising from his guts toward his throat. Sitting up, panting, he imagined himself getting out of bed and running from the stuffy apartment, bolting up the stairs to the roof, inhaling the freezing air, then jumping to the sidewalk below. As he pictured his lifeless body on the ground, he wondered how Jake would react to this, what people would say, how quickly Graham would find out about it. His breathing grew steadier, and he began to relax.

He finally managed to sleep, although he could not remember actually slipping into that state. It must have happened, he felt later, long after Jake had passed out. He didn't think he'd had any dreams, even though unsettling memories of Mr. Hewitt recurred throughout the night, images of his flabby body, his erect penis. But for the most part Randy was aware of nothing until eleven the following morning, when he was awakened by the telephone ringing.

After letting it ring many times, he picked up the receiver. "Yeah?"

"Good morning, baby." Graham's voice had a peculiarly mellifluous tone to it.

Startled, Randy said nothing.

"I've been thinking about you a lot," Graham continued, ignoring Randy's silence and chuckling. "Dakota told me that he met you at The Scrotum. He said you were charming."

Randy lit a cigarette.

"Naturally, I agreed with him. And then I realized how long it'd been since I'd seen you, so I thought I'd give you a call." Graham drew in his breath. "I'm feeling a little better now, baby. Let's get together tomorrow night."

Randy wavered momentarily, then said, "Sure."

"I'm glad you can make it."

Randy drew deeply on his cigarette.

"Come at eight, okay?"

Randy took another long drag. "All right," he said.

"So I'll see you tomorrow, baby?"

"Yeah."

Graham laughed. "Oh, by the way, have you been working on those memoirs of yours?"

Randy was silent.

"Bring them with you. I might want to read some more."

"If…if you want," Randy stammered.

Once Graham hung up, Randy placed the receiver in its cradle and took several quick breaths. The mention of his memoirs had been unsettling; he was still disturbed and even angry that Graham had told Dakota and Denise about the first installment.

But he suspected that he didn't really have to write anything today. Graham's request hadn't seemed that serious; it had sounded like an afterthought. He hoped Graham would forget all about it by tomorrow night.

Jake rolled toward him. "Was that Haircut?" he asked, half asleep.

"No. Graham. He wants to see me tomorrow."

"Oh, yeah? Great." Jake placed an arm across Randy's chest.

"Shit, I wish the fuck Haircut would call. He's got an appointment tonight." He closed his eyes.

Suddenly Randy realized that he had never told Jake about Haircut's fight. He decided to sleep some more. He felt it useless to worry about Haircut or anything else right now; he could explain things to Jake later.

He tried to relax. But as he lay still, he had a fleeting vision of Mr. Hewitt taking a shower. He was calling out to Randy, demanding that he join him. Randy squeezed his eyelids together, and the image faded.

At six-thirty, a frantic Jake shook Randy awake.

"Come on," he cried, "I don't know where the fuck Haircut is. I haven't heard a fucking thing from him. You're going to have to take his place tonight."

Randy tried to take in what Jake was saying.

"Hurry up! Haircut was supposed to see Marcus Philbin in an hour."

"Leave me alone!" Randy moaned.

Jake frowned. "For Christ's sake, just get up!"

Groaning, Randy turned over.

Jake slapped his side. "Get going, okay?"

"Fuck off!" Randy screamed. But he sat up. Still grumbling, he got out of bed and showered. By the time he was dressed, the fog had lifted a little.

He took a cab to Park Avenue and 77th Street, where Marcus Philbin lived with his parents in a duplex apartment. Marcus's family was wealthy and socially prominent; Randy often saw his mother's name or picture in the society pages of the daily tabloids. She and Mr. Philbin were away on one of their frequent holidays. This was when Randy visited their son.

Marcus was in his early twenties, around ten years younger than Randy, and a part-time film student at New York University. He was also a crack addict and smoked constantly during their sessions.

Tonight he was higher than usual, acting edgy and impatient. He told Randy not to bother with the massage, that a hand job was all he wanted.

He was so stoned that he couldn't maintain an erection, no matter how vigorously Randy tried to jerk him off. He appeared to grow frustrated and smoked more, saying he needed to calm down. He offered some to Randy, but Randy shook his head. He found the situation weird enough already.

Growing more frustrated, Marcus put on a cock ring, but when that didn't help him, he wrapped some old rags around the base of his shaft and tied them so tightly that the tip of his penis turned blue. His erection remained ephemeral.

"Maybe if you blew me," he suggested. He inhaled more crack.

Randy had already been working on Marcus for over an hour and was anxious to go home, so he acquiesced. Another thirty minutes passed before Marcus ejaculated. After wiping himself off, he picked up his pipe and started smoking again. Randy charged him for two hours and left.

In the taxi downtown, he decided he would tell Jake that he never wanted to see Marcus Philbin again. But when he entered his apartment, Jake was preoccupied: Just prior to Randy's return, he had heard from Haircut.

"He's in the hospital," Jake told Randy. "I guess he got into some sort of fight at The Scrotum. Had the shit kicked out of him. He's got a broken nose and some cracked ribs. He says he's okay now, but they want to keep him there for a few more days. You know, to do some tests, find out if he's got any other injuries."

Randy lit a cigarette. This mention of Haircut made him feel more uncomfortable.

"You're going to have to fill in for him until he gets out," Jake continued. "I have a lot of appointments lined up."

"But what about Graham?" Randy protested, speaking quickly. "He's not sick anymore. He's gonna keep me pretty busy."

Jake looked concerned. "You're right. That could be a problem." He hesitated, then said, "You're seeing him tomorrow?"

Randy nodded.

"Well, I'll make a few calls. Maybe something can be arranged." Jake picked up the phone.

Randy walked to the bedroom and lay down. He wondered if he should tell Jake about having witnessed Haircut's fight. But what good would that do? The damage was done. And Haircut seemed to be getting better. Besides, Haircut hadn't noticed Randy in the men's room when it happened. Why say anything to Jake and muddy the waters?

Suddenly Melissa Livingstone popped into his head. He then saw Mr. Hewitt in bed playing with himself, pulling Randy to him. He remembered sucking his penis, his high moan as he came, the rancid taste of his semen.

Shuddering, he recalled Marcus Philbin as he'd been that evening, old rags wrapped around his shaft. He felt nauseous.

He forced his thoughts away from this, to the memoir that Graham had asked him to write. He had written so much the first time, revealed things he hadn't recalled in years. And then Graham had betrayed him to Dakota and Denise. He could never write anything else for Graham, he was certain of that.

He heard Jake in the next room, talking on the phone: "It's just for a short time, until Haircut gets out."

Exhausted, Randy closed his eyes. He remained still. Soon he did not hear Jake at all.

He told himself he was sleeping, that this wasn't really happening. But here he was on that plane again, sitting between his father and Mr. Hewitt, and they were having dinner, just as they had done so many times in his dreams years before.

"Eat your peas," Mr. Hewitt said. "You'll need your strength."

"You heard him," Randy's father added. "Do what he says."

Randy raised his fork to his mouth, then stopped. He was sure that he would never be able to swallow anything. He looked out the window. Although the sky was pitch black, he could see that their plane was entering a cloud.

"Here we go!" Mr. Hewitt exclaimed.

Oh, shit, Randy thought, not *this*.

The plane began swaying, rocking, then falling. Their food flew in the air. The passengers around them screamed.

"Not now!" Randy shouted.

"Now's as good a time as any," Mr. Hewitt whispered in his ear.

The plane continued to fall. Randy braced himself for the crash. Then he saw the fire.

"NO!"

"Sweetheart?" Jake was standing above him, shaking his shoulder. "Sweetheart, are you all right?"

Shivering, Randy looked up, not recognizing Jake at first. He appeared pale and ghostly, as if a part of the dream.

"Christ," Jake went on, "you were screaming your fucking head off. What's the matter with you?"

Slowly coming to, Randy stared past Jake at the bedroom wall, noticing that a crack near the ceiling had gotten a bit longer. This seemed ominous. He shut his eyes and realized how easy it would be for him to drift off again. The thought of going back to the dream was horrifying.

"I'm still trying to find someone to fill in for Haircut," Jake said. "Everyone seems to be booked up."

"Oh, yeah?" Randy found a cigarette in a pack on the bedside table and, his hands trembling, lit it. "Listen," he said, "do you have any of that dexedrine you got? You know, the stuff you bought for New Year's Eve."

Jake stared at him. "What for? We're not going anywhere." He sounded both surprised and suspicious.

"Yeah, but..." Randy paused. Then: "It...it's just that I've gotta write something for Graham."

"Now? It's late."

"He'll be really pissed off if I don't come up with something."

Frowning, Jake walked to the bathroom. He returned with the bottle of pills. "Here," he said as he passed it to Randy. "But take it easy on these, okay? I want to keep them around for special occasions."

Randy swallowed a pill. "Don't worry about it. I just want to get some writing done."

Jake grinned. "M'baby, the author." Then he laughed and said, "I'm gonna go make another call. I think I've got an idea." Chuckling, he left the room.

Randy sat on the edge of the bed, afraid he would fall asleep if he lay down again. He knew it would be a while before he felt the effects of the pill and wondered what he would do once he was high.

He thought about his dream, still disturbed by it. It had been so long since he'd had that one, at least fifteen years.

Jake was talking on the phone in the next room: "Yeah, I know it's a hassle. But it pays well."

Randy looked up at the crack near the ceiling. He finished his cigarette and lit another one. Jake's voice faded away.

For a long time, whenever he had thought about Mr. Hewitt, he'd also recalled the TWA crash that had occurred near their hometown shortly after their first encounter, when Randy was ten. His vision of this accident was more vivid to him now than his memory of Mr. Hewitt. He could still see his thinning gray hair, his pink, jowly face, his stiff posture, his large penis. But the mental picture he had of him had become indistinct over the years. The crash, on the other hand—or, rather, the perception he'd had of the accident back then—was clear at the moment, stark and immediate in his mind.

He found it eerie that the week following his seduction was lost to him; he could recall nothing of his life during the days just after he'd left Mr. Hewitt's house that first evening. But he did remember being jolted back to reality by a beating his father had given him a week after that initial visit, although he had no idea what rule he had broken to prompt this punishment. The very next day, TWA Flight 263 crashed as it was making its descent toward the Indianapolis airport, thirty miles from Randy's home.

He remembered the news bulletins, the grim shots of the plane in flames on the runway, the dead bodies on the ground, all covered by sheets. There had been no survivors. At the time, he had wondered how many children were on board and what they had been thinking as they died. It was hard for him to fall asleep the evening he heard the news.

It was then, when he finally did sleep, that he'd first had the dream, the dream that had haunted him for months afterward. It was always the same, their plane crashing as he ate dinner on board with his father and Mr. Hewitt. But the crash itself was the least frightening part of it.

He remembered the rest of the nightmare distinctly: He was on the ground, still in the plane, pinned down by the twisted remains of the seat in front of him, unable to move and surrounded by flames. He looked to his sides. Both his father and Mr. Hewitt were slumped over, and their eyes were shut. He knew they were dead. The fire drew nearer. Terrified, he glanced up and saw through the flames someone coming toward him, a man trying to rescue him. He lifted his hands toward this figure, but, seared by the fire, drew them back. The man reached out for him and pulled him out of his seat, only to drag him deeper into the flames. As the fire enveloped them, he awoke.

It was difficult for him to sleep after he'd had this nightmare. He used to lie on his stomach, going over the dream's images: the plane, the crash, the fire, the lifeless bodies of his father and Mr. Hewitt. Then he thought about the mysterious figure coming toward him from the flames. He tried to imagine what he looked like, since he had never been able to see his face. But each time he tried, he was unable to form a clear picture. He lay awake, frightened. His memory of this faceless man preyed on him.

He started seeing Mr. Hewitt on a regular basis, once every fortnight or so, and attempted to adjust to this new routine. But the acts that Mr. Hewitt asked him to perform—the *frottage,* the mutual masturbation, the occasional fellatio—made him feel ashamed, and he was always glad when they were over. Often he wished that he never had to see Mr. Hewitt again, although he knew how angry his father would be if this were to happen. In the end, he did what Mr. Hewitt asked and tried not to think about it.

One night, a month after he'd first heard about the crash, he was frightened awake for a longer time than usual; his dream had been especially vivid. As he tried to recover from his nightmare, he found himself rubbing his penis against the sheets on his bed and realized he had an erection. He pulled down his shorts and continued his movement, replaying the dream in his mind.

He imagined himself pinned down in his seat, unable to flee, the fire crackling around him. His father and Mr. Hewitt were dead at his sides. Then he saw the shadowy figure coming toward him through the flames, only his eyes clearly visible, glowing like coals, brighter than the plane's inferno. He pictured this man taking his hands, lifting him out of his seat, and, holding him gently, leading him into the fire. As he envisioned the two of them burning, he pushed his penis into the sheet one last time and climaxed. He fell asleep immediately.

For months after that he relived this fantasy over and over, turning what he did into a soothing ritual, a barrier against the terror he felt at night. Soon he started masturbating the moment he was alone in bed. The nightmares stopped; his sleep became more regular.

This fantasy seeped into his daily life. Often it darted into his head during his father's beatings; he discovered if he thought about his dream at those times, his punishments seemed less severe. His father never noticed Randy's detachment; he was always too drunk.

Randy took his fantasy with him to Mr. Hewitt's house, conjuring it whenever they had sex. By the time he had an orgasm, he was no longer conscious of Mr. Hewitt. Instead, as his body shook and Mr. Hewitt laughed, it was the dream figure he saw, the man with the glowing eyes. He climaxed to a vision of this stranger from the flames.

He forced his attention back to the telephone conversation in the next room. Jake's voice was much lower than it had been. Initially, Randy found it impossible to distinguish any words. But as his ears adjusted to Jake's murmur, he could just make out his saying, "It's easy, Adrian. I don't think you'll have any problems."

He was only slightly surprised, yet he felt threatened by the possibility of that affair starting up again. He assured himself that he could handle it; he'd done it before. He would let Jake have his fling and get it out of his system. Jake always came back.

"I can give you a few hints," Jake was saying. "Maybe we can meet tomorrow."

Randy did not want to hear anymore. He felt the dexedrine beginning to take effect, and Jake's words became meaningless.

He suddenly recalled the way things had been for him in 1972, the year he took a trip to Canada with Mr. Hewitt and two years after he'd started fantasizing about the plane crash. He was fairly sure now that he had almost forgotten about his fantasy by that time. He supposed that at some point he'd decided it was childish.

He remembered that whole year vividly. He had been seeing Mr.

Hewitt regularly since their first meeting and had thought then that he had learned to resign himself to the sex, to think of his evenings with Mr. Hewitt as respites from the restraints he felt whenever he was around his father. Often, however, after seeing Mr. Hewitt, he found it difficult to sleep. He didn't talk about this with anyone.

Not that there was anyone he could talk to. His father was incoherent and uncommunicative much of the time, and Randy was a loner at school. Sometimes he heard other boys whispering about girls and telling dirty jokes, laughing about pussies, giggling about faggots. Because he never joined in, they teased him and called him a fruit or a fairy. Then he remembered what he did with Mr. Hewitt and felt exposed. But he knew that he had to keep his mouth shut. Although he didn't care about girls, he didn't want the boys to think he was queer. He tried to block out their taunts and kept even more to himself. Eventually, when Randy did not rise to their bait, the boys left him alone.

Like the boys at school, Mr. Hewitt seemed to think about nothing but sex. If he and Randy were not in bed together, he acted bored. Randy was hurt when Mr. Hewitt ignored what he said and maneuvered him to the bedroom instead of listening to him. But he never protested; he was too intimidated. And he knew what his father would do to him if he did rebel. Yet he hated Mr. Hewitt's indifference; he wanted attention with no strings attached, some consideration for his feelings.

Whenever they were having sex, Randy lay quietly as Mr. Hewitt groaned on top of him, rubbing himself against Randy's groin, his skin sweaty and sticky. Randy closed his eyes and remembered snatches of songs he'd heard on the radio, tunes by Neil Young, America, Carole King. Or he thought about films he had seen, the horror movies he loved, with their packs of murderous rats, carnivorous frogs, huge, scaly reptiles. As Mr. Hewitt ejaculated, he pictured these monsters' eyes—golden, glowing in the dark—until, spellbound, he felt, like them, invincible.

He was sure that his experiences with Mr. Hewitt made him different, as alien in his own way as the creatures in those films. He'd watch the other boys playing ball, joking in the playground ("What did the moron say to the queer?" they'd ask each other) and regret his certitude that he would never be able to join them. Then at home he'd see his father gazing at the television set, making comments about the programs ("That Kojak's quite a guy!") or cursing the "commie bastards" at the Vietnam protests shown on the news. He began to suspect that the boys in the playground would grow up to be just like this, and decided he was glad that he was different, that what he did with Mr. Hewitt set him apart. It made him special. Not a faggot, of course. Just better somehow. Not like the other kids. He didn't care what any of them said, didn't give a shit "what the moron said to the queer." They were idiots.

He started to observe Mr. Hewitt more carefully, studying him as he panted and puffed above him, and wondered what he was feeling, since he didn't feel anything himself. He knew there was more to sex than what he'd experienced thus far, an act he perceived to be invasive. This was particularly evident whenever Mr. Hewitt fondled his buttocks and said, "You've got the best little ass I've ever seen. I'm going up there someday. Later, when you're older. Just wait: You'll like it a lot." When Mr. Hewitt did this, Randy shuddered, dreading the day he would have to submit to this new demand. Then, when he started going through puberty—when his voice began to crack, and he started growing new hair on his body—he was almost certain that day was coming. His suspicion was augmented when Mr. Hewitt made quips about Randy's "getting a beard." Randy feared that this acknowledgment of his burgeoning adolescence might mark the beginning of a change in their relationship.

It was around this time that he and Mr. Hewitt had gone to Canada—the first trip, Randy remembered now, that they had ever taken together.

"It's all settled." Jake, startling Randy, stood before him, grinning impishly.

Randy looked up, then lit a cigarette.

"Adrian Peterson said he'd fill in for Haircut." Jake chuckled. "That word-processing outfit he worked for went under. Adrian's desperate for cash."

Randy found it difficult to concentrate on what Jake was saying. He said nothing.

"What's the matter?" Jake asked, impatient. "You wanted me to fix something up, didn't you?"

Lowering his eyes, Randy noticed Jake's belt, which, he saw, was new, a nice black-leather one with a heavy buckle.

"So what do you think? Is it okay with you? I can't see any problems." Randy stared at him. "Oh, yeah, sure," he said distractedly. "I'm glad you found someone."

Jake frowned. "You should be."

For a second Randy wanted to throttle Jake. He quickly looked down at the belt again.

Jake yawned. "I'm going to bed. I've got a lot to do tomorrow. I think Adrian's going to need some pointers. It's all new to him, you know." He sat next to Randy on the bed, then, with a smirk, added, "I see m'baby's gotten a lot of writing done. Are you gonna be up all night?"

Randy ground out his half-finished cigarette. "I doubt it."

"Well, whatever. But why don't you go to the next room? I've gotta sleep."

"Yeah, right," Randy grumbled, then rose.

Jake took off his boots. "Sorry, sweetheart. But I'll see you later. Have fun."

In the living room, Randy shut his eyes, surprised that he was so agitated. Adrian Peterson was no threat, he assured himself once more; it was just that he didn't want to have to think about him.

He felt a rush from the speed, and opened his eyes. Fuck, he thought, what am I going to do now? He didn't want to go out. And he didn't feel like watching TV either.

He again closed his eyes. Suddenly he saw Mr. Hewitt's summer house in Ontario. He remembered fishing on Lake Huron and walking alone in the woods there at night. He recalled the day excursions he and Mr. Hewitt took in a brand-new, black Lincoln convertible, one to an old British fort, another to an Indian burial site. Finally—briefly, but for the first time in years—he thought about Mark Randall, the attendant at the service station Mr. Hewitt used when he was staying at his summer home.

Jolted, he reopened his eyes; he felt as if he had been dreaming. Then he remembered Mark cleaning the windshield on Mr. Hewitt's car, his chest bare and sweaty, and sensed a vague, nearly forgotten warmth taking hold of him.

He looked down at the table and saw a pen and a pad of paper with some telephone numbers scribbled on it. Impulsively, he picked these up and tore off the top sheet. He lowered the pen and, moving rapidly, wrote, "I was twelve when I met Mark Randall."

He stopped. Clutching his pen, he gazed at what he had just written, thinking about Canada, about his nights in the woods— about Mark.

He lowered his pen to the paper again. It seemed as if he couldn't help himself; he was going to write something after all—something for himself. He didn't have to show it to Graham, he decided. Not all of it, at any rate. Maybe just a few bits, enough to satisfy him— that is, if Graham really did ask to see what he'd done. He could stop any time he wanted to.

He quickly scratched out what he had written before, then started again, writing furiously:

Mr. Hewitt and I took our first trip together in July of 1972. He'd always talked a lot about taking me away somewhere but I figured that was bullshit.

One of the places he used to talk about was this village up in Ontario called Ojibway Sound where he had a summer place. "That's where I go to relax," he'd always say. "That's where I can really be myself." He and his wife used to go there for a few weeks every August. He said it was beautiful around there, that his house was right on Lake Huron and that whenever they were there they'd go fishing and boating and swimming, shit like that. It sounded cool to me.

One night in June his wife was away somewhere so I was with him. We were in bed and he was making stupid jokes about the pubic hair I was getting like saying I had a beard and stuff. All of a sudden right out of the blue he said, "I think you're ready for that vacation I've been promising you." At first I thought this was just some more of his bullshit but then he said real serious, "We can visit Ojibway Sound." I looked at him and asked, "Really?" He said, "I want to go in a few weeks."

It turned out his wife was visiting her sister in South Carolina right after the Fourth of July and Mr. Hewitt thought that'd be a good time for us to get away. So the next day I asked my dad if I could go and he said it'd be okay. He seemed sort of glad that I'd be out of his hair for a while.

I got real excited and thought about the trip all the time. But as it got close to the day we were supposed to leave, I got a little nervous. I'd never spent that much time with Mr. Hewitt before and I wasn't sure what we'd do all day, what would happen up there. I didn't know what he'd expect from me either. But I tried not to think about that too much. Mostly I was just happy to be going.

We left at five in the morning on July 6 and drove all the way to Ojibway Sound in one day. The ride was around fourteen hours, and Mr. Hewitt didn't say much the whole time. I didn't mind though. I was happy staring out the window. It was neat looking out and seeing how everything changed, like the farms and cornfields I was used to seeing sort of disappeared as we got up north, then the highway got narrow and there were all these pine trees on both sides of the road.

The only hassle was the radio. Mr. Hewitt let me listen to the rock station at first but then I guess he got sick of hearing it because after around fifteen minutes he said, "That's enough of that!" and turned the dial to the muzak station. It didn't really matter once we got further into Canada because all we could get was static anyway.

It was starting to get dark when I saw a sign that said "Ojibway Sound 5 Miles." For some reason I felt funny when I saw this. I hadn't said anything to Mr. Hewitt for a few hours. Now I turned to him and asked, "Are we there yet?"

He looked at me and said real quick, "We'll be there soon!" like he was pissed off or something. I thought I'd asked a stupid question so I didn't say anything else. But I felt funnier.

The village wasn't much, just a few old stores and some bars. We drove right through it and headed out on the road towards Mr. Hewitt's house. Right outside of town we stopped at a gas station.

We parked by a pump, then this tall kid walked up to the car. He was older than me, about eighteen or so, and he had on this dark green attendant's uniform with his name, "Mark," written above the pocket on his shirt.

I saw right away that Mr. Hewitt knew him because he said, "Hello, Mark," not too friendly, sort of formal.

It didn't look like Mark seemed too glad to see Mr. Hewitt either. He just stared at him for a second then said, "We were expecting you." He had a Canadian accent but I could tell anyway that he didn't like Mr. Hewitt much.

"How's your father?" Mr. Hewitt asked him.

Mark only said, "He'll be up at your house tomorrow morning." Then he started filling up the gas tank. While he was working I got this weird feeling, like he was watching me. He made me feel nervous.

Mr. Hewitt laughed. "That's Mark Randall," he said. "I've known that kid since he was younger than you are. His father's my handyman Eric. He owns this gas station."

Mark was cleaning the windshield so I looked up at him. He was real tan and had this long light brown hair that came down over the left side of his forehead. He saw me looking at him and stared right back. We just glanced at each other for a second. Then I got embarrassed and looked away.

After that I was even more nervous than I'd been before. When we left the station I was almost wishing that I'd never come on this trip at all.

I was about ready to piss in my pants by the time we got to Mr. Hewitt's. It was right on Lake Huron in front of a woods and huge. Not as big as Mr. Hewitt's back home, but still pretty amazing.

Inside there were all these antiques and old sofas and stuff, everything real expensive looking. The walls were light. Oak, I think. A bunch of stuffed fish were stuck up all over the place. The minute I saw all this shit I thought, "Fuck, what am I going to do here for two weeks?"

Mr. Hewitt had this housekeeper Mrs. Landis who was at the door when we got there. She didn't make me feel any better. She was pretty old, in her sixties I guess. She had this white hair and pale skin. She acted nice with Mr. Hewitt but she completely ignored me. I got the idea she didn't like having me there. She'd turn away if she caught me even looking at her, so I kept out of her way. I remember I wondered if all Canadians were uptight like her.

The funny thing was, Mr. Hewitt also ignored me if Mrs. Landis was near. Once when she was out of the room he winked at me. But other than that it was like I wasn't around. I felt out of place.

Mrs. Landis did fix a delicious dinner though. Roast beef and baked potatoes and peas and salad, apple pie for dessert. Mr. Hewitt opened a bottle of wine and that chilled me out. But I still felt like I wasn't supposed to be there.

Mr. Hewitt didn't talk to me at all while we were eating. He said he was tired from the drive. He did say a few things to Mrs. Landis when she came out from the kitchen, but mostly he just sat there eating and drinking. I kept my mouth shut.

After dinner Mr. Hewitt and I went into the living room and had some brandy. Mrs. Landis washed the dishes, then said goodbye and went to her place in town. I was relieved when she was gone.

"Does she hate me?" I asked after she'd left.

Mr. Hewitt seemed like he was pissed off. "Don't be such a baby," he said. "She just doesn't want to know what's going on between us. She's a religious nut."

I felt sort of ashamed when I heard this, but I didn't want to make Mr. Hewitt any madder so I didn't say anything else. I was tired and a little drunk from the wine and brandy. Nothing was making much sense to me anymore.

Mr. Hewitt had a few more drinks and read the paper. I just sat there trying to be quiet and not bother him. I was still pretty nervous.

Finally Mr. Hewitt said he was exhausted so we went upstairs. We had separate bedrooms right next to each other. Mr. Hewitt told me he wanted to be alone. I went into my room but when I got into bed I couldn't sleep.

I sat up for a while feeling weird and lonely and a little scared. I might of even been homesick. I could hear this owl outside hooting like crazy. That really bothered me. I thought maybe that was what was keeping me awake.

I tried to think about other things, the fishing and swimming and all the stuff Mr. Hewitt said we'd do. But for some reason I kept thinking about Mark Randall, that kid at the gas station. I remembered the way he'd acted with Mr. Hewitt, how they didn't seem to like each other much. Then I thought about how Mark had been watching me and then how we'd looked at each other and how embarrassed I'd felt.

Around an hour after I went to bed, Mr. Hewitt came into my room. He seemed kind of drunk, like he'd had more brandy since he'd left me.

"Hello, boy," he said. "I can't sleep."

He took off his bathrobe and got on top of me. I thought maybe being with him would make me feel better, so I was ready to do about anything he wanted. I didn't have much choice.

At first it was all just the usual shit, like he was playing with my dick and sucking my tits, stuff like that. But then he started twisting my pubes, sort of pulling them. It hurt. That was strange. Then he stuck a finger in my ass, which didn't surprise me or anything, he often did that. But I got this feeling anyway that it was going to be different this time. All of a sudden I knew what was coming.

"Turn over," he said. "You're old enough now."

I freaked when he said this. I mean, I didn't want him sticking his cock in me. I started screaming and shit, shouting stuff like "Not yet!" and "Wait!"

Mr. Hewitt didn't pay any attention. He just laughed and said, "Don't be silly, you'll love it." Then he held me down and pushed it right in.

It hurt a lot. He went up so quick, just ramming it in. I think I must of been squirming and screaming or trying to push him away or something because I kind of remember him saying, "Shut up!" and "Hold still!" I'm not so sure about that though. Mostly it's all a blank. I don't remember much of anything that happened after he started fucking me. Not until he began breathing real hard. It was right then that I could feel him come inside me. It's funny now when I think about it, but as he came I sort of said to myself, "This is sex."

Everything felt like a dream after that. When Mr. Hewitt was done I think he said something like, "How'd you like it?" but I can't really remember too clearly. I'm pretty sure I didn't say anything back. Then he got up and said, "I'll see you in the morning," and left real quick.

I guess I was scared once he left. I could hear that owl outside and I remember thinking that I'd never be able to sleep if it kept on hooting. I must of been a little nuts because I got this idea that I'd go out in the woods and find that fucking bird and kill it.

I turned on the light and got up, but as soon as I was standing I felt this pain in my butt. Then I heard that owl and got pissed off. I looked down at the bed and saw these skid marks and a few little drops of blood on the sheets. The owl hooted again so I turned away real fast and got dressed. Every time I moved I could feel my butt hurting.

I walked out of my room real slow. I felt spaced, like I was sleep-walking or something. I started to go downstairs but for some reason I stopped off in Mr. Hewitt's room first. I could hear him snoring and when my eyes got used to the dark, I could see his body under the covers. For a second I had this crazy idea, like I wanted to pick up his pillow and hold it over his head. He was snoring so fucking loud. But then I looked away from him and saw a pack of cigarettes lying on the table by the bed. He always smoked Kents. I grabbed them and left the room. Once I was downstairs I went out the front door.

It was dark outside, there was no moon or anything, and I could still hear that owl. I walked into the woods behind the house and tried to follow the hooting sound.

After about five minutes I stopped. I was surrounded by trees. Then I heard something right in front of me. I picked up a rock and threw it towards the spot where I'd heard the noise. After I did this I heard these wings flapping and I thought I'd hit it. But then it hooted again so I screamed, "Fucking owl!" over and over until I got pretty hoarse. When I couldn't scream anymore I sat down on the ground.

I almost started to cry, that's how flipped out I was. I stopped myself though. I didn't want to act like a fairy. Instead I took out a Kent and lit it. Then I sat there smoking one after another. Every so often I'd poke the lit end into my skin. Just to see what it felt like. I don't remember it hurting too bad.

The next thing I knew the sun was coming up and I'd smoked the whole pack. I didn't think I'd slept at all but I didn't really know what I'd been doing all night. Fuck, I thought, maybe I did sleep and I've been dreaming all this shit. I looked down at my hands. They were covered with these little burns, ugly ones, red and scabby. I felt like a complete asshole.

When the sun was part way up I got kind of nervous. I didn't want Mr. Hewitt to know I'd been out all night, so I got up fast and ran to the house.

When I got back inside I looked in at Mr. Hewitt. He was still sleeping. I went to my room and got undressed. Then I laid in bed for a while waiting for him to get up.

Around half an hour later I heard Mrs. Landis come in the front door. I listened to her walking around in the kitchen, getting breakfast ready and stuff. She was humming these religious songs real loud. I must of been into listening to her because I didn't even hear Mr. Hewitt when he came into my room.

"Come on, boy, rise and shine," he said. "It's a beautiful day."

Him coming in all of a sudden like that scared me. I rubbed my eyes when I sat up so he'd think I'd been sleeping.

I guess he noticed the burns on my hands when I did this because he said, "What the hell happened to you?" Then he saw the empty pack by my bed and said, "So that's where they went!" I was afraid he was going to be pissed off but he seemed to be in a good mood. All he did was laugh and say, "Crazy kid! Be careful next time."

That whole day was sort of fuzzy. I hadn't slept all night and it all blurs together. I do remember the breakfast Mrs. Landis made that first morning though. It was huge. Pancakes and bacon and sausages and orange juice and biscuits and all sorts of shit. I didn't eat much. Mrs. Landis still wasn't talking to me or anything but I didn't expect her to. I felt ashamed around her. She was sucking up to Mr. Hewitt, saying things like "Can I get you something else, sir?" and crap like that. I remember thinking what a big deal he was even up there in Canada.

Eric Randall, Mark's father, came by just when we were finishing breakfast. I was a little nervous when I met him. He was this big tall guy with a red face and bloodshot eyes. He licked Mr. Hewitt's ass as bad as Mrs. Landis did, talking about the house and everything he'd done there while Mr. Hewitt was away. I mean, everybody seemed to be trying to make Mr. Hewitt happy, old ladies like Mrs. Landis and grown men like Eric Randall.

The funny thing about Eric was that he seemed real interested in me, just like Mark had been. He didn't talk to me, but when he thought I wasn't looking I could tell he was staring at me. That made me more nervous. But I didn't look back at him, not the way I'd looked at Mark.

I don't remember much about the rest of the day. I guess I was tired. I hung out by the lake, but I didn't go in the water. It was too cold. I just laid there in the sun. Eric was doing stuff by the house and Mr. Hewitt was giving him orders the whole time. Every once in a while I thought I saw Eric watching me from where he was working. But that might of been my imagination.

I must of slept some while I was out there because I think I had this dream about Mark Randall. I don't remember much of anything about *it, but when I woke up I felt kind of funny. I ended up going back to the house.*

I knew Mr. Hewitt was going to fuck me again that night, so at dinner I drank my wine fast. Mr. Hewitt even had to open another bottle. He hadn't been saying much to me but then he never did, especially when Mrs. Landis was around. I could tell he was in a good mood though, just like he'd been that morning, because he was smiling as he poured me more wine. "Take it easy on this, boy," he said.

I drank a lot of brandy after dinner and was blitzed when we went to bed. Mr. Hewitt thought it was funny that I was so drunk. I was glad I was because the minute we were in his room he wanted to stick his dick in me again. I was so fucked up that I didn't give a shit. I laid there and let him do what he wanted. The second time didn't bother me like it had the first. I guess the liquor helped.

When Mr. Hewitt was done he made me go back to my room. I passed out as soon as I got under the covers.

I woke up real early with this awful headache, but I felt jumpy and didn't want to stay in bed anymore. I decided to get up and go outside, maybe see if I could find that owl.

I snuck into Mr. Hewitt's room and took his Kents. Then I went out to the woods. I never did see the owl. I ended up just sitting there trying not to think much. It was weird though, because every once in a while I'd remember Mark Randall, the way he stared at me at the gas station.

I burned my hands again that morning. I wanted to stop myself, but I got into it. It was kind of cool seeing how long I could hold the cigarette there.

When the sun came up I snuck back in. This time I made sure I'd left some Kents for Mr. Hewitt. I put the pack on the table by his bed, then went into my room and pretended I'd been sleeping.

From then on, for the rest of my vacation, I'd go out to the woods all the time, either late at night or real early in the morning. I'd stay there 'til the sun came up, then go back to bed and wait for Mr. Hewitt to get up.

I spent the first few days out by the lake. I couldn't do anything else. I mean, Mr. Hewitt was busy bossing Eric around.

At dinner I'd get drunk. That way I didn't mind what Mr. Hewitt did to me later. I'd just blank out.

There was one time when I did come to while he was fucking me. I was stoned out of my mind and it still hurt a lot, but I sort of liked the way it felt anyhow, his cock being up my ass and everything. Just for a minute though. I conked out again after that. I mean, I was really out of it.

I guess I was spaced that whole first week. It's like I'm not too clear about a lot of stuff from that time. Sometimes I didn't even know if I was awake or asleep.

But I do remember when things started to change. It was on this real hot day. That morning Mr. Hewitt and Mrs. Landis were talking about how awful it was, how it usually didn't get that bad up there. Eric wasn't around, he'd called up sick. Since Mr. Hewitt didn't have anything to do, he decided we'd go for a ride in his car. He said he wanted to see this Indian cemetery that was down around ten miles south of us. I was real glad to be getting out.

Just after we started our drive, we stopped at the gas station outside of town. That's where I saw Mark again. It's funny now when I think about it, but as soon as I saw him that day I seemed to forget about everything else that had happened to me since we'd arrived in Ojibway Sound.

The telephone rang. Jarred, Randy froze for an instant, then turned toward the receiver. It was late, after four-thirty in the morning, and although there were several people he could think of who might call at this time—Haricut, for one, but he was in the hospital—he was certain this was Graham.

The phone continued to ring, and he moved his hand toward it, then stopped. He knew Jake wouldn't answer; he usually slept like a log. But he was reluctant to talk with Graham just now; he felt disoriented. Suddenly chilly, he gazed at the sheets of paper spread out before him.

The phone rang for the sixth time. He looked up quickly and grabbed the receiver. "Yeah?"

"Baby?" Graham's voice was thick, much deeper than usual.

"Graham." Randy reached for the pack of Merits beside his story.

"Baby, it *is* you."

Randy lit a cigarette.

"I knew you'd be home, that you'd still be up." Graham's words came out rapidly and were slurred. "You're working on your memoirs, aren't you?"

Randy felt his hand growing moist on the receiver.

"That's a good boy. You see, I've been sitting here having a little nightcap, and it crossed my mind that you might not have taken my request seriously." Sounding raspy, Graham chuckled. "You *are* writing, aren't you?"

"Su...sure."

"Good." Graham laughed. "*Good.* I can't wait to see what you've done."

Neither of them said anything for a moment. Randy could hear the tinkling of ice on the other end as, evidently, Graham raised his glass to his lips.

Finally Graham said, "That's really all I have to say, baby. I just wanted to make sure you were doing what I asked. I knew when I spoke to you this morning that you hadn't done anything then. But I suspected you'd come up with *something.* You know, so I wouldn't be angry with you." He laughed again, then added, "We can talk more later. Just keep writing. And bring it with you."

"Right."

"I'll see you and Hewitt tomorrow then, baby."

Randy hung up, feeling even more peculiar than he had before he'd answered the phone. It was as if he'd been hallucinating and Graham hadn't actually called. He found it eerie that Graham had known he was writing, that he'd been prodding him on.

He ground out his cigarette and glanced down at the sheets of paper. There were fifteen of them filled up with his scrawls. He couldn't believe he'd gotten this far. He looked up at the clock on the wall; it was nearly five. The apartment was quiet, its silence broken only occasionally by the sounds coming from the street four flights below. He again lowered his eyes to the papers and, very high, remembered Graham's slurred, raspy voice, how he'd chuckled during their conversation. Then he recalled Dakota and Denise at The Scrotum and suddenly knew he could not write any more.

Fuck those two, he thought, clenching his teeth; those pretentious cunts'll just laugh at me if they hear about my trip to Canada.

Trying to calm down, he touched the pen on the table. Then, lighting another cigarette, he leaned against the couch, peering at the ceiling.

*

He remembered that sweltering morning, driving into the service station, Mr. Hewitt silent behind the wheel. After they parked by a gas pump, Randy looked out his window, searching for Mark. The lot was empty. Mr. Hewitt, impatient, honked his horn several times. At last, Mark came out from the house behind the station, ambling toward the car.

He was dressed in sneakers and a faded pair of jeans, shirtless, his hair uncombed. Randy gazed at him, certain that he had just gotten out of bed, feeling then as if he himself were coming out of a very deep sleep.

Mark leaned toward Mr. Hewitt's window. "Yeah?" he said, his voice clearly hostile despite its apparent drowsiness. He stared over Mr. Hewitt's shoulder, directly at Randy.

Randy looked away.

"We need gas," Mr. Hewitt replied—curtly, Randy felt. Then he turned to Randy and said, "I'll be right back. Too damn much coffee." He left the car and headed toward the men's room.

As Mark filled the gas tank, Randy watched him cautiously, allowing himself to observe how very good looking he was. He studied his face: his large, dark eyes; the stubble on his chin; his long, brown hair, bleached by the sun. He looked at his bare chest; it was smooth and muscular, lightly covered with sweat, deeply tanned, the nipples even darker, almost purple. He focused on the thin line of hair running from his navel down to his jeans; it disappeared under the denim. He imagined it continuing on, flowing into his pubic hair, and tried to picture his penis, convinced it was large.

Mark finished filling the tank and walked to the front of the car. Randy's eyes followed him, taking in the way his muscles rippled. Mark lifted his arms and ran a rag over the windshield. When Randy saw the hair in his armpits, he wanted to bury his face there, to smell and lick him.

Then he realized Mark had stopped and was again staring at him. Unable to move, he stared back, not lowering his eyes this time, not wanting to. They looked at each other for several seconds. Finally Mark turned his mouth up slightly and, almost imperceptibly, smiled. Randy looked down, blushing.

At that moment Mr. Hewitt returned from the men's room. He paid Mark, and they drove away. But throughout the day, as they rode to the Indian cemetery and walked over its ground, Randy could not get Mark out of his mind.

That night, tired out by the trip and numb from the heat, Randy drank less wine and brandy than usual. After dinner, when Mrs. Landis had gone, he and Mr. Hewitt went to bed.

As he watched Mr. Hewitt undress, Randy studied his body, seeing as if for the first time his soft, paunchy belly, his flabby thighs, his sagging buttocks, the hair on his stubby legs. For a second he felt like kicking his bristly shins and twisting his jowly neck. Then he wanted to disappear.

Minutes later, in bed, as Mr. Hewitt thrashed on top of him, Randy almost started to push him away. The idea of having sex with this sweaty, middle-aged man repulsed him even more tonight; he wasn't drunk enough. But he knew he had no choice.

Closing his eyes, he imagined it was Mark who was on top of him, Mark's thigh he caressed, Mark's tongue in his mouth. He found himself reacting to Mr. Hewitt in ways he'd never before done: As Mr. Hewitt pushed further into him, he responded with thrusts of his own, using his muscles to squeeze Mr. Hewitt's penis, then biting his chest and digging his fingers into his back. He even ejaculated before Mr. Hewitt did, envisioning as he did the thin line of hair that ran down from Mark's navel, disappearing under the waist of his jeans.

"My God, boy," Mr. Hewitt exclaimed when they were finished, "what got into you tonight?"

Randy lay still, not looking at Mr. Hewitt, trying not to see his bloated body.

When Randy returned to his room, he could not sleep at first; the humidity was much too intense. He lay in bed, dripping with sweat, a little nauseous. He thought that if he took a shower he might feel better, but worried that the noise would wake Mr. Hewitt. He touched his skin; it felt sticky, slimy. He quickly drew his hand away, feeling the darkness of the room closing in on him, hearing the owl hooting outside. His heart was racing; he felt as if it were about to leap out of his chest. He shut his eyes and tried to imagine bright sunlight. Then he saw Mark standing shirtless in the lot of the service station, smiling faintly. He touched himself again, no longer conscious of the heat or his perspiration. The beating of his heart slowed, and he drifted off.

He dreamed he was sitting in the dark, frightened and unable to move, pinned down by something pressing against his chest. He saw the fire coming toward him. So I'm here again, he thought, relieved yet still apprehensive. But he knew he had nothing to worry about; the man from the flames would come.

He sensed this faceless figure floating toward him, reaching out and taking his hand, pulling him out of his seat and leading him toward the fire. Together they entered the flames. He felt the fire on his skin, its heat soothing.

He awoke abruptly, damp with sweat, his covers thrown off. The sky was black; it was the middle of the night. He had not been asleep for long. He lay motionless for a few minutes, but unable to sleep, rose and dressed.

He crept to Mr. Hewitt's room, where he found the pack of Kents. Then he tiptoed outside and ran to the woods.

He stopped in a clearing. The air was still, the heat almost as bad as it had been during the day. Sweating, he removed all his clothes and lay on the ground.

Still unsettled by his dream, he thought about Mark, hoping to supplant those old images with a new one. He imagined Mark standing before him naked, his chest glistening, sweat dripping from his nipples onto his stomach, running down that line of hair to his groin. His pubic hair was black and abundant, his penis erect.

Holding this picture in his mind, Randy turned over onto his stomach. The pine needles on the ground pricked his skin. He rubbed his penis against them and came almost instantly. He fell into a deep sleep.

When he awoke, the sun was high in the sky; he could tell it was late. Panicking, he dressed and ran back to the house.

Mr. Hewitt was already awake and at the breakfast table. He frowned as Randy rushed in. "Where the hell have you been?"

"I...I took a walk," Randy stammered. "I couldn't sleep."

Mr. Hewitt saw the Kents in Randy's hand. He chuckled and said, "I see you're up to your old tricks. I've been wanting a smoke." Embarrassed, Randy handed him the cigarettes. He hadn't smoked during the night, so the pack was still almost full. Relieved that Mr. Hewitt's anger had subsided, he sat near him at the table and ate breakfast.

Despite the continuing heat wave, his second week in Ojibway Sound was better for him than the first. Almost every morning he felt pleasantly lightheaded and strangely energized. He drank less at night. The days passed quickly.

Eric Randall had finished his chores, so Mr. Hewitt spent more time with Randy. They visited Fort McIsley, an old British outpost twenty-five miles away. They went swimming and boating, hiking and fishing. Randy caught a few bass. One night Mr. Hewitt took Randy to a restaurant in town called Shirley's. Randy ate the best steak he'd ever had.

As usual, Mr. Hewitt rarely spoke to Randy if they were not in bed; he only commented on the weather or made some other casual observation. But he seemed in a good mood most of the time and, relaxed by his vacation, was fairly patient. Randy in turn felt less uncomfortable with him.

The sole ripples in these otherwise placid days were created by Mrs. Landis. She remained silent around Randy, working about the house, her eyes fixed in front of her, humming gospel tunes and disregarding him. Because of her silence, Randy was convinced that she knew exactly what he and Mr. Hewitt did together. He often wanted to hide, to somehow make himself invisible—though it felt to him as if she were everywhere he went. If he could not actually see her, he could hear her voice. Her presence seemed to burn into him, to remind him of his certainty that she knew everything. He assured himself that this was impossible: There was no way, at least, that she could know about his nocturnal world—which, as the heat wave persisted, had been dominated by Mark Randall.

Every night, after he had satisfied Mr. Hewitt, he lay in bed, unable to sleep. He forced his thoughts away from what he had just done and thought about Mark. After an hour or two of this, he ran off to the woods.

Deep in the woods, safe in a clearing, he undressed and lay on his stomach. Pressing his penis against the pine needles, he conjured up some simple image: the muscles in Mark's arms, his bare chest, the hair in his armpits. Soon his fantasies became more elaborate: Mark removed his jeans and stood before Randy naked. He lay on top of him and rubbed his penis against him. At last he entered him mercilessly, just as Mr. Hewitt had done.

Randy invented dramas: He envisioned Mark breaking into Mr. Hewitt's house, strangling him before approaching Randy. Or he pictured himself being beaten by his dad—until Mark rushed in, killed Randy's father, and swooped Randy away.

Often he imagined himself a pioneer captured by Indians, stripped and tied to a tree. A fire burned at his legs. The Indians formed a circle around him, fended off intruders, and guarded him closely. He was their offering to the gods.

As the flames nipped at Randy's skin, Mark, a renowned explorer, galloped up on a horse. He attacked the warriors, slaughtering them one by one. Victorious, he untied Randy and lifted him onto his steed. Then the two of them rode off together, into the woods.

Randy slept once he had masturbated to his fantasies. But he had learned to be careful about rising with the sun and returned to the house before Mr. Hewitt awoke.

Three nights before they were scheduled to leave Ojibway Sound, he was alone in a clearing, lying on his stomach about to doze off. Suddenly he found himself thinking about the plane crash. When he saw the glowing eyes of the man from the fire, he pushed his penis into the pine needles. The phantom became Mark, naked and sweaty, his penis erect, his moist skin orange as it reflected the flames. Mark took Randy's hand, pulled him out of his seat, and led him forward. As they entered the inferno, Randy ejaculated.

He slept fitfully that night and awoke even before the sun started to rise. He dressed rapidly and sped back to the house, then hopped into bed and slept some more.

When he awoke two hours later, he had almost forgotten everything from the night before. But immediately after breakfast, he heard Mrs. Landis singing one of her gospel tunes in the kitchen, and it all came back to him.

"Yes, Jesus loves me," she sang softly. "The Bible tells me so." Randy recognized the words; he had heard them many times as they drifted out from the Baptist church in his home town on Sunday mornings. He wondered if religion really was a "crock of shit," as his father had said. Perhaps there was a God; perhaps He was watching him. He might consider Randy a sinner. By the time Mrs. Landis had finished her song, Randy had decided to cease his nocturnal escapades.

That evening was even hotter than those that had preceded it. In his own bed after leaving Mr. Hewitt's, Randy lay still, sweating, fighting the familiar impulse to run out of the house. As he listened to the owl outside, he had an odd sensation: Overcome by the heat, he felt as if he were lying in a grave. The sheets pulled up to his chin seemed like piles of earth, protecting him. He slid down toward the foot of the bed, until his head was completely covered. Contented and cozy, he remained submerged for several seconds.

Suddenly he began to panic: He thought he was being smothered. Terrified, he thrust himself forward, up from under the sheets. He switched on the light, jumped out of bed, and threw on his clothes. After retrieving the Kents from Mr. Hewitt's room, he dashed into the woods.

Once he was secure in a clearing, he imagined having sex with Mark in the midst of flames. Afterward he wondered if he had been thinking about hell and if anyone else ever had fantasies such as his. He felt lonely and almost started to cry. He fell asleep instead.

The next day, his last in Ojibway Sound, he awoke anxious and melancholy. He suspected he was upset because he had to go back to his father's, yet his sadness seemed to encompass more than this. He couldn't understand the reason for his mood and was unable to shake it.

At the house, he did his best to avoid Mrs. Landis; he didn't want her scorn to make him feel worse. He played a game with himself, attempting to pretend she did not exist. This didn't work. He then decided that he was glad he had secrets, that he would continue to hide things from people like her.

Eric Randall stopped by that afternoon; Mr. Hewitt still owed him money for his work. Randy watched Eric carefully, attentive to the fact that this big ruddy man was Mark's father. He remembered that he had only seen Mark twice, but was certain that he'd see him again. It seemed inevitable.

When he noticed Eric staring back at him, he looked away.

That night in the woods, he sat on the ground naked, studying the burns on his hands. They had started to heal. He didn't sleep at all. The sun began to rise at five-thirty. He lingered, scanning the trees, then returned to his room, walking slowly.

Mrs. Landis came at six-fifteen to fix breakfast and see Mr. Hewitt off. Even at that hour the heat was stifling. They left at eight. Randy looked at the house one last time, depressed. But as he got into the car with Mr. Hewitt, he began to feel very alert; he hoped they would make one stop before driving back to Indiana.

When they arrived at the service station, Mark was outside, sitting in a chair by the door, smoking. Randy was sure he had been waiting for them. At first Mark didn't stir. He finally tossed his cigarette onto the ground and pulled himself up from his seat.

As he approached them, Randy once again observed his handsome, tanned face, his dark eyes, his long, light brown hair. He was dressed in his green attendant's uniform; the sleeves of his shirt had been cut off, and his brown, sinewy arms gleamed in the sun.

He stopped on Mr. Hewitt's side of the car and leaned toward the window, peering past Mr. Hewitt at Randy. Randy glanced back at him, then downward, stopping when he saw the tufts of hair coming out from under Mark's arms.

"Good morning, Mark," Mr. Hewitt said briskly.

Mark nodded, but did not reply. He kept his eyes on Randy. Randy wanted to look back, but, shy, continued staring at Mark's arms.

"We're leaving, you know." Mr. Hewitt's tone was abrupt.

"My father told me." Mark remained still.

Looking up warily, Randy noticed Mark's eyes. They seemed to be laughing. Mark met Randy's gaze and, gradually drawing back his lips, grinned. Flushing, Randy felt himself smiling as well. He turned away.

"Well, Mark," Mr. Hewitt said, not noticing this exchange, "we need some gas before we go. Take care of that for me. I'll be right back."

Mark stood aside as Mr. Hewitt climbed out of the car, then watched him as he walked to the men's room.

Once he had disappeared, Mark again leaned toward the car's window and, for the first time ever, addressed Randy.

"So, kid, did you have a good vacation?" Although he spoke softly, he sounded sarcastic to Randy.

"Yes...I..." Randy couldn't continue.

Mark smiled. After hesitating only an instant, he opened the car door and sat in the driver's seat. He turned to Randy, his eyes surprisingly serious.

"Your name's Randy, right?"

"Uh-huh."

Mark smiled again. "So tell me, Randy, did that Landis woman give you a hard time?" His voice still had a trace of sarcasm in it, yet he seemed gentle.

Acutely aware of Mark's proximity, Randy said nothing.

"What a tight-assed bitch, eh?" Mark lifted his arm and scratched his head. "She can cook good though, right?"

Randy saw the hair in Mark's armpit and blushed, wanting to touch it.

"That Hewitt's something else, too." Mark chuckled, lowering his arm and resting it on his leg. "He works my dad pretty hard. Serves the old drunk right."

Randy, still uneasy, had followed the movement of Mark's arm, so that his eyes were now focused on his leg. He remembered the fantasies he'd had in the woods and started to get an erection.

"I suppose he gave you a lot of wine every night with dinner. And then brandy afterwards."

Startled, Randy looked up. He couldn't understand how Mark had known this and wondered how much more he knew. His father might have told him some things. But there was something about Mark's tone that made Randy think this was not the case.

"I hope you didn't get too drunk."

"A...a little."

Mark laughed. "Well, it beats going to Fort McIsley. Or to that fucking Indian cemetery. I always hated that."

Randy stared at him, confused. Their eyes locked. Mark's smile broadened. Beginning to understand, Randy looked down.

"I bet he took you out to eat at Shirley's."

Randy raised his head. "Ye…yeah."

"Fuck," Mark exclaimed, "some things never change."

Randy absorbed Mark's face; he thought it could have been his own. Mark was silent, gazing at him. Randy felt as if Mark could see through his skin. He concentrated on his eyes, wanting to disappear in them.

Mark chuckled. "So tell me, man, does he still snore?"

Randy took a deep breath, feeling exposed, naked, yet also strangely animated.

Mark studied him for a moment, intently. He placed a hand on Randy's thigh. When he spoke again, his voice was kind, the sarcasm gone. "You knew, didn't you? I mean, that you're not the first?"

Randy shut out everything except the feel of Mark's touch.

Mark squeezed Randy's thigh. "Relax, kid. He's just a rich fucker. Take what you can. You'll be fine."

"I'm not…" Randy stopped, suddenly excited, unexpectedly grateful. He realized it was true: Mr. Hewitt *was* just a rich fucker. Mark had known it; now he knew it, too. He felt stupid for not having seen it before. But then he had probably known it all along. That didn't matter. The important thing was, he and Mark shared this knowledge. They also might share some of the same secrets. He wasn't alone.

Mark removed his hand from Randy's thigh. "Shit, here he comes."

Mr. Hewitt was emerging from the men's room.

Impervious to this, Randy looked down at Mark's chest and read the name on his shirt. Mark, he thought. *Mark Randall.* He looked further down to Mark's hand, the one that had been on his thigh. I'm Mark Randall, he told himself; Mark Randall is me.

Mark opened the door and jumped out of the car. Glancing back, he said, "Take it easy, Randy. Maybe I'll see you next summer."

Mr. Hewitt grumbled when he saw that Mark hadn't filled the gas tank. Randy watched Mark as he worked. When Mark was finished, Mr. Hewitt gave him a small tip. Mark pocketed the change and returned to his chair outside the station's door. Mr. Hewitt and Randy rode away.

They drove south, down the narrow road that led out of Ojibway Sound, passing miles and miles of pine forests, getting nothing but static on the radio. After driving for several hours, Mr. Hewitt turned the dial and got a faint signal from the muzak station. Soon the pine forests were gone and the signal became clearer. A few farms appeared, then cornfields.

Randy was still at the service station, outside on the chair beside the door.

He saw himself sitting there, hot even with his shirt off, smoking cigarettes as he listened to the traffic, absentmindedly stroking his bare chest. A car drove in, and he stood. He filled the gas tank and washed the windshield, making small talk with the man behind the wheel. Then he returned to his chair and sat in the sun again, waiting for the day to end. He had some beers after work, ate, got undressed, and went to bed. The next day was the same. It wasn't such a bad life.

So wrapped up was he in his daydream that he almost wasn't conscious of their entering Indiana, did not really know they had passed the state line until Mr. Hewitt said, "Well, boy, we're almost there." Randy looked out the window and saw the familiar landscape. "Shit," he muttered, "I'm home."

He thought about Mark for years after that, though Mark was killed the following fall in a car crash. The accident happened while he was driving drunk on a road outside of Ojibway Sound. According to Mr. Hewitt, it was his own fault. "Crazy kid," he said when he told Randy the story, "he never could hold his liquor."

Randy continued to have fantasies about Mark, especially when he was with Mr. Hewitt. He imagined himself with Mark in the flames, bathing in heat. He saw the hair in his armpits, the sweat on his skin, the muscles on his lanky body. The fire then swallowed them both.

Writhing on top of Randy, Mr. Hewitt groaned and ejaculated. Randy, far away, scarcely knew he was there.

Sometimes he felt guilty about fantasizing in this way; he was afraid that if he didn't stop himself, he would "grow up queer." But he was convinced that he would not do this forever; he had his plans, after all.

Shortly after he had returned from Canada, he vowed to leave Indiana as soon as he could. He promised himself that he would move to New York City and become a famous writer or an actor, get married and have a couple of children. He would leave Mr. Hewitt behind him. Mark Randall would fade away.

Later, when he was grown and living in New York, he laughed if he thought about his early ambitions. The promises he had made to himself in those days seemed so naive, so childish. Of course, he remembered, he *had* been a kid back then; he had not yet learned that such resolutions were only made to be ignored.

It was eight in the morning; the apartment was silent. Staring at the clock, still on the couch, Randy did not know where the past three hours had gone.

High but very tired, he looked down at the fifteen sheets of paper on the table before him, then thought again about Dakota and Denise, about how amused they had been by his first story. That didn't matter, he assured himself; they'd never hear about this one. He would never write the part about Mark. And he'd only show Graham a bit of what he had done, just enough to keep him happy.

He gazed at the words on the paper; they seemed to be shimmering, alive. He wondered how he could have even started this, and was furious with himself. Moving blindly, he grabbed the pages and ripped them to shreds, allowing the pieces to fall on the floor. Once the debris had settled, he glanced at the torn paper. Relieved, he leaned back on the couch.

A few minutes later, he bolted up. Fuck, he thought, what have I done? Now he had nothing to show Graham. He stood and paced back and forth across the room, only stopping when he noticed on a shelf next to the television set the copy of *Summer Swan* he had stolen. It had been so long since he'd read it, he had almost forgotten about it. He walked to the shelf, picked up the book, and took it with him to the couch, then, the moment he got there, turned to a page in the middle.

"Your memories are intense," he read. "A part of him is still here. But the more you remember, the more you are aware that he is gone. Yet keeping his memory alive is foolish. The world has moved on. It is time for you to move as well."

Randy stared at the words, not understanding any of them; he only knew that they were a part of Graham's legacy. He wondered if he, too, could have been a famous writer if things had been different. Then he smiled, feeling that such speculations were absurd. He looked up from the book. This is the way things are, he told himself. He could change nothing.

He sat still and heard the faint sound of Jake snoring in the bedroom. After listening for a moment, he picked up the pen and, scarcely conscious of his actions, began writing on the pad of paper:

What happened then seems so far away. You don't give a shit anymore. You want to turn to everyone you meet and say, "Do whatever the fuck you want, it's over." But you don't have to tell them that. They've always done what they pleased anyway. What you say doesn't matter.

He stopped, puzzled. He read what he had just written, and found that it sounded as strange to him as the passage he had read from Graham's book. He didn't know where his words had come from or what had prompted them. He read what he had written several more times, but still could not comprehend anything.

Well, he thought, at least I have something to show Graham. It wasn't much, but it would have to do. It was almost nine, and he was exhausted.

IX

At six that evening, Randy was awakened by laughter and a babble of voices in the living room. At first he was confused: still vaguely aware of the dexedrine he had taken the night before, cloudy about the previous day's activities, and perplexed by a nagging suspicion that he had forgotten something important. Then, once he was more awake and his ears had adjusted to the sounds coming from the next room, he realized with dismay that Adrian Peterson was in the apartment with Jake.

"That's cool," Adrian was saying. He giggled. "I think I can handle *that.*"

Adrian and Jake both laughed raucously. Speaking softly, Jake said something else. Although Randy was unable to make out his words, whatever he had said made Adrian laugh even more.

"Right!" Adrian exclaimed. "I know *just* what you mean!"

Still in bed, Randy was furious. But he felt he had no right to be angry. Jake *had* informed him about the arrangement with Adrian. And it was necessary, Haircut being in the hospital. Of course, he knew that there was more than business involved in Jake and Adrian's dealings. Nevertheless, he told himself once again—as he had been doing since that night at The Scrotum—this renewed affair was no threat to him. Actually, he remembered, Jake had remarked only recently that Adrian was "just another tired East Village faggot."

A pretty one, Randy had to admit, but a cliché nonetheless. He had always thought that Adrian—with his closely cropped blond hair, his perfectly toned gym body, and his waxed, hairless chest—resembled every other gay man he saw, dressed as he invariably was in strategically ripped jeans, combat boots, and a tight muscle T-shirt. Jake had told Randy that Adrian clipped his "pubes" as well as other "unsightly" body hairs. He even shaved his legs. Apparently he wanted to achieve the smooth, sculptured look that so many queers admired.

"You have to admit he's hot," Jake had said when Randy mocked Adrian's painfully studied narcissism.

"Yeah," Randy replied, "if you're into someone who looks like a porn star."

Adrian was very much a part of the East Village scene. On those few occasions when Randy went out to a club or bar, he would usually see Adrian, posing on the edge of the dance floor, chatting with friends, cruising the room, dancing rapturously. They rarely acknowledged each other. Even so, in addition to a shared carnal knowledge of Jake, they had several similarities.

For starters, they were both uncommonly good-looking. But

Adrian was much fairer than Randy, compactly built, with guileless blue eyes and clear skin. He looked vulnerable. Randy, however, knew—for he had heard it from certain club kids and seen it a few times himself—that Adrian could be one mean queen. Like Randy, Adrian claimed to be an actor. Yet he was as lax as Randy in pursuing his career and never made it to auditions. He had supported himself until now at a series of undemanding jobs with flexible hours. Such a schedule enabled him to stay out late at night, so that he could be sure he was one of the first to visit all the new clubs.

He had many older "friends," men who took him to dinner and helped him with his rent and bills. How much he actually gave each of them in return was a subject of amused speculation amongst his acquaintances at the clubs. They did know that he was looking for someone "secure," someone with a fat bank account, a good trust fund or a top job, and a summer house on the Fire Island Pines.

He'd ended his first affair with Jake after he met just such a man, one Jonathan Richardson, a homely but generous heir to a liquor fortune. Adrian and Jonathan had spent the previous summer together on The Pines. Unfortunately for Adrian, Jonathan terminated their relationship in the fall. According to club gossip, Adrian's greed was so transparent that it eventually became obvious even to the gullible Jonathan.

Now Adrian appeared to be on the make again. Randy assured himself that as soon as he met another wealthy man, this second affair with Jake would come to an abrupt halt.

But it seemed that Adrian had fallen on hard times. The very fact that he'd agreed to a business arrangement with Jake indicated as much. In the past, Randy had always had the impression that Adrian looked down on him, that he did not approve of the way in which Randy supported himself and Jake. It wasn't anything Adrian said that gave Randy this idea. Rather, it was Adrian's haughty manner, the clear disdain he exhibited toward Randy whenever they were thrown together in social situations.

Randy felt Adrian's superior attitude pretentious and patently absurd. What he did with his older "friends" was probably identical to what any common street prostitute did with his johns. And yet Randy suspected that Adrian would never before have agreed to a crass exchange of cash for a hand job or anything else of that nature; he had always conveyed the impression that his sexual favors were more precious than that.

Evidently he'd had a change of heart. And now, as he had consented to take Haircut's place, he even seemed ready to move beyond the sensual massages that Randy usually provided, to go "all the way" and be "full service."

Just then Randy was drawn out of his thoughts by another burst of laughter pealing out of the living room.

"Shit, Jake," Adrian cried gleefully, "that's flawless!"

Randy swirled around and glared at the bedside clock. It was past 6:30; he had just a little over an hour to prepare for Graham. He didn't feel like facing Adrian, but feared it was inevitable. He crawled out of bed and into the shower, then dressed slowly, hoping a miracle would occur, that Adrian would be gone by the time he was ready.

When he walked into the living room, Adrian was sitting next to Jake on the couch, their legs pressed together.

"Sweetheart!" Jake exclaimed, moving away from Adrian as he smiled at Randy.

Adrian lit a cigarette, his eyes darting up and down Randy's body, as if appraising his outfit. His face seemed to register disapproval of Randy's plain blue shirt and baggy jeans.

"I've been showing Adrian the ropes," Jake continued, flushing slightly.

"Uh-huh." Randy stood still. He felt awkward and was anxious to leave the apartment.

"It's all probably boring to you," Adrian remarked. "You're such an old pro." He laughed, then dragged on his cigarette. "I've still got a lot to learn, though. Jake is being very sweet. He's teaching me everything."

Randy gazed at Adrian, uncomfortably aware of his own rage.

"So what time are you meeting Graham?" Jake was now sitting on the opposite end of the couch from Adrian, as far away from him as he could get without leaving his seat.

Ignoring Jake, Adrian picked up a sheet of paper from the table in front of him. "I see you're a man of many talents, Randy. I'm impressed."

Randy looked down and, appalled, saw that Adrian was holding the piece he had written for Graham the night before. He realized he had forgotten about writing it and leaving it there.

"Come on, Adrian, leave m'baby alone!" Jake attempted to yank the sheet from Adrian's hands. But Adrian grasped it tightly, staring down at the writing.

"'What happened then seems so far away,'" he read, his enunciation overly dramatic and heavy with sarcasm. "'You don't give a shit anymore. You want to turn to everyone you meet and say, "Do whatever the fuck you want, it's over."'" He stopped, giggling. Then, smiling, he said, "Frankly, my dear, it looks like you don't give a damn."

"Enough, Adrian!" Jake grabbed the paper from him and passed it to Randy.

"Oh, I'm sorry!" Adrian's voice was syrupy. He continued smiling at Randy. "The last thing I wanted to do was upset you. I think it's *fabulous* that you're writing. Really, I do. I just wish I could have read the rest of it. You know, the stuff we found on the floor. It's a pity you tore it up."

"Yeah, sure." Randy blushed, finding that Adrian's false, mocking tone augmented the discomfort he felt now that he recalled everything from the night before—this fragment of writing and the memories that had inspired it. He folded the sheet of paper and put it in his pants pocket, then started to turn away.

"Oh, sweetheart," Jake cried, changing the subject, "I heard from Haircut."

Randy stopped. "Oh, yeah? How is he?"

"He's getting better. But he got some bad news: They did a few tests and found out he's positive."

"Positive?" Randy pictured Graham's thin, bony body, his overly prominent rib cage. He quickly focused on Jake's neck; there was a hickey there. He felt his rage dart to the surface once more, overpowering everything else. Glancing up, he glared at Jake, then, looking down again, tried to control himself.

Adrian shrugged. "Well, he's always been one of the biggest whores around."

"They also found a lot of alcohol in his blood." Jake appeared to be avoiding Randy's eyes. "They've talked him into going into a rehab at St. Vincent's. It's a mess. His mother shows up all the time. Comes in from Queens every day. Haircut told me she's always pulling these crazy scenes and shit. I guess she's really freaked."

"Another drama queen," Adrian chortled. "Just like Haircut."

Randy turned toward Adrian, more confused now than angry. He was trying to take in all this information, but was having a hard time.

"None of this really surprises me," Adrian went on. "We've always known Haircut was a lush and a slut."

Randy looked at Jake. "Wha...what's he going to do in rehab?"

"He'll..."

"Oh, he'll go to a lot of AA meetings," Adrian cut in. "So many fags are doing that these days."

"Yeah, you're right," Jake agreed. "It'll probably do him some good."

Randy glanced at his watch; it was nearly 7:30. "I've gotta go," he said abruptly.

Adrian grinned. "So soon?"

"I'm supposed to be at Graham's at eight."

"Well then, do have fun. We'll be thinking of you."

Randy frowned, wishing he had never even met Adrian Peterson.

Jake stood and walked to Randy, then kissed him on the cheek. "Yeah, listen, sweetheart, take care, okay? And be good. I'll see you later."

Before leaving the apartment, Randy went to the bedroom. Shaky as he was, he felt he needed to take something. He searched Jake's drawers and found the bottle of dexedrine, then glanced toward the door to make sure Jake was not looking in. He swallowed a pill.

He walked west, his mind reeling from his encounter with Adrian and from everything Jake had told him. The situation with Haircut was disturbing. Randy was shocked that the hospital had suggested he go to their rehab. Of course, Haircut *did* overdo it sometimes, but then so did a lot of other people. He wondered if the doctors weren't overreacting. He was glad that he wasn't in Haircut's position. Then there was the news that Haircut had tested positive. And now he was about to see Graham again.

He thought about Graham's waxen skin, his emaciated chest and thighs. Although the fact that Graham was sick had been obvious at their first meeting—or at least Randy recognized this now—he tried not to dwell on his illness. Actually, it seemed as if the sweetness had become a part of Graham's personality.

Haircut's positive status was different. This was the first time anyone, including Haircut, had learned of it. Randy wondered if he would have to watch Haircut deteriorate or if, as had happened with so many others, Haircut would merely disappear. Randy had never liked him, but they were closely connected. The idea that someone so familiar might wither away and die in this manner terrified him.

Growing more agitated, he stopped to light a cigarette, shielding the flame from a strong gust of wind that was shooting up the street. Suddenly he recalled himself perched on top of Graham's penis, semen dripping out of his asshole. But he had been stoned then, he remembered. And it hadn't happened again.

He shuddered, looking at his watch; it was nearly eight. He had to move. He didn't have time to worry about things like this; he was anxious to see Graham. He hoped their session tonight would make him feel better. There was something about Graham that felt right—his fame, maybe, the fabulous life he had led, an aura he projected.

Of course, he would have to be careful if they did have sex again. He'd made a mistake with him. He'd been careless with others, too. Sometimes all those precautions just seemed futile. The world was fucked, and he was going to die eventually anyway. Besides, everyone was lax occasionally, and they weren't all sick.

He hurried across Sixth Avenue. Chilly, he stuffed his hands in his pockets, feeling the sheet of paper. He wondered how Graham would react to his piece; he knew it wasn't the sort of thing he was expecting.

For an instant he thought about Mark Randall, recalling, too, his dream of the plane crash. He then found himself thinking about the sweetness again. Enough! he told himself. He couldn't imagine what the sweetness had to do with his early life.

He turned onto Perry Street, aware of the uneasiness he experienced whenever he was about to visit Graham. Then he again thought about some of the things they had done together and, remembering Graham's penis pushing into him, increased his pace. Despite his apprehensions, he hoped something would happen tonight. He'd just have to be cautious.

At that moment he recalled something Haircut had said weeks before, that every gay man had the sweetness, it was only a matter of time. Well, Randy thought, it looks like Haircut's about to prove his point.

He approached Graham's building, walked up the front steps, and rang the buzzer. He waited for what seemed a very long time. Finally the door clicked.

X

The first thing Randy noticed when he entered the building was its overwhelming silence, the eerie stillness that penetrated all its floors. He climbed the stairs, expecting to find Graham at the top, greeting him in the hallway. But when he got there, Graham was nowhere to be seen. He saw that Graham's door was ajar and edged toward it. He cautiously walked in.

The apartment was almost completely dark, its only light provided by the small lamp on the table near the leather couch. At first he thought that he had made a mistake, that this was not Graham's apartment at all. But when he saw the portrait of Madonna on the wall, he knew he was in the right place. Graham was not in the room. Randy stood motionless, his stomach starting to churn.

He heard the sound of a toilet flushing, then listened to Graham's footsteps as he walked from the bathroom to the bedroom, coughing frequently. A few seconds later, Randy looked to his left. Graham, smiling slightly, was shuffling toward him, coming out through the bedroom door.

"Hello, baby," he said softly. "Sorry I took so long. It's just that I had this wicked case of the shits."

He was dressed once again in his bathrobe and slippers. But, Randy noticed, he had lost a great deal of weight since they had last been together, so that now his robe seemed to hang like dead skin over his emaciated body. His face had no color whatsoever; Randy thought that he could detect his skull.

Graham leaned over and brushed Randy's lips with his own. Randy nearly pulled away. But then he looked up and, reassured by a familiar gleam in Graham's eyes, felt his old attraction to this man—the strange stimulation he experienced whenever they were together—coming back.

Graham touched Randy's right hand. His skin felt cold. "Come on, baby," he said, "let's have some fun."

These words were spoken playfully, yet they seemed to Randy hollow and forced. He felt torn between a longing to withdraw into himself and a disquieting empathy, as if he, too, were wasting away.

They sat on the couch, Graham breathing with some difficulty. Randy lit a cigarette, then turned to the photograph of Dennis sitting on the table next to him.

Graham began coughing violently. Randy quickly extinguished his cigarette and looked back at him, not knowing what to do.

"Fuck!" Graham exclaimed once his coughing had subsided. "I can't stand this! I'd been feeling better until a few hours ago."

"Was...was the smoke bothering you?" Moving tentatively, Randy placed a hand on Graham's thigh. "I'm sorry. Really. I won't do it anymore."

"No, no, it's not that at all!" Graham pulled away, impatient. A moment later, he cried, "I've had enough of this shit! Let's get high!" He abruptly stood and, walking very slowly, left the room.

Immobile, Randy stared at the photo of Dennis. He recalled Dennis's uncanny resemblance to the Jamie Gilmour of *Teenage Butt Juice* and thought about Mark Randall. Then he remembered the piece he had written and grew more apprehensive, again unsure how Graham would react to it. He almost wanted to flee.

Graham returned, carrying two glasses of gin and the bottle of dexedrine. Sitting next to Randy, he placed the drinks on the table and took out two pills. He passed one to Randy. "Here, this should help us both."

"But I…" Randy stopped. He already felt high and was not sure he wanted to take more speed. Holding the dexedrine, he took a swig of his drink.

"Come on, baby." Graham washed his own pill down with gin. "What are you waiting for?"

Randy wavered, then put the dexedrine in his mouth and raised his glass to his lips.

"Good boy!" Graham grinned.

He swallowed the pill.

They were silent for a few minutes. Graham, fidgeting, finished his drink quickly. He appeared to be waiting for the speed to kick in. Randy stared into space, thinking about the piece he had written, wondering when Graham would ask to see it. He wanted to light another cigarette, but was afraid smoke would cause Graham to cough again.

At last Graham said, "Let's go to the bedroom, baby. I think I'd like a massage."

Surprised, Randy looked at him. "You want one now?"

"I think it would help a lot. Anyway, it's something to keep us busy while we're waiting to get high."

Randy, relieved, stood. Maybe Graham's forgotten about the story, he thought; he was pretty drunk when he called last night.

He suspected things would not move beyond the massage stage now; sex was certainly out of the question, seeing how sick Graham was. He recalled Haircut's morbid remark, and knew it was better that they not do anything. He felt disheartened.

He followed Graham to the bedroom, then stood by the bed, holding his drink tightly. Although he had seen this room before, he'd never bothered to take it all in. The general impression he'd had was that of an orderly space, everything neat and clean. But tonight the bed was unmade, the sheets falling down onto the floor. Clothes, used tissues, papers, and books lay scattered everywhere. The room itself felt exceedingly warm and close, which aggravated Randy's discomfort.

Graham lay down, but kept his bathrobe on. Randy, hesitant, sat next to him.

"You haven't undressed," Graham said.

Smiling uneasily, Randy touched Graham's robe. "What about you?"

Graham sighed. "Don't worry about me, baby. It's a little cold, that's all. I've got to be careful. But I want to see you starkers. I mean, you're still well, aren't you?"

Randy gulped his drink. "Yea…yeah, sure." He undressed.

Once he was naked, he again sat next to Graham. He did nothing at first.

"Come on," Graham said, "what's your problem? Just carry on as you normally would."

"Okay." Randy swallowed the rest of his gin, then placed his glass on the bedside table. He climbed on top of Graham and began rubbing his shoulders gingerly, caressing the material that covered his skin.

Graham closed his eyes.

Randy moved his hands down Graham's back, working his way toward his buttocks. He felt the second pill he had taken augmenting the effects of the first, and focused on Graham's bathrobe, finding its deep blue color breathtakingly rich. He watched as the blue in the robe seemed to swirl in circles before him, forming strange patterns and designs, changing hues, becoming almost purple. Motionless now, he stared at the robe, transfixed, his hands resting on Graham's lower back.

He heard Graham snoring, and saw that he was asleep. Fuck, he thought, what should I do? He worried that, despite the speed, Graham would sleep for the rest of the night. For a second he was afraid Graham was dying, then, shuddering, decided this was impossible, that Graham wasn't *that* ill. He remained still, his legs pressed against Graham's sides, listening to the sound of his heavy breathing.

After several minutes, his legs grew numb, and he felt restless. Shifting his body forward, he moved his hands up to Graham's shoulders, pulling the robe down slightly and kneading the skin. He saw how incredibly thin Graham had become, the bones in his back clearly visible, more prominent than they had been before. He studied his flesh, fascinated by its pallor. As he continued the massage, he thought he could feel the flow of Graham's blood through his veins. Soothed by this and by the sound of his breathing, he surrendered to the heat in the room. The warmth now seemed pleasant and luxurious.

He felt Graham's rib cage expanding and contracting and took hold of his own penis, which had become erect. He lay down, stretching out on top of Graham, wrapping his arms around his chest, rubbing his groin against his robe. Graham groaned. Randy paused, then continued, moving warily this time.

As he moved, his eyes wandered to the table next to the bed. There, near a lamp, he saw a photograph of Dennis he had never before seen. He stopped in order to fully absorb it: Dennis, looking flushed, was dressed in a tuxedo and holding a glass of champagne. He appeared to be in a large club; Randy could discern in the background hundreds of people dancing under strobe lights. Laughing, Dennis had turned from the camera toward these dancers, as if about to join them. Randy wished he could have been there, moving onto that crowded floor and dancing with Dennis.

He noticed something else on the table, a thick leather book with a marker in its middle, and wondered what it was. There was no title on its cover, nothing at all. He decided it could be only one thing: Graham's diary.

He reached out toward it, then pulled back. Graham would be furious, he knew, if he caught him reading his diary. But he was desperate to see it; he was certain it would answer many questions he had.

He extended his hand toward the book once again. At that moment, he felt Graham stir.

"What...?" Graham raised his head.

Randy lowered his hand to Graham's side.

Graham looked back at him, appearing confused. Then, coming to, he exclaimed, "Right!" He shook his head and laughed. "Oh, baby, I feel so much better! Like a new man! Dexedrine is the real miracle drug!"

"Yeah." Randy blushed. Apparently Graham had not noticed anything.

Graham raised his shoulders. "What are you doing, baby? I mean, why are you lying down? Get up! You feel heavy. I want to move."

"Sorry." Randy slid off Graham's back, then sat on the side of the bed, his penis now flaccid.

Graham, stretching, sat up. Randy gazed at him, realizing that he did indeed look somewhat better: His face, though still pale, had more color than before.

Graham tweaked Randy's nipple. "What about that story you promised me?"

"Story?" Randy looked away, staring at his empty glass.

"Why, of course. I want to read it." Grinning, Graham rose. "But let's have another drink first, okay?" He picked up Randy's glass and, his pace unnaturally quick, left the room.

Shit, Randy thought, he remembered the fucking story after all. He wondered what he should do; he was now convinced that Graham would not be pleased with what he'd written.

Graham returned with their gin.

"Here, baby," he said as he passed a glass to Randy. "So let's have a look at this new masterpiece of yours."

Randy took a long sip of his drink. Then he gripped his glass and glanced downward, saying nothing.

"Well? Where is it?"

Randy peered up over Graham's shoulder at the photograph of Dennis. "I...I didn't write anything."

Graham squinted at him, for a second appearing puzzled, even, Randy noted with surprise, hurt. But then, reddening, he sucked in his breath. "You what? I thought you were working on it last night."

"I couldn't. I didn't have time." Randy now wished that he had left earlier, right after he'd arrived.

"You didn't *have time?* Graham's voice cracked. "What bullshit! That's not what you said when I talked to you."

Randy continued staring at the picture of Dennis, avoiding Graham's eyes.

"I gave you plenty of notice. Not to mention the money I've been sending you."

Randy swilled some of his drink, still unable to look directly at Graham. Scarcely aware of what he was saying, he mumbled, "And there was that night with Dakota and Denise." As soon as he'd said this, he felt his heart pounding and wished he could take his words back.

Graham started coughing again. He gulped some gin and managed to stop. Then, almost whispering, he murmured, "Dakota and Denise?"

"You…you told them about the first story."

"So?"

Randy glanced at Graham, then immediately downward.

Graham moved closer to him, leaning forward. "It wasn't a secret, was it?"

Randy said nothing.

Graham, too, was quiet for a moment. Then he said, "Ah, yes!" and placed a hand on Randy's leg, allowing it to rest there. When he spoke again, his voice was low, peculiarly earnest: "Look at me, baby."

Randy looked up. He noticed that Graham's face had softened, that his anger seemed to have subsided. This unexpected softness only heightened Randy's uneasiness.

"I gather thinking about Hewitt makes you uncomfortable."

Randy thought he heard a slight apology in Graham's tone and found this embarrassing; he preferred his earlier reprimand.

Graham smiled, a gleam returning to his eyes. He spoke, sounding lively, perky: "Well, it shouldn't, baby. We've all known people like him."

Randy peered over his shoulder once more, at the photo of Dennis.

"So many kids have been fucked with, just like you. You hear about it all the time."

Randy looked away from the photograph. "What do you mean?" he asked, perplexed.

Graham laughed. "Why, it's only natural. There's so much repression around."

"Repression?" Randy bit his lower lip.

"Repression, yes. And guilt. You know, don't you, that most of us are afraid of the things we desire? We *do* live in a Puritan culture. When we act out, we feel guilty afterwards. So we try to suppress our urges." Graham laughed again. "Or find some compliant child who won't threaten us. Some sexy little morsel like you."

Randy felt as if Graham were speaking in a foreign though vaguely familiar language. He was relieved that the conversation seemed to be moving in another direction and found himself hypnotized by the flow of Graham's words.

"I'm sure Hewitt was abused, too. When he was young, I mean. Most pedophiles were. As he got older, he probably tried to fight what he felt. There are so many other agendas, after all. But his desires got the best of him. They always do. Too many juicy young butts around, everywhere you look."

Randy wanted to stretch out on the bed, to float on his high.

"We all have our agendas. And our urges. Often they contradict each other. But we carry on anyway. Secretly." Graham hesitated before adding, "Of course, all of this repression and guilt creates monsters. Like Hewitt, for instance." He grinned. "Or, for that matter, like me."

Randy noticed that Graham's skin appeared to be swirling just as his robe had done earlier, that the pores seemed alive and throbbing. He studied his face, fascinated, relaxing under its spell.

"What you went through isn't all that unusual," Graham continued, still smiling. "You should try to enjoy the memories. And be grateful that you started at such a tender age." He paused, as if trying to decide what to say next. At last he lay down, taking Randy's hand and pulling him forward. "Come on, baby, lie next to me. I'm afraid I'm still a little weak. But I want to tell you a story."

"Okay." In a daze, Randy curled against Graham, feeling then as if he were in a dream, watching himself from above the bed.

Graham cupped a hand between Randy's legs. "I want to tell you about someone I knew."

Randy listened, soothed by Graham's voice, staring at the book he thought was a diary and the photograph of Dennis directly behind it.

"He was a boy very much like you," Graham began, almost purring. "You know, a Midwestern child. Strong. Very pretty. Beautiful, really. And rather ruddy. But a little terror! Always getting into trouble. He loved speeding down streets on his bike, swearing, frightening old ladies. Or tossing rocks through the windows of his school, picking fights with other kids, stealing trinkets from the stores at the mall. All his teachers were mystified; they couldn't

imagine what was wrong with him. But the boy didn't give a shit."
Graham laughed, caressing Randy's inner thigh. "I can just see him
now, whizzing down that street, his hair flying in the wind. He was
absolutely gorgeous."

Randy inched closer to Graham, his eyes glued to Dennis's image.
"He and his father lived in this housing tract near the outskirts of
town. Alone. His mother had deserted them when the boy was a
baby. She'd had enough, I suppose. You see, his dad was this big,
dumb bruiser who worked at a factory or mill or something like
that. Very blue collar. Every night he'd go to this bar after work and
come home drunk. Then he'd sit in front of the TV and drink beer,
not saying much of anything. But he always had this strange look on
his face, like he was preoccupied. Every once in a while he'd threat-
en to discipline the kid, but he usually just let him run wild. They
kept out of each other's way.

"The boy thought he liked his freedom. Sometimes, though, he'd
lie awake all night. He had no idea what was bothering him, and yet
he'd always end up frightened. Naturally, he didn't talk about this
with his father; he couldn't talk to him about anything. He just grew
up recklessly, like some feral little weed."

Graham stopped, noticing Randy's distant gaze. It was still fixed
on the photograph of Dennis. "Baby," he asked, squeezing Randy's
thigh, "are you paying attention?"

Randy pulled his eyes from the photograph and stared at
Graham. "Yeah, sure."

"Well, good." Graham peered past Randy toward a corner of the
room. It almost seemed as if he were searching for something. Then,
returning to Randy, amused, he said, "It gets better, baby. Really,
much better. Besides, it might help you. You're going to like it a lot,
I promise."

Randy placed his head on Graham's chest, closing his eyes.
Graham continued, his words coming out clearly, simply, as if he
were speaking to a child.

"He was very young when he realized how beautiful he was. It was
right after his father hung this tacky, full-length mirror in their

bathroom. The boy was around eight years old, I think. About that. At any rate, he started studying his reflection in this mirror whenever he was alone, if his father was at work or away somewhere. For hours at a time. He liked what he saw. He told himself that, even if he was just a kid, he was a good-looking one, better looking than anyone he knew. He was sure others would see this, too, someday.

"But things didn't really get interesting until he was older, when he started going through puberty. You know what that's like, don't you? Well, picture this: The boy grew tall and supple. His voice started to change. Now, when he looked in the mirror after showering, he saw his cock surrounded by this lovely, light, silky hair. His chest was broader; his muscles were more pronounced. He'd stand there looking at his body, running his hands over his skin. Then he'd masturbate.

"Well, one night while he was doing this, his father staggered into the bathroom, just bolted right in, without knocking or anything. He was totally bombed, of course. The boy was stunned, shocked. The father, too. He stopped right in his tracks and turned a deep, deep red. He couldn't look at the boy's face. But he stared at him anyway. Oh, yes, he stared! For quite a few seconds. Then he stuttered, 'I…I thought I heard something,' and lurched out of the room.

"You can imagine how embarrassed the boy was. But he thought about it afterwards and decided that since his father was drunk, he'd probably forget what he'd seen. Then the boy remembered his father's expression as he'd stared at him; he'd never before seen him look so interested in anything." Graham moved one hand across Randy's groin, the other up and down his back. "He got excited and looked in the mirror. He saw his smooth skin and the silky hair around his dick." He held Randy tightly. "Then he took hold of his cock and masturbated. Came in a big, lovely spurt."

Graham relaxed his grip as he moved a hand around Randy's penis. It was partially erect. "Is this turning you on, baby?" he asked, as if surprised. "That wasn't my intention." He smiled. "Not at all."

Flushed, Randy lay still, his stomach fluttering. He placed a hand on Graham's emaciated chest and stared at him. Graham's smile almost seemed to have obliterated his face. His skin looked taut and red, and no longer appeared to be swirling.

Graham gazed back at him. Slowly his smile faded. Randy thought that he looked disturbed.

"I just want to help you," Graham said a moment later, now speaking deliberately. "Let you know you're not alone."

Randy felt as if he were sinking into Graham's eyes.

"So shall I go on?"

Randy nodded, once more closing his eyes, conscious of nothing but the sound of Graham's voice.

"It was right after this that he began to notice little changes in his father's behavior. Nothing major, mind you, just subtle things. They still didn't talk much. But sometimes in the evening, at dinner or if they were watching television together, he'd see his father staring at him. If he looked back, his father would look away.

"When this first happened, he thought his father was angry with him for some reason or another. He even thought he could see rage in his eyes. But then these incidents occurred more and more frequently, and the boy started to find them flattering. They made him feel grown up. He hoped that, since he was older, the two of them would begin to have more things in common. Every day now, he thought something else would happen, something that would bring them closer. So he waited."

Graham took a deep breath. Randy opened his eyes, feeling Graham's hands on his back and groin, his touch cold yet soothing.

"Well," Graham continued with a sigh, "it went on like this for a while, until the boy was around fourteen or so. At about that time he was suspended from school for some silly reason. Stealing money from a classmate, I think. Of course, it wasn't the first time he'd misbehaved there. But it was the most serious incident, and his father was notified.

"Before, whenever the boy had been in trouble, his father hadn't cared. It was like it was easier for them both if these things were ignored. But this time the school called on a day when his father had stayed home from work. He'd gone on a bender the night before and gotten totally pissed. When the boy returned that evening, his father was waiting for him."

Graham increased the pressure of his hand on Randy's groin.

"Christ, what a scene that was! His father was blasted, completely out of his mind. He began screaming things like, 'You've gone too far this time!' and 'I've let you get away with too much!' At last, when he was hoarse from shouting, he stopped and just stared at the boy. This flipped the kid out. I mean, he realized his father was looking at him in that weird way. His father didn't say anything at first. Then he mumbled, 'I should have done something before,' and stared at the kid a little more. The boy didn't know what to do. He wanted to shout back, but he found it hard to look at his father. Finally, after a minute or so of this, his father ordered him to lean over the kitchen table and drop his pants."

Graham paused. Randy felt the icy pressure of Graham's hands, and was more aware of the churning of his stomach, of the perspiration falling down his brow.

Graham placed a hand under Randy's chin, raising his head so that Randy had no choice but to stare straight at him. He looked stern, his expression serious, not at all like it had been at the beginning of his story. Randy again felt himself sinking into his gaze.

"The boy was amazed," Graham went on, his voice low, not quite a whisper, "absolutely freaked. First of all, he'd never seen his father angry like this before. And then hearing this strange order! Later he remembered thinking how bizarre it had seemed. But he didn't want to give in, not without a fight, so he screamed, 'Fuck you!' at his dad, just spat it out.

"Well, his father was in no mood to take any crap. He clenched his fists, then slammed the boy right in the jaw.

"The boy was even more shocked now. His father had never done anything like this before. He thought he was dreaming, or maybe that his father was playing some weird game. But then his father grabbed his arm and cried, 'Do what I say!'

"The boy started shaking. But you can bet that he did what his father asked then!"

Graham removed his hand from under Randy's chin, easing it down his chest and stomach. He took hold of Randy's penis and massaged it. Randy shut his eyes.

"Once the boy had leaned over the table and lowered his pants, his father took off his belt—this really thick, leather one—and looked down at him. The boy thought he heard him say something like, 'Nice.'

"But he didn't have time to think about that, because his father began whipping him, just cracking the belt down on his round little butt. The first blow was horrible, but the boy was determined not to scream. Each strike after that was harder, but he never did cry out.

"At last his father stopped. He was panting. The boy was in a daze. Then his head cleared, and he discovered that he had an erection.

Randy opened his eyes, aroused despite the churning of his stomach. He stared over Graham's shoulder at the photo of Dennis. Graham continued massaging him.

"They remained where they were for a while. You know, the boy leaning over the table, his father standing above him. His father finally told him to go to his room; he was stammering as he spoke. The boy looked up at him; he seemed huge. He felt embarrassed and began walking away.

"Then he heard his father call, 'Wait!' and he stopped. But his father didn't say anything else. He only looked at his son in this strange way, like he was begging him for something. The boy was confused, yet in a way he felt energized. After a few seconds, though, he couldn't take any more. He turned away from his father and hurried upstairs."

Suddenly Graham pulled his hand from Randy's penis and started coughing furiously. Randy was scarcely aware of this, focused as he was on Dennis's photograph. He was lost in the image—and still experiencing Graham's story.

Graham stopped coughing and was silent for a moment. Then, speaking faintly, he said, "Sorry about that, baby."

Randy turned to him. He appeared drained, as pale as he had been earlier, when Randy had first arrived. Randy wanted to look away, but Graham gripped his arm.

"The story's almost over," he said unsteadily, his voice having lost any playful tone. "Just a little bit more, and then we'll do something else."

Succumbing to the force of Graham's grasp, Randy fell against his chest, holding onto his sides as he sank into his ribs.

Graham resumed the story, speaking breathlessly, again moving a hand down to Randy's groin.

"He took a shower—a long, hot one—and let the scalding water run over the welts on his ass. Whenever he touched his cock, he knew how excited he was. This alarmed him. But he was sure there was more to come. Later, he realized he had been anticipating what was about to happen for months.

"He climbed out of the shower and grabbed a towel to dry himself. He sensed someone else in the room almost immediately. He quickly turned to the mirror and, as he had half expected, saw his father's reflection. He was standing in the bathroom's doorway, staring. The boy looked down, then up again. His father was gone.

"He was trembling as he went to bed. Naturally he couldn't sleep. Instead he lay quietly in the dark. Soon he felt his father crawl under the covers beside him. He smelled beer on his breath and thought he could hear him crying. Then his father touched his chest. 'I'm sorry,' he whispered.

"The boy didn't budge; he was much too frightened. But he knew he had to do *something*. After stopping himself several times, he put a hand on his father's arm.

"The instant he did this, his father slipped out of the robe he was wearing and climbed on top of him. He kissed him on the neck and said things like, 'Denny, please!' and 'Oh, my little Denny, I'm so sorry!' Then he started moaning, sort of crying again, moving back and forth and rubbing his cock against the boy. The whole time his chest was right up on top of the kid's face."

Graham played with the tip of Randy's penis. Randy squeezed his eyes shut.

"The boy was rigid at first, completely uptight. But as his father kissed him on the mouth and caressed him, he smelled the sweat on his body and became excited, erect. He was sure what they were doing was wrong. Yet he couldn't forget the looks his father had been giving him recently. He decided that maybe, just maybe this was the way it was meant to be. At least it felt right at the moment. Without thinking about it anymore, he wrapped his arms around his father's back and clutched his shoulders tightly."

Graham moved his hand down Randy's shaft. "It went on like this for a few minutes, both of them moaning and gasping and carrying on. At last his father grunted and cried, 'God!' in this awful, cracking voice. His body shook with these little spasms. Then he squirted his come all over the kid's stomach. Once he'd come, he rolled off of the boy, turned away from him, and curled up by his side, completely out of breath."

Randy opened his eyes and looked at Graham, finding his pale, nearly expressionless face ghostly and beautiful. He felt Graham's hand on his penis, stroking its head. The room seemed to be closing in on him, its warmth reassuring.

"The boy was surprised that his father had rolled off so quickly, and was afraid to move. He waited. Finally he eased over to him and placed a hand on his shoulder.

"His father pulled back, then sat up and yelled, 'Don't! Don't ever do that again!' He was absolutely furious. He didn't say anything else for a while. The boy just lay there, stunned. When his father did speak again, it was in this low, low voice, so low the boy could barely hear it. 'It never happened,' he said, or something like that. Then he shot out of bed and stumbled out of the room.

"The boy was really frightened now. And ashamed of what they had done. He wondered if it had been a dream. Then he told himself that it had not been real, that he hadn't actually had sex with his father—and if they *had* done something, what they'd done had not been sex at all."

Graham stopped, still stroking Randy's penis, lightly now. Randy waited for his story to continue, but he said nothing else.

"So what happened then?" Randy asked.

Graham stared at him, appearing distracted and a little discomposed. Then, shaking his head, he laughed. "Why, the kid was awake for hours, he was so turned on. Had to masturbate in order to sleep. And in the morning, at breakfast with his father, it was like nothing had gone down."

Randy edged his penis toward Graham's, expecting more.

"Of course," Graham went on, a faint smile on his face, "that wasn't really the end. What they had went on for years. On the sly, naturally."

"What...what do you mean?"

"Well..." Graham paused before going on: "As I said, they pretended nothing had occurred. The boy went back to his old ways. Eventually he got into more trouble. Many times, over and over. Every time he misbehaved, it would happen again. You know, the beating, then the sex. His father was always drunk, of course. But neither of them acknowledged anything. It was just a little game they played, one that kept them amused for a very long time."

Randy waited. Then he murmured, "What happened to the boy?"

Graham's smile vanished. When he spoke again, his words were clipped: "Why, he got tired of it all. Moved to New York. Became a prostitute. Then he died."

Randy tightened his grip on Graham.

Graham gazed at him, his expression momentarily grave. Looking away, he noticed their drinks, both unfinished. "We've hardly touched our gin," he remarked, suddenly cheery. "I think I'd better freshen them up, don't you? We can't possibly drink *these*. They're much too watered down."

Pulling away from Randy's grasp, he stood, grabbed the glasses, and sauntered from the room.

Randy remained inert, thinking about Graham's story. It had left him feeling queasy, and he could not get it out of his head.

To him, the weirdest thing of all was that it had turned him on. Obviously this had been Graham's intention, since he had fondled him during much of his narration. He must have wanted to have sex. But if that was the case, why had he gotten up? They were already high; the gin could wait.

He turned toward the photograph of Dennis, certain he was the boy Graham had been talking about. It had been as though he were hearing a page read from Graham's diary, one on which Graham described everything he knew about the early life of his now-dead lover.

He wondered if he should let Graham know his suspicion, then remembered Graham's reaction the last time he had mentioned Dennis's name. Perhaps reciting this very personal history had upset

Graham. He had been calm enough at first, but by the end of his story, he had acted a little agitated—although it was never easy to tell exactly what Graham was feeling.

He studied Dennis's face, his tousled hair, his flushed skin, his brilliant smile, then imagined him naked, getting beaten. He found this image disturbing yet stimulating.

He was amazed by how much they'd had in common. But Dennis had slept with his father. He pictured his own father lying on top of Dennis. Then he imagined being in Dennis's place, getting humped by his dad. He shivered, assuring himself that he could never have done that. It was one thing being with Mr. Hewitt; what Dennis had done was completely different.

Still, he was curious to know what it had been like for Dennis, how often his father had done it, how many years it had been before Dennis had tired of it. He wondered if Graham was ever intrigued by such speculations, if thinking about things like this put him "in the mood." Then he recalled the piece he had written about his trip to Canada and regretted having torn it up. He was certain Graham's reading it would have led to other things.

But he *had* written something else, he reminded himself. He could show that to Graham. He'd make sure they were safe this time. He didn't want to think about *that*, though.

"Baby, what's wrong?"

Graham walked in with their gin. His voice sounded a bit too sweet to Randy.

"You look morose," he continued, sitting on the bed. "I hope my story didn't depress you."

Randy bolted up, accepting a glass from him. "No. No, I liked it. Really."

"Well. good. I thought you would." Graham smiled, looking, Randy thought, rather puckish. "I'm sure you've guessed that I made the whole thing up."

Randy took a huge swig of his drink. *"What?"*

"Yes." Graham laughed. "I'm a writer, remember? It was just a fable I invented. A fairy tale, so to speak. To teach you a lesson. I wanted to show you what happens to bad little boys."

For a second Randy believed this. But as Graham continued chuckling, he was again convinced that the story had been true. He decided this wasn't important; there were other things to think about. He inched closer to Graham and placed a hand on his thigh. Graham pulled away from him. Smiling strangely, his tone peculiarly petulant, he said, "You disobeyed me, you know. I asked for a story, but you didn't bring me anything." He touched Randy's chest, then, slowly, twisted his nipple. "We'll have to do something about that, won't we?"

Randy winced. Speaking quickly, he blurted, "But I did write something."

"What's that?" Graham was no longer smiling. He stared at Randy, his gaze malevolent. "What do you mean? Don't tell me you've been holding something back!" He drew his hand away, raising it slightly, as if he were about to strike Randy's face.

Randy cringed, instinctively preparing himself for a blow. "I was just...I just didn't think it was very good."

Graham glared at him. "I believe that's for me to decide, isn't it?" He abruptly lowered his hand and, surprising Randy, laughed. "I fooled you, didn't I? You really thought I was going to hit you."

Randy swilled his drink, trying to calm down. Graham's game had unnerved him.

Graham's expression again turned serious. "So where is it?"

"In...in my pocket."

"Go get it."

"Okay." His heart throbbing, Randy retrieved the sheet of paper from his pants, then returned to the bed, passing it to Graham. "It's not much."

Frowning impatiently, Graham set his glass on the table. "Again, that's for me to decide. Why don't you just sit down and shut up?"

Randy obeyed. Seated on the edge of the bed, clutching his gin, he watched as Graham read, waiting for him to finish, deciding as the minutes passed that he had to be reading it many times.

At last Graham looked up, scowling. "You're absolutely right. It's nothing."

Randy lowered his head and stared at his feet. "I...I told you so."

Graham was silent for what seemed an inordinately long time. Suddenly he grabbed Randy's arm, yanking it. "Look at me!"

Randy did as he was told, peering into Graham's eyes, frightened by the apparently blossoming fury he detected there. He wondered if Graham was serious this time, if he was actually angry, or if he was playing another game.

"This is not what I asked for, nothing like it at all." Graham held the paper before him, furrowing his brow melodramatically. "'But you don't have to tell them that,'" he read, hurling the words out contemptuously. "'They've always done what they pleased anyway. What you say doesn't matter.'" He stopped, gazing at the writing. Then he ripped the sheet into tiny fragments and threw the pieces in the air.

Randy followed them as they floated down to the bed.

"You knew what I asked for! You knew I wanted to hear about Hewitt! But you gave me this piece of crap instead!"

Randy's eyes remained fixed on what was left of his work.

Graham again grabbed his arm. "I told you to look at me!"

Randy looked up and, seeing how red Graham's face was, became much more frightened. Yet he also felt excited, expectant. This *is* a game, he told himself.

"After everything I've done for you," Graham cried, "all this time. And now you disappoint me. You..." He began coughing. Grabbing his gin from the table, he gulped half of it down. As his fit subsided, he lay back on the bed, then pulled Randy toward him. "Come on," he murmured, "let's see what we're going to do about this."

Shaking, Randy lay down.

Graham placed a hand on his groin. As his breathing became more regular, he squeezed Randy's penis, twisting it. "So, baby," he whispered, "how are you going to make it up to me?"

Randy squirmed, starting to sweat. He was getting an erection. "Maybe you should fuck me!" he spat out. Once he had said this, he was startled by his words, surprised that he had been able to say anything. Everything became hazy.

Graham tightened his grip on Randy's penis, twisting it even more. "I see the boy's getting a little angry. We'll definitely have to do something about that. After all, I told him such a nice story. And what did he give me?" He dug his nails into Randy's shaft. "He gave me shit!"

"Cunt," Randy mumbled softly. He no longer knew what he was saying.

Smiling, Graham sat up. He raised a hand above Randy's head, then lowered it across his face, striking him forcefully. The sound of the slap reverberated in the room. "Didn't you learn anything from my little fable?" he asked.

Randy lay on his side, stunned. He felt as if he were watching himself in a film. Somewhere above him, he heard himself say, "Why don't you just get a belt and beat me?"

Graham stared at him, his eyes animated. "You really want me to beat you?" Leaning forward, he pinched Randy's penis and grinned. "I see you've learned something after all."

Far away, Randy said nothing.

Graham stood. "Right!" he exclaimed. He walked to a closet on the other side of the room.

The sound of Graham's movements roused Randy slightly. He lifted his head and, as if through a fog, saw Graham remove a thick belt from a hanger.

"This one should do quite nicely," he was saying.

Deep in his guts, Randy felt an abeyant panic struggling to come up. He pushed it away and, rigid, closed his eyes.

He heard Graham approaching, then felt him take hold of his sides. "Come on, baby." Graham pulled Randy off the bed onto the floor.

Kneeling, Randy pressed his chest against the mattress, turning his head to one side and raising his buttocks. He kept his eyes shut, fascinated, listening as Graham knelt behind him. He felt Graham's breath on his back, then his tongue slipping into his asshole. He relaxed, aroused, allowing himself to open up, to take Graham's tongue and swallow it. He heard himself moan. Then he felt Graham pull away.

"Yes!" Graham whispered, standing. He caressed Randy's anus with one finger, then gently slapped his left thigh with his other hand.

Randy started to fade.

The belt struck his buttocks, jolting him back.

"Little shit!" Graham cried. He again cracked the belt on Randy's buttocks, much harder this time. "Stupid fuck!"

His eyes wide open, Randy listened to himself scream.

Graham lowered the belt over and over, shouting, "Cocksucker! Pretty boy! Cunt!"

Then the blows weakened and came down less frequently. Randy heard Graham above him, his voice nearly a whisper: "You've done it too often, fucked me over too much. Little cunt, I'll kill you!"

It stopped. Suddenly—alarmingly—Graham started coughing, having a fit worse than any of the previous ones. Randy heard him toss the belt onto the floor and felt him, still coughing, fall onto the bed.

He opened his eyes and saw Graham lying on his side, coughing and shaking. He stared at him, frightened yet numb.

At last the coughing tapered off, and Graham seemed to relax. He remained still.

Moving up from the floor onto the bed next to Graham, Randy, too, lay quietly. He focused on his smarting buttocks, seeing everything that had just occurred, himself kneeling on the floor, leaning across the mattress. He had felt during those moments as if he had been in that position his entire life. Looking past Graham's body at the photograph of Dennis, he became convinced that Dennis had been in such positions many times.

He moved closer to Graham, pushing his groin against his back and throwing an arm across him. He tucked a hand under his bathrobe and massaged his penis.

Graham grunted and rolled over, facing Randy. "Umm?" he mumbled, as if he had been asleep. "Baby?"

Randy continued playing with Graham's penis; it was slightly erect.

Graham grasped Randy, then, very slowly, removed his robe and climbed on top of him. He took hold of Randy's legs and spread them apart.

"Wait…" Randy began. But he could feel Graham's penis pressing against him, a wave of dexedrine rushing through him. He felt as if he were drifting away. He drew back his legs and arched his buttocks up toward Graham's groin.

Graham tried to enter him. His penis, though, was still not completely erect and slipped out. He stopped moving.

Randy clung to Graham's shoulders; they were quivering.

Graham tried once more, but all traces of his erection had disappeared. He slid off Randy and lay on his back, then, barely audible, murmured, "I think you'd better go."

"What?"

"I want you to go," Graham said weakly. "I'm not feeling well."

Randy found it hard to take in his words. But then they sank in, and he sat up. "Can't I stay?" he pleaded. "Maybe spend the night?"

"No. Definitely not."

Randy gazed at him, feeling a rush of anger well up inside. Reeling, he rose. "Okay," he said.

He found his clothes and dressed, then turned toward the bed. Graham was still on his back, his eyes now shut.

"Is it all right if I piss before I leave?" Randy asked. He glanced back and forth around the room. Although his anger seemed to have subsided, he found it impossible to look directly at Graham.

When he received no response, he hurried to the bathroom.

Once there, he stared into the mirror above the sink. His face appeared incredibly red to him, the veins in his neck unusually prominent, terrifyingly so. He had to look away. He stood still, then, scarcely conscious of what he was doing, lowered his pants and masturbated. He ejaculated on the tiled floor. When he was finished, he buckled up. As he did, he noticed a bottle of pills sitting on the sink. He grabbed it and took one out; it was dexedrine. He wondered if Graham kept several bottles in the house. He decided that he did. He put the pill in his mouth and swallowed it. Then he stuffed the bottle in his back pocket and returned to the bedroom.

"I'm going," he said to Graham, his voice low.

Graham's eyes were still shut; he appeared to be sleeping.

Randy turned away, suddenly certain that he no longer wanted to be here. He walked to the front door and let himself out, then ran down the stairs.

XI

The moment Randy entered his apartment, he knew it had been a mistake to take the third pill. All the lights were on, providing a startling contrast to the subdued lighting at Graham's and to the dimness of his building's hallway. He felt nearly blinded. He closed his eyes, but, disturbed by the yellow, coiling patterns that he saw when he did this, immediately reopened them. He waited for Jake to call out and acknowledge his return. There was only silence. He remained by the door, focusing on the brown wall in the entryway, watching as its surface seemed to twist and turn, to breathe. Frightened, he hurried further into the apartment.

The living room was in a shambles, pillows from the couch thrown about on the floor, items of clothing scattered everywhere, ashtrays overflowing with cigarette butts and pot seeds. He noticed a pair of black underpants sticking out from under an easy chair and leaned over to pick it up. The brand was Calvin Kleins, which Jake never wore. He threw the underwear back down forcefully.

"Hello," he called out, not expecting a response.

When no reply was forthcoming, he became angrier. It was obvious that Jake was out with Adrian.

He continued to the bedroom. After hiding Graham's pills in his top bureau drawer, he stretched out on the bed and, hoping to calm down, switched off the bedside lamp.

The coiling patterns returned, and the light shining in from the living room cast a harsh, unsettling glow on everything. This bothered him, but he did not feel like getting up to turn the light off. Instead, he thought about his night with Graham. He realized he had not been paid.

He put a hand on his buttocks, wondering if they were red. He was sure that he could feel a warmth there, a tingling sensation emanating up from under his pants. He felt like masturbating again, but remained motionless, his hand still on his buttocks, thinking about Graham's diary, his story, the photograph of Dennis, the leather belt, and the beating.

As he mulled over the night's events, one thing in particular stuck in his mind, something Graham had said: "Of course, all of this repression and guilt creates monsters. Like Hewitt, for instance. Or, for that matter, like me."

Randy did not know why, but this remark colored his memories of the night's session and nearly overshadowed everything else. He thought about what he and Graham had done, and decided that if

Graham was a monster, then he must be one, too. He had submitted willingly to Graham's demands; they had been in it together.

He wondered if his submitting in this way meant that he was repressed, guilt-ridden like the monsters Graham had talked about. He had never thought of himself as repressed; since he'd left the Midwest, he had tried to be free. And, he felt, since he'd met Graham, he had started to understand much more about what freedom could entail.

Of course, there were moments when he worried about the future, about what he would do when he was older and could not support himself as a masseur. But he tried not to think about this; things seemed to have worked out so far.

What had happened tonight, however, perplexed him. He was amazed and somewhat alarmed that the beating had been his own idea. But he'd been high. And he was even more stoned now. Things would make more sense later, once he came down.

As he stared at the white bedroom walls—taking in the way they appeared to be melting, conscious of the warmth that seemed to be heating up his blood—he thought that he could feel his whole life floating within him, flowing through his veins, moving inexorably toward his buttocks, toward his kneeling on the floor in front of Graham, toward the belt cracking down on him. This beating had felt right at the time, and he knew that if he had to relive the session, he would want to submit in the same way once again.

Was that freedom? he asked himself. Or *are* Graham and I monsters?

He continued staring at the melting walls, trying to relax. Then Haircut popped into his head.

What a sick queen! he said to himself, as he had many times before. And now Haircut was positive and going to a rehab! But were the two of them really that different? Both filled their hours in similar ways: seeing clients, watching TV, smoking pot, and drinking.

He tried to picture Haircut in a hospital bed, withdrawing from drugs, dying. This image faded, and in its place he saw Dennis's photograph. Then he again saw himself kneeling naked on the floor, getting beaten by Graham. He imagined himself getting tied up, flogged with a whip, singed with lit cigarettes, matches, and candles. At last he saw himself dead, in a grave next to Haircut and Dennis.

He closed his eyes and thought for a moment that he was finally going to sleep. But the jagged, yellow patterns returned, strokes of lightning now, and he bolted up, wide awake. The walls still appeared to be melting. He shot out of bed and dashed to the window.

Looking out, he saw the early-morning sun; light sparkled on the sidewalks. Where the fuck is Jake? he asked himself. The silence of the apartment felt overwhelming. He returned to the bed, then gazed at the clock on the bedside table. It was eight, much later than he'd thought.

He lay down again, wondering if Jake would ever return, if he himself would ever sleep, or if he would lie awake here forever, seemingly drifting in the air above a melting apartment.

He sat up quickly. You're just stoned, he told himself. But he didn't want to be alone anymore, in bed waiting for Jake, unable to sleep. He thought about going out to get some fresh air.

Then he remembered that Haircut was at St. Vincent's—in the West Village, near Graham's. He could walk there in half an hour. He wondered if he should visit him, and tried to ignore a sudden twinge of guilt, a memento from his night at The Scrotum. He decided going there would give him something to do, that by the time he returned, Jake would be back. By then, he was sure, the speed would be out of his system and he'd be able to sleep.

The fluorescent lights at St. Vincent's seemed abrasive, the people in the waiting room pale and menacing. Randy couldn't understand why he had come; he didn't really consider Haircut a friend. Well, I owe him one, he thought, and I'm here now; I might as well go through with it.

He walked to the information desk and stood before the nurse behind the counter. She was short and heavy, with pallid skin and long black hair tied up in a bun. He noticed a large mole on the right side of her chin. He stared at it, wondering if it was indeed, as it appeared to be doing, inching its way down toward her neck.

"Yeah?" she asked him.

Randy glanced up from the mole and into her eyes. They looked bored and mean. "I want to see Haircut."

"*Who?*" The nurse's tone was frosty. She glared at Randy, appearing to him threatening.

Then he remembered that, of course, she would not know Haircut by that name; he would be Doug to her. He tried to recall Haircut's last name; it had been a long time since he'd heard it. He finally thought it had come to him. "Doug O'Connell?" he said hesitantly. The nurse turned to her computer. Randy studied her mole, fascinated by the way it seemed to be wiggling, overpowering her face. The nurse looked up and snapped, "You mean Doug O'Connor?"

"I...I guess so."

She sighed. "He's on the fourth floor, room 407."

"Thanks." Randy started to walk away.

"Just a minute."

He stopped and looked back. The nurse appeared even heavier now, and her skin seemed to glow ominously.

"You can't go up there yet." She spoke sharply, pronouncing each word distinctly.

"What?" Randy found what she had said incomprehensible; he was distracted by the waves of light that seemed to surround her head.

"Visiting hours start at nine. And you'll need this pass." She held out a long piece of plastic.

Moving methodically, Randy took it from her.

"Wait over there." She motioned toward an area where a few dozen people were seated on rows of benches. "You've still got fifteen minutes."

Confused, Randy followed her instructions.

Once he had seated himself, he stared at the person sitting on the bench directly before him, an emaciated, balding man wearing a studded leather jacket. Randy took in his face, noting that, like everyone else he'd seen since arriving at the hospital, he was pale. But his pallor was more extreme than the others' and was augmented by his emaciation. Looking away, Randy thought of Graham. He remembered the way he had been at the end of last night's session, drained and apparently sleeping, and realized that in his preoccupation with the beating, he had almost forgotten about the evening's conclusion: Graham's impotence, his abrupt dismissal of Randy, the way he had drifted off.

Randy wondered how he was this morning, if he was feeling better—and if he would call to set up another appointment.

Maybe he's dead, Randy thought, shivering.

The man in the leather jacket started coughing loudly, and Randy noticed for the first time small lesions on his face, purple blemishes. He thought he was seeing things and closed his eyes. When he reopened them, the lesions were still there, the purple vibrant. Repelled yet fascinated, he realized this man had the sweetness. Like Graham, he thought. Like Dennis. And soon, of course, Haircut would have it, too.

The man stopped coughing. Looking up, he caught Randy's eye and, with a faint smile, winked at him.

Randy turned away quickly.

He noticed someone else seated across from him, a small, weary-looking woman, heavily made-up, with bleached blond hair and very red lips. She sat on the edge of her seat, holding an unlit cigarette and chewing her lips. Her eyes darted restlessly around the room. On the floor next to her feet was a large Macy's shopping bag; a box of Oreo cookies poked out from its top. Every once in a while, she touched the box, as if to make sure it was still there. Occasionally she put the cigarette in her mouth and took an imaginary puff. Although he could hear nothing, Randy had the impression she was talking to herself.

He glanced at the clock on the wall; it was nine. Almost magically, several people stood at the same time. Others followed.

Yawning, Randy stood, too. He wondered again if he really wanted to go through with this visit. But he felt unable to resist the movement of the crowd, and so he followed them. He entered an elevator and, in a trance, got off on the fourth floor with several others.

He looked around, dazed, having forgotten the number of Haircut's room. The white corridor looked like an immense, writhing tunnel, leading to another world. He couldn't decide whether or not to flee. Then he saw the woman with the Macy's shopping bag standing near him, still holding her unlit cigarette. She seemed confused, too.

"Holy Christ," she muttered to herself, "where're the nurses when you need 'em?"

Randy stared at her. The lipstick she wore obscured her mouth; it was as if she had a large, bright red sore just above her chin.

"You lost, hon?" she said to him. She put her shopping bag down. "This always happens to me. I can never get the fucking room number straight." She coughed, then cleared her throat and asked, "So who're you looking for?"

"Doug O'Connor." Randy found it strange to be using Haircut's real name.

"Oh, yeah? Are you a friend of Dougie's?" The woman beamed, her red lips parting to reveal yellow, tobacco-stained teeth. "Well, I'm his mom. Who're you?"

"Randy."

"Nice to meet'cha, Randy. Glad you could come. Dougie hasn't had many visitors." Craning her neck, she looked around. "So where the hell are the nurses?"

Randy saw that, although she was shorter than her son, she looked very much like Haircut the few times he had seen him in drag.

A nurse walked past them.

"Listen, lady," Haircut's mother called to her, "can you tell us where Dougie O'Connor's at?"

The nurse stopped. "So it's you," she said, only partially amused.

Haircut's mother scowled. "Just tell me where he's at, okay?"

"I told you yesterday," the nurse sighed impatiently. "Room 407. Down the hall and to your left. Try to remember this time." Frowning, she hurried off.

"Bitch!" Mrs. O'Connor muttered as she left. "Well, screw her!" She looked at Randy. "Come on, hon, let's go see Dougie."

Exhausted, Randy followed her, struggling to keep up. He felt as if he were swimming beneath the surface of an ocean, exploring an immense underwater cavern, its walls white and shimmering.

They found Haircut in his room lying on his side facing the window, his back to them. Randy noticed that brownish roots were showing beneath his dyed black hair.

"Dougie," his mother called out, "look who's here!"

Haircut did not budge. "Hi, Ma," he muttered lethargically.

Mrs. O'Connor plopped down on a chair beside the bed. "Come on, you've got a visitor."

Haircut said nothing.

Randy remained by the door, feeling awkward and self-conscious, somewhat guilty and a little frightened. He looked at Haircut and observed the way his hospital gown parted in the back to reveal wan, freckled skin. For an instant he thought that he detected a lesion there, then realized this was only a particularly large freckle.

"Turn around, Dougie. Randy's come to see you."

Sluggish, Haircut rolled over toward them. His nose was swollen and his left eye black. "Randy?" he murmured, puzzled. "What the fuck are *you* doing here?"

"Watch your mouth," his mother exclaimed. "Is that the way you talk to your friends?" She turned to Randy: "Don't be shy, hon, have a seat."

Randy approached the bed cautiously. "How...how're you feeling, Haircut?"

Haircut grimaced. But his previously listless eyes were more alert. Speaking rapidly, his voice thick with sarcasm, he answered, "Oh, just swell! It's the answer, right? I mean, haven't I always dreamed of staying here at Trump's St. Vincent's?"

His mother interrupted him: "What's this 'Haircut' shit? Do your friends call you that? What's wrong with Doug?"

"Ah, Ma!" Haircut turned back to Randy and, embarrassed, said, "Look, you can't stay here long. I've got this fucking recovery group I've gotta go to in ten minutes. In the rehab, on the eighth floor."

"I thought they would've moved you there already," his mother threw in, exasperated. "Jeez, haven't they done enough tests yet?"

Still standing, Randy felt lost, and wondered once more why he was here.

"I told you before," Haircut explained, obviously irritated. "They've gotta do a little more blood work here before they move me up there and feed me all their bullshit. But they make me go to their meetings now anyway. I guess they can't wait to start brainwashing me." Almost sheepish, he looked at Randy. "You wouldn't believe the crap they put me through. All this shit about twelve steps and surrendering and how unmanageable my life is. Fuck, it's come to this! It's definitely not the answer, really!"

Randy had been watching Haircut's lips move and did not understood a word he'd said.

"Come on, Randy," Mrs. O'Connor motioned toward a chair next to hers. "Take a load off your feet."

Randy sat on the chair. No one said anything for a moment. Finally, as if attempting to break the silence, Haircut sneered, then remarked, "So that was quite a night at The Scrotum, wasn't it, Randy? It fucked me up pretty good."

Randy gripped the arms of his chair. Haircut's skin seemed to be changing colors, turning bright orange.

"Scrotum?" Mrs. O'Connor asked. "What scrotum?"

"Shit, Ma, never mind!"

Haircut's mother looked as if she were about to thrash him. Instead she leaned over and grabbed the box of Oreos from her shopping bag. "Here," she said to him, "have some of these. They're your favorites. And I brought you a lot of other junk: peanut butter, ginger snaps, brownies, all the stuff you love."

Haircut pushed the cookies away. "I haven't eaten that crap in years."

"Yeah, right, you were too busy with the drugs."

"Cut it out, Ma!"

"You know you shouldn't do that shit. Or the drinking either. Look at your Uncle Tommy."

Haircut rolled over, so that he again faced the window.

Chuckling, Mrs. O'Connor spoke to Randy: "Look, he's gonna pout. He's just a big kid, really."

"Ma!" Haircut groaned.

"Well, you are." She opened the Oreos and took one out, then offered the box to Randy. "Have a cookie, honey. Don't pay no attention to him."

The idea of eating anything revolted Randy, but he accepted one, since he was touched by Mrs. O'Connor's offer. When he tried to eat it, he was unable to swallow; his throat was too dry. The soft, chewed piece remained on his tongue. When it finally did go down, he was afraid he was going to choke.

Mrs. O'Connor poked Haircut's back. "Get over it, Dougie. Talk to Randy. I mean, he's the only one of your friends who's bothered to come here."

"Leave me alone!"

Mrs. O'Connor shrugged. "What are we gonna do?" She stuffed a second Oreo in her mouth. "You want another one, hon?" she asked Randy.

Randy shook his head; he was still holding the first, unfinished cookie. He sat on the edge of his chair, wondering if the room really was growing smaller. Then he stared at Haircut's back, convinced it was covered with lesions.

Haircut turned around and spoke to him: "Look, Randy, I think you should get out of here. It's not a good time. I've gotta get dressed and go to that fucking meeting."

"We've still got a few minutes," his mother informed him. "And I'm not going anywhere. Your doctor said he'd talk to me today."

Relieved, Randy stood; he'd been wanting to leave since he'd arrived. "No...no, really, that's all right. I...I just wanted to see how you were."

Haircut flushed, again looking embarrassed. "Oh, well thanks. Maybe some other time."

Mrs. O'Connor stood, too. "Yeah, that was real sweet of you, honey. I just wish you didn't have to go so soon. You shouldn't let Dougie get to you. Now come here." She drew Randy to her and, standing on her tiptoes, planted a wet kiss on his cheek. Randy noticed that her breath had a stale odor to it, a pungent combination of cigarettes and onions.

"You're a nice kid," she continued, patting his arm. "Not fucked up like some of Dougie's other friends. So don't be a stranger, you hear? The next time you gotta stay longer."

Randy pulled back, resisting an urge to wipe away the cookie crumbs she had left on his cheek. The room seemed to be swirling. He thought he was going to faint.

"You okay, hon?"

He tried to focus his eyes. "Oh, yeah, sure," he mumbled. Then, barely aware of what he was saying: "Well, it was nice meeting you. I'll see you guys later."

Haircut sat up, resting on his elbow, glum. "Yeah, see you, Randy."

Randy looked down; Haircut's head appeared to be on fire. He turned away, feeling better as he moved. "Bye," he said.

"Bye, hon," Mrs. O'Connor called after him.

He dashed out of the room to an elevator.

XII

Randy took in the brisk, cold air, hoping to get a grip on himself as he stood before the hospital's entrance. He wondered why he had come here in the first place and if it was safe for him to go home yet. But he was exhausted and couldn't think of another place to go. He decided Jake was bound to be back by this time; it was almost ten.

He considered hailing a cab, but instead walked east, thinking that the exercise would do him good; he hadn't been to the gym or even worked out at home for weeks. And he felt he needed time to come down, to sort everything out.

He walked quickly, only partially aware of the frigid gusts of wind rattling the awnings of the shops he passed, wanting to ignore the other pedestrians, most bundled up in their winter coats. Despite the chill, the sunshine was bright, blinding, and he regretted not having brought his sunglasses. He thought he saw a sharp shaft of light shooting out toward him from a store window, and accelerated his pace.

As he sped down 8th Street, his mind, too, was racing, whizzing over his evening with Graham. He thought about Haircut as he had just seen him, sick, his mother nearby. Soon his recollections of the hospital mingled with his memories of last night's session, and he became more and more edgy, dissatisfied, tired, anxious to be home and in bed, shielded from the shoppers he passed, these strollers who all seemed to have the face of the man with the lesions in the studded leather jacket.

He reached Avenue A, immensely relieved. Disregarding the panhandlers around Tompkins Square Park, he ran down the last few blocks to 4th Street.

He plodded up the stairs, feeling as if he were about to collapse. Then, as he approached his floor, he heard music coming from his apartment, blaring out so loudly that it shook the banister.

Well, he thought, at least Jake's home.

Jake was seated on the couch in front of the television set. Although the sound was off, he was staring at a morning talk show, smoking a joint and nodding his head in time to the blasting music. It was not until Randy was standing directly before him that he acknowledged his presence or even appeared to have seen him.

"Sweetheart!" Jake's voice was drowned out by the music playing. "Where've you been?" He held up the joint. "Want a hit?"

As Randy took the joint, he noticed a large red-wine stain on the front of Jake's light-blue T-shirt. He took a toke and passed the joint back to Jake, then saw how bleary his eyes were.

"So what've you been doing?" Jake shouted above the music. He inhaled on the joint.

Randy could not hear a word he said. Turning quickly, he walked to the CD player and switched it off. "Do you mind?" he asked. The sharpness of his tone surprised him. "It's late."

Jake peered at Randy, amused, his eyes twinkling dully. "Sure, sweetheart. Anything for m'baby."

Another voice pealed out from the bathroom: "Hey, Randy!"

Dismayed, Randy realized it was Adrian Peterson.

Jake chuckled. "Adrian's busy shaving his legs." He took another drag on the joint, then handed it to Randy.

"What?" Randy raised the joint to his lips, staring at the television screen. The talk show host was interviewing the President's brother, who, Randy knew, was a recovering coke addict and an aspiring rock star.

"I didn't think you'd care. You know, about him being here and everything. I mean, you don't, do you?"

Randy turned back to Jake. The amusement he'd detected before appeared more obvious: Jake now seemed to be laughing at him. Randy found it difficult to breathe.

Adrian walked in, dressed in a pair of bikini briefs, the material embellished with cartoon images of frolicking panda bears. He was wiping shaving foam from his legs with a soiled purple hand towel.

"Hello, hello," he cried as he dropped the towel onto the floor. "How're you doing, Randy? I got bored watching TV, so I thought

I'd smooth my legs out a bit." He eased himself down onto the couch next to Jake.

Randy stared at Adrian's glistening chest. He found it grotesquely well-defined. Only a few tiny stubbles of hair poked out near the right nipple, marring an otherwise perfectly sculptured look.

"So, Randy," Adrian continued with a smile, "I guess I'm not a virgin anymore. Not after I met Franklin Kent last night." He leaned forward and took the joint from Randy's hand.

Randy nodded, then looked down at the floor, recalling Franklin Kent, a blandly handsome prep-school teacher who often called Jake to make an appointment. He stared up at Adrian's chest again; the stubble seemed to have grown at a startling rate in the few seconds that had passed since he'd first noticed it.

Adrian sucked on the joint. "It was a cinch: I told him he was the coolest, most brilliant person I'd ever met. That got him going. But he just wanted to jerk me off. I guess he was afraid of catching something." He took another toke. "The only problem was, afterwards he kept trying to psychoanalyze me. You know, like he wanted to know why I was doing what I did, stuff like that. Please, give me a break! What a fucking hypocrite!"

Jake smiled. "A lot of them do that."

"Oh, yeah?" Adrian glanced at Randy. "Does that happen to you much?"

Randy was absorbed in his perusal of Adrian's stubble and did not hear the question.

Adrian looked at him for a second, then said, "Hey, man, Earth to Randy: Do you read me?" When Randy did not reply, he laughed. "Wow, are you spaced or what?"

Jake laughed, too. "I guess m'baby's pretty high." He grabbed Randy's leg and pulled him forward. "Come on, sweetheart, why don't you sit down and cool out? Tell us what you've been up to."

Randy moved away from him, trying to adjust his vision. What he could see was hazy and indistinct; it was as if he were partially asleep. He sat on the floor, then lay on his side, leaning on an elbow and resting his head on his hand.

"So," Jake asked, "where've you been?" His red eyes looked impish.

"Oh, leave him alone," Smirking, Adrian threw an arm across Jake's shoulder. "He doesn't have to tell you everything, does he?"

Coming back, Randy turned away from them toward the television screen and watched the President's brother play his guitar. The show's host was beaming in the background.

"I'm sure you had a better time than we did," Adrian went on. He extinguished the joint and emitted an exaggerated sigh. "After I saw that Franklin character, Jake and I decided to celebrate. You know, toast my loss of innocence. We ended up taking some speed and going to this party I'd heard about. What a mistake that was!"

"It wasn't that bad," Jake protested.

"Come off it! The only people there were a bunch of plague fags."

Randy pulled his eyes from the television and looked at Adrian. "Plague fags?"

"Yeah, you know, tired old queens from the seventies. All those losers who still can't believe The Mine Shaft and Studio 54 are gone."

Randy remembered lying against Graham's shrunken chest, Dennis's photograph on the table beside them.

Jake squeezed Adrian's leg. "You're so cruel," he said, grinning. He glanced down at Randy and winked mischievously.

"Not cruel, sweetie. Accurate." Giggling, Adrian fell back against the couch and moved closer to Jake.

Randy gazed at them, his vision becoming indistinct again. Despite this, it was infuriating to see Adrian with Jake. And Jake seemed to be gloating. He felt like dashing at their throats.

Then he told himself that he was being paranoid, that Jake and Adrian's affair would end soon enough. He shouldn't have smoked that joint. He was already exhausted.

As he stood, he felt as if he were using all his remaining strength. "I'm going to bed," he mumbled.

"Sure, sweetheart. But don't you want another joint first?"

Adrian pinched Jake's bicep. "Let him be. Can't you see how ravaged he is?"

Shaking, Randy walked away.

In the bedroom, he lay down. The room was spinning. He could hear Jake and Adrian, still giggling in the next room. Although their voices were clear, he felt distant from them, as if he were lying on the other side of the world.

Their voices faded, and he saw himself in a hospital bed. A woman was applying an ointment to his wounded buttocks. At first he thought she was Ellen. Then, surprised, he recognized Mrs. O'Connor.

"Hi, hon," she said. Her grin was a leer. "You're a nice kid, you know that? I'm gonna come around here more often."

Randy felt himself sinking into the mattress. It seemed to devour him. As he crawled under the covers, he had the impression that he was lying beneath the earth. At ease, he fell into a deeper, dreamless sleep.

He awoke to the alarming sounds of doors slamming and drawers banging. The noise cut into his sleep, aggravating the throbbing in his head, the pain he felt there as he opened his eyes. He quickly shut them again, but by now it was too late: The pain had spread across his eyes, working its way through his leaden sinuses, down to his dry mouth and parched throat, to his hacking chest, to guts that threatened to heave. He hurt all over, and was sure that he'd died and gone to Hell. He couldn't imagine where else he was. Then, as a drawer slammed one more time, he moved a hand down his side to his buttocks and, in an instant, remembered everything. He groaned.

"Shit," he heard Jake murmur. He listened as, evidently, Jake kicked the chest of drawers. "Shit," he murmured again, louder now.

This voice felt to Randy as if it were piercing his head, cracking it open and exposing its nerves. He rolled to one side, away from Jake. The sounds continued: the banging, the slamming, Jake's mumbled curses. He squeezed his eyelids together, and was blinded by a harsh, bright light, yellow, then red. Jake slammed another drawer shut. Randy could take it no more. "Why don't you shut the fuck up?" he screamed.

The noises stopped. Randy opened his eyes. He rolled onto his other side and looked up.

Jake was standing by the chest of drawers, his clothes rumpled, his face rigid and red. Despite the painful fuzziness of his hangover, it was clear to Randy that Jake was still high, probably much higher than he'd been earlier.

Jake stared down at Randy, appearing startled but, Randy thought, vaguely contemptuous. Gradually his expression relaxed a bit, and he offered a weak smile. "Sweetheart," he cried blandly, "you're awake." He looked over at the chest of drawers and, his smile vanishing, muttered, "This place is a fucking pig sty."

These words tore through Randy's shredded skull, and he felt his blood racing through his brain.

Jake walked to the bed and sat next to him, then slapped the covers above his thigh. "So, is m'baby going to get up or what? It's night already. Almost eight."

Randy moaned, his head on fire. He rolled onto his stomach. "Leave me alone!"

Jake drew in his breath. "So it's going to be this again, is it?" He let out a short, dry laugh and stood. "What a lazy slug you are!"

Randy heard him walk away, then, shaky and queasy, listened as he opened a drawer. He looked up. Jake had pulled out a lavender shirt, and was holding it in front of him, squinting at it.

"Are you going out?" Randy asked haltingly.

Jake acted as if he had not heard the question. He continued staring at the shirt and, nodding his head, said, "I guess this is clean enough." He removed the T-shirt he was wearing.

Randy leaned over on one elbow. He felt his pulse pounding. "So where are you going?"

Jake turned to him, grinning slyly. He threw on the lavender shirt and tucked it in. "We took some more speed, so now Adrian's taking me to this new club that's opening, a huge place up on Broadway. It's supposed to be fabulous."

Randy felt a wave of nausea churning up within him. He was afraid he was going to retch.

"It's amazing," Jake continued, "but Adrian seems to know *everyone*. At least the people who count. He has such cool friends."

The nausea passed, but the throbbing in Randy's head was even more wrenching than it had been.

"It's funny," Jake went on, speaking rapidly and chuckling, "but

I didn't really know how bored I'd been until I hooked up with him again. I mean, there's so much *out there*." Randy glared at Jake, the sudden hatred he felt oozing inside him, as if another manifestation of his hangover. "So where is he now?" he spat out. "At his place getting dressed. I'm supposed to meet him there in ten minutes." Jake glanced into the mirror above the chest of drawers, then stared at Randy. "Why, sweetheart," he asked, seemingly surprised, "you're not jealous, are you?" He smiled.

Jake's tone sounded simpering to Randy, the astonishment it expressed obviously feigned. "Why don't you just go?" he yelled, his voice cracking.

Jake's smile remained frozen in place for a second. Then it faded. "Christ," he exclaimed, "what's your problem? I mean, get over it!" He paused. When he spoke again, he seemed calm but chilly. "I don't know when I'll be back, so don't bother waiting up, okay?" He laughed. "Not that I have to worry about *that*." He headed toward the closet.

Randy watched him take his leather jacket from a hanger, then put it on and walk to the door. He was convinced that if he had a gun, he would use it. But he could barely move; it was all he could do to shout out, "I hope you both fucking die!"

Jake stopped in his tracks, just by the door. He looked back at Randy and grinned. "Piss off, sweetheart, okay?" he hissed, then slammed the door behind him.

Randy remained inert for a few minutes, the pain in his head horrid. He finally threw his legs over the side of the bed and sat up. He looked around. The room seemed desolate, empty despite the dirty shirts and socks scattered on the floor, its silence hideous. He felt absolutely alone. For a moment he wished Jake was still with him, that they had not argued.

Overcome by nausea, he had to lie down. He closed his eyes and remembered Jake standing in the doorway, glaring at him. He saw Adrian giggling and, jarringly, Haircut in his hospital bed. He squeezed his eyelids together, attempting to clear his head.

He tried to think of other things—Graham, Dennis, the life

those two had led—but kept seeing Graham in his room at his apartment, sleeping, looking exactly the way he had the last time Randy had seen him. His skin grew paler, even tauter and more emaciated than it had been. Tiny lesions cropped up here and there. His breathing became more labored, painful and erratic. Soon he was dead.

He imagined Graham's funeral, an elaborate affair, one attended by the press and many celebrities. Dakota and Denise were among them, dressed in black outfits, carrying, for reasons Randy could not explain, umbrellas. He pictured Graham in an open casket—his hands folded before him, his eyes shut—and saw himself standing near the front of the throng, staring into his lifeless face. Then, just for a second, as he drifted off, it was he himself he saw lying there—a world-famous personality mourned by an immense and glittering crowd.

A hand was on his stomach, moving toward his groin, a body squeezing against him, warm, slightly moist. Fingernails grazed his skin. He shivered. The hand slipped his briefs off across his thighs and clutched his penis roughly. His muscles tightened. It inched its way further up.

Then a voice whispered, "Sweetheart"—slowly, thickly—and he knew that, of course, this was Jake. A sweaty Jake. Beery. Bombed.

He felt Jake lumber up on top of him, keeping one hand between his legs, a finger inside of him, probing.

His muscles remained tense.

Jake rolled off and kneeled beside him on the bed. He took hold of Randy's legs and eased them back.

"No," Randy said—firmly, he was sure. "Not that. Not now." He looked up and, in the early morning light, saw Jake, large and naked. Familiar.

Jake was smiling. "Is m'baby still angry?" he asked. He chuckled softly, then released Randy's legs and again lay on top of him.

"But Adrian…" Randy began. He stopped. Jake was warm, his penis hard. He felt his own muscles slackening.

"Oh, Adrian," Jake rasped. "Yeah, Adrian. He met some rich

prick at the club." He pressed himself against Randy's groin, and moved back and forth, breathless.

Randy shut his eyes. Tentatively at first, he touched Jake's back, massaging it. He followed Jake's movements, breathing carefully, and slowly became erect. He knew it was easier this way.

Jake bit Randy's neck and ejaculated. He lay quietly, catching his breath. Neither said anything. Then, without warning, surprising himself, Randy started to cry.

"Sweetheart?" Jake was startled. "M'baby?"

Randy's sobs became louder. Wanting to muffle them, he threw his arms around Jake's back and pushed his face into his chest.

"Oh, sweetheart," Jake slurred. *"Sweetheart.* It's just that I need space sometimes, that's all."

Randy continued sobbing. Jake stroked his head. Within fifteen minutes, both were asleep.

PART TWO

XIII

Randy stayed in bed for much of the next week and a half, yet never felt as if he had slept enough; he was preoccupied by the fact that he'd had no word from Graham. Jake was no help in getting him out of this mood; he spent hours away from home, insisting he had business to take care of. Randy knew he was with Adrian— evidently the "rich prick" from the club had been just a one-night stand—but didn't have the will to protest. He preferred his absence to Adrian's hanging around their apartment, which was unbearable. He told himself that Adrian and Jake's affair would end soon, that inevitably one of them would tire of the other. In the meantime, Jake always gave him a joint and a few dollars for food and cigarettes before he left. Not enough, Randy thought, but better than nothing.

The wretched weather only increased his lethargy. Three days after his last session with Graham, it started to snow. For several hours it looked as if a major storm was developing. The snow became sleet, then a heavy, stubborn rain, which persisted for days. He kept his blinds shut; there was little daylight anyway.

It was unusually quiet outside: He could hear no arguments drifting up from the drug dealers who congregated in front of his building, no music blasting out of passing boom boxes. Whenever he went to the store, the streets were almost deserted. He braced himself against the icy winds and freezing rains, did his chores, then hurried home.

If he wasn't in bed, he watched television—everything, anything, whatever was on when he was awake: the morning talk shows, the afternoon soap operas, the situation comedies at night. He discovered that pot was the perfect complement to this activity. Contrary to his experiences with it in the past, if he sat very still, staring at the TV, its effect was not unpredictable at all: Used in this way, it never made him paranoid.

He listened, fascinated, to the post-op transsexuals on *Jenny*

Jones; the celebrity authors on *Regis and Kathie Lee;* the battered housewives on *Oprah.* He learned to recognize Lorna from *Another World,* Sheila from *The Bold and the Beautiful,* Opal from *All My Children.* Even the sitcoms, which he had always thought dumb, didn't bother him now. It didn't matter if they weren't funny; the laugh track was soothing.

Whenever Jake happened to be at the apartment, he watched TV, too, making comments that Randy found irritating.

One afternoon, during a particularly heavy downpour, he asked about a soap that was on, "Is this the one with the gay kid on it?"

Randy looked at him as if he were an idiot. "No way! That doesn't come on until three."

"Oh, yeah? Adrian told me it was this one."

"That just shows you how much he knows."

They had another joint. As soon as there was a lull in the rain, Jake rushed off. Adrian was taking him that night to a gallery opening in Soho.

Randy tried not to fret too much about Jake and Adrian's being together. Instead, he often thought about Graham and Dennis, and saw himself living a life like the one he imagined theirs to have been, charmed and glamorous, passed in a world of unlimited freedom. He was so wrapped up in this fantasy that, when he did hear from Graham, he almost felt as if he were speaking with a ghost, an apparition from his own imagination.

The call came on a Tuesday afternoon, eleven days after they had last been together. Randy had just finished the joint Jake had left him the night before and was about to watch *The Guiding Light.*

When he first heard the phone, he thought it was Jake calling to explain his absence. Not wanting to listen to any absurd excuse, he did not pick up the receiver for several rings. But he finally gave in, regretting, as he often did, that he had never bothered to buy an answering machine.

"Randy?" asked the voice on the other end, its timbre weak but unmistakably Graham's.

Before Randy could say anything, he was disconcerted by a brief but vivid memory of himself kneeling naked on the floor and leaning across Graham's bed. He nearly hung up the phone. But then, listening to Graham's voice, drawn to it, he looked around. Despite the items of clothing scattered about, the apartment seemed barren, its graying walls desolate.

"Baby?" Graham went on, his pitch much higher. "Baby are you there?"

"Oh. Yeah." Randy reached for the pack of cigarettes sitting on the table near him. His hands shaking, he took one out and lit it.

"Sorry I haven't called, baby, but I haven't been well. Not at all. They almost had to take me in. You know, to the hospital. I thought I was a goner."

Graham's voice had a pathetic, pleading quality, strange for him. Randy relaxed his grip on the receiver.

Then Graham laughed, and, though his voice was still weak, his old tone returned. "Well, I think I'm a little better now, baby. Not well enough to see you, I'm afraid, but I will be soon, I'm sure. I'm not dead yet. They've started giving me all these new drugs."

Randy took a drag on his cigarette, recalling Haircut as he had been in the hospital. His vision grew fuzzy. "I'm glad. I've been worried."

"Oh, really? I suppose you should be." Graham chuckled. "But never mind. Besides, I'm sure you've been having a ball. I can just imagine what you've been up to."

Randy noticed a pair of Jake's jeans on the floor. "Not much," he remarked.

"Oh, no? Why don't I believe you?" Graham laughed again. "Anyway, baby, I'm sending a messenger around to your place this afternoon. You'll be there, won't you?"

"Sure."

"Well, good. Because if you remember, I didn't pay you the last time you were here. I want to make it up to you. And give you a little something extra. You know, something to keep you going while I'm recuperating. Just to make sure you don't wander off."

Randy had forgotten that Graham owed him money. "Don't worry about it. I'm not going anywhere. Not in this fucking weather." Turning away from the jeans, he suddenly wished that he could see Graham that evening. "Thanks a lot for thinking of me, though," he said. "I can use it."

"It's nothing, baby, nothing at all. I'll take care of you. Just be good." Graham paused, then added, "And stay well." He chuckled once more. "I'll see you very soon."

After hanging up, Randy sat still for a few minutes. The television set was just on the other side of the room, but he no longer wanted to watch it. He felt disappointed. And bored. He suspected that he had been vegetating for too long; Graham's call had made that clear. He supposed he'd been waiting for Graham to perk him up—although he had known Graham was sick and had even feared the worst.

It appeared that his apprehensions had been groundless: Apparently Graham was getting better. Even so, Randy was certain that he would have to wait to see him—and in an empty apartment, with nothing to keep him occupied except the joints Jake left him and the TV. That prospect seemed depressing and dreary.

He recalled the pills he had stolen from Graham; he couldn't understand how he had forgotten about them. Maybe I'll take one and go out, he thought—that is, after the messenger gets here. But where?

He considered visiting Haircut again. Yet the idea of going back to the hospital, of seeing Haircut in bed, his mother hovering over him, was frightening. He was sure he could come up with something better than that.

Then he remembered a bar he used to frequent, Mike's, a tavern on Second Avenue which had been there on and off since the seventies. This was where he had first met Jake. Since that time, he had held for it a certain affection, a sentimental attachment, but he had not been there or even thought of it much in a while.

He walked to the bedroom. The pills were in his top bureau drawer, just where, in his fog, he had hid them days before. He swallowed one, then went to the window and cracked open the blinds. Amazed, he saw that the rain had stopped and that the sun was breaking through the thick clouds. More people were on the street. It even looked as if it had grown warmer, as if the city was about to get an early taste of spring. He decided going to Mike's might not be a bad idea.

Stretching his arms above his head and yawning, he returned to the bed and lay down, anticipating the first rush of the pill.

He knew Mike's was a dive, a large, dark space, hot and close, not immediately inviting. But for many years it had been the most popular spot in the East Village, the first real gay bar in the neighborhood, attracting punks from Alphabet City, actors and playwrights from La Mama, writers from the St. Mark's Poetry Project—plus assorted detritus from the street, random queens who, when Mike's first opened, had been relieved that they no longer had to shlep to Christopher Street at night. Mike's became what Randy had assumed was a scene, albeit, back then, a subdued one, completely different from the more aggressive joints, the backrooms and leather bars near the piers, which usually made him uncomfortable. Mike's had been a neighborhood place, nothing more, nothing less.

From the time Mike's opened at three in the afternoon until it closed at four the following morning, every stool at the bar had been taken, occupied by the heavy hitters who practically lived there: the middle-aged artists, the speed queens and transvestites, the lesbians with their spiky dyed hair, their black leather jackets and tight, ripped jeans. Far in the back were two pool tables and the dance floor. It was there that Randy had stood, sipping his drink, watching the dancers, sometimes meeting one-night stands.

On Mondays, Mike's had shown old movies, musicals by Busby Berkley, campy epics with Maria Montez. At happy hour, they served free hors d'oeuvres, soggy meatballs and greasy chicken wings. The jukebox had an eclectic selection: Motown and acid rock, disco and early punk, new wave, rockabilly, tinny singles distributed by local bands. Randy used to listen as Marvin Gaye gave way to Janis Joplin, the Talking Heads to Bryan Ferry, Bob Marley to Iggy Pop. Time seemed pleasantly jumbled; decades drifted effortlessly from one to the next. Late at night, at around three in the morning, when Diana Ross sang "Love Hangover," the drag queens near the front joined in.

Then he met Jake and stopped going as often.

*

The buzzer rang, startling him. He thought he might have been sleeping, until he stood and realized how stoned he was.

It was the messenger with Graham's package, which contained five hundred dollars in cash. There was also a short note: "I'll be sending more, baby, in a few days. So be good. And keep in touch. It's all a bore, isn't it?"

Randy pocketed three twenties, disappointed that he would not be seeing Graham sooner. He went to the bedroom and stuffed the rest of the bills next to the dexedrine in his bureau drawer, then glanced at the clock on the bedside table. It was four-thirty. He knew Mike's wouldn't be too crowded; the only people there would be those steady customers from the old days who still congregated by its bar every day at this hour. He walked to the window and peeked behind the blinds.

What he saw outside nearly blinded him at first, accustomed as he was to the dim interior. The sun was out, shining dazzlingly now, the clouds completely gone. Dozens of passersby paraded up the street, most of them having discarded their winter coats in favor of leather or denim jackets. Acquaintances stopped to chat, laughing happily. A group of boisterous Latino boys walked by, one of them carrying a huge boom box. Randy drew open the blinds, then listened as a soft salsa floated up to him. He closed his eyes and let the warmth of the sun wash over his face. A wave of contentment passed through him, merging with the speed and the music. He felt as if he were dissolving into the air.

The salsa faded, and he opened his eyes. The boys had moved on; he could see them up the street, near the corner at Avenue A. Excited, he nearly felt like running out to join them.

He turned away and looked around, realizing he could not stay here a minute longer.

At the bottom of the stairs, on the first floor of his building, he noticed some large boxes and five pet carriers outside the studio apartment near the landing. A cat mewed shrilly inside one of the carriers as a thin, fiftyish woman fiddled with her key, trying to open the apartment's door. She's kind of pretty, Randy thought, even if she is old. The cat mewed again, more shrilly now.

"Quiet, Despair," the woman murmured. She leaned forward toward the carrier. "We'll be in soon, baby. Just shut up for a minute."

Randy decided she had to be the new tenant that the building's superintendent had mentioned to Jake a few days before, Sylvia Radicatti. He remembered Adrian laughing at her name.

She stared at him, and he thought she looked friendly. Jake had always warned him against getting too close with any of their neighbors. "You don't want them to know any of our shit," he'd said more than once, "and we don't want to know theirs either." But Randy felt expansive and invigorated; he'd been more or less alone for days.

"Hi," he said.

"Hey." Sylvia smiled, brushing her long, grayish-brown hair back from her forehead.

"Moving in?"

"Right." The cat mewed, then hissed. Sylvia again leaned toward the carrier. "Come on, Despair. Can't you be good like your brothers?" She turned back to Randy and, speaking rapidly, asked, "Say, listen, do you know anything about these locks? I can't seem to get the door open."

"Sure, I guess so." Randy walked over.

"My old man was supposed to help me move," Sylvia continued, her words gushing out, "but he probably got hung up. I had to bring all this shit over in a cab by myself."

"Let me see what I can do." Randy turned the key in the lock, which had been affected by the damp weather. He was high, but was used to the idiosyncrasies of his own lock and after several attempts was successful.

"Wow, that's great! I thought we were going to be stuck out here forever." Sylvia brushed her hair back and asked, "So do you want to come in or something? Maybe have some juice? I can run out to the store and get some." Suddenly she sneezed. She moved her hand up to her nose and touched it familiarly. "Damn allergies!" she exclaimed as she ran a finger across her nostrils. Then: "So why don't you come in? I mean, we're going to be neighbors now and everything."

Randy found her face extraordinarily lively, expectant and eager, her pale skin almost transparent, a little unreal. He thought it might be nice to talk with her some more; the speed was making him feel chatty. But he didn't want to risk upsetting Jake. "No. Thanks anyway, though. Maybe later. I want to go out. It's beautiful outside."

"Yeah, I'll say. It's been so fucked lately."

Randy motioned toward the carriers. "These all cats?"

"Yeah, five of them."

"*Five?*" Randy knew the apartment she was moving to was tiny.

"Uh-huh. Despair, Sloth, Avarice, Envy, and Anger. There used to be three more, Lust, Gluttony, and Pride, but the poor babies died."

"Those are pretty funny names."

"I thought so. I named the first ones after the seven deadly sins. Then I called the youngest 'Despair.' They say that's the worst sin of all."

Despair started whining again.

"Shit, Despair, be quiet, please! We'll be there in a second." Sylvia laughed. "She's the only girl. I never did have her fixed."

"Oh, yeah?"

"I couldn't stand the idea." She ran her words together, an impassioned edge to her tone. "I mean, I had to do *something* with the boys. Otherwise, they'd spritz all over the place. And it's a pretty simple operation. The vet just has to snip them right off. But it's different with a girl. Messier. Like she's gotta be opened up and everything. I couldn't put Despair through that."

"Yeah, I know what you mean." Randy had not heard a word she'd said; he was much too fascinated by the way she moved as she talked, abruptly, constantly, stroking her hair, touching her nose, chewing her lips.

"Now, of course, she's in heat all the time. Never leaves me alone."

As if to confirm Sylvia's words, Despair howled.

"Oh, Despair, you really are too much!"

"Let me help you with this stuff," Randy offered.

"No, that's all right. I mean, I've gotten this far. I guess I'll be okay." She sniffled and ran a finger across her nose again. "By the way, my name's Sylvia Radicatti. What about you?"

"Randy."

"Well, listen, Randy, I better get moving. But come over any time. We can talk."

"Yeah, sure."

"And thanks for the help."

"Right. See you."

As Randy walked out the front door, he could hear Sylvia sneezing and Despair howling. "Damn, Despair, be quiet!" she cried. "It's almost over."

Outside, he paused in front of the building, overwhelmed by the sun's brightness, certain that the temperature had risen at least thirty degrees since the last time he'd been out. He watched the cheerful pedestrians strolling past him, and listened to their radios playing salsa, disco, and top-forty hits. It was a cacophony he found exceedingly harmonious in the sunlight: The music seemed like an extension of himself, and he in turn a part of a dizzying melody. He walked as though floating, moving dreamily, conscious of a blur of contented faces passing by, of soothing melodies, of a pleasant heat rippling across his skin. He took off his jacket, in a happy daze.

Three blocks from his apartment, on 7th Street and Avenue A, he came to a partially demolished building. He stopped, sure this place had been intact the last time he had passed by. He knew it well; it was where Jake had bought pot for a while years before, when they had been living together for around ten months. Several times a week back then—that was '82, Randy remembered—Jake used to run over here and pop into the little bodega on the building's first floor, "The Candy Store." There he bought nickel bags, sometimes dimes, sometimes more. Then he returned to their apartment and got high. Afterward, if Randy wasn't out on a session with a client, they usually had sex.

Thinking back, Randy found that period special, his memories of it pleasantly nostalgic: His relationship with Jake was still fresh; it felt good to be with someone, a relief to have an anchor. He decided then that he never wanted to be alone again.

Things had been so different. He'd been much younger. And, of course, that was before the sweetness really took over.

He sat on a nearby stoop and, melancholy, turned to the building.

The demolition had never been completed; only the top three stories had been razed, leaving the ground floor, its jagged walls poking up toward the clear sky, and an enormous pile of rubble, bricks and heaps of trash. The garbage looked as if it had been collecting there for months. He was sure the demolition had been an illegal one; someone obviously hoped they could make some quick cash from the bricks and any other goods they could excavate from the site.

Two shabby-looking men—junkies, Randy supposed—were sorting through the debris, scavenging.

"What do you want this shit for?" one of them was saying. "Let's go."

"Wait, man," the other said. "I gotta piss."

Randy studied the second man, who was emaciated, his skin pasty. Sort of like Graham, he thought. He wondered if this junkie was sick, too.

He turned away quickly. The sun was uncomfortably hot. He felt as if he couldn't move.

Two boys strolled by, one of them carrying a large radio. It was playing rap at a high volume, which increased Randy's agitation. The boys were walking rapidly, and the music soon faded. Sweating, Randy turned back to the junkies, who were now heading east. He looked at the building where The Candy Store had been, wondering if he was in the mood for Mike's after all, thinking that perhaps he should just go home.

As he stared at the razed building, he again recalled his early life with Jake. It was during those years that the sweetness had crept up around him. For most of that period, however, even after the heavier backroom bars and bathhouses were shut down, Mike's remained a familiar place where he could have a drink late at night.

Leaning back, he lit a cigarette.

In those days, he'd had no real friends who were sick. But in the mid-eighties, he began sensing the presence of the sweetness wherever he went. There were persistent telltale signs: A friendly bartender disappeared from one of the clubs. Haircut mentioned a mutual acquaintance who, ill, had gone home to live with his parents. Randy ran into someone he hadn't seen in months and noticed how much weight he had lost. There even seemed to be a nebulous gloom in the air, a dim distress he detected in the people he knew whenever he ventured out on the town.

But he had already been with Jake for a few years by then and thought he was safe. He knew that, apart from his clients—and he did nothing dangerous with them—he had sex only with Jake most of the time.

For a while it appeared as if some had lost interest in sex completely. Dozens of bars had closed, and many people seemed to be attempting to become celibate or remain monogamous. Randy's business was bad; evidently the hand jobs he offered had a diminished appeal.

This dry spell had a markedly adverse effect on Jake's disposition. "Christ," he complained, "they're all so uptight. I mean, a lot of them even use rubbers for a fucking blow job. Give me a break!"

Randy made do with the clients he still had and tried not to aggravate Jake if he was in a volatile mood. But as Jake had been involved in a few affairs by that time, it was obvious to Randy that their "honeymoon" was over. Mike's became a comforting haven where he could retreat whenever they had a fight.

Business picked up again in the late eighties. It looked as if his clients had grown tired of restraining themselves—or, perhaps, merely became accustomed to the presence of disease. New, wilder bars opened in the East Village—Dirt!, The Scrotum—as well as jerk-off clubs on 14th Street, dilapidated storefronts on Avenue D, raunchy holes where patrons could be seen strolling about naked, hooking up with partners before moving off to darker rooms in the back.

Randy was never at ease in these bars; he preferred Mike's, which reminded him of the earlier, plague-free era. It was reassuring for him to know that it had survived. Then, in 1990, the unthinkable occurred: Rocked by the new, more freewheeling competition, Mike's shut its doors. For almost a year it had a sign outside that read, "Closed for Renovations."

Randy was stunned when he first saw this. For a few days he felt strangely vulnerable. It was as if, with Mike's closing, a fragment from his past, a part of himself, had been erased. Now that it was gone, Mike's assumed an importance it had never had before.

He drifted through the routine of his days, putting up with what he learned to consider minor inconveniences—Jake's affairs, which were becoming increasingly frequent; their squabbles—trying to ignore the dissatisfaction gnawing at him, an uneasiness only aggravated by the grimness he sensed pervading the city. He often looked back at the world he had known at Mike's—at the many assignations he had made, at the music he had listened to then, at life before the sweetness—and viewed it all with a nostalgia which, at other times, he knew it did not deserve.

One night, in the spring of 1991, Haircut showed up with some news. "It's the answer!" he exclaimed. "Old Mike's is reopening! New decor, new owners, new everything. What a hoot! It's got to be better than it was. I mean, it used to be so tired. There's a party there this Saturday night."

The three of them went to the opening together. Although he usually did not like going out anymore, Randy had looked forward to the evening and had bought a new shirt for the occasion. He secretly hoped that this night would prove auspicious, that in some mysterious way it might mark the end of the gloom he had felt building up in New York and in himself for the past five years.

There was the expected, anticipatory mob outside, although this was a tense, impatient swarm totally unlike the relaxed clientele that Randy remembered being at Mike's before. They seemed angry, resentful of the wait, as if they did not have a lot of time to waste. For the entire hour that Randy stood outside, he was sure he could feel their anger surging through him.

Once they got in, the first thing he noticed was the huge screen above the bar, the same screen where, years before, he had watched Carmen Miranda in *The Gang's All Here*. What he now saw there was an impossibly blond boy standing nude at the top of a hill, his back to the camera, staring seductively over his shoulder, bending forward and fingering his anus.

The club had been completely renovated, the back of the bar, the area that once contained the pool tables and the dance floor, sealed off. Flimsy curtains floated down across an entryway to what was, apparently, a dark back room. Dozens of patrons clustered near its entrance.

The jukebox was in the same place, just by the bar, right next to the cigarette machine. It was not in use that evening. Instead, Randy heard a techno mix seeping out of innumerable speakers, offering only snatches of one melody before moving on to something else. He wanted to leave, but stayed for most of the evening.

Jake and Haircut immediately deserted him; they couldn't wait to try out the room in the back. Left on his own, Randy watched as intoxicated queens with fashionable haircuts staggered around lecherously, many approaching him in an aggressive, relentless way that was more reminiscent of the old leather bars than of Mike's from the past.

One was especially persevering, a handsome, cocky man wearing a tight, orange T-shirt, with a shaved head and, on his left cheek, a long, nasty-looking scar. His name was Eddie, and he followed Randy everywhere.

Randy attempted to ignore him. But as the night dragged on and he became more intoxicated, he felt his resistance to Eddie weaken. Hot and claustrophobic in the thickening crowd, unable to locate Jake and Haircut, he tried some of Eddie's coke. Once he was high, he noticed how muscular Eddie's arms were, how his jeans fit snugly at the crotch. When Eddie asked him for the fifth time if he'd like to go to the back room, he agreed. Surrounded by others doing the same, he sucked Eddie off.

Eddie left as soon as Randy had finished. Ten minutes later, still not seeing Jake and Haircut, Randy fled.

He had not been back to Mike's since.

"Where you goin', bitch?"

Randy looked up. A large, ferocious-looking man and a haggard, furious woman were arguing in front of the rubble beside the partly demolished building, both dressed in filthy clothes and clearly high. The woman was trapped, blocked by the man hulking in front of her, but trying to get away.

"Had enough of your shit, JT!" she cried. "Enough bullshit!"

JT grabbed her arm and pulled her toward him. "What?" He raised his hand above her. "Yeah, well what about that dope? The fifty bucks?"

"You're talking shit again."

He slammed her against a car parked beside the curb. "Don't fucking lie to me, Delphine. You've fucking asked for it!"

For a second Delphine looked terrified. But then, glowering determinedly, she shoved her way past him, hurrying east. "Go fuck yourself, JT. Just fuck yourself."

JT caught up to her and again grabbed her arm. "Fucking bitch!" They both moved on, JT shouting, "Fifty bucks, bitch, fifty bucks!"

Randy sat motionless, relieved that they were gone and that nothing worse had happened. He felt squeamish and, despite the warmth, was shivering. There had been something about those two—an intensity, an expressive, almost passionate squalor—that reminded him of Eddie, of his faint, unpleasantly musty odor, the way he had grasped Randy's head, the sour taste of his penis.

He and Jake had never discussed what occurred at Mike's reopening, and he had tried not to think about it afterward. He didn't know why all of this bothered him today, but it did. Remembering everything made him miss the old Mike's even more.

He felt a rush from the dexedrine, then, for an instant, saw Jake as he had looked when they'd first met there, younger and laughing. He gazed at the nearby rubble. Now that the sun was beginning to set, it was covered by the shadows of neighboring buildings. He lingered for a minute, his eyes on the debris, then threw on his jacket and rose from the stoop.

XIV

"Take Me to the River" by the Talking Heads was playing when Randy entered Mike's, a tune he recognized from years before. Haircut had told him that the jukebox was still used here in the afternoon, that taped mixes did not come on until the evening crowd took over. He stood still, feeling a rush from the speed. Suddenly everything seemed magical, as if he'd returned to the Mike's of long ago.

Once his eyes had adjusted to the room's low lights, he looked toward the bar and saw around twenty men, much like the ones who used to hang out here, poets, painters, and neighborhood queens.

Maybe not the exact same crew, he thought, but close enough. Nearly floating on the music, he headed toward the bartender.

He stopped when he saw further back in the room someone he'd seen in the neighborhood, a fortyish man with a beard and long graying hair. Jake had once identified him for Randy as a playwright named John Stanley. According to Jake, John had written epic plays for transvestites in the seventies. Now he was holding a drink and talking with two very effeminate men, one tall and gangly, the other shorter and obese. Noticing Randy, he looked at him cautiously and briefly smiled.

Randy caught himself smiling back. Self-conscious, he turned away; he wasn't sure that he wanted to talk with anyone. He walked to the bar and ordered a gin. When the drink arrived, he grasped his glass and hurried to the jukebox.

He studied the list of songs, reading the names: Marvin Gaye, Marianne Faithful, the B-52s, Patsy Cline. The words seemed meaningless; he couldn't concentrate. Somehow he knew that John Stanley was still staring at him.

He turned around. John was gazing at him even as he talked with the men beside him. Randy met John's eyes, and John looked down. Disconcerted, Randy, too, stared at the floor. When he raised his head, John was whispering something to his friends. All three were looking at Randy now, the fat one grinning broadly, John smiling faintly, almost shyly, the other openly leering. Randy lit a cigarette. Although he was embarrassed, he found this odd, disparate group fascinating, and could not turn away.

A new song pealed out, another one Randy recalled, by the Tom Tom Club. He felt a stronger rush from the pill, and the music seemed to envelop him. Then he saw the trio from the bar walking toward him, John's friends pulling him forward. They appeared to be moving in time to the song's beat, their steps synchronized. Under the spell of the sounds coming from the jukebox, Randy watched them approach.

They formed a circle around him, blocking his view of the rest of the bar. He found it difficult to focus on any one of them.

The fat one spoke first. "Hi, sugar," he said, his voice unnaturally high, with just a trace of a Southern accent. "I'm Fey. Fey Ray. Fey with an 'e,' Ray without the 'w.' You may have heard of me."

Fey looked even more obese than he had from a distance. Randy found his immensity overwhelming. "I...I'm Randy."

"What a fabulous name!" Fey beamed up at Randy, his round face lightly rouged, his hair a dark, greasy blond. He was wearing a pink blouse, with three large stains on its front visible in the bar's subdued light. This blouse was hanging out above a pair of tight, ragged jeans, much too small for him, his huge stomach straining the waistline, barely contained by the pants' top button.

He motioned toward the gangly man next to him. "Meet Stella, sugar. Stella Dallas. Another sick queen."

Stella offered Randy a wispy smile, one, it seemed, meant to be seductive. He was one of the homeliest people Randy had ever met, tall and reed thin, the acne scars on his face highlighted by his heavy makeup and by the bright red cowboy shirt he was wearing. As Stella's smile broadened, Randy noticed that one of his front teeth was missing. The others were decayed.

Stella took a Kool from his pack of cigarettes. "Got a match, hon?" He inched closer to Randy.

"Yeah, uh...sure." Randy found a lighter in his coat pocket and, his hands shaking, leaned toward Stella.

Taking the light, Stella brushed against Randy's thigh. "Thanks," he purred.

Fey grabbed Randy's arm and pulled him away, then pointed toward John Stanley, who was standing back slightly, clutching his drink.

"Now this fabulous queen is John Stanley." Fey let the apparent weight of these words sink in. "You've heard of *her*, haven't you? She's a genius. She made us stars."

Randy looked at John, whose timidity, now that he was closer, was painfully clear; it seemed as if he preferred being overshadowed by his more flamboyant companions. He was dressed in an old, faded sweater and a pair of jeans that were equally worn. At first he did not acknowledge Fey's introduction, which Randy found surprising, considering the way John had been smiling at him from the bar. But at last, glancing past Randy's shoulder, he raised an arm and weakly shook Randy's hand. Randy saw that he was blushing.

"We've been admiring you," Fey went on.

"I'm sure she could see *that*," Stella interjected. He blew out a smoke ring. "You're so obvious. But she's such a beauty, she's probably used to it."

Fey glared at Stella, then returned to Randy. "Don't mind my sister. She's been on the rag all day." He scowled at Stella again before continuing: "Anyway, sugar, we were just talking about this play we're doing. John thinks it's time."

"Play?" Randy took a swig of his drink. He had lost track of the conversation's drift, wondering if he should know who Fey and Stella were, if Jake had ever told him anything about them. The name "Stella Dallas" sounded familiar.

"*Cocks in Space*," Stella offered. "You remember that, don't you? We did it the first time twenty years ago, with Silver Pam and Toothless George." He raised his cigarette to his lips, studying Randy, then shook his head. "No, I suppose you're too young—just a baby, really."

John looked as if he were about to say something. Stroking his beard, he stopped himself, gazing over Randy's shoulder.

"It was fabulous!" Fey cried. "I was the talk of the town."

"*You?*" Stella chortled. "Why, no one even noticed your lardy old butt up there, way back in the chorus. They were watching me."

"What about that number I did with Nora Nipples? 'Hudson Hussies'? We brought down the house."

"Two minutes in a three-hour show! Hon, you had a lot to learn."

"And you…"

John intervened, speaking for the first time, his words slurred: "You were both stars. And still are. They'll see."

Fascinated despite his confusion, Randy finished his cigarette, then lit another. He felt as if he were watching some underground film from the sixties, like the one he'd seen with Jake a few years before. There was no need for him to say anything, he decided; he'd just let things happen.

"We *are* stars," Fey said to him. "The last of them. The other goddesses are dead."

Randy thought of Graham. He wondered if he'd ever known Fey

and Stella, if they'd run in some of the same circles. That seemed a possibility.

"Don't be stoo-pid," Stella drawled. "Not all of them. I know for a fact that Pepper's running a vegetable stand in Illinois, with that hunky husband of hers. You know, the cute farmer she met at Macy's."

"The rest are dead, though," Fey insisted. "Or dying." He turned back to Randy with a sigh. "There just aren't any stars around anymore. These new queens, they're nothing. Hacks. We did it all years ago."

"Lip-synching trash," Stella agreed.

"Yes, but…" John began tentatively.

Randy noticed how glazed his eyes were, how he swayed as he stood there. It was obvious that he was very drunk.

"But there are others out there," John went on after a moment, staring at Randy. He gulped the last of his drink. "There always have been."

"A few maybe." Stella pointed at Randy. "Like you, hon. You're *flawless.*"

"She's right, sugar." Fey's pitch grew higher. "You'd be perfect for the play."

"I…I don't know." Randy felt himself blushing. He stared at Stella, then at Fey, taking in their rouged, flushed faces, their keen eyes, finding them both startling, larger than life. He turned to John, who, though still gazing at him, was swaying more now, as if about to pass out. "I haven't acted in a while."

"That's all right," Stella assured him. "All you gotta do is stand there. You're gorgeous. They'll love it."

John lifted his glass to his lips. Seeing it was empty, he asked, "Does anyone want another drink?"

"Nah, let's tip," Fey replied. "I'm broke. We can go up to my place. I've got those tuies Crystal gave me."

"Tuies?" Randy finished his gin.

"Tuinols, hon," Stella explained. "You'll love 'em."

Fey laughed. "I'll say!"

Stella ran his fingertips across Randy's hip. "So you're coming, aren't you?"

"I…maybe."

"Oh, come on, sugar," Fey exclaimed. "We'll show you the costumes we're making for the show."

Still swaying, John mumbled, "Yes. Please. I'd like to talk with you some more."

An old Motown tune blasted from the jukebox. "Okay," Randy answered, suddenly excited.

"So let's tip," Fey cried.

They walked north, Randy gnawing his lip as he sucked in the warm air. It didn't seem like early February at all, more like May. He looked at the sky; the moon was full, nearly golden. As he moved, John Stanley beside him, he felt extraordinarily light. He was having an adventure.

A few feet in front of them, Fey and Stella took no notice of the temperature. They were in their own world, chattering incessantly.

"Did you see Sister Dexie in there?" Fey was asking.

"Oh, yes!" Stella lit a Kool.

"She's gotten so grand! Wouldn't even look at me. Why, that bitch has been on her knees all over this town!"

"Had every dick. A regular Hoover."

"And her ass, sugar! Wide as the street! It hurts even thinking about it."

"A real size queen!"

"Loves those pechungas!"

John Stanley said nothing. Staggering beside Randy, he could barely stand. Randy expected him to keel over at any moment.

But he was intrigued. This man's shyness was appealing. And he saw how Fey and Stella looked up to him. As John lurched along, Randy caught him casting surreptitious glances in his direction. He wanted to talk with him; the dexedrine was giving him courage.

He turned to him, the light from a street lamp shining down, and studied his long, bony face, his graying, unkempt beard. Despite the dim light, Randy could detect little veins running across his nose. He was not particularly attractive, though he looked as if he might have been at one time.

As John tottered along, reeling, stumbling from the lamp's light into the shadows, he began, for reasons Randy could not explain, to resemble Graham. This resemblance was vague—a faint expression on his face, puzzled yet amused—and immediately faded.

Startled, Randy looked ahead at Fey and Stella, listening to them dissing and shrieking, taking in their demi-drag, their straggly, castoff clothes. With their frequent references to long-ago events, they seemed to have emerged from another era, the one he'd heard Jake and Graham talk about so often, a time when life had been loose and free. He recalled that old underground film he had seen, remembering a platinium-blond transvestite shooting speed and talking nonstop with a silent, beautifully coiffed brunette, a debutante, who was lying fully clothed next to him on a bed, chain-smoking cigarettes. He suspected that Fey, Stella, and John had known them. He had found the contrast between this stoned drag queen and the aloof heiress alluring, weirdly decadent; it reminded him of all the stories he'd heard about those days, when everything was supposed to have been fluid, spontaneous, new.

He looked back at John, hesitating. At last he said, "It's…it's a beautiful night, isn't it?"

John stopped for a second. Randy was afraid he was going to collapse. "You think so?" he slurred. Then he staggered on.

"I…I mean, it's so warm."

"Everything's gorgeous when you're young," John murmured. He weaved back and forth precariously.

Discouraged, Randy said nothing else. He wondered if John would be able to make it to Fey's apartment.

Fey lived a few blocks away on 14th Street, in a small place he shared with his grandmother, just above Combat Jo's, his grandmother's bar.

"You'll love Jo," Fey gushed as they approached the building.

"She's a trip," Stella concurred.

"Worked in vaudeville down in Atlanta when she was five. 'Marmalade Jo,' they called her."

Stella chuckled. "The queen was a star even then."

As Fey opened the front door, Stella pinched Randy's thigh. "Later, hon," he whispered.

Recoiling, Randy lit a cigarette. He told himself that he shouldn't worry, that Fey was harmless, John bombed. Stella might get a little heavy, but he could put him off.

Fey's apartment was on the fifth floor, at the top of a steep flight of stairs. John, tottering, made it up with some difficulty, following the other three. Fey and Stella giggled at his inebriation all the way. Once inside, Fey switched on an overhead light. Randy noticed a thin black cat scampering away to hide.

Fey laughed. "Oh, Piewacket, there you go again."

"That beast has always hated us," Stella observed.

A shrill voice cried out from the rear of the apartment: "Frankie?"

Randy looked to his left, toward a small room at the back. The door was open; light from a night lamp drifted out. He could see an old woman lying on a narrow cot inside, dressed in a faded blue nightrobe, her head partially raised, hair white and disheveled, her face a mass of wrinkles. She appeared to be at least eighty.

"Frankie," she called again, "is that you?"

"Right," Fey answered.

"Well, pipe down," she barked. "Combat Jo's beat."

Fey strolled to the door. "You okay, Jo?"

Jo grunted, then frowned. "Just beat."

"So who's watching the bar?"

"Little Kevin," Jo muttered drowsily. Yawning, she lowered her head onto her pillow. "God, there were drunks all over the place this afternoon. Brawls, everything. You'd think it was Saturday night." Her eyes suddenly alert, she again lifted her head, attempting to see past Fey's bulk. "Is Lester here, too?"

"Yeah, Stella's here."

"Well, listen, you two queens keep it down, okay? This old broad's dead." Turning away from Fey, Jo resumed napping.

Fey looked at the others. "She's out like a light. Probably took a couple of her pills." He headed toward the kitchen to his right. "I'll get some candles."

Stella ran after him, crying, "Don't forget the tuies!"

As soon as they had gone, John stumbled to one of the three mattresses that were spaced out on the floor. He kneeled on it for a second, staring at the wall, then abruptly fell over and passed out.

Sweating, Randy looked around, trying to disregard John's inert body, his discordant wheezing. The room was meagerly furnished: Besides the three mattresses, there were only two small tables, each holding an overflowing ashtray and old movie magazines, *Photoplays* and *Silver Screens*. Strips of pink and red gauzy material and little piles of multi-colored glitter were everywhere. There were no lamps, just the overhead light. The white walls were grimy, discolored by smoke, and adorned with three posters advertising films starring Kim Novak: *Picnic, Vertigo,* and *The Legend of Lylah Clare*. He walked to this last one, drawn to its vivid red background. The yellow lettering listing the stars seemed to be sparkling.

"You like Kim, sugar?" It was Fey, who was standing behind him, three dark blue candles in one hand, a bottle of pills in the other. Stella, holding two more candles, four paper cups, and a jug of red wine, was beside him.

Randy lifted a hand to his forehead, wiping sweat from his brow. "Yeah, I guess so."

Fey tilted his chin and fluttered his eyelids, imitating Kim's pose from the poster. "People say I look like her. A little heftier, maybe, but still."

"Kim has nothing on Barbara!" Stella snapped.

"Barbara?" Randy felt the room growing warmer.

"Why, Barbara Stanwyck." Stella looked at Randy, for a moment impatient, as if he thought him dense. Sighing, he said, "She was the greatest star of all."

"Oh, yeah?"

"Of course. When she died, her spirit came to me." He gazed directly into Randy's eyes. "She's with me all the time."

Fey plopped himself down onto one of the mattresses. After placing the pills and candles on the floor, he glanced at John's motionless body. "I see she's gone," he remarked. Then he looked up at Randy and patted a space next to him. "Come on, sugar, make yourself comfortable."

Stella stretched out on the third mattress. "You should come over here. It's cozier." He set the wine and candles out before him.

Randy wavered, then quickly sat next to Fey. Once he'd seated himself, he felt something under his right leg. Moving slowly, he reached down and touched a soft, furry object. He grasped it carefully and lifted it up to the light; it looked like a dead animal. A little black mouse, he thought. His heart started pumping wildly.

Stella screamed, "Yikes! What's that?"

Fey studied the object in Randy's hand, giggling. "Oh, that Piewacket! The demented thing smothered all her kittens."

Randy looked down at what he was holding, his stomach churning, and dropped it on the floor.

Fey leaned forward and scooped it up. Holding it gingerly between his right thumb and forefinger, he darted to a brown paper bag lying against a wall and tossed it in. "I thought we'd gotten rid of all of those," he said as he returned to his seat. "We started finding them around the house yesterday."

Grinning, Stella turned to Randy. "What a mad queen, right?"

Randy clutched his legs, running his hands against the denim of his pants.

"Where is that beast anyway?" Fey looked to his left. Piewacket was huddled in a corner at the back of the room. Seeing Fey's gaze fixed on her, she dashed to Jo's room and jumped onto her cot.

Stella guffawed. "Wretched animal! Horrid creature!"

"The beast!" Fey cried. "*The beast!*"

They both laughed uproariously.

Randy sat still, scarcely breathing, his eyes wandering over to Jo. The light floating out of her room seemed eerie, ominous. He could see the back of her head, her mop of white hair, the shoulders of her faded nightrobe. She was covered by an old red comforter, with Piewacket perched on top of her legs, hovering there nervously, staring back at Randy, who quickly looked away.

Stella was pouring wine into the paper cups. "Drink up," he said as he passed the cups around.

Randy took a large gulp, then looked toward John's body, listening to him snore, watching his rib cage move up and down, wondering when he'd awake.

"Cheers!" Stella exclaimed. He sipped his drink.

"Yeah, cheers!" Fey echoed. He turned to Randy. "Sugar," he said softly. "Sugar, sugar, sugar. I'm so glad you're here."

Randy swallowed the rest of his wine, then noticed how the folds of flesh under Fey's chin seemed to be swelling, undulating. He sat up. "I've gotta go."

Fey and Stella looked at him, appalled. "No!" Stella cried vehemently.

Fey grasped Randy's shoulder, his grip firm. "Sugar, the party's just starting." He stopped and peered straight at him. Then, speaking slowly, his voice momentarily deep: "Let's take those tuies. That'll make you feel better." He reached down to the floor for the bottle of pills and poured five of them onto the palm of his hand. They were small and white. He handed one to Randy.

Randy held onto it tightly, convinced he would not be able to walk if he tried. The room was unbearably hot. He felt paralyzed.

Stella poured more wine into his cup. "Hon, you need a refill."

"You sure do," Fey added, his pitch again high.

Randy put the pill in his mouth and let it rest on his tongue for several seconds. At last he raised his cup to his lips and gulped it down, swallowing with it all his wine.

Fey and Stella each took two. "Fabulous," Stella murmured. He picked up the wine jug and turned to Randy. "Here, let me pour you some more."

Randy held his cup out toward Stella. He could feel the wine he'd already had flowing through him, joining the dexedrine. Stella refilled his cup. Randy took a slug. The warmth of the room began to feel tolerable.

Fey lit the candles as Stella switched off the light. Randy sipped his drink and watched the flames flickering in front of him, entranced by the shadows they cast on the wall.

"Do you think I was nuts to take two?" Fey asked Stella. "You know how I get."

"Well, you did, Blanche, you did!" Stella replied.

They roared, then started chattering again, their words becoming indistinct to Randy, their voices indistinguishable, a constant murmur, blending in with John's snoring, with the light drifting out of Jo's room, a light that, for an instant, seemed to be coming from Piewacket's eyes. He helped himself to more wine, losing track of the time, fascinated by Fey and Stella, by everything he imagined they had seen and done, finally relaxing, thinking that perhaps he should join the conversation.

"I know Graham Mason," he blurted. As soon as he'd said this, he blushed.

Fey stared at him, taken aback. Randy was afraid that he was annoyed by the interruption. But then, laughing, Fey gasped, "Oh, I see!"

"Oooo!" Stella shrieked. "Graham Mason!"

His stomach fluttering, Randy searched in his pockets for his pack of cigarettes. "Do...do you know him?"

Fey grinned. "Not really. But we used to see that demented queen everywhere."

"Yeah, what a sickie!" Stella leaned toward Randy and offered him a light, grazing his arm in the process.

"My, my, my!" Fey giggled uncontrollably. He paused to catch his breath before inquiring, "And Miss Dennis: Did you know her, too?"

Randy dragged on his cigarette. "N...no."

"Another sickie!" Stella threw in. "A real grunge queen!"

"Oh, yes!" Stella proclaimed. "The stories I've heard! They make *me* blush!"

"That's saying something!" Stella cried.

Randy gripped his cup and leaned forward. "Like...like what?"

Just then John Stanley grunted and, rolling onto his side, farted loudly.

"Good one!" Stella screamed.

Fey waved his hands in front of his face and wrinkled his nose emphatically. "Phew!" he exclaimed. He and Stella burst out laughing.

Randy poured more wine into his cup, waiting for them to stop and tell him more. But when they managed to contain themselves, they seemed to have forgotten all about Graham and Dennis.

"Where's the music?" Stella demanded. "It's time for the Yma!"

Fey shot to his feet. "Yes!"

"Do the Yma, girl! Do the Yma!"

Fey looked down at Randy. "And we can show you our costumes, the ones from the show."

Stella smirked. "Listen, you dizzy thing, we haven't even gotten around to making them yet."

Fey glared at him, motioning toward the gauzy material strewn on the floor. "We can improvise, can't we, bitch?"

"Just get the Yma."

Randy watched Fey scurry to a second bedroom situated next to Jo's, becoming aware then of another surge of warmth passing through him, this time an extremely pleasant one. He began to feel buoyant, lighter than the air, though heavy, too, incapable of speaking. After tossing his cigarette into an ashtray, he fell back onto the mattress and gazed at the ceiling, wondering how it had ever gotten to be so white, how the shadows cast by the candles could be so beautiful.

"Are you okay, hon?" Stella was leaning over him, running his fingers through his hair.

"What's the Yma?" was all Randy could say.

Fey rushed in, carrying a portable tape deck and two cassettes. "What's the Yma?" He seemed shocked by Randy's ignorance. "Why, sugar, she's Yma Sumac. An Andean princess. A stunning chanteuse."

"Amy Camus from Brooklyn, you mean." Stella squeezed Randy's arm and laughed. "She started spelling her name backwards when she went to Hollywood."

"Well, she's fabulous anyway." Fey's face was glowing. "One of the greatest stars ever."

"A real diva," Stella agreed. "Her range is flawless."

"She can sing in any pitch: soprano, bass, and everything in between."

"Tweets like a bird, and roars like a bear. She's a camp!"

On his back, Randy peered up at them, their words drifting past him, certain he was floating on an ocean—or maybe asleep, dreaming. Whatever I'm doing, he thought, it's all—well, it's strange, but still sort of fabulous.

"Are you ready, sugar?" Fey inserted a cassette into the tape deck.

Randy closed his eyes and listened to the sound of cymbals clashing, to violins and a harp, a lilting chorus, a booming orchestra. A woman started singing, her voice high, then higher, rising to the ceiling, twilling, chirping, the highest soprano he had ever heard. Then, without warning, this voice seemed to descend to the floor, growling, becoming a deep, deep bass, a guttural, thunderous sound.

He reopened his eyes. Hazily, as the candles' flames quivered and Yma wailed, he saw Fey lifting some of the thin material that was lying everywhere, wrapping it around his immense frame, across his face, dancing slowly, gracefully—surprisingly so, considering his heft—flowing miraculously.

The music quickened, and Fey rose up on his toes, twirling, allowing the material to fly with him, to become a veil, a shimmering, magical cloak. Light appeared to be shooting off of him as he moved faster, faster, a blur of colors, of pinks and reds.

Stella stood near him, reaching down to the floor and scooping up the glitter lying in piles there, lifting it and sprinkling it on the spinning Fey. "Dance, slut, dance," he cried joyously.

Randy watched Fey's shadow dance on the wall. He closed his eyes again.

The music seemed exotic, foreign, ancient, like the scores for those old fifties epics he had seen on television, the ones he used to watch with Jake on Sunday afternoons. He peeked through his eyelids and saw Fey become a slave girl, a captive dancing for her master, her king, a conquering warrior. He was in a palace.

With an orchestral flourish and a trilling in Yma's throat, the music changed. He heard a torch song, an old standard, like those records he had listened to at Mr. Hewitt's years before, when he had been in his living room, waiting for him to finish his drink, for them to go to the bedroom. He felt sweat running down his sides.

Yma began chanting in Spanish, her voice rippling from soprano to bass. Distantly, as if through a mist, he saw candles flickering, Jo's night lamp, John's body, Fey dancing—Stella, too, now. The music faded.

He hadn't slept, he was sure of that; he could still feel the speed, under the tuinol, beneath his lethargy. But for a time—for hours, it seemed—he had been convinced that he had left the room, that no one else was around. He had been conscious of almost nothing.

Now he could see Fey and Stella leaning over him, both grinning, the candles burning dimly around them, and he could tell that his pants were down around his ankles.

"Oooo, it's a big one!" Stella observed approvingly.

"Yes, indeed!" Fey exclaimed.

Torpid, Randy shut his eyes. He felt breath on his groin, coming nearer. He knew it was Stella.

"Gum her, bitch!" Fey cackled.

He felt Stella's mouth on his penis—licking the shaft, closing in on the head—teeth (some missing), gums. He wanted to pull away, to move, to leave, yet was certain that he couldn't. He had no choice about what happened to him; it was best to lay still.

"Work it!" Fey shrieked. "You've got a limp noodle there."

Randy felt himself floating, again drifting away. This is a dream, he told himself; when I wake up, it'll be over.

"Oh, sugar, you've got her now!"

He was in the air, flying over the street, looking down at Mike's, at the demolished building where The Candy Store had been. He saw the rubble and, at the edge of the debris, Fey, Stella, Jake, Adrian, Graham, Mr. Hewitt. His father, too. But he was so far above them, their faces were blurred.

Then he spotted smoke, a fire shooting up out of the ground. It hissed and howled furiously, and swallowed them all.

"What's this shit?"

Randy opened his eyes. He could just make out the candles' flames, the light from Jo's room, two indistinct heads. Fey and Stella, he realized. Then, far off, someone else. A man. Standing above them. It was John.

"Christ!" John roared, enraged. "Can't faggots ever think of anything else?"

Stella backed off of Randy and jumped up. "Oh, come on, girl, chill out!"

Fey, too, was indignant. "She wanted it!"

John said nothing. Appearing surprised by his own anger, he started swaying.

Randy didn't move.

John put one hand to his beard, steadying himself, briefly staring down at Randy. He looked away, then, hesitantly, at Randy once more. He paused, stroking his beard. "Are you okay?" he asked.

"She's fine!" Stella snapped. "Why don't you just go back to bed?"

Randy sat up, unsteady, and peered past John toward the light in Jo's room. She was sleeping, her back facing him. From a corner of one eye, he saw Piewacket fleeing to the kitchen. He looked back at John, who, disconcertingly, was still gazing at him, Fey and Stella beside him. Randy lowered his eyes, then saw his bare legs and groin. He quickly pulled up his pants and, blushing, said, "I…I think I better go."

"No!" Fey cried.

John leaned toward him. "Are you sure?"

"Stay," Stella pleaded.

Shaky, Randy stood. "It's late."

John looked at Fey and Stella, his anger returning. "What the fuck did you give him?"

"Just a little tuie," Fey replied meekly. Then, again indignant: "You knew we were gonna take them."

"I forgot." John glanced down and mumbled, "Too fucked up." He looked up again, glaring at Fey. "Jesus, he's probably never taken that shit before!" He turned to Randy. "Are you sure you're all right?"

"Ye…yeah." Randy studied Fey and Stella; their faces appeared bleary. He felt himself weaving and was afraid he was going to pass out. He focused on John, seeing the light from the candles flickering behind him. His skin was very pale. Randy stood still, breathing deliberately. His balance slowly returned.

"This won't happen again," John said a moment later. "Trust me."

"No, sugar," Fey added, contrite now. "We were just having fun."

Randy stared at John's head, fascinated by the light encircling it, by the waves of color that seemed to be shooting through his hair. John's voice echoed in his brain. "Trust me," he had said. Randy wondered what he had really meant and why he had bothered to say this.

Fey grabbed a *Photoplay* and a pen from one of the tables, then passed them to Randy. "Give us your number. Maybe you can help us with the show."

"Or even be in it," Stella squealed.

Randy took the magazine and scribbled on its cover. He handed it to John.

John swayed and gazed backed at him, ashen. Then he stumbled away, clutching the magazine.

"Well...well, I'll see you all later." Randy headed toward the door. Fey and Stella came with him. "I'll call you tomorrow," Fey said as he let Randy out.

Randy stared past Fey and Stella, seeing John in the background, prone on the mattress. Wavering, he answered, "Yeah, see you."

He stood on the street, uncertain where he was. It was drizzling, and the temperature had dropped precipitously; the warmth of the day was completely gone. As he tried to orient himself, he almost felt as if nothing he had experienced in the past few hours had really happened. Winter had returned. He suspected he'd awake and again find himself in bed, waiting for Jake.

The drizzle became rain; he was getting soaked. He looked up and read a street sign. He was on Third Avenue and 14th Street. A taxi passed. Chilly, he stretched out his hand.

xv

He slept fitfully, not conscious of any dreams yet disturbed by a feeling of disgust. When he awoke early in the afternoon, he listened to the heavy rain outside. Things seemed exactly the way they had been for the past few weeks.

Then he heard Jake and Adrian enter the apartment, both of them giggling. Fuck, he said to himself. He lay on his side, trying to ignore them.

"Where's m'baby?" Jake cried from the living room. "He should hear about the party."

"Where else?" Adrian replied. "The beauty's sleeping."

"Let's go tell him about it."

"Aw, c'mon."

"Nah, he should get up anyhow."

They stumbled to the bedroom. Randy pressed his eyelids together, pretending to be asleep.

Jake threw himself down onto the bed next to him. "Sweetheart, you'll never guess where we've been."

Randy lay still. He sensed the beginnings of a headache just behind his right eye.

Jake patted a space on the bed and spoke to Adrian: "Come on, Addie, relax."

When Randy felt Adrian seating himself next to Jake, he bolted up. "What do you want?" he screamed.

"Why, sweetheart!" Jake seemed surprised by Randy's outburst. "I wanted to see how you were."

Randy took in their red, boozy faces, glaring at them.

"We didn't mean to bother you," Adrian said jauntily, faintly sarcastic.

"It's just that we had an unbelievable night." Jake spoke with an enthusiasm that revolted Randy. "Addie knows this guy who works for Donald Trump. We had dinner with him earlier. Well, sweetheart, he ended up inviting us to this party at Trump's apartment!"

"Huh?" Randy grabbed a cigarette from his pack on the bedside table. He wondered if this story were true and how much of it he would have to hear. At the same time, he knew that he would have liked to have gone to Donald Trump's himself.

"You wouldn't believe where he lives," Adrian gushed. *"Incroyable!"*

"Right." Randy gazed past them toward the living room.

"Everyone was there," Adrian went on. "Celebrities, models, stars. Plus all these rich hebes and society cunts."

"And you haven't even told him the best part." Jake was grinning.

"Hold on, I was getting to that."

Randy raised his cigarette to his mouth and chomped down on the filter. When his teeth came together, he thought his head was going to explode.

"Adrian met this agent," Jake explained, excited. "You know, for models."

"He used to be with Zoli," Adrian continued effusively, "but now he's started his own business." He paused—for effect, Randy felt—then said, "He wants to use me. He says I have the look they want."

"Very nineties, didn't he say?" Jake's smile grew wider.

"Yeah, that's right. He wants me to call him tomorrow."

"Addie's gonna be famous."

"And rich!"

Randy took a drag on his cigarette, sneering.

"Isn't that fabulous?" Jake asked.

"Yeah, right." Randy drew in more smoke, hearing little.

"So what's m'baby been up to?" Jake ran his fingers across the blanket covering Randy's legs.

Randy peered at him. He found his face much too cheerful, his grin unbearably smug.

Adrian chuckled. "I hope it was glamorous."

"I doubt if I can compete with you!" Randy snapped, exhaling smoke in Adrian's direction. He felt his left cheek twitching.

"Oooh, a little touchy, I see!" Adrian picked up Randy's pack of cigarettes, took one out, and, after removing a silver lighter from his shirt pocket, lit it. "You don't mind, do you?"

Jake squeezed Randy's leg. "Don't be so uptight, sweetheart. We were just curious." Randy noticed that his eyes were twinkling.

"Yeah," Adrian concurred, "tell us what you've been doing."

Randy looked downward, then up again, glancing past Adrian. "I went out."

"And?" Adrian grinned. Moving languorously, he tapped his cigarette against an ashtray.

"I met these people."

"It gets better all the time."

"Who, sweetheart?" Jake reached under the blanket and massaged Randy's leg.

"John Stanley," Randy answered quickly. "You know, that playwright. And these two drag queens, Fey Ray and Stella Dallas."

"Oh, god," Adrian gasped, "*them*!"

"Yeah, I remember those two," Jake remarked.

Adrian laughed. "I heard they died years ago."

"Well, they didn't!" Randy shot back furiously. "I thought they were funny."

"Well, yes, I suppose they could be, in a seventies sort of way."
Adrian lifted his cigarette to his lips and dragged on it slowly, then
giggled and said, "They must be pretty ravaged by now. I mean, they
hit their peak years ago. And they were supposed to have been pretty bad back then."

"You're right," Jake agreed. "Did you ever see that old film they
were in?"

"Which one? They made so much crap."

"I don't remember the name. But they were so fucked up, completely demented!"

Randy's eyes darted from Jake to Adrian. He found Adrian's pretty, beaming face revolting and wished he had never come home, that
he had stayed at Fey's. At least it would have been better than this.

"You should be careful who you hang with," Adrian said to him.
"You never know who's gonna see you."

Jake pinched Randy's leg and laughed. "He's right, you know."

Wrenching away from him, Randy tossed his cigarette into the
ashtray and, naked, jumped out of bed.

"Sweetheart, where are you going?"

Randy did not look back. "Out," he mumbled as he pulled on his
jeans.

He heard Jake stand and say, "But it's pouring outside."

"Let him go," Adrian said. "He's obviously got some sort of crank
on."

Randy listened as Jake returned to the bed. He threw on his shirt
and buttoned it, then quickly walked to the closet and found his
coat.

"Is m'baby gonna be gone long?"

Taking long strides, Randy hurried out of the bedroom.

"Wait, sweetheart!" Jake called after him.

Randy headed for the front door. The last thing he heard before
he left the apartment was Adrian's voice: "See you, Randy!"

He ran down the stairs, then stopped at the bottom, out of
breath. His head was pounding, and he felt drained. Images of Jake
and Adrian floated before him, both prone on his bed and giggling.

He lit a cigarette and focused on the hallway's wall. Its whiteness seemed blinding; he had to look away.

As he stood still, he heard an old song by Joni Mitchell, from an album he vaguely recalled. He inched his way toward the music, which was coming from Sylvia Radicatti's apartment. When he realized what he was doing, he turned away, paused, then dashed out of the building.

The rainstorm was torrential; he could barely see across the street. He didn't know where to go. It was freezing.

He noticed a tall, heavyset man approaching him, the only other figure on the block, wrapped in a thick, black blanket and lurching through the downpour. A blast of wind shot up the street. He threw his cigarette onto the sidewalk and rushed back inside.

He stood in the hallway and listened to the music coming from Sylvia's. The album was "Blue"; he remembered liking it a long time ago, when he'd heard cuts from it at Mike's. He tried to recall if he had been with Jake. He remained still, then edged up to Sylvia's door. After staring at it for a few seconds, he rapped lightly.

There was no answer. He could hear nothing except the music and cats scampering across the floor. He started to suspect that Sylvia had gone out and left the radio on. Then he heard her sneeze. He knocked again, harder this time.

The music stopped. "Yeah?" she called out. "Hugh?"

Randy stuffed his hands in his pockets and fingered his change. He wondered if Hugh was Sylvia's "old man," if she was expecting him. He backed away.

"Get off that table, Sloth!" he heard her cry. He listened as she ran to the door.

She opened it quickly, her smile brilliant. But when she saw Randy, her smile faded. She regarded him carefully, as if trying to place his face. Slowly her smile returned, halfhearted.

"Hey," she said, "what a surprise. Randy, right?"

Randy stared back at her, thinking she looked tired, older than she had the day before, frumpy. She was wearing jeans and a wrinkled blue sweatshirt, and was holding a cat in her arms. He caught a slight odor of soiled litter wafting out from the apartment. "Am...am I...Is this the wrong time?"

"No, no, I need a break. I've been working like a dog trying to get all this shit together. Moving's hell." She spoke rapidly and fluttered her hands, just as she had when they'd first met, and seemed distracted. Even so, her eyes were glowing, almost fiery. "Come in, come in," she continued absently, pushing a loose strand of hair from her face. The cat jumped out of her arms. "Don't mind the mess."

Randy walked in. Once she'd shut the door, he again became aware of the cat litter, its odor more evident inside. Cats encircled him, rubbing against his legs, one—Despair, he remembered— mewing persistently. He thought of Piewacket and her dead kittens, and glanced up over Sylvia's shoulders.

Behind her, he saw the boxes that had been in the hallway—just one of them appeared to have been touched—as well as a futon pulled out into a bed; a table in front of this, littered with papers, a paperback book, and some aluminum foil; and a computer and an old phonograph on the floor.

"I told you it's a mess," she said. "But never mind." She gestured toward the opened futon. "Sit down."

"I…I can't stay. I just wanted to know if you had any aspirin."

One of the cats leapt onto the table and started to play with the papers. "Get down, Greed!" she screamed, then looked at Randy. "I don't think I have anything like that here. Sorry, but…I don't like to use that shit. Got a headache?"

"Uh-huh. A real bitch."

She raised a hand to her chin, apparently considering several options. Decisive, she exclaimed, "Listen, what you need is some juice."

A lilt in her voice made Randy feel that her enthusiasm for his presence had grown. "Juice?"

"Yeah, something natural, fresh. I was just about to make some for myself." She sniffled, then walked to the kitchen in the back.

Hesitant, Randy took off his coat and sat on the futon, his eyes following her. "I don't want to bother you. I mean, are you expecting someone or something?"

Sylvia stopped behind a counter strewn with peeled carrots. A small juicer was to her left. "No…I mean, yeah, but…" She grabbed one of the carrots and grasped it firmly. "Why would you think that?" she asked, her tone suddenly sharp.

"It's just…" Randy looked toward the front door, wondering when he could leave.

Sylvia was silent for a moment, still gripping the carrot. At last she snapped, "Well, he's late. Actually, he was supposed to be here last night." She paused. Then, vehemently: "Men are pigs, don't you think? Scumbags. Excuse my French." She stuffed the carrot into the juicer's funnel.

Randy stared at Sylvia, her words ringing in his ears. The unexpected anger she'd displayed seemed to ripple down his spine and settle in his lower back. He pushed the palms of his hands against the futon, concentrating on her face. It was flushed. But she was smiling now, albeit weakly.

"I don't know why I'm talking to you like this," she said, calmer, somewhat embarrassed, "but maybe you know what I mean." She gazed at him, her expression thoughtful. "Yes, I think you do. I'm psychic, you know." She switched on the juicer and pressed down on the carrot. Then she stopped and remarked, "Really, I'm glad you're here." She shoved the carrot in forcefully.

Randy listened to the machine whir. Orange liquid seeped into a green plastic glass. He glanced at the juice, becoming nauseous, sure he could never drink it. He looked up at Sylvia. Her furrowed, determined face had an intensity that he found a little frightening. He wondered if he could ever like her. He'd thought that he did yesterday. He wanted to now. But he felt that she talked too much—or, rather, knew that what she'd said (and the way she'd said it) made him uncomfortable.

Sylvia grasped another carrot and cried, "Almost ready. Just one or two more." She crammed it into the juicer, then loudly, above the machine's roar, asked, "So tell me about yourself. You're gay, aren't you?"

Randy wasn't certain that he had understood. "What?"

"Gay."

A cat jumped onto the counter, sniffing at the glass. Sylvia pushed him away, back to the floor. "Not now, baby. Your mother's busy." Then, to Randy: "Well, are you?"

Randy sensed a twinge of anger rising with the air from his chest. He'd found her question intrusive, although he didn't know why. He answered anyway: "Yeah, I guess I am."

"I thought so. You're too good-looking not to be. All my friends are." The whir of the juicer stopped. She raised a hand to her head and stroked a strand of her hair, twisting it, then, frowning, said, "Except for Hugh, that is."

Randy felt a draft of cold air blowing in from a partially opened window. He reached for the pack of cigarettes in his coat pocket.

Sylvia lifted the glass, which was now full. "There, that's ready." Holding it carefully, she headed toward Randy. Two cats followed her.

"I…I don't think I really want any." Randy clutched an unlit cigarette.

Sylvia stopped before him. A drop of orange liquid dripped over the green rim of the glass in her hand. One of the cats rubbed his head against her leg. "Is something wrong?" she asked, puzzled.

"No, I…it's just that I don't like that stuff much."

Sylvia stared at the glass. Then, seeing his cigarette, she laughed. "Oh, I see. But smoking doesn't bother you." She raised the juice to her lips, took a quick sip, and shook her leg, driving the cat away. "Please, Avarice, you just ate." She sat next to Randy. Another cat jumped onto her lap.

Randy closed his legs tightly together and shifted away from her. "You don't mind if I smoke?"

Sylvia ran her fingers across the cat's fur. "Sure, go ahead."

He lit his cigarette, then held onto the used match.

"Just use the floor. I haven't gotten around to finding an ashtray yet." She pointed at the unpacked boxes. "It's in one of those somewhere. I've never smoked myself." She hesitated, then mumbled, "Of course, Hugh smokes like a chimney."

Randy took a long drag on his cigarette, kneading the fabric of the futon's cover with his free hand. Neither of them said anything. He felt as if Sylvia were examining his every move, waiting for him to speak. He wanted to leave and yet, because of a peculiar eagerness he could intuit in her, was certain that she didn't want him to. He supposed she needed company. He remembered the rain outside and Jake and Adrian upstairs, and crossed his legs.

Sylvia tilted her head forward. "Are you okay? I mean, did something I say annoy you?"

Randy detected a thin line of carrot juice on her upper lip, then, as she leaned further toward him, thought he noticed a dim empathy in her restless eyes.

"I hope you didn't think I was being nosy," she continued, stroking the cat with one hand, a strand of her hair with the other. "You know, when I asked if you were gay and stuff."

"No, that's all right." Randy saw that her eyes were blue, limpid, a little watery. He felt himself relax slightly.

"It's just that…" She coiled the strand of hair around one of her fingers, pensive. "It's just that you seem so nice. And we're neighbors and all. At first you surprised me when you came by, but then… well, I guess I realized that I wanted to get to know you. You know, I hadn't talked to anyone since yesterday. It was making me edgy. And then Hugh never showed up last night. I couldn't call him. My phone's not connected yet. I mean, I tried this morning on the pay phone across the street, but he wasn't home."

"Oh, yeah?" Randy stared at the gray in her hair, wondering how old she was, what she had looked like when she was younger. Beautiful, he thought.

"You're not much of a talker," she observed, laughing. "I like that. But then you must think I'm such a chatterbox. I had a shrink once who told me I was too open. Nowadays he'd probably talk about me having no boundaries or something. Anyway, he thought that was because I might have been abused when I was a kid." She shrugged. "Who knows? I stopped seeing him years ago."

Wincing, Randy looked down at the papers on the table in front of him. One of them was her lease.

"They talk a lot of crap," Sylvia went on, her voice contemptuous. "The one I saw just wanted to know about the men I dated, why they were all so horrible."

He moved his eyes past the papers to the book beside them, a lurid-looking novel called *Savage Surrender,* and studied its cover, drawn in. A brutally handsome man standing at the top of a lush, verdant hill hulked over the pale, dark-haired woman quivering before him, a hint of passion in her eyes. The sky was overcast, the trees behind them bent in the wind. The man's shirt was unbuttoned, his chest hairless, rippling with muscles, his long blond hair flowing down his back. The woman was dressed in a low-cut, red-velvet gown and had backed away from him. But the man was grasping her shoulders—firmly, it seemed to Randy—and it was evident from the look on her face, reluctant yet eager, that she was about to fall into his arms.

"He was a fucking quack," Sylvia was saying, "a real prick."

Another cat nuzzled against one of her shins, mewing. "Oh, Despair," she cried, "is my girl jealous?" She pushed the first cat off her and leaned forward to pick up Despair, who settled in her lap. "There, there, baby," she murmured, petting her, "Mama's here." She looked at Randy, then saw that he was staring at the novel. "Oh, you noticed that thing? Well, I wrote it."

Randy raised his head, his interest tweaked. "You're a writer?"

Sylvia grinned. "Not really. I mean, my stuff's just a lot of crap. You know, romance novels. Hugh's always giving me shit about them, says they're drivel."

"But writing must be cool."

She laughed. "Nah, it's like any other gig: It pays the bills."

He slid back, resting an elbow against the futon. Maybe I should tell her about Graham, he thought.

"Listen," she said, "are you sure I can't get you anything?"

"No, I'm fine." He ground his cigarette on the floor, glancing at Despair, fascinated by Sylvia's nimble movements as she caressed her back.

"I feel sort of ashamed that I freaked out earlier," she continued, a little sheepish. "You know, when we were talking about Hugh. He's not so bad really, just sort of spaced. You get mad at your boyfriends, don't you?"

"Uh…yeah, sure." Randy gripped the cover of the futon, wondering what Jake and Adrian were doing, how long they would stay at the apartment. He gazed at the paperback on the table.

"Sometimes I envy you gay men. It's like you're all so free. Things must be a lot easier." She paused, then, her voice faltering, added, "At least they must have been a few years ago." Another pause. "Sorry."

Randy looked up, wondering how Graham was. He caught a glimmer of sympathy on Sylvia's face, obvious even as her eyes darted about the room. She's a writer, too, he thought, weird but kind of nice. And interesting. He stared at her for a second, then, flushing, peered down at *Savage Surrender,* then at the aluminum foil on the desk. He noticed a residue of white powder there.

Sylvia took a deep breath. Randy looked at her. She was blushing. Apparently she had been following the path of his gaze.

She laughed nervously and said, "I guess you caught me. But...I mean, you take drugs occasionally, don't you?"

"Yeah...that is, every once in a while."

She smiled, relieved. "I don't like to do them much, but, you know, with all this moving and stuff ... well, I needed a little perk."

Randy studied the aluminum foil. Not much of the powder was left.

"You want a toot?"

Randy looked at her. "Is there any more?"

"Sure. Hugh's dealer has great coke."

Randy wondered what it would be like to get high with her. He didn't want to go back upstairs. He didn't want to go anywhere.

"Okay, that'd be great."

"Hold on, I'll be right back."

Pushing Despair onto the floor, she dashed to the kitchen and searched through a drawer, then returned with a tiny plastic bag full of white powder, a hand mirror, a razor blade, and a straw. Once she had seated herself, she tipped some of the powder onto the mirror and, using the razor, scraped up six lines. She sliced the straw in two.

"You first," she said. "It's really excellent stuff. Uncut."

They each did three lines. After her third one, Sylvia giggled. *"Mio caro!"* she exclaimed, grinning avidly and sniffling. "The best! Really, don't you think?"

Randy pulled himself up from the mirror, allowing the coke to slither down his sinuses, enjoying the bitter taste at the roof of his mouth. He nodded, answering, "Yeah."

Sylvia fell back onto the futon, her arms over her head, then quickly sat up. "But we need music, don't we? I mean, what's coke without some sounds? Is Joni Mitchell okay with you? The rest of the stuff's still packed."

"Sure." Randy felt the coke easing its way down to his throat; its taste was pleasantly acrid. His headache was gone.

Sylvia hurried to the phonograph and put on "Blue." The first song that played was the one Randy had heard in the hallway. He tried to remember what it was called.

"I love this one," Sylvia remarked as she sat. "It came out about the time I met Hugh."

"Yeah, I…" Randy took out a cigarette. Joni Mitchell trilled mournfully in the background.

Sylvia leaned in his direction. "What's that?"

"Well, I…I remember it, too."

"But you're so young. You must have been just a kid back then."

"Yeah, but…I mean, it was an oldie when I first heard it, but…" He dropped his eyes to the floor. "Well, it still makes me think of some things."

"Oh, yeah? Like what?"

He looked up; Sylvia's eyes were sparkling. He lit his cigarette. "You know, the late seventies. Or maybe the early eighties. People. A lot of stuff."

Sylvia smiled. "Yeah, I do know. That was the end of a really special time. You caught just a glimpse of it." She drained the last of the juice from her glass, then asked, "So what do you remember most?"

He stared at her face—inhaling smoke, hearing the music, everything startlingly vivid—and saw there a distinct curiosity, speckled with something else, a trace of kindness, perhaps. He wanted to respond to her question, to talk about the past. He knew she would understand; her unwavering expression told him that. But words seemed difficult.

With a quick little yelp, Despair leapt onto Sylvia's lap. "Oh, baby," she cooed, stroking her fur, "you've come back to Mama. Good girl." She gazed fondly at Despair, then off toward the kitchen, murmuring once again, "A really special time."

Randy tried to speak, but found himself unable to. He waited for her to say more. She suddenly appeared younger, less tired, her eyes bright, her skin glowing. She's been around a while, he told himself, she's probably seen a lot. Maybe she'd have some good stories to tell. And hearing her might give him words.

Two more cats settled at her feet, huddling together.

Petting Despair, Sylvia resumed talking: "What I liked was the freedom we had then. The sixties were great. I was a real beauty, you know, just like you." She ran a hand through her hair, laughing lightly. "I was all over the place. But to tell you the truth, I didn't know what I was doing. It wasn't until the seventies that I actually learned how to enjoy myself. That's when I met Hugh." She played with a strand of her hair, hesitating. "We never lived together, but... well, he got to me. He was this activist, a pretty famous one. Organized all these war protests, worked in the ecology movement. I'd heard a lot about him before we even met. And when we did meet, I couldn't believe he was interested in me. I mean, he seemed important, powerful." She lowered her hand to Despair, grasping her. "After we started going out, he taught me things. Took me to demonstrations, talked about politics. But it wasn't just that, he... well, he showed me stuff, things I'd never done before, like..." She blushed. "You know what I mean, don't you?"

"I...I'm not sure." Randy looked at the wall, seeing Jake, then Graham. He wanted her to stop, yet was desperate to hear more. He threw his cigarette onto the floor.

"You know. In bed. He did things that...I mean, I really lost myself. I loved the fact that I had no control over what we did."

He had a transient, startling vision of a much younger Sylvia, naked and enthralled, a huge, hairy man on top of her, pressing himself against her groin, her legs thrown over his shoulders. He dropped his eyes to the cover of *Savage Surrender*, to the man with the heaving chest, then quickly averted them toward the kitchen. He tried to focus on the juicer.

"Oh, shit, am I embarrassing you?" Sylvia's face was crimson. "I guess I'm embarrassing myself. But...I don't know, I just knew you'd understand. Gay men always do." She giggled, then added, "Besides, I'm absolutely ripped. You want some more?"

Randy wondered why she was telling him so much, then remembered John Stanley, how he'd mentioned trust. Sylvia trusts me, he thought. He looked down and saw that she was tapping out more coke.

"Come on," she said, passing him the straw, "let's not waste it."

He leaned over and, as if from an immense height, sucked in two lines. He fell back across the futon. Sylvia's voice gushed above him, overwhelming Joni Mitchell.

"Hugh loves coke. Always has, ever since I met him. We had such great times for a while." She stopped, her eyes narrowing.

Flat on his back, Randy looked up at her, suspecting that a new, troubling thought had entered her head.

Abruptly angry, Sylvia muttered, "I'm not sure when he became such a motherfucker. Probably when I started getting old." She emitted a sharp, bitter laugh.

He gazed at the bags under her eyes, which seemed to be drooping in the glow of the overhead light. They made her appear vulnerable. He wanted to touch her, just her arm, let her know he'd been through things, too.

"He's always hanging me up," she continued, her fury increasing. "Running after some young twat, some new piece of ass." She clasped Despair, then stared at him, bewildered. "Fuck, why am I talking to you like this? You're just a kid."

He remembered what she'd said about the shrink she'd seen, how he'd told her that she might have been abused, then wondered if he could mention Mr. Hewitt to her. He didn't want to say too much. But he was sure she'd never react the way Dakota and Denise had; she'd never laugh at him.

"It's so hard sometimes," she went on, looking away. "You know, growing old. It's like it happened overnight. One day I was this young thing, everyone after me, and then…well, fuck Hugh anyway!"

He took in her face, her watery eyes, and worried that she was about to cry. He wanted to tell her something, talk about Jake, his affair with Adrian. But he was afraid to say anything, knew he could never be open with her, never tell her about his clients, those men with their sweaty demands, talk about the money they gave him, how he shared this with Jake. He felt himself blushing.

"It hasn't been good for a while," she murmured. "Seems like I'm by myself most of the time these days. Jesus, it's depressing!"

He imagined her alone, waiting for Hugh, and wondered how anyone could treat her in this way. He couldn't envision Hugh, what was like. But he was convinced that he didn't deserve Sylvia, that she didn't deserve *this*. He sensed a wave of hatred welling up in his guts and grasped for words. Sputtering, he cried, "But…but why do you put up with it?"

The music stopped. Sylvia stared down at him. A wispy smile appeared on her lips but quickly disappeared, replaced by a blank, stony expression, one Randy found impossible to read. She peered at him for a second, then smiled again, thinly. "You wouldn't know, would you?" she asked disdainfully. "I mean, what it's like. You're young."

He looked away from her, at the ceiling. The connection he'd felt started to float away, as if carried off by the draft which was once again apparent. He wanted to hold onto it, change the subject, chatter about anything else. Then he realized he could talk about Graham. He hadn't had a chance before. Now it seemed important that he do so.

At that moment, outside in the hallway, Adrian's piercing voice rang out clearly: "Come on, Jake, we're late!"

The cats at Sylvia's feet darted up, awakened by the sound. They ran to the kitchen. Hissing, Despair jumped from Sylvia's lap and followed them. Two more cats emerged from the back of the apartment and joined the other three.

Randy shot upright and drew his legs together.

Sylvia fixed her eyes on him, studying him carefully, then laughed and drawled, "Oh, I see." Her words were weighted with sarcasm. Even more pointedly, she added, *"Friends?"*

Rattled, Randy looked toward the kitchen and saw the cats hiding behind the counter. He heard Jake in the hallway: "All right, Addie, all right. Christ!" The front door slammed. They were gone.

He immediately stood and said, "I've gotta go."

Sylvia looked at him, her dry amusement rapidly fading. "Oh, okay," she answered tersely. She raised a hand to her hair and, her expression softening, asked, "Do you have to?"

"Yeah, I…I've got some stuff to do."

"You'll come back, won't you?"

He caught a pathetic edge in her tone and felt a tug pulling him toward her. He considered staying, telling her about Graham, maybe talking about Dennis, too. But the vulnerability he saw on her face was becoming frightening, a little repellent. He started to back away. "Sure, I'll…I'll come back later. Or you can come up to my place."

She frowned, as if trying to decipher his words, then quickly smiled and exclaimed, brightly, "Great. Maybe tomorrow."

"Okay."

He hurried to the door. Sylvia and the cats followed him. Despair rubbed her head against one of his calves, mewing.

"Later," Sylvia said as she let him out.

Despair howled.

Indications of Adrian's recent presence were everywhere: Items of his clothing were scattered about the bedroom, socks, underwear, and jeans dropped on the floor, a dirty green shirt thrown across the bedstand. His essence seemed to hang in the air, along with the still-powerful odor of his cologne. Motionless by the doorway, Randy took it all in, regretting that he had ever left Sylvia's, that he hadn't stayed with her and shared some more lines. He was coming down, which made what he saw appear all the worse.

He sat on the bed, then noticed two used glasses and a tube of lubricant on the bedside table. His pulse became animated, and he forced his eyes away, recalling Sylvia. Hugh *is* a motherfucker, he thought. The hatred he had felt downstairs returned. He suspected that her whole life had been difficult.

He turned to the bedside table. On the rim of one of the glasses was a smudge of lip gloss. That's Adrian's, he told himself; Jake never uses that shit. He gazed at the glass, thinking of Adrian's thin, smarmy lips. He grabbed it. "Pigs!" he screamed, hurling it against the far wall. The sound of it smashing was immensely satisfying. "Pigs!" He stared across the room at the pile of broken glass, breathing quickly. Then he stretched out on the bed.

He felt something beneath him and reached down to pull it up. It was his copy of Graham's book *Summer Swan,* the one he had stolen months before. He couldn't understand how it had gotten here, who had been reading it. Not Jake, he was certain; he never read anything. Yet he didn't want to think that Adrian had touched it. He almost tossed it on the floor. Instead he held onto it for a few seconds before, impulsively, turning to a page near the end.

"Any trust is a betrayal," he read. "What you see is only a part of it. Once you have peeled back the layers of his lies, you uncover the truth. It is a horror that even you had not imagined."

He looked up, unsettled. He couldn't remember having read this passage before. He looked down and read it again, then several more times. The telephone rang.

Graham! he thought. He grasped the receiver. "Yeah?"

"Oh, sugar, it's you!"

Although the piping voice was familiar, Randy had a difficult time placing it; he had been too absorbed in his attempts at understanding Graham's words. Then it came to him. "Fey?"

"Yes, sugar," Fey answered, laughing. "I told you I'd call. We want you to come over. John says we've gotta get moving on the play."

"When?" Randy realized he was glad to hear Fey's voice. What had happened the night before didn't seem important anymore.

"Well, tonight's out. I've gotta watch the bar for Jo. But tomorrow would be good." Fey giggled, then added, "I hope we didn't freak you out too much last night. We get carried away sometimes, particularly around beauties like you. We won't do it again. John gave us more hell after you left."

"That's okay." Randy reached over to the bedside table and found a pack of cigarettes.

"John went upstate this afternoon, you know. To her parent's."

"He…he did?"

"She almost didn't make it, she was so hungover. But they're loaded, so we forced her to, pushed her out the door."

Randy took a cigarette from the pack and lit it. He wondered if he wanted to go to Fey's now that John wasn't going to be around.

"She's not gonna be gone long," Fey continued, as if reading Randy's mind. "Just overnight. She's gonna ask them for some money. We've gotta find a theater and everything. Plus a cast. All that's not cheap these days, sugar, believe me."

"So he's gonna be back tomorrow?"

"Sure." Fey chuckled and asked, "What time are you gonna come?"

"What time do you want me to be there?"

"Oh, whenever you want." Fey sounded thrilled. "In the afternoon, I guess. Not *too* early. But come."

"Okay."

"You remember where we are?"

"Yeah, I think so."

"So we'll see you, sugar. It'll be flawless."

Randy hung up, excited. He had a plan, something to do for a change. He was sure he'd be safe with Fey and Stella; John Stanley would see to that. Anyway, the play would keep them busy.

There was one thing he anticipated above all else: He knew that he'd have many opportunities to speak with John. He wanted to ask him questions, find out more about what it had been like years before. He just hoped that John wasn't going to be too drunk.

Looking at the bedside table, he saw the remaining glass, Jake's, an inch of beer at the bottom. He took one last drag on his cigarette and dropped it into the liquid, enjoying the hissing sound of the ember sizzling out. Then he crawled under the covers, fully clothed, and switched off the light.

"Any trust is a betrayal," he whispered, approaching unconsciousness. He pushed his face into the pillow. Sylvia floated before him, laughing, then mournful, surrounded by darkness. He wished he'd been able to talk about Graham with her.

XVI

The building's boiler broke down that night. Randy awoke at four in the morning, freezing, his covers pulled up to his nose. There had been intermittent problems with the heat throughout the winter. Whenever Jake complained, the superintendent assured him that he was taking care of things.

Shivering, Randy rolled over, noting that Jake was not there. "Motherfucker," he muttered. He bent his legs toward his chest and curled into a ball, trying to ignore the cold. Hearing the wind outside, the familiar pounding of the rain, he recalled Sylvia, then wondered if Hugh had shown up. He drifted back to sleep.

He dreamed he and Sylvia were alone in a house, each in bed

though in separate rooms, both rooms on the ground floor. Lying beneath numerous blankets, he peered through a small opened porthole onto the street. He was certain he was in New York, yet felt as if he were in another, possibly foreign place—London, maybe, because of the thick fog he saw—or in a small town somewhere, perhaps in the Midwest. He watched pedestrians stroll past. No one looked in.

Then Graham walked by. Randy called out to him. Graham leaned over and poked his head into the room. Randy noticed how extraordinarily thin he was.

"Oh, there you are, baby," Graham whispered. "I've been looking everywhere for you." He fell onto his knees and tried to squeeze through the porthole. It started to shrink, closing in on his waist, and he dissolved into the fog.

"Graham!" Randy cried. "Graham?" There was no response. The light disappeared, and he sensed a body lying next to him, an icy hand unzipping his pants. He suspected this was Hugh. The hand slipped under his shorts and grasped his penis. He felt his erection pressing against its chill.

He opened his eyes. A body was indeed beside him, Jake's, his frigid hand clutching him. He quickly moved back, drawing his penis away. "Fuck off!" he screamed. "Why don't you just take it to Adrian?" His words seemed to roar across the room and echo against the walls.

Jake frowned, looking shocked and a little hurt. "What do you mean, sweetheart?" He edged up to Randy and tried to snuggle against him. "The heat's off again. That fucking super never takes care of anything. Your baby's cold."

"That's your problem." Randy turned over, his erection wilting. He stared at the bedside clock. It was two—in the afternoon, he supposed. He remained still, wanting to sleep. Then he saw Graham as he had been in the dream, dissolving. Breathing rapidly, he threw his legs over the side of the bed and sat up. He no longer noticed the chill.

Jake crawled over and touched his side. "Sweetheart?"

Randy pulled away, cringing. "It's late," he said, a resolve in his tone that felt unfamiliar. "I've got things to do."

"Oh, yeah?" Jake sounded surprised. He slid a hand under

Randy's shirt and massaged his lower back. "I thought m'baby and I could have a little fun. We haven't done that in a while, have we, sweetheart?"

Randy jumped up and found his shoes. "Forget it, I'm busy." He grabbed a cigarette from the pack on the bedside table and, sneering, asked, "So where's Adrian?"

Jake flushed. Then a tiny smile slipped onto his lips. "With that agent. You know, Harold Lynch, the guy he met at Donald Trump's. Adrian called him this morning. Harold told him to come right over."

Randy detected a trace of pride in Jake's voice. He lit his cigarette and snapped, "I suppose it's Harold who's gonna be fucking Adrian now."

Jake widened his eyes, his smile vanishing. "Shit, sweetheart," he exclaimed, seemingly wounded, "why are you being such a bitch? This is business."

"Yeah, *right.*" Gripping his cigarette, Randy hurried to the closet and seized a light-blue shirt from a hanger.

Jake remained on the bed. "So…so what's m'baby doing today?"

Randy removed the shirt he was wearing, dropped it on the floor, and ground his cigarette out beside it. He turned around and gazed at Jake, then was convinced that he saw an imploring look on his face, an uncertainty there that was touching. He listened to the rain outside and felt a draft on his bare chest. He took a step in Jake's direction.

Jake stretched out an arm. "Stay," he murmured. "Please. I've gotta meet Adrian in an hour, so we don't have much time."

Randy froze. The vulnerability he'd caught in Jake's expression a moment before was gone, replaced by a miniscule grin. "Fucking cunt!" he shouted. He threw on the shirt he'd been holding, ran back to the closet, and grabbed his coat.

Jake leapt out of bed. "What did I say?"

Randy glared at him, incredulous. "You really don't…" Shaking, he tossed on his coat.

"Sweetheart!"

Randy sprinted from the bedroom.

"Sweetheart!" Jake called again.

The apartment door slammed behind Randy.

*

The wind was as bad as the rain, bursting across the block in sharp gusts. Randy stood under the awning in front of his building, having brought no umbrella. He had neglected, too, to bring money with him, and considered dashing back upstairs. Yet the idea of seeing Jake, of hearing his feeble excuses and listening to his stupid lies, revolted him. He couldn't go back; he had to move.

He sped north, thinking of Jake. He worried that he might be overreacting and tried to push his anger down. He began to run. He barely noticed the downpour.

By the time he reached 14th Street and Third Avenue, he was winded and completely soaked. He stopped, unable to locate Fey's building. Nothing looked familiar: There was no bodega he recognized, no newsstand or restaurant. It was unusually dark for this time of day, and the wet, nearly deserted block appeared peculiarly alien. Frightened, he searched for a cab. Then he remembered that he had no money.

A figure stepped out from a doorway and veered toward him. His stomach heaving, Randy hurried east, looking downward. But the figure was quicker than he, and was soon at his side.

"Hey, man, I'm hungry."

Randy glanced up and saw a boy, probably no older than fifteen, with greasy blond hair, jaundiced skin, and loose, shredded clothes. He was filthy, dirt running down with the rain on his face, and he had a rancid odor. Despite this, Randy felt that he would have been pretty if it weren't for his odd little grin and his unsettlingly dull eyes, which shifted blankly from Randy to the street, then back to Randy. He's really nuts, Randy thought, and walked faster.

The boy thrust himself in front of him. "Come on, man, give me some change. You can afford it." He scratched his arm, muttering words that were incomprehensible.

Randy tried to walk around him, but the boy, smiling weakly, blocked his path. "I'll suck your cock," he whispered.

Randy pushed past him and rushed on.

The boy ran after him. "Fucker!" he screamed. "I'm sick and tired of you and all your rich faggot friends. You've caused me to lose hundreds of thousands of dollars. If you don't fucking get it back for me, I'll fucking slit your throat!"

A voice rang out above the rain: "Give it a rest, Danny!"

His heart thudding miserably, Randy looked up. Fey was a few yards away, emerging from a tiny store and carrying a brown grocery bag, an old gray poncho draped over his huge frame.

The boy looked up as well. "Fuck off, faggot! Mind your own fucking business." He picked at his arm. "Fat, fucking homo!"

Fey scooted over, then stood before him, leaning forward. He was at least six inches taller than Danny and three times his weight. "Listen, sugar," he growled, his voice uncharacteristically deep, "go peddle your slime at Bellevue."

"Fuck off!" Danny exclaimed once more, less vehemently this time.

Fey grabbed his arm and leaned further toward him. "I'll break your fucking neck!"

Danny stared back, his eyes wide open, his lips quivering. For a second Randy thought that he looked like a child, a frightened little boy. It seemed as if he were about to cry.

"You heard me," Fey roared. "Get lost! Crawl back to your hole!"

Danny glanced up, now scowling, no longer childlike. Randy was certain he was going to lunge at Fey. Instead, after pausing briefly, he lurched away. "Motherfucker!" he screamed over his shoulder.

"Crazy sleaze!" Fey screamed back at him. Then, to Randy, his pitch instantly higher: "That's all we need, right, sugar? Some demented faggot hassling us! That one's always hanging around here. Everyone knows her. Stella told me she used to be kept by this rich fashion fruit, some piss-elegant queen. I guess the kid freaked out and Miss Pissy got tired of her." He turned toward Danny's departing form, which was stumbling west, then looked at Randy and, breathy, said, "Anyway, we've got enough problems with John."

"John?" Drenched and shivering, Randy gazed at Fey, wanting to rush home.

"She's a mess, right?"

"What…?"

"Come on, we'll talk about it inside. We're drowning. I mean, sugar, you look like a mop."

The grocery bag in his arms, Fey strutted toward a nearby apartment building. It did not look at all familiar to Randy. He remained where he was, trying to forget about Danny, to decipher what Fey had said about John. At last, reluctant, he joined Fey.

"She's ruining everything," Fey complained as he opened the door. "How can we do the play if she's not around?"

They walked into the hallway. Again Randy recognized nothing. He gripped the wet denim of his jeans. "What…what happened to John?"

Fey wrinkled his brow and stared at Randy. "You really haven't heard?"

"Heard what?"

"Why, John's in a rehab. She called this morning. At *nine*. That mad queen was so bombed when she arrived at her parents…well, they just checked her right in. Said they'd cut her off without a penny if she didn't stay there."

Shivering even more than he had done outside, Randy thought of Haircut, then tried to find a reason to leave. He wanted a drink, a pill.

"Don't worry, sugar, we'll figure it out. Stella's at the apartment. And I just bought some beer."

"Yeah. Yeah, sure." Dazed, Randy followed Fey up the stairs.

Stella was waiting inside Fey's apartment, standing by the front door. His distress mirrored Fey's.

"I can't believe she did this to us," he cried when they entered. He spoke as if Fey had never left. "I mean, hon, a *rehab!*"

"She's a beast," Fey sighed. "We've always known that."

Stella stood on his toes and looked inside the bag in Fey's arms. He crinkled his nose, moaning, "Oooo, Colt 45! That's a nigger's drink! How could you?"

"Listen, sugar, it was on sale. You know we're broke. I went to Jo's bar, but that bitch Kevin wouldn't give me anything."

Randy remained by the entryway, uncertain as to what he should do. Stella hadn't even acknowledged him. He looked toward the living room, seeing, as he had the last time he'd been here, piles of glitter and strips of gauzy fabric strewn across the floor. Further in, he noticed Jo in her room, on her cot, dressed in the same blue nightrobe she'd worn before, Piewacket asleep beside her. She was awake, sitting up and reading a *Photoplay,* her face bright red, covered with several layers of makeup. He wondered if they had found all of Piewacket's kittens.

"Don't just stand there, sugar," Fey said to him. "Come on in, dry off. We've gotta get started, figure out what we're gonna do."

Stella motioned toward the bag Fey was carrying. "Gimme one of those beers, will you?"

"Calm down, girl, don't get your pussy all tied up in knots. I bought three six-packs." Fey dropped the bag onto the floor by Randy's feet. Stella dove into it and grabbed a can.

Randy slowly moved to the living room. He could hear Jo in her bedroom.

"Farley Granger!" She looked up from the *Photoplay,* her expression merry, and spoke to Fey. "What a pansy, right, Frankie?"

"Leave her alone, Jo," Fey called back to her, laughing. "You know that old queen's dead."

"Sure, but he was still some fruitcake." Chuckling blithely, Jo continued reading.

Randy stood by the living room's three mattresses, one hand in a coat pocket, grasping his pack of cigarettes. He wished he had the nerve to bolt out the door.

Fey pulled his poncho over his head and tossed it onto one of the mattresses. He was wearing a Hawaiian shirt, patterned with bright orange flowers set against a vivid blue and green background, the colors vibrant under the overhead light's glare. As before, his jeans were much too tight.

"Sit down, sugar," he said to Randy. "I mean, you're gonna be here for a while, aren't you?"

Stella sidled over and grazed one of Randy's arms with his fingertips. "Why don't you take off those clothes? We'll dry them out for you."

Randy flinched, shrinking away from him.

Fey chewed on his lower lip. "Slut!" he muttered at Stella. His face relaxing, he turned to Randy. "Look, we're not gonna eat you. Or rape you either." He raised a hand to his mouth and giggled. "John'd never forgive us for that."

Clutching his beer, Stella grinned. "I'll say! She made *that* clear. She wants you for herself."

Randy blushed. "It's…it's not like that."

"What's that, sugar?"

He couldn't look back at Fey. "I mean, I…I've got a boyfriend at home."

Stella slugged down some beer. "Of course you do, hon. A beauty like you!"

Fey frowned. "Look, bitch, you're making her nervous!" Again smiling, he spoke to Randy: "Relax, sugar, have a seat. Tell us all about your man."

Randy backed away from him, down onto one of the mattresses.

Fey ran to the entryway and grabbed the grocery bag from the floor, then returned and sat next to Randy. Stella sat on Randy's other side.

"Is she big and hairy?" Fey gushed, pulling two beers from the bag. "A real macho?" He passed one can to Randy and kept the other for himself.

"And her pechunga," Stella added, "tell us about that. Is it huge?"

Fey glared at him.

"Oh, chill out, hon!" Stella cried. "Why don't you just hand me another one of those vile 45s?"

With a sigh, Fey complied.

Randy let his eyes wander to Jo's room. She was still reading, grinning happily, Piewacket by her side. He swallowed half of his beer, then turned back to Fey and Stella, wondering if it was safe to leave yet, if Jake was at Adrian's.

Stella seized a Kool from a pack on the floor, lit it, and, a fresh beer in one hand, hopped to his feet. "Listen," he said to Fey, pacing in front of him, "we've gotta figure out what we're gonna do. You know, about John. And the play."

"She'll be back," Fey insisted. "She promised me that. She'll never last at that rehab."

"Yeah, sure, but…" Stella took a quick puff on his cigarette. "Shit, we've gotta do something now. John wanted the play to be ready in six weeks. He said if we opened in time, we'd probably get an Obie."

Randy swigged his beer, finishing it, then reached into his coat pocket for a cigarette and looked down at the floor, wishing he were still in bed, that he hadn't gotten so angry with Jake. But Jake's a fuck, he thought.

"What's the matter, sugar?" Fey touched Randy's arm.

Startled, Randy edged away from him.

"Oh, come on!" Fey cried, indignant. "I told you we're not gonna do anything to you. I mean, we've already had you. Besides..." He studied Randy, momentarily pensive. Then, his voice much softer: "Why, sugar, you really are upset about something, aren't you?"

"Wha...what?" Randy looked back at Fey, surprised by his tone, which was gentle for him, and by his expression, unusually serious.

Stella returned to the mattress and sat beside Randy, leaning toward him. "Have another beer, hon. Tell your sisters what's bothering you." He grinned, then, eager, asked, "Did you have a fight with your husband?"

"She doesn't want to talk about it with *you!*" Fey snapped.

Randy opened a second beer and lit the cigarette he was holding, unable to look at either of them, not knowing what to say or do.

"Come on, sugar," Fey continued emphatically, "you said you'd help us with the play. That'll make you feel better. You'll forget about everything, whatever it is that's bothering you."

"Yeah," Stella agreed, "it's gonna be a real trip. And there's a part in it that's perfect for you."

"I don't know, I..." Randy drew on his cigarette, staring down between his legs at the mattress. He was sure he'd never said he'd be in their play; he'd only promised to help them out. "I don't think I'd be right."

"Get over it, hon." Stella gulped some beer. "You'll be flawless."

Fey glowered at him. "Lay off, girl. She can make up her own mind."

"Beast!" Stella hissed.

Just then a voice pealed out from behind them: "I see you queens are up to your usual shit."

Randy turned around. Jo was shuffling out from her bedroom, her robe partially opened, enabling him to see the pink slip she was wearing beneath it. As she moved closer to them, he stared at her chest, noticing how soft the skin there looked, how pale it was, almost as white as her hair. He found the contrast with her rouged, lined face amazing.

"You two are always carrying on about something," Jo cackled. She ambled up to Stella, who was smiling back at her, a beer in one hand, a cigarette in the other. "Give me one of those Kools, will you, Lester?" she said to him.

Stella passed her the pack of cigarettes. "You wanna beer, too, Jo? All we got is this piss Fey bought."

"Nah, I gotta work. I told Kevin I'd be down at the bar by five." She lit a cigarette and, for the first time, looked at Randy. She seemed amused. "So who's the pretty boy, Frankie? I've never seen this trick around here before."

Randy's eyes darted from her chest up to her face, then down to her chest again. He observed a cluster of thin blue veins running across her wrinkled cleavage, visible above her slip.

"That's Randy," Fey answered. "She's gonna help us with the play."

Jo grinned. "So, Randy, are you gonna be one of their cocks?" She puffed on her cigarette and chuckled. "You know, in space."

Randy glanced up. "Well, uh, no I...I'm just helping them out a little."

"Be careful," Jo laughed, "it's a bad business. *Cocks in Space*, my ass. Who cares about a bunch of faggots on Venus?"

"But, Jo, it's gonna be fabulous," Fey protested. "Really."

"Yeah, sure." Jo took another drag from her cigarette. "They don't know entertainment for shit these days, haven't for years. And you told me yourself all those old queens are dead."

"We'll find new stars," Stella insisted.

"Sure, sure."

"Don't you remember, Jo?" Fey leapt to his feet. "Andy loved it the first time we put it on."

"Andy Schmandy!" Jo harrumphed. "That queen's dead, too."

Randy gazed into Jo's bedroom and saw Piewacket on the cot, perched on her hind legs, staring toward the living room. When he looked at her, she jumped onto the floor and hid in a corner.

"And that John Stanley," Jo was saying, "I don't know how you all can put up with *him*. What a wacko! You won't see that queen for a while, believe me. You might as well kiss your play's silly ass good-bye and get some real jobs." She crushed her half-finished cigarette in an ashtray and said, "Like maybe the both of you helping me out at the bar."

Randy lowered his eyes, then lifted a strip of fabric from the floor and balled it up in his right hand.

"John's a genius!" Fey persisted. "And she'll be back soon. She promised."

"Yeah, yeah, yeah."

"Barbara had problems, too," Stella threw in. "Some of her pictures got delayed for months. She told me so."

"Oh, right, Stanwyck!" Jo chuckled. "Get over it, Lester, grow up!" Grabbing another Kool from the pack, she turned away, muttering, "Well, girls, have fun. I'm gonna go douche. This bitch has gotta *work.*" She lit the cigarette in her hand, then looked back at Fey. "Listen, Frankie, I wanna see you down at the bar later, okay? Kevin says it's gonna be packed tonight. Some sort of Ukranian holiday."

"But, Jo…"

"Just be there!" Her cigarette dangling from her lips, Jo sauntered to the bathroom.

No one said anything for a few seconds. The silence made Randy uneasy. He dropped the fabric he was holding, wondering if it was true what Jo had said, that John wouldn't be back for a while. He grasped his beer, but found that he'd finished it.

Fey reclaimed his seat on the mattress and spoke to him: "Don't pay attention to Jo. She doesn't know what she's talking about."

"Right," Stella concurred. "I mean, she's flawless, but…well, she can be a horror sometimes."

"She doesn't mean any harm," Fey said, still to Randy. "She's just senile."

"Yeah, sure." Randy looked downward, extinguishing his cigarette and lighting a new one. He felt numb.

"Sugar, what's wrong? Come on, cheer up!"

Randy looked up at Fey's beaming face, then at his shirt, at the bulk of his chest straining against the flowery material.

"There're a million other husbands out there," Stella offered, moving closer to him.

"That's not it," Fey interjected, testy. He turned to Randy and murmured, "You miss John, don't you?"

Randy peered past him, taking a deep drag on his cigarette.

"She'll be back," Fey promised. "I told you that. Really, she will. Even sooner than we think."

"Yeah, hon. Why don't you just chill out and have another beer?" Stella reached into the grocery bag and passed a can to Randy.

They were silent once more, for nearly half a minute. Randy opened his beer and took a fast slug. He wondered what Jake had thought after their fight, if he was thinking about it now.

Fey jumped up. "I know what she needs. Yes! Listen, sugar, it's time for Miss Trixie!"

Stella clasped her hands together and squealed, "Oooo, Trixie!"

Fey scurried to a far corner of the room and found his tape deck and a cassette, then hurried back and held the tape up for Randy. "Some peddler was selling this on St. Mark's Place yesterday. Believe me, sugar, we snatched it right up. It's Miss Trixie's best. I hadn't heard it in years."

"It's *fabulous*," Stella chimed in. *"Flawless."*

Randy gazed at the cassette in Fey's hand, an album called "Frugging with Trixie and the Wonders." The photograph on its cover was of three young black women, each with straightened hair, all three dressed in loose shirts and casual slacks, their clothing luridly colorful, lime green, chartreuse, and pink. They were dancing, hands on their hips or flung in the air, and grinning wildly, teeth sparkling.

Fey leaned toward him, enthusiastic. "You like Miss Trixie, don't you, sugar?"

"Yeah, sure." He remembered being ten or eleven and seeing an article called "A Go-Go World" in a back issue of *Life* magazine, one he'd stolen from Mr. Hewitt (it had been old even then), reading about Chubby Checker and The Peppermint Lounge, the Twist and the Frug. That was when it all began, he thought. He wondered what Graham had been doing at that time, where he'd been.

Impatient, Stella puffed on his cigarette. "Come on, hon, let's hear her."

"Right!" Fey swung around, away from Randy. "Miss Trixie!"

Randy eased back and watched Fey insert the cassette into the recorder. A smile slipped onto his face.

The tape's quality was poor, scratchy; the music sounded as old as it was. The moment the orchestra's tinny introduction began, Stella shimmied up and, in a flash, started dancing with Fey, both of them twisting and frugging, warbling with the Wonders.

"Oh, baby cakes!" sang Fey, echoing Trixie.

"Sweetie pie!" Stella answered, continuing the refrain.

They spiraled up and down and threw their hands in the air, singing jubilantly, nearly subsuming the sound of the tape: "I love you, baby cakes! You're my sweetie pie!"

The floor was shaking, the music booming. From the corner of one eye, Randy saw Piewacket scamper out of Jo's room to hide in the kitchen. He focused on Fey and Stella, studying Fey's brightly flowered shirt, its colors blurring as Fey frugged madly, his movements agile. Skinny Stella was clumsy, stumbling across the fabric on the floor, waving his arms awkwardly above his head and grinning, his decayed teeth prominent. The music washed over Randy. He thought it sounded great, catchy, even beautiful, and wondered if he'd ever heard it at Mike's. He realized there was nothing to worry about. He was with friends; he could trust them. And John would be back soon.

"Baby cakes," Fey and Stella sang to Randy, urging him to join them, "can't you tell I adore you? I love my baby cakes. You've got me, sweetie pie."

He finished his beer and grasped another one, wanting to stand, to dance and sing, too, then decided it was better to just watch, let the music blanket him.

"Baby cakes, you've got me begging. Make me yours. I'm mad for my sweetie pie."

Twirling wildly, Fey lifted his right leg behind him, leaning forward, his arms stretched toward the glare of the overhead light. The orchestra reached a crescendo.

And then the music stopped.

"Jesus Christ!" a voice shot out from behind their backs.

Randy turned around. Jo was standing beside the tape deck, dressed in bright red slacks and a checkered work shirt, her hands on her hips. She had applied more makeup, and her face was even redder than before.

"Don't you queens ever quit?" she complained, irked but laughing. "A girl can't hear herself think!"

Smiling back at Jo, Stella ceased his movements. Fey continued to dance, shaking his huge hips and twisting obliviously, shouting the words of the now-silent music: "You've got me begging, baby cakes. Make me yours, make me yours."

"Come on, Frankie," Jo screamed at him, "relax!"

Jo's command penetrated Fey's fog, and he fell forward, then broke his fall by throwing his hands to the floor, at the same time flinging his hips up. His jeans ripped apart at the seat, revealing an immense pair of baggy shorts, their red and yellow polka dots sticking out through the torn seam.

"Fuck!" Fey gasped, turning crimson. Loosing his balance, he slipped again and finished his descent, landing on the floor with an enormous thud.

Jo and Stella began to howl.

"Look at that queen!" Stella roared. He pointed at Fey's shorts. "She's Little Dot."

"He's a Lulu all right!" Jo shrieked, her face scarlet.

Randy stared at Fey, who was now prone on the floor, his legs curled into his chest, giggling uncontrollably. This is too bizarre, he thought, and yet . . .

He started to laugh, softly at first, a bit frightened by the sound. As his eyes darted up to Stella and Jo, both of them doubled over, overcome, then back to Fey, who was rolling about yelping, his laughter grew stronger, bursting forth in breathless peals that overpowered the others'. It all seemed ridiculous. He fell back onto the mattress, consumed by his mirth.

"Look at her!" Stella motioned toward Randy. "She's gonna die!"

Seeing Randy's condition, Fey and Jo squealed.

"She's bursting!" Fey shrieked. He rolled onto his stomach and kicked his legs.

"Pretty boy's gonna piss in his pants," Jo whooped shrilly.

Their laughter went on for several minutes, loudly and uproariously, until, tears running down her face, Jo glanced at her watch. "Jeez, look at the time. You queens are gonna make me late again."

"Sure, Jo." Fey could not stop chuckling. "Go."

The merriment continued after Jo left, only slightly more sub-dued. Randy, like the others, could not contain himself.

Exhausted from laughing, Fey swept an arm across the fabric by his feet. "Come on, you bitches!" He moved up onto the mattress next to Randy. "We gotta work, start getting all this crap together."

"Yeah, yeah." Stella gulped his beer and, suppressing a giggle, burped.

Randy stared at the fabric, which appeared to stretch out for miles in front of him, reams and reams of pink and red strips, acres of gauzy material lying next to mountainous heaps of glitter. Trying not to laugh, he asked, "What are we supposed to do with this anyway?"

"Yeah, hon." Stella grabbed a piece of fabric. "How are we gonna make costumes out of all this shit?"

Fey creased his brow, then, in a rapid movement, reached under the table nearest him and found a pill bottle. "This'll do it," he said as he unscrewed the cap. He tapped three black pills into his hand.

Randy gazed at the pills resting on Fey's palm, shining under the overhead light. "What are those?" he asked. He searched for his cigarettes.

Stella raised a hand to his mouth and guffawed.

"Why, sugar, you've never seen them? They're really hard to get nowadays." Fey passed one of the pills to Randy. "These are black beauties." He handed the second pill to Stella and, slugging his beer, took the third one himself. Then, again to Randy, excited: "You know, *speed.*"

"Oh, right." Randy's eyes wandered to the kitchen, where he noticed Piewacket peeking through the doorway. He looked down at the shiny black pill he was holding. It was sticky from his perspiration. What the fuck, he thought. He placed it on his tongue.

"Fabulous, sugar! Now let's get moving." Fey grabbed a strip of fabric from the floor with one hand and switched on the recorder with the other.

In the next few hours, he played Miss Trixie's tape eight times.

It was after midnight when Randy stumbled through the door-way to his apartment, giddy from the chaos at Fey's, sorry it had ended when Jo returned and ordered Fey down to the bar. Inside, he heard the telephone ringing in the bedroom. He ran to it, but stood still once he got there. It's just that fuck Jake, he thought. He decided not to answer. The phone stopped after twenty rings.

He lay on the bed, waiting for the two tuinols he'd taken just before he left Fey's to kick in, noticing then a note on the bedside table. He picked it up and stared at the words, trying to decipher Jake's careless scrawl. Each letter leapt at him, disconnected from the others. He squinted his eyes, until he was able to make sense of it.

"I've gone out," it read. "Don't know when I'll be back. I hope you've calmed down. That weird woman downstairs stopped by, Sylvia something. Said you invited her over. What the fuck's going on? J."

He read this three times, then crushed the paper into a ball and threw it on the floor. "Cunt!" he muttered, stretching out on the bed. He gazed at the ceiling, taking fast breaths. He didn't want to be here.

The telephone rang again, jolting him. Furious, he sat up and grabbed the receiver.

"What?" he screamed.

"Oh, baby," came the voice on the other end, speaking indistinctly. "Baby, I've found you at last."

Despite the faint tone, Randy knew who it was. He felt his palm growing moist on the receiver. "Graham," he whispered.

"Yes, baby, it's me, back from the dead. I've been trying to reach you. For hours. Did you get the money I sent you?"

"Yeah," Randy mumbled, "thanks a lot." He paused. Then, quickly, scarcely aware of what he was saying: "I've really missed you."

"Oh, and I've missed you, too, baby. You'll never know." Graham started coughing violently. Controlling it, he murmured, weaker, "I've missed those tight little buns of yours. Thinking about them is all that's kept me alive, I'm sure."

"When can I see you?"

"God knows, baby, I certainly don't. I'm sick as hell, have been ever since I talked to you the other day. Another relapse, unfortunately. I'm better than I was, I suppose, but still wretched." He began coughing again, his fit this time alarmingly sustained.

Randy lay back on his bed, suddenly dizzy. "Are…are you okay?" he asked as the coughing died down.

"It's…I'm all right." Graham was wheezing. "This has been happening all day. My doctor said it'd be a while before those drugs I've been taking start to help." He took a long, raspy breath. "But he said I'd get better. Then we can get together, baby, I promise." His coughing erupted once more.

Clinging to the receiver, Randy asked, "Should…shouldn't you be, you know, resting, taking it easy or something?"

It took a moment for Graham to recover. Annoyed, he snapped, "Don't worry about it! Christ, I can't sleep anyway! It hurts to lay still."

"Sor…sorry." Randy turned onto his stomach, his dizziness worse. The tuinols were beginning to take effect.

"I'd better go," Graham said hurriedly. "Fuck, I can't even talk on the phone anymore."

"But when…?"

"Please. Let me go. I'll call you as soon as I can." Coughing, he managed to say, under his breath, hoarsely, "I love you, Dennis."

"What?" The room began to spin.

Graham hung up.

Randy threw down the receiver. Everything was reeling. He closed his eyes, and it all disappeared.

XVII

In the weeks that followed, Randy received money regularly from Graham, but heard nothing from him. He did his best not to worry—after all, he reasoned, it's going to take time for Graham to get better—and tried not to invent morbid scenarios, as he was prone to do. Every day he took at least one pill from the bottle of dexedrine he'd stolen, which helped him gloss over everything.

If he and Jake were alone together, they watched television mutely and smoked joints—although Randy couldn't concentrate on the screen if he was with Jake; he was much too conscious of his flaws. He noticed that Jake was getting a slight paunch, that his hairline was receding and his feet smelled. While watching TV,

Jake liked to pick at his toenails, a habit Randy had ignored before. Now it revolted him.

"Shit," he complained one afternoon as Jake scraped the cuticle of his large left toe with a roach clip, "that's disgusting. It's making me sick."

Jake glanced up, flushed. "Jesus Christ," he answered tersely, "you're such a fucking prig. Mind your own fucking business." He put the clip down and gazed at the TV. Their silence resumed. Within five minutes, he was working on his toe again.

Randy kept a mental inventory of Jake's faults, which he loved to review, picturing Jake's face, always sneering. He found that this augmented his anger in a pleasing way, providing a gratifying heft to their silence.

This silence was made more conspicuous by the fact that Jake did not see Adrian as often as he had, only two or three times a week. Apparently Adrian was busy with Harold Lynch and his prospective modelling career.

"Adrian's networking," Jake enthused. "You know, he and Harold have gotta go to all these fashion parties, shows and shit."

Catching a defensiveness in Jake's tone, partially hidden by his boastful voice, Randy only smirked.

One morning he was in bed sleeping when Jake rushed in.

"Get up," Jake cried, shaking Randy's shoulder. "Right now."

"What?" Drowsy, Randy opened his eyes. Jake was standing above him, his jaw protruding. Randy rolled over.

"Come on." Jake again shook Randy's shoulder, more forcefully this time. "Franklin Kent's expecting you."

"Fuck off!" Randy wrapped his pillow around his head. He had been with Fey and Stella until four that morning. "What's the matter with Adrian? He can jerk Franklin off."

Jake sat on the bed and placed a hand on the blanket, over Randy's leg. He's gonna try and sweet talk me, Randy thought, shifting away.

"Sweetheart, please." Jake's tone was softer, pleading. "Adrian's having some pictures taken. You know, for his portfolio. Harold arranged the shoot days ago."

"Well then, *you* go see Franklin." Randy gripped his pillow, pushing it further against his ears.

"*Sweetheart.*" Jake squeezed the blanket above Randy's leg. "You know that'd never work out. Franklin likes 'em young. Anyway, he asked for you." He slipped his hand under the blanket and caressed Randy's thigh.

Randy sat up wearily, afraid he would never be able to get back to sleep. He reached over to the bedside table for his cigarettes and lit one, then stared at Jake. His eyes looked alert, his expression tense. Randy dragged on his cigarette, too tired to argue.

Jake's lips parted, and his face started to relax. "M'baby'll do that for me, won't he? This one time?" He pinched Randy's thigh. "Come on, get dressed."

There was just then an edge to Jake's voice, smugly imperious. Randy pulled his leg away. "No!" he shouted, suddenly determined.

"*What?*" Jake grabbed one of Randy's cigarettes, his face turning bright red. "So what are you gonna do, hang around here? Or go see those fucking queens?" He lit the cigarette. "Jesus, what a waste!"

"What's it to you?" Randy cried. "I'm not asking you for anything." This was true; Graham had sent him money the day before.

"Oh, right, you've got Mason to take care of you now, don't you?" Jake inhaled on his cigarette, fuming. "God, you're pathetic! I mean, what are you gonna do when Graham…?"

Randy became aware of his heart thudding furiously. He ground out his cigarette and lit a fresh one. "What's that?"

Jake laughed dryly, ending with a short little snort. "Oh, never mind. Do whatever the fuck you want."

Randy threw his cigarette into the ashtray and lay down, again gripping his pillow and wrapping it around his head. "Why don't you just shut the fuck up, okay? Leave me alone!"

Jake crushed his cigarette out next to Randy's, then stood. "Little shit!" he muttered. He stomped out of the room.

Randy clutched his pillow. He could hear Jake in the living room, making calls. Let the motherfucker find someone else, he thought. The fury he was experiencing seemed to waft through the room's heavy air and pour down with the rain he heard outside. He wanted to feel nothing, to drift away.

He listened to Jake on the phone: "It'll be easy, Roger. Franklin's a pussy."

He remembered Roger, a buffed, muscular actor he'd met at The Scrotum the year before. What an asshole! he said to himself—but then Jake is, too. He raised his knees to his chest and curled up tightly.

"So you know where he lives?" Jake's voice sounded louder, horribly so. "Yeah, that's right, two blocks from Barneys."

Randy squeezed his eyelids together. His heart felt as if it were ripping his chest apart. He wanted to get up and find his pills.

"Okay, so I'll see you later."

He heard Jake drop the phone into the receiver and return to the bedroom.

"Well, sweetheart," he said, his voice rippling with sarcasm, "you can get your beauty rest now. Roger's gonna take care of Franklin."

Randy pretended he was asleep.

"Sweetheart?"

He didn't move.

Jake was silent until, a moment later, Randy heard him tiptoe to the bureau by the wall, open a drawer, and rifle through its contents.

Randy shot up. "What the fuck do you think you're doing?"

Jake looked over at him, startled, a wad of bills in his hand. "Oh, sweetheart," he said gently, his anger no longer evident, "I didn't want to bother you. I found someone for Franklin, and I...I was gonna go out. I just wanted to...you know, I was gonna borrow some money from you."

"Well, you can't. It's mine. Put it back."

Jake arched his brow. "Oh, come on!"

"I said put it back!"

Jake glared at him. "Fuck, what about all the times I gave you shit? What about that?"

"I earned it!"

Jake stood rigidly, shocked. Furious, he dropped the bills into the drawer and banged it shut. "Fucking A, I was gonna pay you back!"

"Yeah, sure." Randy grabbed a cigarette.

Jake squinted, glowering at him. "God, you're a fucker! A real jerk!"

"You'd know, wouldn't you?" Randy lit his cigarette and met Jake's eyes.

Jake's face was immobile, crimson. "Asshole!" he hissed, creeping forward.

Randy's muscles tightened. It looked as if Jake were about to pounce on him. He felt ready, prepared for anything.

Jake continued to glare at him. Finally he screamed, "Why don't you just go fuck yourself?" He sped from the room.

"Yeah, run, motherfucker!" Randy shouted after him.

The apartment door slammed.

Randy's heart was beating madly. He smoked several cigarettes, unable to move. What an asshole, he said to himself, what a fuck, what a pig. He started to feel dizzy and lay down. For a second he couldn't breathe. He bolted up, gasping, and glanced at the bedside clock. It was past noon. Fey and Stella'll be awake by now, he thought.

He jumped out of bed and darted to the bureau, still dizzy, though less so than he'd been. He opened a drawer and saw his money, next to it his dexedrine. He tossed two pills into his mouth, found his clothes on the floor, and threw them on. He wavered, catching his breath, until his dizziness was almost gone. Then he returned to the bureau and grabbed the wad of bills from the drawer. He wanted to stop at a bank on his way to Fey's and open his own account. He'd always used Jake's in the past.

As the weeks flew by, Randy's arguments with Jake became common. They fought about everything: Randy's refusal to see clients (although Jake had a knack for finding replacements); what they'd watch on TV; who was monopolizing the blankets in bed. When they weren't arguing, they talked even less than they had before. Jake wasn't around a good deal of the time, despite Adrian's involvement with Harold Lynch. Randy had no idea what he was doing.

He enjoyed stopping off at Sylvia's to snort coke. There he found himself lulled by the old music she played and soothed by her chatter about the past. They went to movies, romantic comedies and tearjerkers—"silly pictures," Sylvia called them. But for the most part, they stayed at her place, just the two of them and her cats. He didn't talk much, yet he liked being with her, seeing a friendly face. The spell was only broken if Hugh entered the conversation. Randy still hadn't met him and didn't want to.

His evening at Fey's and the play Fey and Stella were planning took up much of his time throughout March. It didn't matter to him (or, it seemed, to Fey and Stella) that their progress in creating costumes was snaillike, that they spent more time gossiping or dancing than they did working, that the pile of fabric on the floor remained enormous, the completed costumes few. When it became obvious to Fey that John Stanley's ambitions for the play were too grandiose—they had not as yet managed to find a performance space, let alone a cast—he and Stella decided they would scale the production down and cut out all the scenes except their own, turn it into a showcase for the two of them, an outlet for their long-dormant talents. "We were the stars anyway," Fey declared. "We're the ones people want to see." Randy didn't care what they did; he was having fun.

John had not returned, although, Fey said, he and Stella spoke to him daily. "She's coming back soon," Fey insisted. "She's sick of that rehab. Just a few more weeks and she'll be here." Randy liked being reassured. He missed John—inordinately, it seemed to him, since he had only met him once. At times his memories of John merged with his recollections of Graham, so that neither's face was quite distinct from the other's. He found this surprising, yet somehow it made sense to him.

He was fascinated by Fey and Stella's stories, and liked hearing about their lives during the sixties and seventies. Those decades jumbled together in their rapid banter, but this didn't matter to him. The sixties, the seventies: He couldn't see the difference. He only knew that he hadn't been there and that the sweetness had not been around.

He was particularly intrigued by the tales they told of Max's Kansas City, a steak-and-ribs restaurant on Park Avenue South, closed now for many years. Every night in those days, they explained—sometime in the sixties or seventies, Randy didn't know exactly when—they'd get high on some drug, usually crystal meth, then head for Max's, for its rear dining room, a dimly lit, cluttered space with works by contemporary artists on the walls. According to Fey and Stella, this was a room that attracted some of the more flamboyant residents of New York: the trendiest artists and writers, pretty boys, models, speed freaks, coke and acid heads.

"It was demented," Fey shrieked. "Sugar, we were all stars then." They met celebrities there. Fey mentioned a noted Italian director who came to Max's at least once a month to scout for faces, "freaks" to appear as extras in his films. Stella talked about a prominent Hollywood starlet who had a fling with Amanda Jade, one of Fey and Stella's intimates, a renowned transsexual. But the main attractions, they claimed, were the regulars at Max's, especially the more eccentric ones. These habitués could be counted on to provide a show every night.

Priscilla Douche liked to dance on table tops, then strip to her panties as she sang in a distinctive, husky voice, "There's No Business Like Show Business." Johnny Mouth gave blow jobs, his specialty, to any man who wanted one, usually in Max's men's room. Toothless George, a tall, hirsute Southerner and the heir to a tobacco fortune, dispensed shots of methedrine while dressed in nurse's drag.

"They were all so sick," Stella gushed approvingly.

"Flawless," Fey agreed.

Anything, they said, could happen there, at least from midnight until four or five in the morning. Everyone was free, wild and open, much more so than people were now. And whatever they did, there were no dire consequences.

Hearing this, Randy wondered what his life would have been like if he had been in his twenties years before. He remembered the fabulous things Graham had talked about, the glamorous clubs, the gallery openings, the Broadway premieres and film screenings, and felt that it had been different back then. Today's world didn't seem right to him. He wanted more.

On the last day of March, a grim Sunday, just after he'd roused himself at six in the evening, Randy learned that Jake was about to go to the Fire Island Pines for a week.

"Harold went to California on some business," Jake told him, the glee in his voice blatant. "He's letting Adrian use his summer house out there." He paused before he added, leering, "It's gonna be great. I mean, the only thing to do on The Pines this time of year is fuck."

Randy tried to ignore the tightening of his gut, a prickling on his skin. "Do whatever the fuck you want," he mumbled, "I don't give a shit." The very mention of Adrian's name grated on him—although Jake hadn't talked about him in over a week. Let the motherfucker get it while he can, he thought; Adrian's gonna dump him again anyway.

"You gotta admit, sweetheart," Jake drawled, his leer growing broader, "Addie's got the best butt in town."

Randy froze, then clenched a fist and, in a barely perceptible movement, started toward Jake. Shaking, he stopped himself. "Why don't you just fuck that faggot to death?" he cried. "See if I care."

"Why, *sweetheart*," Jake sneered, placing a malicious emphasis on the last word.

"Fucking cunt!" Randy ran to the bedroom, found his dexedrine in the bureau drawer, and swallowed three.

"I'll be gone when you get back," Jake called as Randy rushed to the front door.

"Great!"

Jake laughed. "Stay high, sweetheart!"

Although it was frigid outside, Randy perspired as he moved, hurrying toward Fey's across flooded streets. It had been raining all day, as it had been for weeks, but had stopped for the moment. It looked as if it could start again at any time. Everything he saw appeared dank: the few pedestrians who passed him, bundled up in their jackets, folded umbrellas under their arms; several panhandlers, all soaked, asking for change; even the street lamps, shining out through the moist darkness. He wanted to kill Jake and was considering ways he could do it—with a knife or a gun, or with his bare hands—when he came upon two teenage girls standing by a used-clothing store, huddled together and laughing.

"It was awesome," one of them was saying, drawing a strand of long black hair across her full red lips.

"So awesome," the other agreed, grinning.

This second girl was carrying a radio, and Randy heard a song coming from it, a man's falsetto voice lilting sweetly:

Oooh, baby, those nights,
the night we met,
the night you left.
Oooh, baby, those nights.

He stopped in his tracks, startled by an unexpected pull that he sensed in his depths. An orchestra followed the refrain, then a chorus of women, chiming in:

Oooh, baby, those nights,
those nights,
Oooh, baby, those nights.

Mellow, he thought, then wondered why that word had popped into his head. He'd heard this song before, but could not remember when; he just knew it was old. He edged his way to the store, keeping his distance from the girls, hearing the man's voice:

The night we met, baby,
the night we kissed.
Oooh, baby, those nights.

He was overcome by a feeling of loss, one so deep he was afraid he was going to cry. He stared into the store's dark window, at a display of bright spring shirts and light khaki pants.

"C'mon, Yvonne, let's go," the first girl said to her friend. "Johnny's waitin' for us."

"Sure, all right," the second girl replied eagerly.

They moved on, giggling, taking the song with them. Randy heard the chorus fading:

Bring back those nights, baby,
bring them back.
Oooh, baby, those nights.

The girls turned a corner, and the music was gone.

It started to drizzle, then pour. Randy remained by the store, unable to move, gazing at the rain washing down the window, blown against the pane in gusts. He stared at his image in the glass, barely visible, at the patterns flowing across it, sparkling under the street lamps. The glowing, effervescent water made him think of Fey and Stella, Graham and Dennis, their lives. It circled his face, touching its edges, giving it a brief, garish tint. As it trickled away, his reflection again became obscure. He studied his likeness, pulsating dimly, and saw that he was drenched, that his hair was plastered to his forehead, appearing to him like peeling layers of skin. He found himself grotesque, a deformed, hideous thing.

Just then, in the glass, he thought he saw Mr. Hewitt's face leering in the shadows. He reeled around. No one was there.

He wiped his brow and took several deep breaths. The words of the song he'd heard came back to him:

Oooh, baby, those nights,
those nights.
Oooh, baby those nights.

He felt the sense of loss creeping up on him once more and, terrified, rushed off.

He was still agitated when he arrived at Fey's, and Fey and Stella didn't help. Both were in foul moods.

"Come on," Stella moaned as Fey inserted a Ronettes cassette into the tape deck, "not them again."

"So what do you wanna hear?" Fey asked, irritated. "Miss Trixie?"

"No!" Stella shrieked emphatically. "Shit, we've been listening to those sixties bitches for weeks. How about something different, some disco diva?"

"Jeez!" Fey switched on the recorder. "Get over yourself, sugar. I hate that shit."

"Disco's fabulous!" Stella insisted. "It makes me think of hunks in leather bars."

Randy imagined Dennis dressed in leather. He leaned forward and found a cigarette.

"Forget it," Fey snapped, adamant. He turned up the volume on the tape deck. "We're gonna listen to this."

"Girlfriend," Stella hissed, "you're a beast."

Randy stared at the fabric on the floor, at the two costumes Fey and Stella had managed to create, a pink tutu for Fey and a shabby-looking red-velvet gown, which Stella was supposed to wear in his final scene. They planned on making at least ten more.

Fey and Stella continued to bicker.

The next day Randy awoke at noon, not remembering having come home or going to bed. Jake had not returned; Randy assumed he had already gone to The Pines with Adrian. Fucking shits, he thought, and rolled over.

He remained in bed for most of the afternoon. Occasionally he thought of the song he'd heard and tried to recall when he'd heard it before. The memory of it made him melancholy; he didn't know why.

At four, a messenger arrived with an envelope from Graham. It contained several large bills but no note. After stuffing the money in his wallet, Randy stared at the handwriting on the envelope. It looked weak and insubstantial, and this unsettled him. Gripping the envelope, he hurried to the telephone, wanting to hear Graham's voice. He was unable to make the call; he worried that he'd be bothering Graham or, worse, that there would be no answer. He walked to the TV.

A talk show was on. The host, a stocky, dark-haired woman, was interviewing three married couples. All the wives had remained with their husbands despite the fact that they were beaten regularly.

"How can you do this to yourself?" the host asked one of the women, a thin blond seated next to her husband, a pale man with a red mustache. "Don't you..." She looked directly at the camera, a rapt concern on her face. "Don't you have any *self-esteem?*"

The woman started to cry. "But, Jeanette," she sobbed, her voice cracking, "I *love* him. We love *each other.*"

Her husband nodded his head in assent.

Randy's stomach started to churn. He felt submerged in the voices coming from the screen. He switched off the TV and rolled a joint, staring at a shirt of Jake's on the floor. He wished something would happen, that something would change.

He smoked the joint, then decided to go back to sleep. Reaching into his pants pocket, he found one of the tuinols that Fey had given him the night before and swallowed it. He rose, grabbed a beer from the refrigerator, took off his clothes, and crawled into bed. He drank half of his beer and smoked two cigarettes. Then the tuinol kicked in.

He dreamed he was with Fey and Stella at Max's, a large, cavernous club, much like The Scrotum. In the back, he could see hundreds of men cramped together in a small, bright room. Some wore leather, others nothing at all. A woman dressed only in her panties danced on a table.

The crowd dissolved, and he saw Graham in a corner, caressing Dennis, who was nude. He watched Graham stroke Dennis's penis, running his other hand across his chest. Erect, he glanced at Graham's face; he was now John Stanley and was crying.

In another corner, he heard a cracking sound. He whirled around and glimpsed Mark Randall tied to a column, naked. Mr. Hewitt was behind him, holding a whip. A dozen men surrounded them, masturbating. Mark's buttocks were red.

In the distance, a song started to play:

Oooh, baby, those nights,
the night we met,
the night you left.
Oooh, baby, those nights.

He awoke with a start, then realized the music he was hearing was coming from the street. He listened to it:

Bring back those nights, baby,
bring them back.
Oooh, baby, those nights.

He had a piercing vision of the gas station in Canada, of a bare-chested Mark ambling across its parking lot toward Mr. Hewitt's car. A song floated out from inside the station, coming from a radio:

Oooh, baby, those nights,
those nights.
Oooh, baby, those nights.

He stared at Mark's tawny skin, longing to touch it. The song ended, and he heard the mellifluous voice of a woman announcing, "That was the mellow sound of Chris Jackman." Mark reached the car.

Trembling, he came back, sobbing. He cried for half an hour. Exhausted, he turned onto his stomach. His sobs gradually subsided. He lay quietly, recalling his dream. A warmth rippled through him. Gripping his pillow, he rubbed his penis against the sheets and closed his eyes.

He saw himself as Dennis at Max's, now a dark, squalid club, the smell of poppers in the air. Disco music blasted as hundreds of men stood nearby, all sweating and staring at him. He passed through the crowd effortlessly, his eyes darting from face to face, searching. Hands grasped at his buttocks and groin. He ignored them.

He stopped when he reached a pitch-black room, its darkness impenetrable. He could feel the press of bodies against him, sweaty flesh, and could hear the rustle of denim and leather, a smacking of lips, soft moans. Relaxing, he felt a penis sliding against his thigh. He clutched it instinctively; it was erect, thick, immense. The darkness around him parted. He was sure then that he had found the most beautiful, most desirable man at the bar, in the universe really. He could feel it in the pounding of his own cock, in the beating of his heart. He fell to his knees, onto the floor, which seemed, because of his calm, like the aisle of a church. He lowered his lips to the penis in his hand, kissing its tip and licking its shaft. The calm overwhelmed him.

Outside, he saw other men on the street, their arms draped over each other's shoulders, strolling in the early morning light, a seventies light. Their smiles were bright, and all had a startlingly healthy glow to them, a glow of sex, of satiation, a glow that came from their certainty that they were living in Paradise.

He opened his eyes, roused by a sharp, cold draft. He became aware of a moisture beneath him and sat up, shaking. He forced his mind back to the room, trying to clear his head. But he couldn't stop thinking that his life was over, that he'd missed it. Dennis was dead. Graham was dying. Those had been times unlike any seen before or since. They would never be seen again.

Although he couldn't remember, he suspected that he'd taken another tuinol. He could see by the light outside that it was the next day. His skull felt as if it had been shattered. The telephone was ringing. With a lumbering motion, he rolled toward it, then saw himself lift the receiver to his ear. "Yeah," he whispered.

"Baby," a voice cried, excited, "baby, it's me! All better now, completely well!"

Randy stared at the wall before him. The voice sounded like Graham's. It can't be him, Randy thought; he's too sick. The receiver felt heavy in his hand.

"You're not sleeping, are you? Come on, get up, it's almost noon. I want you to come over. Now. As soon as you can."

"Right." Randy lay back on the bed and burrowed down toward the blankets.

"Listen, you got that money I sent you yesterday, didn't you? You can take a cab."

Randy shut his eyes. The covers were warm, the sheets snug against him.

"You *are* coming now, aren't you?" The voice sounded impatient. "I really can't wait, you know."

"Yeah. Yeah, sure." He reopened his eyes and lay still.

"Well, *good.*" A giggle. Then: "Look, Dakota's supposed to call me, so I've got to go. But don't be long, you hear?"

"Uh-huh." Randy felt his head sink into the pillow.

"Good. Good, baby. I'll see you very soon then. Oh, yes, I can't wait." There was an abrupt click.

Randy tossed the receiver onto the bedside table, curled up, and pulled the covers to his chin. I'm dreaming, he told himself. An instant later, he was asleep.

Suddenly the ceiling light was on, its glare horrid. He was almost blinded. He could just make out a nude figure, Jake's, pacing back and forth in front of the bed. Where the fuck did he come from? Randy wondered.

"Oh, sweetheart, sweetheart," Jake moaned, "I've missed m'baby so much."

Randy raised a hand to his eyes, blocking out the light. Specks of red and green floated before him.

"I've been so bad to m'baby," Jake continued, nearly sobbing, his voice more forceful. "Really bad. How could I trust that cocksucker, that hustler, that little fuck?"

Randy watched as the specks seemed to fly around him.

Jake sat on the bed and lowered his head onto Randy's stomach, clutching his knees. "You'll forgive me, won't you, sweetheart? I'll be good. It'll be just like old times again, I promise."

Randy heard his own voice, coming from behind him, its tone steady: "So what happened?" He was surprised that he was able to talk at all.

Jake shifted a hand down between Randy's legs and rubbed a finger against his anus. Randy shivered. "That doesn't matter," Jake said. "Me and m'baby are together, that's all that's important."

"What happened?" Randy's tone had become harsher, yet he wanted to remain detached. He wanted to sleep.

"Oh, sweetheart, don't, please," Jake wailed, hurt. "I've had such a hard time."

Randy attempted to stare at Jake's face, sensing a sadness there. He lifted his right hand and, for a second, moved it toward him. Shuddering, he stopped himself, looking away.

Jake inserted his finger into Randy, massaging his sphincter. Randy's back stiffened. He tried to remain numb. Jake leaned toward his neck and kissed him lightly on the throat. "Addie's just a little shit," he muttered. Sheepish, he gazed plaintively at Randy.

"What happened?" Randy asked again, his voice now icy. He pulled his hips away from Jake, forcing Jake's finger to slide out.

"It's just…" Jake was flustered; his face turned red. Speaking frantically, he murmured, "It's just that Harold Lynch called to say he was coming back early, that he was gonna come out to The Pines. He said he wanted to see Adrian and…and…" He narrowed his eyes, then, incredulous, cried, "Jesus, Addie made me *leave!* I mean, shit, sweetheart, I'd just gotten there and everything. Harold wasn't even gonna arrive for another day."

Randy noticed beads of sweat on Jake's upper lip. He nearly laughed.

Jake stretched out on the bed and lay there, breathing erratically. He threw an arm across Randy's chest and curled against his side. "Baby, baby," he whispered, "m'sweet, sweet baby."

Randy could smell fumes of alcohol emanating from Jake.

Jake lifted his head and glanced at him, grinning—like an idiot, Randy thought. "Isn't m'baby happy? Aren't you glad I'm back?"

Randy was silent.

Moving impetuously, Jake crawled on top of him and grazed his neck with his lips. "Let's forget about those fucks, okay, sweetheart? They're all just cunts anyway." He lay across Randy, completely covering him.

As Jake's weight pressed into his groin, Randy began to perspire. He pushed at Jake's chest and tried to wriggle free. "Get the fuck off of me, okay?"

"What?" Jake sounded surprised. He took hold of Randy's arms and rubbed his penis against him. "C'mon," he mumbled, "don't be such a cocktease. I just wanna be nice to m'baby, that's all."

Randy smelled Jake's fetid breath, felt his flesh, his paunch, his sweat dripping onto his face. He pronounced each word distinctly: "I…said…get…off."

Jake laughed, then ran his tongue across Randy's lips, attempting to slip it into his mouth. "Sweetheart," he murmured with a smile.

Randy felt his stomach heaving. Clenching his jaw, he raised a knee and rammed it into Jake's gut. "Motherfucker!" he screamed, darting up.

Jake fell onto the bed, clasping his stomach, in shock. "Jesus Christ!" he gasped. He caught his breath and, recovering rapidly, hurled himself at Randy, forcing him down. Then he crawled onto his chest, straddling his sides with his legs and clutching his arms. "What the fuck do you think you're doing?"

Randy's reply came out in a rapid burst: "I'm just sick of your shit, that's all, you fucking pig!" He tried to raise his arms to shove Jake off, but Jake's grasp was too strong.

Jake's mouth was hanging open, his eyes woozy. Randy felt smothered, crushed. He dug his nails into Jake's legs and made another, more desperate attempt to push him off. Jake's grip remained firm. A grin appeared on his lips, and he produced a short, odd laugh. "You really want it, don't you sweetheart? That's what this is about." He slid down and grabbed Randy's legs, pulling them up.

"Cocksucker!" Randy spat out, twisting frenziedly. He kicked at Jake's groin, but missed.

Jake laughed once more. "C'mon, sweetheart, it's been too long." Pushing Randy's legs further back, he thrust himself toward him.

As soon as Randy felt Jake's penis begin to enter him, his blood rushed to his brain, and his arms shot up, clasping Jake's throat with a power that amazed him. "Don't touch me, motherfucker!" He tightened his grip. "Don't ever touch me again."

Jake fell back, Randy on top of him, clinging to his neck. Jake gagged. Randy relinquished his hold on his throat and began pummeling his chest, his legs, and his face. "Motherfucker!" he screamed. "Cocksucker!" Jake covered his head with his hands and rolled over, shouting, "Jesus, you crazy fuck!" but Randy continued to pound on him, ignoring his cries, striking him repeatedly.

Terrified, Jake pulled himself away. He jumped off the bed, his complexion red, drops of blood trickling from his nose. "You're fucking nuts!" he shrieked, his voice quivering. He glared at Randy, then, turning quickly, ran to the bathroom and locked the door.

Randy stared at his hands, panting. He wanted to follow Jake and break down the bathroom door. He knew that he had the strength. Sweat streamed down his sides. He remained on the bed, listening to the water running in the bathroom. He hoped Jake was in there cringing, suffering.

Suddenly he began to tremble, sensing a dread, a familiar feeling of emptiness creeping up on him. He didn't know what to do.

Then a thought came to him.

"Fucking psycho!" Jake bellowed over the sound of running water. "Shit, you need help!"

Randy was not listening. He was thinking about the phone call he'd received earlier. His memory of it was fuzzy, yet he was certain now that it hadn't been a dream. Graham had recovered. He'd asked him to come over. He was late.

He searched for his clothes.

XVIII

Randy's conviction that Graham had recuperated became more and more palpable as he rushed west, the relief that he was experiencing overwhelming everything else and pushing him onward. It wasn't until he reached Sheridan Square that he noticed how warm it was and realized the sun was out and shining brightly. Spring had arrived, for good this time, he was sure. He paused, allowing the sunlight to flood across his face and into his pores. He felt free. Jake doesn't matter, he told himself; Graham's well.

He saw under his open coat that his shirt, damp with sweat, was hanging out over his pants. He had neglected to tie one of his shoes. He laughed as he crouched down, feeling a hint of the dexedrine he had taken before leaving his apartment. He straightened up and was dazzled by the sunshine. He closed his eyes, then reopened them. Everything seemed to come together in a blast of whiteness: mothers with strollers sauntering by, young children beside them; men in leather jackets, ambling down Christopher Street toward the piers; a few businessmen in suits and ties, talking on cellular phones. He looked up at a clock just above the doorway to a tobacco store and saw that it was ten past three, almost twenty-four hours since he'd gone to bed the previous afternoon. I'm late, he thought; Graham's going to be pissed.

He hurried across Seventh Avenue, then stopped in front of an outdoor café, trying to remember how to get to Graham's building. It had been so long since he'd been there, he'd forgotten the exact route. The café's terrace was packed with diners wearing summer clothes, women in flowered dresses, men in thin shirts. He glanced to his left, hoping to find Perry Street, and observed a tall, dark-haired boy, seedily handsome, gyrating next to a pay phone. He appeared to be dancing to some tune in his head.

Just then, to his right, Randy heard a voice calling out to him: "Randy?"

Jarred, he turned, but could see no one he knew.

"Randy!"

He suddenly noticed a familiar figure in the distance, twenty yards away, standing by a table in the terrace of the café. "Haircut," Randy whispered.

Haircut ran out from the terrace and up to him, beaming. "Randy," he cried, "this is the answer!" He threw his arms around Randy's neck. Randy stiffened. Oblivious to this, Haircut hugged him. "How've you been?"

Randy backed away, studying Haircut. His skin was rosy, his hair completely dark, apparently its natural color, longer, straggly and unstyled. It all seemed unreal.

"How's everything?" Haircut asked.

Haircut's tone was different, too, Randy felt, not at all caustic. He wondered when he'd gotten out of the hospital, what had happened to him since then. "Fine, I guess," he answered.

"That's good." Haircut smiled.

Randy stared over Haircut's shoulders at the boy by the phone, who, swinging rhythmically back and forth, was removing his shirt. He could think of nothing to say.

Haircut broke the silence: "I was just talking about you."

"Oh, yeah?"

"Yeah. Actually, I've been thinking about you a lot."

Randy looked down at the sidewalk.

"You were the only one who bothered to come and see me at the hospital, you know. I mean, besides Ma." Haircut wavered before, a little shyly, adding, "That was real nice of you. I was a bitch then, I know, but…well, I'm really grateful for it. I owe you an amends."

Randy pictured Haircut as he had been that day, remembered the lesions he'd seen on his skin, which was now so clear. He reached into his shirt pocket for his cigarettes, edging further away.

"So what's happening?" Haircut continued cheerfully. "How's Jake?"

"Ok...okay." Randy lit a cigarette and muttered, "The same."

"Right." Haircut gazed at him.

Randy blushed. Speaking rapidly, he said, "I've been real busy."

"Yeah?"

"Uh-huh. I've been meeting all these new people. This woman, Sylvia, moved in downstairs. And I've been working on this play, with Fey Ray and Stella Dallas. You know, those drag queens."

Haircut laughed. "Oh, sure, I've heard of them. They were in those movies back in the sixties." He stopped, frowning. "Don't they do a lot of drugs or something?"

"No...no, not really." Randy could not look at Haircut. "I mean, no more than anyone else."

Haircut shook his head. "I don't know about that. I heard they did. But anyway, as long as you're okay..." He hesitated, then, in a burst of enthusiasm, announced, "Listen, I just got ninety days."

"What?" Randy peered at him. He had no idea what he was talking about.

"Ninety days clean and dry. I'm sober."

"Oh, yeah?" Randy drew on his cigarette, trying to think of an excuse to leave.

"Yeah, I'm going to meetings. Every day. It's the answer, really."

"Meetings?"

"You know, AA."

Randy's eyes darted over to the boy by the phone, who, bare-chested, was lifting his arms in the air and swaying. Randy grasped his cigarette, desperate to move on. It was late.

"I've surrendered," Haircut explained. "I mean, Randy, my life was *so* unmanageable. You of all people know what a mess I was."

"I...I guess so."

"I'm different now." Haircut's voice seemed a bit uncertain. "I really am, don't you think?"

"Uh-huh, sure." Randy concentrated on the boy, who, seeing Randy, winked.

"You should come with me sometime," Haircut offered, once

again eager. "You know, to a meeting. They're fabulous. And a lot of them are gay. Believe me, it's the best place to meet men these days."

"Right." Randy was finding it difficult to stand still. He noticed the boy thrusting a hand down the front of his pants.

"I'm dating someone myself," Haircut went on. "Met him the third day I was there. I mean, I wasn't supposed to get involved with anyone the first year. My sponsor told me that. But then…well, the important thing is progress, not perfection, don't you think, Randy? And I couldn't help it." He looked downward, reddening, and, softly, nearly inaudibly, said, "He's old and he's fat, but he loves me." Lifting his head, he motioned toward the café. "He's over there now."

Randy turned toward the café's terrace and glimpsed a heavy, middle-aged man sitting alone at the table where Haircut had been. When this man saw Randy staring at him, he smiled and waved. Randy turned back to Haircut.

"Leonard's helped me a lot," Haircut explained effusively. "You know, with everything that's been going down. When I found out I was positive, I freaked. And then getting sober! But Leonard's real serene. He's been in the program for years, worked all the steps."

"Steps?" Randy noticed that the boy by the phone had unfastened the top button of his pants and moved his hand further in toward his crotch. Looking away, Randy checked the clock above the tobacco store. It was three-thirty.

"You've heard of the Twelve Steps, haven't you? Leonard's teaching me all about them. I'm learning how to turn my shit over." Haircut glanced behind him at Leonard, who was grinning at them from his table. Returning to Randy, Haircut said, "Why don't you come over and meet him? He's cool. You'll really like him."

Randy saw the boy staggering away from the phone. Still gyrating, he looked back over his shoulder and winked at Randy one last time. "I…I can't," Randy replied. "I'm late."

Haircut stared at him. "Seeing a client?" Then, immediately: "Sorry. It's none of my business."

Randy again felt himself blush. He wished Haircut would disappear, that he hadn't run into him. How the fuck am I gonna get away from here? he wondered. "I…I'm not doing that anymore."

"Oh, no? Me neither. I can't now that I'm sober."

Randy crushed his cigarette on the sidewalk and mumbled, "I'm seeing a friend."

"*Friend?*" Haircut appeared confused. Smiling faintly, he said, "Oh...oh, right." He stopped before uttering, quickly, "Does Jake know about this?"

"Jake can go fuck himself!" Randy spat back. Once he'd spoken, he was surprised by his words and the vehemence of his tone, shocked that he had even been able to say this.

"Oh, I see." Haircut's eyes briefly twinkled; for that instant he resembled his old, chafing self. Randy thought he was about to laugh. But then, abruptly serious, Haircut looked down at Randy's shirttail, evidently noting for the first time that it was hanging out. "What's going on, Randy? I mean, tell me the truth, is everything really okay?"

"Yeah. Sure." Irritated and edgy, Randy found it hard to speak. "Look, I...I've gotta get going."

"Oh, okay, but..." Haircut turned his head toward Leonard, then looked back at Randy and, earnest, asked, "You've got my number, don't you?"

"Uh-huh." Randy started to move away.

"Call me."

Randy tried to smile. "Okay, sure."

"Or I'll come and see you."

"Right."

"This week, maybe?"

"Sure."

"Great. I'll be there."

Randy spun around and, nearly running, sped west.

The sunlight began to feel relentless, the unexpected warmth of the day stifling. Desperate to reach Graham's, he tore off his coat, pushing through the throng of pedestrians, which seemed to be growing thicker, closing in on him. He felt nauseous. Nothing was distinct, just a glaring mass of light. A car alarm sounded in the distance. He stood still; he thought he was going to faint. Gasping, he sucked air into his lungs, then looked upward. He saw a street sign; he had reached Perry Street.

The world came back into focus. He heard laughter and noticed two women passing him, chatting amiably. He realized he was smiling at them and that they were smiling back. Music was coming from somewhere, an old disco hit. He sprinted to the street sign and turned left.

He knew where he was now, remembered every building, the trees in front of them, the restaurant on the corner. He found Graham's brownstone and read its number, 152. The numerals seemed to shoot out at him. I'm here, he told himself; it's where I belong. He thought of Haircut, his rosy expression, his words, then stared at a dark window on the building's top floor, one he knew was Graham's. *That's* the answer, he decided.

He bounded up the steps, but stopped at the front door, recalling himself naked on Graham's floor, kneeling, leaning over his bed. His head was pounding. He lifted a hand and clenched his jaw. Moving decisively, he rang the buzzer.

Two older men walked by, one with a beard. They were arguing. "No!" the bearded man cried. "No, that's not it at all!"

"What is it then?" the second asked, exasperated. "What do you mean?"

They continued east, and their voices faded.

Randy rang the buzzer again, then stood quietly, wondering if Graham's call had been a dream. Maybe I'm still asleep, he thought; maybe this isn't happening.

Suddenly Graham's voice boomed through the speaker. "Who is it?" he screamed, sounding angry. A pause. Then, louder, even angrier: "What do you want?"

Shaking, Randy leaned over. "It's…it's Randy." His voice was almost a whisper. He worried that he'd made a mistake.

"What's that?"

"Randy," he said, still tentative but more distinctively.

"Oh, well, it's about fucking time!" The door clicked.

Randy pushed the door and walked in. He stood in the building's hallway, adjusting to the dimness. Loud music was drifting down from upstairs. He knew it was coming from Graham's. Graham really is well, he thought, unsettled yet relieved. He crept to the foot of the stairs, then, walking lightly, started up.

At the top, Graham's door was open. He could see no light inside, but music blasted out. "Oh, baby," a male voice sang. "Oh, baby, come on!" Cautious, he approached the door and knocked. There was no answer. His heart rapped in his chest. He wondered if Graham was playing a game and knocked a second time. Again, no response. He waited a few seconds, then slipped past the door.

Inside, all the blinds were drawn. One small lamp was on in the living room. Beside it, on the leather couch, he saw Graham sitting absolutely still, dressed in light tan slacks and a mauve sweater.

"Graham?" Randy mumbled. The music in the background nearly drowned out his voice. He threw his coat on the floor by the door.

Graham looked up. Randy thought that in the half light his complexion appeared healthier than it had before, rosy like Haircut's. He moved closer.

"Well, well, well, baby," Graham sneered, "it's you at last." He lifted a thin arm, leaned back, and switched off the CD player on a stand to his left.

Randy studied his pink face, observing how emaciated it still was, how just under his eyes, the color was running. He realized then that Graham was wearing makeup.

"What are you looking at?" Graham asked peevishly. Chuckling wanly, he murmured, "The paint?"

"Paint?"

"Yes, baby, paint." Graham produced a tiny smile and touched his cheek. "Courtesy of Estée Lauder. I mean, baby, after all, appearance is everything."

"I…"

"One has to pretend, you know. The doctors can only help so much." Turning away, Graham picked up the drink sitting on the table beside him, took a sip, and fixed his eyes on a wall. A frown appeared on his lips, and he looked at Randy. "You are aware," he said deliberately, his voice harsh, "that you're very, very late."

"I…I'm sorry, I…"

"No excuses!" Graham snapped. He peered straight at Randy. "I told you that I wanted you here immediately."

Randy felt as if Graham's eyes were impaling him. He tried to meet his gaze, but found it impossible. The blush Graham wore seemed to be eddying across his brow and around his nose. Randy looked down at the floor.

"But never mind," Graham continued, softening. "Come here. Let me look at you."

Randy didn't move.

"Come on."

Flinching, Randy took a step in his direction.

"Hurry up, baby."

Randy crept to his side.

Graham stared at him, his eyes glazed. Randy focused on the colors that appeared to be billowing across his cheeks, tiny waves of pink and red.

Graham lifted a hand to Randy's thigh, then raised it further to his shirt, sliding his fingers under it onto his stomach. He pressed his thumb against his navel. "So," he whispered, "you're here." He lowered his hand and unbuttoned Randy's pants. "Did you miss me?"

Randy felt Graham's hand against his skin. He quivered. He was getting an erection. "Ye…yes."

"That's good." Graham forced his hand under Randy's jeans and took hold of his penis. "I missed you, too." He ran his fingers across the shaft, pinching the skin, then, brusquely, pulled his hand out and said, "But we can play later, baby. I think we should get high first."

At that moment, he had a violent coughing fit. His face turned scarlet. Frightened, Randy looked up at the portrait of Madonna on the wall and gazed at the knife in her hand. It appeared even sharper than he remembered. He gripped the rim of his pants pocket. His erection disappeared.

Graham's coughing eased. He stared at Randy, scanning his face and body, disoriented. Recovering, he grabbed Randy's shirttail, then let go of it. "God," he remarked disdainfully, rasping, "you look like a sow."

Randy lowered his eyes. "I…I was in a hurry. I fell asleep after I talked to you and…and I didn't know what time it was. I wanted to see you."

"Oh you did, did you? I'd say you have an odd way of showing it. Four hours late, indeed!"

Randy glanced up, then down again.

Graham glared at him, breathing unevenly. His face relaxed, and he slapped Randy's thigh. "Anyway, baby, what's done can't be helped." He reached out and found a pill bottle on the table beside him. "I think we need some of these dexies. I took two half an hour ago, but that's not going to be enough. I mean, I had to do *something* while waiting for you to get here, so I'm afraid I had just a bit too much to drink." He grinned. "I don't have the constitution I once did, you know."

Randy inspected the bottle in Graham's hand. "Are...are you sure...do you think...?"

Graham glanced up and, irritated, exclaimed, "Don't patronize me! I'm a big boy. I told you I'm well."

Randy blushed, then looked away. "Sor...sorry."

"Yeah, right!" Graham twisted the cap off the bottle and poured five dexedrine into his hand. He passed two to Randy.

Randy took them. "Thanks."

Graham swallowed three and leaned back against the couch, closing his eyes. "We should be there soon, baby. Actually, those pills I took earlier seem to be working. I think I can feel something coming on right now."

Still standing, Randy swallowed the pills he was holding. He wished he had a drink, but Graham hadn't offered him one. He waited for Graham to speak.

Graham opened his eyes, gazing at him. "So, baby, you really are here." His voice was soft, a little hazy.

Randy started to sit beside him.

Graham held out a hand. "No, stay there. Let me look at you some more."

Randy pulled back, sensing Graham's eyes on him, which made him erect again.

"Why don't you take off those filthy clothes?"

Randy met Graham's gaze. It seemed as if his eyes were boring into his skin, straight through to his core. He looked away, up at the Hockney sketch of Dennis, nestled beside Madonna's portrait. Dennis was sitting on an easy chair, his thick brown hair tousled across his forehead, a cigarette in one hand, a drink in the other. Shivering, Randy looked down and unbuttoned his shirt.

"Great, baby. But do it slowly."

Randy slipped out of his shirt and dropped it on the floor. He stood stiffly, feeling Graham's eyes on his chest. He stared at Graham's face, at the colors that seemed to be streaming across it, lush ripples of red, the shades hideous yet beautiful. He leaned over and removed his shoes and socks, then straightened up.

"Yes," Graham whispered, "that's good." He placed a hand on his own pants and unzipped them, extracting his penis, partially erect, prominent against his tan slacks. He played with the tip.

Randy slid his jeans down his legs and stepped out of them, naked.

Pressing his hand against his shaft, Graham smiled. He was completely erect now. "You want it, baby?"

Randy moved forward.

"Go ahead," Graham murmured. "Can't you see how much better I am?"

Randy kneeled in front of him, observing from the corner of an eye the sketch of Dennis. He thought he remembered some words that Graham had spoken to him on the phone one night around a month before, "I love you, Dennis." He may have dreamed it. Lowering his head, he took the tip of Graham's penis in his mouth.

"That's right, baby, keep going."

Randy moved his tongue across the shaft. Graham thrust his hips up. Randy gagged.

"Come on," Graham laughed, "you can take it."

Increasing his pace, Randy shut his eyes. Graham's penis pushed against his palate.

Graham thrust his hips further up and shoved down on Randy's head. Randy recalled his fight with Jake, everything that had happened between them earlier. He slid his mouth over Graham's shaft.

"Easy, easy," Graham said, "mind the teeth."

Randy slowed down. Working steadily, taking in Graham's shaft, he thought about the Hockney sketch, Dennis and Graham's life together, that phone call of Graham's.

Graham thrust his groin forward. Randy squeezed his eyes more tightly together, seeing, quickly, Jake grinning at him, Mr. Hewitt stretched out on his bed. He started to choke.

"Keep it up. Don't give out on me now." Graham forced his penis toward Randy's throat.

Randy felt as if he were going to retch. Graham wasn't like this with Dennis, he thought; he loved him. Gasping, he pulled his head up, away from Graham's groin.

Graham leaned forward, narrowing his eyes. "What the fuck do you think you're doing? Why'd you stop?"

"I...I couldn't breathe." Catching his breath, Randy stared at Graham's face, at the shades of red that appeared to be flying across it, down his thin neck, over thick veins. Just then he hated him.

"You couldn't breathe?" Graham glared at Randy. "Christ, don't you do this all the time?"

"No, I..." Randy stopped, his pulse throbbing. He waited a few seconds, then, speaking rapidly, said, "I mean, why can't we just...?" He stopped again. Turning, he peered at Dennis's portrait, and for a moment thought he saw something oblique there, in Dennis's expression, on his handsome face, in his languid eyes.

His erection gone, Graham zipped his pants and, unsteady, stood. "Forget it! I'm in no mood for your shit anymore. You're not worth it. You've kept me waiting long enough today. I'm late."

Randy looked back at Graham. "Late?" He hesitated, wishing then that they'd never stopped, that he could relive everything that had just happened. He didn't want to have to leave, to return to his life. He touched Graham's leg. "Late for what?"

Graham moved back. "Why, late for Dakota's, of course. I told you, didn't I, that I have to go there? Dakota's giving a cocktail party for Denise. It's her birthday." He rocked forward, then stood still, regaining his balance.

"Can...can I come?" Randy blurted. As soon as he'd spoken, he blushed.

"Oh, please! My first time out in weeks, and I'm supposed to take *you* with me?"

"But..." Randy turned his head toward Dennis's portrait, trying to grasp what he'd seen there.

Catching the object of Randy's gaze, Graham snarled, "What are you looking at?"

Randy glanced at the floor.

Graham glowered at Randy, his breathing spasmodic. Randy thought that he was going to attack him, beat him. That might be a relief.

Graham continued to stare at him. The anger in his expression eased. He closed his eyes, reopened them, and ran a hand across his brow, examining Randy, distracted, puzzled. "No," he muttered to himself, shaking his head, "no." Then he spoke to Randy, his tone unexpectedly gentle, a tremor beneath his words: "What do you want from me anyway?"

Randy looked up. He didn't know what to say.

"You realize I can't bring you to Dakota's? Denise wouldn't like that."

Randy was silent.

"So do you want to stay here? Wait for me? Would that make you happy?"

Almost imperceptibly, Randy nodded.

Graham said nothing, backing off slightly. Randy peered at the floor.

Grinning, an impish lilt in his voice, Graham cried, "Well, all right. I suppose I can trust you." He giggled. "We might even have some more fun later on." Weaving, he started to walk away. Then he stopped and, looking at Randy, said, "Make yourself comfortable, baby. There's some gin in the kitchen. And help yourself to the pills. I'll only be a few hours."

Randy slipped up from the floor onto the couch. The leather felt cool against his skin. He watched as Graham, apparently searching for something, fumbled around the living room.

"Where the fuck did I put my coat?" Graham asked, speaking to himself. His frail body reeling, he began to cough.

Randy looked downward, afraid that Graham was going to collapse.

But Graham controlled his fit and, flushed, managed to say, "I know I threw it somewhere."

"I...I don't think you'll need it." Biting his lip, Randy reached down to the floor and clasped his shirt.

Graham eyed him. "Oh, no? Not even in my condition."

"It's really warm out there."

"Oh, is it now?" Graham paused. Then, jaunty, he smiled and exclaimed, "Yes! That's it! Winter's over! I'm high! I think I've recovered at last!" A headlong spring in his gait, he hurried to the door.

Randy took a cigarette from the pack in his shirt pocket, then lit it, clamping down on the filter, concentrating on Graham's back. "Graham?" he mumbled through his teeth.

Graham didn't hear this. "See you, baby," he called to him, turning his head, amused and unnervingly vivacious. "Be good. I'll be here again before you know it." Chuckling, he opened the door. "Oh, yes, I'll be here." He rushed out.

Randy leaned against the couch. He could hear Graham coughing as he started down the stairs, then singing faintly, "Oh, baby! Oh, baby, come on!" He drew on his cigarette, staring in front of him, taking in the dim apartment. Graham's voice disappeared.

He was alone.

XIX

He remained on the couch for nearly an hour, scarcely aware of time passing, but acutely conscious of the apartment's murky gloom and of distant voices floating up from the street. The walls of the room appeared to be spinning into tiny waves. He found this strangely soothing.

A draft caressed his skin. He glanced behind him at the Hockney sketch, at Dennis, his lips fixed in a half-smile, then, searching for the pill bottle, turned away. On the table beside the couch he saw the photograph of Dennis in a bathing suit. He looked astonishingly beautiful, his hair damp against his brow, his chest lightly muscled, smooth and pale. Here, too, he was smiling halfheartedly, his expression compelling, a mystery.

The draft breezed past Randy. Shivering, he found the pill bottle, grasped it open, and tapped out a dexedrine. He threw the pill into his mouth and sat still, his arms pressed against his chest. He decided he needed a drink. He waited a few seconds, then slowly rose to his feet. Proceeding carefully, he walked to the kitchen.

He switched on the fluorescent light, raising a hand to his eyes to shield them from its glare, and stood in the doorway, wobbly, adapting to the brightness. Once his eyes had adjusted and his equilibrium returned, he looked toward the kitchen sink and saw a half-filled bottle of Bombay Gin surrounded by half a dozen empty bottles, all lying on their sides, and many used glasses. He moved to the sink and picked up a glass. There was a trace of clear liquid at the bottom, a dead fly floating on top. He turned on the faucet to rinse it out, seeing as he did this a pile of dirty dishes in the sink, one caked with a moldy red sauce. A cockroach scurried across it. He ran the glass under hot water, and the sauce slithered apart. Mold slid down toward the drain, taking the cockroach with it. He watched, gripped by the insect's struggle, then filled the glass with gin and took a fast slug. After switching off the light, he returned to the living room.

He stood by the Hockney sketch, holding his drink, probing Dennis's face. He could feel the speed he'd taken earlier, joining the gin as it eased its way into his depths. Geoffrey'll be back soon, he thought. He stared at Dennis's tenuous smile, enigmatic in the faint light. He wanted to know what he'd felt when he was with Graham, to learn how he'd lived his life.

Then he recalled the book he'd seen on his last visit, the one he'd thought was Graham's diary. It had been out in the open, conspicuous on the bedside table in Graham's bedroom. He wondered if it was still there. He wavered, his eyes on Dennis's face. At last, clutching his glass and cigarettes, he hurried to the bedroom.

The room was even more disorderly that it had been the last time he was here, blankets and dirty sheets tossed about, joining the clothing, papers, and used tissues on the floor. There was a stale odor in the air, not quite foul. He felt the draft. Chilly, he continued to the bedside table.

The book was gone, its absence making a framed photograph achingly prominent. He slumped onto the bed, placing his glass and cigarettes on the table, and studied the photograph, the one of Dennis at a club, flushed and laughing as he headed into a huge, strobe-lit crowd on a dance floor. Randy wondered when this had been taken and where.

He gulped some gin, then looked around him. He knew the diary had to be somewhere; Graham couldn't have thrown it out. Noticing a chest of drawers by a wall, he jumped to his feet and darted to it. He yanked the top drawer open and gazed inside, but saw only a mass of papers: bills, scribbled notes, a few prescriptions, and a manuscript. He tried the other two drawers. Again nothing, just sweaters and shirts in one, socks and underwear in the other. Turning around, he stared at the debris on the floor, searching. He returned to the bedside table, grabbed his gin, and finished it, then peered in front of him, sucking in air. There was a closet at the far end of the room. He rushed to it.

He paused by the closet's door before cracking it open. It was dark inside, but he could tell that the closet was spacious. A chain cord dangled from the ceiling. He pulled on it, and the overhead light came on. Hanging in front of him was an array of clothing unlike anything he had ever seen Graham wear: at least a dozen pairs of jeans, most expensive-looking, a few worn and frayed; long shirts, some black, some white, others brightly colored or checked, all partially rolled up at the sleeves; five leather jackets, each appearing new; burnished black-leather pants. Randy was sure these clothes had belonged to Dennis. He moved inside.

He ran a hand across a pair of black jeans, fondling the denim, and raised the label on its back toward the light. It read Fiorucci. He drew the pants from their hanger and held them to his groin, then slid them on. They were tight—skin-tight, the way they were supposed to be, he knew. He edged forward, becoming erect, aware of the fabric of the pants rubbing against him. His eyes scanned the shirts and settled on a turquoise one, the most beautiful shirt he had ever seen. He took it from the hanger and held it to his face, sniffing it, convinced he could detect a trace of cologne on its collar. He slipped into it, savoring the feel of the soft material on his skin, and found that it fit perfectly. One shoulder fell down over his upper arm. He remembered that the shoulders of certain shirts worn in the early eighties had done this. As he tucked in the shirttail, his hand brushed his erection.

He returned to the bed and sat for an instant, then abruptly rose and raced back to the chest of drawers. He pulled the top drawer open. His eyes settled on the manuscript inside. *"After Death,"* he read, "by

Graham Mason." He'd never before seen this title. This is Graham's new book, he thought. He touched the top page and let his hand rest there, stroking the paper. He finally gripped the manuscript and lifted it to him. He was astonished by how much of it there was.

Suddenly he saw from a corner of an eye something in the drawer that had been hidden under the manuscript, that book, the one he'd suspected was Graham's diary. In one brisk motion, he dropped the manuscript on top of the chest of drawers, leaned over, and scooped the book up. He sped to the bed with it and stretched out, then turned to the first page.

Before him was a full-page, black-and-white photograph of Graham and Dennis, and he knew then that this was a photo album, not a diary. It was leather-bound and thick, and did look like a lot of old journals he'd seen in period films. Even so, he couldn't understand how he had been so mistaken.

He examined the picture beneath its plastic sheathing. Dennis was dressed in a leather jacket and checkered pants, and was slightly hunched over, his expressionless eyes veering off to his right. A mid-thirtyish Graham, more formally attired in a jacket and tie, stood beside him, an arm flung across Dennis's shoulder, his smile cold and effete, derisive. Randy could see other people in the room, women in glittering gowns, men in tuxedos, a few in leather. Abstract paintings were on the white wall behind them. He decided this was an opening, and tried to imagine what it had been like.

There were four photographs on the spread that followed, all of a dinner party. Their colors were faded, so that they appeared older than the photo on the previous page. Graham was seated at the head of the table and was beaming in every shot. He looked as if he were in his late twenties here, fit and healthy, his thick, dark hair impeccably styled. There were three others at the table, two women and a man, and a birthday cake in the center. The women were dressed in colorful jumpsuits, the men in bright dinner jackets and ruffled shirts. Everyone was laughing. Randy was certain, because of the bottles of wine and hash pipes near them, that they were high. He recognized no one besides Graham at first, although he felt as if he should. He was sure these others had been famous; all of Graham's friends seemed to be.

Just then, in the background of the photo at the bottom of the right-hand page, almost hidden in the shadows, he noticed Dennis. He was much younger than the other guests, probably around seventeen, and was standing discreetly to the side, in the distance behind the table, looking to his right, downward, shyly. His skin was tanned and his hair long, falling past his shoulders, bleached from the sun.

Randy stared at the photograph, amazed that this self-effacing youth was the same person as the apparently confident Dennis he'd seen in other pictures. For a second the walls of the room seemed to move toward him. He focused his vision, then turned back to the first page, again noting Graham's chilly smile and Dennis's wayward eyes, which, dull and blank as they were, appeared bored by the scene around him. He returned to the photos of the dinner party. Dennis's diffident figure looked like a ghost's. Clinging tightly to the edge of the album, he turned the page.

In the next four pictures, Dennis was lying on a bed in his underpants. Randy took in the fine hair on his legs, then his face. He was pouting—seductively, Randy thought. He recalled Jamie Gilmour, the boy from the magazine that Graham had shown him, and was struck, as he had been before, by Dennis's resemblance to him. Erect, he felt his eyes wander down to Dennis's crotch. He allowed them to rest there for a moment. Then he moved on.

He flitted through the book quickly, in a trance, glancing briefly at each photo, thrilled by the fact that he was looking at the past. Apart from the picture on the first page, the album seemed to be laid out in chronological order, and he could see how Graham and Dennis changed in telling ways from page to page. Dennis's hair became shorter and darker, Graham's sprinkled with gray. The ruffled shirts and bright jackets of the early pictures were replaced by tight T-shirts and pants, army-and-navy surplus items, combat boots and leather. Later, they wore clothes that Randy remembered from his early days in New York, jackets with wide lapels and sleeves, black shoes with polished toes, thin ties and thinner belts, square boxy shirts and suspenders. But the glamour of their lives was constant, Randy felt, the clubs, parties, openings, and dinners consistently alluring, their world charmed.

Three-quarters of the way through, he came to a photograph much like the one on the first page. It was in color this time, but was apparently taken at the same event, for Graham and Dennis were standing in that same crowded room, and from what Randy could make out, the people surrounding them were identical. This picture, however, was blurry, and Dennis and Graham's faces were maddeningly indistinct. Randy turned back to the first page, then started to browse through the album again, carefully this time, probing their expressions in each picture, realizing there was something he'd missed before, more subtle than their hairstyles and clothing, something he found hard to pin down.

For one thing, he could perceive a burgeoning confidence in Dennis as the album progressed. In a print that came just after the ones of him in his underpants, it was evident that he had grown more at ease in Graham's world. His hair had been cut, styled like Graham's, parted to the side so that it fell down over his forehead, and he was dressed in black-leather pants and a dark shirt, chatting with friends at a party, laughing and obviously happy. The next few pages contained comparable photos: Dennis in elaborate outfits, strutting across a gallery, seated at a formal dinner, dancing at a club. Randy was awed by the exuberance of his eyes and by the huge smile that was always on his face. He could feel himself smiling back at him.

A picture near the middle of the album made him stop. Here Graham and Dennis were on the couch in the living room, a dozen glasses on the table beside them. Randy was certain there had been some sort of party going on. What grabbed his attention was the unmistakable anger he saw on Graham's face, a threatening gleam in his eyes that made Randy squirm. He was glaring off to his right, away from Dennis, and his hands were on his knees, locked on the kneecaps. He seemed to be trying to restrain himself. Dennis was glancing at him cautiously, and his eyes were downcast.

In the photos immediately following this one, they were still on the couch, but this time it was Dennis glaring at Graham, who was bleary-eyed here and clearly inebriated. Dennis's posture was upright and stiff, and Graham had wrinkled his brow, so that he looked pained and disturbed. Randy wondered what had been going on, if Graham and Dennis had argued, and if so, why.

He moved on, then, several pages later, was struck by two shots that came just after the point where he'd stopped before, both shots on the same page. In the top one, Graham and two burly men, unfamiliar to Randy, were dressed completely in leather. Dennis was on the floor by Graham's side, crouched on his hands and knees, nude save for a leather jock strap and a dog collar around his neck, a chain leash attached to it. He was looking at the floor, his face hidden. Beside him, Graham was gripping the leash and grinning—sneering, Randy decided. He wondered what Dennis had been thinking.

The picture directly below this one was nearly as intriguing. Here Graham was lying fully clothed on the couch. His shirttail was out and his eyes closed, his mouth hanging open. Evidently he had passed out. A shadow, the photographer's, fell across his body. That must be Dennis, Randy thought. He found it odd that he had taken such a shot, and tried to envision what had prompted him to do so.

He returned to the photograph above this, moving his eyes from the leash to Dennis's thighs, noting how strong they looked. He slid a hand under his pants toward his groin and let his eyes stray down Dennis's leg. Just above the calf, he saw a distinct mark, a purplish bruise. He gazed at it for several seconds, then, with a shock, realized it was a lesion.

He hurried on, hoping to erase this image from his mind. But shortly thereafter, in pictures that followed, he discerned a change in Dennis's complexion and overall aspect, an alteration that, slight at first, was more apparent on every page.

Dennis was getting thinner and paler, his skin taut around his cheekbones, his eyes hollow. His flamboyant outfits and leather gear, so prominent in earlier pictures, were gone, his clothing now restricted to old T-shirts and jeans. There was also a gravity in his expression, a weight there totally unlike the uninhibited demeanor he'd displayed before. Randy perused each photo assiduously, his stomach fluttering.

Near the end of the album were several shots of Dennis, painfully thin, sitting at a desk and writing. In the last of them, Graham stood by his side, leaning against the desk. He looked disheveled and intoxicated, and was laughing, as if at Dennis. Frowning, Dennis appeared annoyed or possibly distraught. Randy remembered the stories he'd heard, how Dennis had started writing just when Graham had stopped. He couldn't imagine what had happened.

He saw only one more photo after this one, of Dennis, once again in leather, heading toward the apartment's front door, his head turned as he lifted an arm, waving over his shoulder, his eyes lowered, the set of his face rigid. His leather pants were loose around his hips, and his skin was pasty. He looked completely emaciated. Randy was startled by this image, seeing Dennis so ill, leaving the apartment, wearing the sort of outfit he seemed to have discarded pages before. He found it hard to take his eyes off him.

The next few spreads were empty. He flipped past them, ready to go through the album yet again, to study it even more carefully. But then, on the page just before the last one, under the plastic sheathing, he saw a manila envelope. He thrust a hand under the plastic, grabbed the envelope, and opened it quickly. There was a photograph inside.

He held this in front of him, his hands trembling, staring at a black-and-white glossy of Dennis, nude, strapped to a chair in Graham's living room, ropes drawn tight across his wasting body, his mouth gagged. His feet were tied together, his hands behind his back. His eyes were closed. He almost looked dead. Despite the gag in his mouth, he was smiling. And he was erect.

At that moment, a voice booming above Randy shattered the silence of the room: "What the fuck do you think you're doing?"

Randy twisted around and saw Graham by the door, rocking from side to side, his arms stretched out toward him, his clothing rumpled, his makeup smeared. He reeked of alcohol. Randy froze.

Graham stood weaving, glowering at Randy and breathing rapidly. Then he bolted up to him and whisked the photo from his hand. "Fucking cunt!" he screamed. He raised an arm and forcefully slapped Randy's face.

Randy pulled away, stunned, his head ringing. He lifted his hands to his chest and attempted to cover the turquoise shirt.

Seeing this, Graham cried, "Take it off, you little shit! Take it off right now! Christ, how dare you!"

Randy could not stir. Dazed, he tried to think of something to say. "Why…why are you here?" he managed to ask.

"What?" Graham moved back, wheezing, squinting his eyes, as if distracted. "Why, that cunt Denise..." He stopped. Then, with a snarl: "What do you mean, why am I here? It's my fucking apartment!" He leaned over and gripped the front of the shirt Randy was wearing. "I said take that fucking thing off!"

Shaking, Randy unbuttoned the shirt and removed it. He threw it beside him on the bed.

"Everything!" Graham roared. He began to cough with an alarming force, his face turning red, then fell on his side next to Randy, curling into a ball. "God," he moaned.

Randy's vision started to blur. The room was spinning. He wanted a drink.

Graham lay curled beside him, coughing. His fit eased, and he sat up, taking hold of Randy's thigh, grasping the jeans he had on. "Take them off!" he shouted. "Get out! Go!" He pushed at Randy's leg.

Randy, quivering, stood and unfastened the pants. He felt dizzy.

His breathing labored, Graham stared at the photograph, which was still in his hand. "What a fucking sneak you are!" he gasped. "I can't believe you did this to me." He glared at Randy and cried, "Come on, take those fucking things off!"

Randy slid the jeans down his legs, then stood still. Everything was spinning around him.

Graham looked at the photo, silent. Wary, Randy watched him, afraid to budge. He thought he was going to faint.

Graham raised his head. "Well, what are you waiting for? Aren't you going?" Although his tone was still angry, his voice was lower.

"Please, I...I didn't mean..." Randy clutched at his chest. "I just wanted to know..."

"What?" Graham kept his eyes on him, his gaze deliberate. He peered down at the photograph in his hand, then back up at Randy, exploring his body. Suddenly he smiled. Then he giggled.

Randy felt himself flushing. The spinning stopped.

"Oh, right," Graham said, his tone softening. He seemed amused yet singularly intrigued. Still smiling, he lifted a hand to his chin. "You want to know about Dennis."

Hearing Dennis's name made Randy flush even more. It sounded strange, jolting, coming from Graham.

"But why, baby?" Graham's voice was now almost gentle. "Why

are you so interested in him?" He narrowed his eyes. "Do you feel like you've been there, too?"

"I...I..." Randy looked down at the floor.

Graham glanced at the photo, then laid it beside him. He patted the mattress. "Come on, let's talk. Sit down."

Randy hesitated, then inched his way to the bed. He sat close to Graham, pulling his legs together and placing his hands on his knees. Graham smiled at him, weakly. Randy lowered his eyes. They settled on the photograph, next to Graham's hip.

"He learned, you know," Graham mumbled, following Randy's gaze, his words barely audible and slurred. "He learned that you can't escape. The world's just become a shithole. We're all monsters. I told him that a million times."

Randy focused on Dennis's thigh, seeing something there he hadn't noticed until then, a red mark. It was, he grasped, a welt, a deep one.

Graham motioned toward the manuscript sitting on top of the chest of drawers. "It's all in my new book, of course. I see you've found that, too." He laughed. "I hope it was enlightening for you."

Randy stared at the welt, oblivious to Graham. It appeared to be opening up before him, expanding across Dennis's thigh.

"But then you probably didn't read any of it, did you, baby? You never will, I'm sure. Let's just get high again, and I'll tell you all about it." Graham paused. Then, an edge in his tone, he exclaimed, "No, that's not what I'm going to do. That's not it at all. I'll just..." He paused once more, chuckling this time. "Listen, baby," he continued, impassioned, "remember when I used to talk about writing with you, what I told you then? Remember, baby? Show don't tell?"

Randy watched as Dennis's thigh seemed to vanish, engulfed by a swirling mass of red.

"But maybe it wasn't you that I said that to, maybe it was him." Graham touched Randy's hip, kneading the skin between his fingers. "Anyway, baby, it doesn't matter." He stood. "I'm going to get the pills and some drinks. When I get back I'll..." He smiled. "Well, baby, then you'll learn all you need to know. Yes, baby, I'm going to *show* you everything."

XX

Afterward, at one in the morning, as he lurched home from Graham's, Randy thought about a song that had been playing there for much of the night: "Shatter me, shatter me in pieces, you can't kill me." All the while, Graham flailed above him. Now, moving guardedly across streets that shimmered under the street lamps, he was sure he could hear this tune, feel it in the air, skulking around him, suspended with the warmth that remained from the day. He sensed it surging into his core.

He passed few people as he walked, and most of them appeared ghostly, amorphous creatures barely there. Occasionally a face became distinct and seemed to leap out at him, its head preternaturally large, eyes bulging and red. These apparitions pushed him forward, although he couldn't walk too quickly. Any hasty movement made him conscious of his thighs.

Only once did his haze lift, on St. Mark's Place and Second Avenue, when, waiting on the southwest corner for a street light to change, he thought he saw Adrian Peterson whizzing by on rollerblades, wearing a tight black T-shirt and skimpy denim shorts. Adrian's on The Pines, he told himself, his head reeling, the street a glimmering pool of light. That's not him; this is a dream.

His apartment seemed scarcely more real than the street. All the lights were out, and Jake's clamorous snores spewed forth from the bedroom, piercing the darkness. He turned on a lamp. Everything was dim, looking ethereal yet hardly serene. He crept to the living room and, cautious, sat on a chair in front of the television set, easing his buttocks onto the seat. Numb, he switched on the set and turned the volume high.

"Yes!" a voice boomed from the screen, howling with laughter.

Randy saw that the voice came from a man standing near a desk at the center of a stage. Apparently he was the host of the show. A pretty blond woman, dressed in forest-green slacks and a loose silk blouse, stood beside him. A dog was running in circles by their feet.

"Good girl!" cried the host with a giggle and a smirk.

"Oh, Jeff," his guest shrieked, giggling as well, "you're too much."

Just then Jake called out from the bedroom, "What the fuck?"

Randy watched as the dog stopped, then began circling madly in the opposite direction. The host's grin grew broader.

"Jesus Christ," screamed Jake, "turn that fucking thing down! Shit, I'm trying to sleep."

Randy stared at the laughing host. His gleeful eyes appeared to be shooting out from the screen. It felt to Randy as if they were penetrating his skin.

"Where've you been anyway?" Jake shouted. "I hope the fuck you've come to your senses."

Randy tried to focus on the dog. She was moving so quickly that he could barely detect her. All he could see were spirals, hundreds of them, overwhelming everything.

"So have you been with those queens? Come on, are you deaf? What've you been doing?"

Randy said nothing.

"Well, fuck it then. Just keep it down. I wanna sleep. We'll talk about it later. You've got some explaining to do."

Randy remained silent.

"Randy?"

Randy gazed at the spirals as they absorbed the screen.

Even now, after all that had occurred, he couldn't forget how Graham had been when he returned to the bedroom, two glasses of gin and the bottle of dexedrine in his hands, how, suddenly, he seemed oddly melancholy, his expression grim, how he sat on the bed and silently gave him a glass and two pills, then, turning away, found the photo album lying near them. He picked it up and leafed through it. Randy was afraid to look at him. And yet he felt at that point as if a fog were lifting; each instant of time became etched in his brain.

Neither spoke at first. Randy only clutched his glass as Graham, breathing heavily, flipped the pages.

After several minutes of silence, a half-smile appeared on Graham's lips. "Yes," he whispered.

Randy glanced down and saw that he had come to the photographs of Dennis in his underpants.

"Yes," Graham said once more, still whispering, a remote yet pronounced tinge of sadness in his voice. He sighed. "And now it's gone." Randy raised his head. Graham seemed lost in the album, his eyes glistening. Randy thought he could see the makeup on his face twisting into tiny red circles. "What's that?" he asked.

Graham looked up, confused, evidently not recognizing him. His eyes were unfocused as he gazed past Randy at the wall. Randy wanted to touch him, lean against his frail chest, but found that he couldn't. The circles of red that he saw on his face were becoming larger, frightening.

Jerking his head back and glancing at Randy, Graham regained his focus. He frowned and took a slug of his drink. "Never mind," he said. He peered at the album, then in an abrupt motion, tossed it aside and jumped up. "Enough of this shit! We've got things to do."

Randy leaned forward and gripped his kneecaps. "Wha...what?"

Graham stood still, his hands on his hips, the smile on his face frozen. He waited for what seemed to Randy an eternity. At last he said, "I want you to lie on your stomach."

"Huh?" Randy stared at him, then muttered, "Oh." He lowered his eyes to the floor. "Oh, yeah." He thought that he understood. He lifted his eyes to Graham and, his voice quivering, asked, "Is...is it the belt?"

"The *belt?*" Graham's smile evaporated, replaced by an expression of an almost-exaggerated severity. Randy felt waves of fear, then excitement creeping across his shoulders and down his sides. He leaned back toward the mattress.

"Oh, right, the belt." Graham laughed harshly. "Well, I suppose that's a start." He gazed at Randy, murmuring, "Come on, baby, lie down."

Randy took a long breath. Then he stretched out, turning onto his stomach, becoming erect. He watched as Graham walked to the closet and moved inside.

A second later Graham emerged carrying a large duffel bag. He returned to the bed, set it by his feet, unzipped it, and pulled out several cords of rope. Kneeling on the floor, he leaned over Randy and pressed his lips against his buttocks, then slid his head down and slipped his tongue into the crack. He pulled back, laughed, and, leaning over again, bit Randy's left thigh. He pinched him, lightly slapped his buttocks, and stood. "Relax, baby," he purred. "I'm going to go put on some music."

"Yeah. Yeah, sure." Completely erect now, Randy closed his eyes.

"What the fuck's going on?"

Startled, Randy became aware of Jake standing before him, wearing a pair of baggy white briefs. He was directly in front of the television set. Randy shivered. He wanted to push Jake away, kick him in the groin.

Jake moved his eyes down from Randy's face to his tousled shirt, then back up to his face. Hesitant, he raised a hand to his chin, squinting at Randy. "What's the matter?" he asked him, his voice softer. "What happened to you? I mean, you look…" He stopped.

Randy sat still. He felt as if he couldn't move.

Jake bent down and touched his arm. "Come on, what is it?"

Randy cringed and pulled away. He was unable to look at Jake and said nothing at first. Then, his words garbled, he mumbled, "I saw Adrian." He had only a vague notion of what he was saying.

Jake inched back. "You what?"

"I saw Adrian." Randy leaned to his side, gazing past Jake's hips at the TV.

"That's impossible." Jake flushed. "You know he's not back yet. He's still on The Pines." He stood aside, studying Randy, his mouth hanging open. "Jesus," he exclaimed, "what did you take? And you smell like shit."

Randy stared at the television screen. The host and his guest were seated at the desk, both laughing. "God, Jeff!" the woman yelped.

"Listen," Jake said, turning the volume down, "I've gotta piss. Why don't you go to bed? You look like you need some rest." He started to walk away.

Randy kept his eyes on the TV, his ears attuned to its sound. The host and the woman were still laughing, more frantically now. "That's what you told me," the host gibed. "You told me that last night." The woman twisted her head up. "Jeff!" she tittered. The audience screamed with laughter and burst into applause.

Jake continued toward the bathroom, then stopped and looked

at Randy. He furrowed his brow. "Sweetheart?" he muttered, his eyes fixed on him. Then, speaking quickly: "I'll be right back. We could both use some sleep." He moved on.

Randy hadn't understood a word Jake had said. He felt much too subsumed by the audience's applause.

Jake reached the bathroom and shut the door.

Randy gazed past the screen.

He recalled lying across Graham's bed, his arms and legs stretched out, tied to the bed posts, thick ropes binding him tightly, music blasting from the next room. Above this, he heard Graham laughing. "You're pathetic, you know." Despite his laughter, Graham's tone was almost tender. "Just a cheap little whore, a two-bit hustler."

Randy pressed his erection against the mattress, closed his eyes, and clenched his hands into fists. The rope chafed into his wrists.

"But that's why I love you, baby. Haven't I always told you that?" Graham unbuckled his belt and pulled it from his pants. "So then, are you ready?"

He listened as Graham snapped the belt against the floor, and beyond this, heard the music: "Shatter me in pieces, you can't kill me."

"One. Two. Three." Graham paused. Then, with a terrifying force, he flung the belt across Randy's thighs.

Randy's eyes shot open, and his body jerked spasmodically. The shock and the pain nearly obliterated everything. The ropes tying him to the bed seemed to tighten further. Panting, he waited for the second blow.

But it didn't come. All he could hear was the music: "Shatter me, shatter me, you'll never kill me."

Shaking, he peered behind him and saw Graham crouched over, reaching into the duffel bag by his feet.

"You know, baby," Graham said, smiling up at him, his right hand deep in the bag, "I don't think the belt is going to be enough this evening."

Randy gripped the ropes extending from his arms.

"No, baby, tonight I think we need something special." With a flick of his arm, Graham yanked a long black whip from the bag. "Let's try this, okay?"

Seeing the whip, Randy coiled his chest up and pulled at the ropes. Sweat prickled his sides. He made an unsuccessful attempt to lift a hand toward Graham. "Don't hurt me!"

Graham giggled. "Come on! You've never complained before."

Panic leapt from Randy's stomach to his throat. He thought he was going to vomit, but forced his nausea down and wriggled uncontrollably. The ropes seemed tauter than ever.

Graham stood above him, gulping his drink and chuckling.

For an instant, Randy thought that he heard Mr. Hewitt's laughter, a hideous, throaty guffaw. His heart rapped hard in his chest. He listened to a voice coming out of his mouth, not his own, he was sure. "Cocksucker!" it shouted at Graham. "Motherfucking cunt!" Squirming, he pushed his groin into the mattress, realizing then that he still had an erection.

"Oh, baby," Graham laughed. "Baby, you're turning me on." Clenching the whip, he lifted it in the air and held it over his shoulder.

"Don't fucking touch me!" the voice cried. Randy heard the music in the distance, the lyrics no longer audible, its sound a wail.

Graham grinned. He started to lower the whip.

Randy's blood rushed through his veins, straight to his head. "Wait!" the voice screamed. He now knew that it was his. "Please!" Nothing he said made the slightest difference.

He shifted in his seat, wincing, feeling the welts on his back and thighs rubbing against the chair. The toilet flushed in the bathroom. He glanced at the TV. The host of the show had put on a Swiss mountain hat with a green feather sticking out from its top. The woman seated beside him was touching it and smiling.

"I got it in Zurich," the host explained, a sardonic lilt in his tone. "You like it?"

The woman pulled back and studied the hat. "It'll do," she replied with a laugh.

Jake called from the bathroom: "Is m'baby ready for bed?"

Randy stared at the wall, completely still.

He wasn't sure how long Graham had whipped him, towered over him, flinging the whip across his back and thighs, screaming things

like, "You cunt! You worthless piece of shit!" He knew he'd strug-
gled, pulled at the ropes that restrained him, hurled himself from
side to side, in shock and agony, enraged, yet erect the whole time.
It ended when Graham began to cough, a sustained hacking fit.
He collapsed onto Randy's back, on top of the welts that had risen
there, panting, but laughing, too.

"Fucker!" Randy shrieked, in pain. He heaved his hips up, forcing
Graham off.

Graham rolled to Randy's side, coughing and giggling. "Baby,
baby," he gasped. His fit died down. He slipped his shoes from his
feet and took off his pants, along with his boxer shorts. He threw
them onto the floor, then grabbed Randy around the waist. "Come
on, baby."

No longer conscious of the pain, Randy tried to shove his elbow
into Graham's chest, but found that he couldn't move freely enough
to do so. "Motherfucker!"

Graham pinched Randy's nipple, climbed on top of him, and
pushed his erect penis against his buttocks.

"Eat shit," Randy murmured. He thought that he'd spoken in
anger, that he'd spat the words out, but they came out as a moan, a
caress. He felt himself move his hips up.

Graham let out a rasping cough and started to enter him.

Randy pressed up against Graham. He stopped. Moving quickly,
he pulled his hips down. Graham's penis slid out. "Wait," Randy
said, "don't you have any...?"

Graham grasped Randy's chest, pulling him back. "You're dying
for my cock, aren't you, baby?" With a sudden, sharp movement, he
again thrust his penis into him.

Randy felt as if he were being sliced open, as if Graham's penis
were splitting him apart. He rammed his buttocks up against
Graham's groin.

"Little shit!" Graham shouted, shoving down on Randy's shoulders.

"Shut the fuck up, cocksucker!" Randy lifted his groin off the bed,
until Graham's penis seemed to be piercing his guts. This isn't safe, he
thought, then nearly laughed. What is? The world's a fucking shithole.

Graham took a deep, irregular breath and stopped moving.
Wheezing, his penis still in Randy, he placed his head on Randy's

shoulder and sighed. Randy thought that he was going to cry. But he only lay quietly. Then he laughed. His hands crept up from Randy's chest to his neck, and he ran his fingers across his throat. "You know," he whispered in Randy's ear, "I could kill you right now." He fondled Randy's Adam's apple. "Then I could fuck your rotting corpse."

Not absorbing this, eager for Graham to continue, Randy cried, "Do it! Just do it!"

Graham moved his hands down to Randy's groin and grabbed his penis. "No, baby, that'd be too easy." He pulled out of Randy, then, with a frightening ferocity, thrust himself back in. "You're going to go with *me*."

"What?" Randy froze. He understood. Graham pulled out, then pushed into him again. Randy's eyes dropped to the floor. Lying beside the bed was the photograph of Dennis tied to a chair. He saw the rope stretched across Dennis's skin, the smile on his face, his erection.

With another quick thrust, Graham ejaculated. He lay on top of Randy, catching his breath. Then he stood. "That was good, baby. I'm just going to go pee."

Randy's heart was racing. He was desperate to move, to get up and dress, go. Graham's semen trickled between his legs. He peered at Graham, who was weaving by the bed, wearing only his mauve sweater and a blue shirt underneath that, his face pale beneath its running makeup, a hand cupped under his now-flaccid penis. "Untie me, okay?" Randy asked, his voice shaky.

Inching toward him, his movements unsteady, Graham grinned. "You want me to untie you?"

"Yeah."

Graham's teeth gleamed. "Well, all right. But first say 'please.'"

"Huh?" Randy stared at the streaks of mascara under Graham's eyes.

"Say 'please.'"

Randy was silent. Then, under his breath, he did what Graham had demanded. "Please," he muttered. He glanced down at the photograph of Dennis, then back up at Graham. The mascara appeared to have completely obliterated his eyes.

Graham continued to smile at him. "Make it 'pretty please.'"

Flushed, Randy complied.

"Good. Good boy." Graham leaned forward, so that he was directly over Randy. "Yes, baby, you're a *very* good boy." Giggling, he clutched his penis and released a stream of urine on Randy's back.

"Jesus, sweetheart, you're freaking me out!"

Randy looked up. Jake had his hands under his arms and was trying to pull him out of his seat. "Leave me alone!" Randy screamed. He kicked at Jake's shins.

Dodging Randy's foot, Jake pulled harder. Randy wouldn't budge. "Please, sweetheart!" Jake let go of his arms and moved back. "Christ, what's wrong with you tonight? I mean, you're completely out of it. You aren't still angry, are you? About our fight? About Adrian? Believe me, that's over."

"Fuck off!" Randy stared past Jake at the television set. The show's credits were rolling. In the background he could see the host standing by the desk. The dog had returned and was circling the host's legs. The blond woman was in her seat, laughing and applauding.

"Listen," Jake offered, "there're some pills in the bathroom. Maybe those'll help."

"Pills?" Randy shifted his eyes from the TV, back to Jake.

"Yeah, you know, to make you sleep." Jake again took hold of Randy's arm. "Come on."

Randy felt himself go limp. Jake pulled him up. Randy stood unstably, then, staggering, let Jake lead him to the bedroom.

Once there, he sat on the bed. Jake left to find the pills. When he came back, he gave the bottle to Randy. Randy took three.

Jake kneeled on the bed and unbuttoned Randy's shirt. "I'll help you undress, okay?"

Randy said nothing.

As Jake removed the shirt, he noticed Randy's back. "Fuck," he exclaimed, shocked, "what happened to you?"

"I..." Randy stopped.

Jake touched one of the welts lightly. "Shit, sweetheart, who did this?"

"I...I..."

"Come on." Jake sounded angry. His face was red. "I'll kill the motherfucker."

Randy wavered. Then, half-whispering: "I did it to myself."

Jake pulled his hand from the welt. "You what?"

Randy spoke again, louder and more clearly this time: "I did it to myself."

His anger dissipating, perplexed, Jake almost started to smile. He stopped himself and stared at Randy, the lines around his mouth taut. "God, you're more fucked up than I thought you were. I mean, if you don't want to tell me what happened, about this rough trade of yours or whatever it was—well, that's your business. But shit, sweetheart…"

Shaking his head, he gazed at Randy, frowning, more confused.

Randy couldn't look at him.

Speaking rapidly, Jake murmured, "Let's just go to sleep. Things'll be better in the morning."

Randy found it hard to grasp what Jake had said. He took off his shoes and pants, then, moving carefully, lay down and curled into a ball.

Jake undressed and stretched out beside him. He turned off the light, grazing Randy's shoulder with his arm. Randy stiffened. Jake pulled away and rolled over. " 'Night, sweetheart," he mumbled uneasily.

Edging toward the other side of the bed, Randy didn't answer.

He couldn't sleep, even after the pills that Jake had given him took effect. He wondered if he had slept at Graham's. That didn't seem possible; he'd been so high on speed. And yet there was that dream.

After Graham untied him, he'd found that he was still unable to move; he felt glued to the bed, frozen. He didn't know why this was so. Just a moment before he had wanted to leave. Now it was as if he had nowhere to go.

Graham fell down beside him almost immediately. "I'm exhausted, baby," he muttered, his voice abruptly drowsy, weaker. He switched off the bedside lamp. "Let's just rest a bit."

He had no idea how long he lay there, smelling the urine on the sheets and on his back, listening to Graham's heavy breathing, his gasps, his hoarse coughs. Hours perhaps, or maybe just a few minutes.

Graham only stirred twice. The second time he threw an arm across Randy. "Denny," he whispered. Randy moved to him and pressed his head against his chest. He felt his skin's warmth. A cold draft blew past him; it seemed to be coming from Graham's depths. He slid away.

It was shortly after this that the dream came. He was with Haircut, outside that café on Sheridan Square. Haircut was gesticulating frenetically, pointing toward the café's entrance.

Randy couldn't quite hear his words. He stared at him. His hair was long, longer than he'd ever seen it, falling down his back, well past his shoulders, lighter, too, more blond than it had ever been, radiant in the bright sunshine.

Haircut continued talking. A broad smile broached his face. Just then Randy heard him distinctly. "Come inside," he was saying. Randy shook his head.

"Please." Haircut's smile grew wider. "It's the answer, really. You can order coffee, tea, something sweet. It's much better, safer." A beam of sunlight fell directly on his head, and his hair turned a brilliant golden hue, blinding Randy. "Come on, Randy," he went on, "we can have cake!"

At these words, Haircut's feet rose from the ground, and he ascended into the air. Randy watched him drift up, over the café, far past it, until he reached the white, puffy clouds that floated above the earth. Moving beyond them, he vanished in a deep blue sky.

Randy came back from his dream with an unfamiliar sense of calm, a feeling of lightness and freedom. He didn't know where he was and didn't care. The room was dim, lit only by the illumination slipping in through the cracks of the blinds, coming from the street lamps outside. A clock on the bedside table told him it was a quarter before one. He sat quietly, taking languorous breaths, watching specks of dust fluttering in the rays of light, enjoying the silence. Then he heard a sigh. He turned and saw Graham. He was sitting up, gazing down at his lap. Randy remembered everything, and his heart throbbed violently. He stared at Graham and realized he was holding the photo album. He wondered how well he could see it in the dark.

Graham sighed again, then started to sob. "Oh, baby, baby," he cried softly, peering up from the album toward a wall. "Baby, I'm sorry. Oh, so sorry!" He glanced back at the album, sucking in air. His breath caught in his throat, and he let out a piercing wail: *"Baby!"*

Terrified, Randy shot up from the bed and dashed to the living room. He found his clothes in a heap on the floor, his coat by the entryway. Once he'd dressed, he bolted out of the apartment and down the stairs, stopping at the bottom. He could still hear Graham's screams. For a second he considered returning to him. But then, suddenly, he knew that he could not go back, that he could never go there again. He threw the front door open and lurched into the night.

PART THREE

XXI

The voices coming from the living room were muffled. Randy only recognized Jake's. "Three days!" he was saying. "I can't fucking believe it."

Torpid, Randy rolled to the other side of the bed, about to fall back asleep. Then a woman's voice came through to him. "Maybe I should go," she said. "I didn't want to bother you. It's just that I haven't seen him in a while." Shit, Randy thought, that's Sylvia. What the fuck's she doing here? He heard a third voice, a second man's: "It's his bottom, I know it." It was Haircut.

Now alert, Randy pulled himself up. He opened his mouth, trying to form words, but nothing emerged.

"What do you mean?" he heard Jake ask. "What the fuck are you talking about?"

"You know, his bottom," Haircut answered. "He's gotta hit one before he can get sober."

Sylvia interrupted them: "I really better go."

Randy started to throw his legs over the side of the bed. He felt a welt on his thigh rubbing against the bedsheet and lay down again.

"You're so full of shit," Jake muttered, apparently speaking to Haircut. "Just because you fucked up yourself, that doesn't mean everyone else is as bad as you."

"I'm sorry," Sylvia began, "I…"

"Look, Jake, I don't mean any harm." Haircut's tone was firm. "It's just that when I ran into him the other day, he seemed…well, I don't know, really lost, I guess."

Randy took a deep breath.

"Christ!" Jake exclaimed. "Why don't you just mind your own fucking business."

Randy exhaled, gasping one word: "Haircut." As he spoke, he was startled by the strength of his voice and by its unexpected clarity. It seemed to shoot back at him from the bedroom walls.

The conversation in the living room stopped. Randy shut his eyes.

271

"Sweetheart?" Jake called to him. He sounded apprehensive. "Sweetheart, are you awake?"

Randy squeezed his eyelids together. He heard footsteps hurrying toward the bedroom, coming to him. He waited for a moment, then opened his eyes. Jake was at the foot of the bed, looking down on him intently. Haircut and Sylvia hovered by the doorway.

"Are you okay, sweetheart?" Jake sat on the edge of the bed and touched the cover above Randy's legs. Randy edged away. "I mean, shit, m'baby's been in bed for three whole days. I didn't know what to think."

Randy glanced past Jake at Haircut, focusing on his dark hair, for an instant astonished that it wasn't blond, golden like it had been in that dream. He almost expected to see him rise into the air and drift from the room, float out some open window and fly away. "Hi, Haircut," he whispered.

Beaming, Haircut walked toward him. Sylvia hesitated, then followed.

Haircut stopped by the bed. "I told you I'd come. I wanted to see how you were."

"Me, too," Sylvia added, standing a few inches behind Haircut. She produced a tiny smile. "I've missed you."

Randy tried to smile back at her, but couldn't. The eagerness that he saw in her eyes and heard in her voice made him squirm.

"Those queens have been calling all the time," Jake threw in, smiling slightly himself. "You know, Fey and Stella. They wanted to know where you were, said something about a play."

Randy looked from Jake to Sylvia, then at Haircut. They were all staring down at him. He wanted to pull the covers over his head and go back to sleep.

"You really gave me a scare," Jake went on. "I couldn't get through to you at all."

"Yeah," Haircut said, almost to himself, "I'm glad I stopped by. I knew something was up."

Sylvia inched forward, tilting her head toward Randy, her eyes wide open. "Can I get you something? Some juice, maybe? Would that make you feel any better?"

Randy gazed at her. He felt as if he could vanish in her avid eyes. "No. No, I'm fine."

Haircut glanced at his watch, then at Randy. "Shit, it's late. I've gotta go. I mean, I've been here for more than an hour already. I've got this meeting I've gotta catch. But listen, Randy, I'll be back again as soon as it's over, I promise."

Jake leaned on Randy's legs, pulling them toward him. "Don't bother. M'baby's gonna be fine."

Randy twisted away, peering at Haircut. "Meeting?"

Haircut grinned. "Yeah, I told you about that the other day, remember? AA?"

Jake chortled. "Right, we wouldn't want you to miss *that*."

Randy sat up. His stomach was heaving, and he became aware of the welts on his back and thighs. They were still tender. An obscure feeling of uneasiness crept over him.

"I...I really can't stay either," Sylvia said to him. "Hugh's supposed to be stopping by. But please, let me know if I can do anything for you."

Jake squeezed Randy's leg. "Don't worry. M'baby and I have everything under control."

Randy pulled away from him, his eyes on Sylvia. "Hugh?" He spoke half unconsciously. "But...but why?"

"Huh?" Sylvia's gaze was restless, darting about the room. "Well...I mean, he promised he'd take me to some film."

"Oh. Oh, right. Sorry." Randy's uneasiness grew worse. He searched for his cigarettes, then, before finding them, turned toward Haircut, who had moved back a bit, as if preparing to leave.

Jake again took hold of Randy's leg. "Come on, relax. Things are gonna be fine."

Randy felt nauseous. The room seemed to have become much smaller and unendurably hot.

Haircut spoke to him: "So I'll see you later, Randy. In a couple of hours, after the meeting."

Thrusting himself from Jake, speaking rapidly, Randy asked, "Can I come with you?" Once he'd spoken, he was amazed by his words. He hadn't intended to say this.

Jake let out a quick snort. "Jesus, sweetheart, what do you wanna do that for? You don't need that crap."

Randy leapt from the bed and found his jeans and shirt on the floor. "How the fuck do you know?" He held onto his clothes, dizzy, keeping his back to the wall. He wanted to hide his welts.

Delighted, Haircut smiled at him. "You really want to come with me? Now? I mean, do you think you're ready?"

"Yes!" Randy's dizziness passed. He pulled on his shirt, carefully, then his pants.

"Are you nuts?" Jake flushed. "God, you might as well join some fucking cult."

Randy slipped his shirttail under the waist of his jeans.

Running her fingers through her hair, Sylvia mumbled, "I guess I'll go downstairs."

Haircut turned to Jake. "Leave him alone. Can't you see he needs it?"

"You don't know what the fuck you're talking about." Jake grabbed Randy's pack of Merits from the bedside table, struck a match, and, his hands unsteady, lit a cigarette.

Randy saw his shoes on the floor and put them on, then looked at Haircut. "Let's go."

"Sweetheart!" Jake grasped Randy's arm. "Come on, you gotta rest. You've been sick. You don't want to get into all that shit."

Randy drew away from him, snatched his cigarettes from the table, and headed toward the doorway. "Are you coming?" he said to Haircut.

"Yeah. Yeah, sure." Haircut hurried to his side.

Sylvia vacillated, glancing from Jake to Randy, then at Jake once more. "Thanks a lot," she murmured to him, following Haircut.

Jake ignored her. "Sweetheart, come on."

"Fuck off!" Randy shouted over his shoulder. Then he fled.

The heat was hideous. This was the worst April day that Randy could recall. The afternoon sunlight seemed to be shooting through his skin, to his core. Dazed, he did his best to keep up with Haircut's rapid pace. More than anything, he wanted a drink and a pill.

"Jeez, I'm glad you decided to come," Haircut told him as they rushed west.

"Uh-huh."

"Don't forget to call me 'Doug' when we get there. Everyone in the program does. Haircut's over. Doug's more real. I mean, it's me."

"Sure." Sweat trickled from Randy's armpits down his sides. He wished he'd never come out, that he'd stayed in bed. What the fuck am I doing, he wondered, going to some fucking AA meeting?

"You'll love the rooms," Haircut continued, walking even faster. "They're really cool. The people there, they understand. AA's a safe place."

"Safe?" Randy suddenly remembered Graham's penis pressing into him, pushing toward his guts. It happened again, he thought. He'd forgotten about that. He bit into his lower lip. Two women passed, arm in arm. One of them was wearing a thin white T-shirt and had thick gray hair, piled on top of her head in a bun. The second was much younger, in her early thirties, Randy supposed, and her hair was short and dark. She put her head on the older woman's shoulder.

"The meeting's up there in that church." Haircut pointed in front of him. "We're a little early. It doesn't start until five. That's good. You can meet some of my friends."

Randy froze, seeing a large group, mostly men, standing beside a church several yards before them, at the corner of 5th Street and Third Avenue. He didn't want to move any further. "Look..." he began.

Haircut smiled at him, his eyes twinkling. He seemed amused. "Yeah?"

"Look, this is a mistake. I...I..." Randy stared at the group by the church. He was astounded by how many of them there were, at least thirty, probably more. "I better go home. I've been sick. I should be in bed."

Haircut pulled at his arm, laughing. "Come on, you're just shy. We all are at first. You've been isolating too long."

Randy heard a woman's voice in the distance, screaming, "I'm going to kill someone before I fucking kill myself!" He glanced to the left of the church and saw a heavy-set woman with spiky red hair kicking a trash can. "I'm going to kill someone before I kill myself!" she cried again. "That's right. You'll see." Few paid attention to her.

His hand trembling, Randy reached into his shirt pocket for a cigarette. "Wh...who's that? I mean, is she in AA?"

Haircut nodded. "Yeah, that's Jude."

"Jude?"

"She's got issues, a lot of rage."

Randy lit his cigarette and raised it to his lips. "Oh, yeah?"

"Uh-huh." Haircut sighed. "She can't see how simple it is. All she's gotta do is work the steps. Just turn it over, surrender."

"Surrender?" Randy felt totally confused. He watched as Jude kicked the trash can once more.

"Motherfucker!" she screamed. "I'm going to kill those fucking cunts!"

"She's a painter," Haircut explained. "It's her ego, I guess. She can't get past that. She's pretty famous."

"Really?"

Jude kicked at the can again, missing it this time, then stood still, her eyes on the church's brick wall.

"She had this show in Soho last year. It got her a lot of publicity." Haircut giggled. "That's 'cause she likes to paint pictures of her pussy."

"Pussy?" Randy drew deeply on his cigarette. He wasn't sure what he wanted to do. He couldn't go home. But all of this was scary.

"You know, her vagina. That's all she does, just paints pictures of it." Chuckling, Haircut added, "By now, she's got the most famous pussy in town."

He was interrupted by a voice calling to him: "Dougie!"

Randy saw a short, bone-thin man standing at the outer rim of the crowd by the church and beckoning Haircut. He appeared to be in his late thirties.

"Ralph!" Haircut answered. "Girlfriend!" He ran to him and threw his arms around his neck, kissing him on each cheek.

Randy stayed where he was. Haircut wasn't looking at him, and he considered slipping away.

Haircut turned to him. "Come on, Randy, what are you doing? Come here. I want you to meet someone."

"Yeah, okay." Wary, Randy approached them, clutching his cigarettes tightly.

Haircut gestured toward his friend and grinned. "Randy, this is Ralph. Ralph T., I guess I should say. He's the answer. It's like he's gotten me through all sorts of shit." He spoke to Ralph: "Be nice to Randy. He's new. It's his first day."

"Oh, really? Well, congratulations, Randy." Ralph pulled back, taking in Randy's face, then moving his eyes downward and scanning his body. Leering, he glanced up. "Just a chick, are you? That's good. Welcome."

Randy tried to look at Ralph, but couldn't. He appeared much too thin. His face was pale and spotted with two purplish lesions, one to the left of his bulbous nose, the other, more prominent, high on his forehead, just beneath the widow's peak of his thinning blond hair. Randy was sure that he was sick. The welts on his buttocks started to itch. He gazed over Ralph's shoulder at the crowd behind him, focusing on a large, muscular woman in jeans and a flowered blouse. She was talking with three men and holding a liter of Diet Coke, sipping it through a straw. Randy detected the trace of a mustache above her upper lip.

"So," Ralph went on, a mischievous gleam in his eyes, "when did you…?" He paused, smiling. "Well, Randy…" He chuckled and looked down, surveying Randy's thighs. "How can I put this delicately? Oh, hell, when…?" Another, more dramatic pause. Then, cackling: "When did you hit your *bottom?*"

"I…I…" Randy noticed in the crowd a fat, middle-aged man and a fortyish woman pushing their way toward Haircut and Ralph. The man was Leonard, Randy realized, the person he had seen with Haircut at the café on Sheridan Square.

"Doug!" Leonard cried. He lumbered up to Haircut, his heft more apparent as he walked, and squeezed his arm. "Honey, I've been looking for you."

Haircut grinned. "Me, too."

They hugged.

Randy looked at the woman who had arrived with Leonard, taking in her tanned, lined face, her grayish hair, her blue eyes. She was wearing new, expensive-looking jeans, a green silk blouse, and a blue riding jacket. Randy found her bearing intimidating, too calm. There was a jeweled brooch pinned to her jacket. He suspected she was rich.

"Hello," she said to him, self-assured but friendly. "I'm Aggie."

"I…I'm Randy."

Aggie smiled. "I haven't seen you around here before. Is this your home group?"

"No…that is, well…"

Haircut interrupted him: "He's new, Aggie. Just coming in. Today."

"A chicky." Ralph winked at Randy.

Leonard leaned forward, speaking to Randy for the first time: "Oh, right, I remember you. We saw you the other day, on Sheridan Square."

"Yeah, I knew when I saw him then that he'd make it to the rooms." Haircut threw an arm across Randy's shoulder. "I just didn't think it'd be so soon."

Randy pulled back and ground his cigarette on the sidewalk, then lit a new one.

"So do you have a sponsor?" Leonard asked him.

"A sponsor?" Randy took a long drag. He could see Leonard's protruding stomach pushing against the buttons of his shirt.

"You know, someone's who's been here for a while, to help you out. You'll need one, especially now, during the first ninety days."

Randy looked past Leonard at the crowd. The woman holding the Diet Coke was listening to the man on her left. Her eyes were grave, and she was nodding vigorously. A shabby, solitary man on the church steps to her right started to sob. An older man rushed to him. "It's all right," he said. "It'll pass." The sobbing man glanced back nervously. He wavered, then, tears streaming down his face, retreated into the church. These people are all nuts, Randy thought.

Haircut was talking to Leonard: "Come on, Len, give Randy time. Maybe we'll find someone for him upstairs."

Behind them, Jude thrust her foot forward and shrieked, "Fucking cunts! I'll kill them!" She kicked the trash can, knocking it over.

"And she's off!" Ralph laughed.

Everyone roared.

Randy perused the crowd, which appeared to have grown larger, although most of the faces had begun to blur. Slightly to the side, standing alone, he saw someone he hadn't noticed before, a man close to his own age, slender and handsome. His skin was tanned, accenting a thin scar on his left cheek. Randy thought that he looked familiar, though from where he wasn't certain. The man stared back at him. Their eyes locked. Randy looked down at the sidewalk.

Far to his right, he heard a voice he recognized, speaking tentatively: "Randy?"

He looked up. A figure was emerging from the crowd, approaching him. It was John Stanley.

Seeing John, Haircut bristled. "You know *him?*"

"Ye...yeah." Randy drew on his cigarette, his eyes on John, shocked to see him here, not sure that he was glad to run into him now. He wanted to go home.

"I'd avoid him if I were you. He's toxic." Haircut paused, then mumbled, "Just a suggestion, of course."

John arrived, sneering at Haircut. "Suggestion?" His inflection was sarcastic. "Which one is it this time?" Speaking to Randy, he asked, "Did he tell you to keep it simple? Work the steps?"

Randy studied John, still disoriented at seeing him—although, he then remembered, John *had* joined AA. He looked healthier: His skin had more color, just as Haircut's did, and he had gained a little weight. But there was a biting edge to his voice, which made him sound much harsher than he had that night at Fey's.

"Hello, *John,*" Haircut muttered, moving away from him.

Leonard and Ralph cast disdainful glances at John, but other than that did not acknowledge his arrival. Only Aggie seemed to appreciate his presence: She was smiling.

Randy noticed how John affected the others, and this made him uncomfortable. He explored the crowd, hoping to find the handsome man he'd seen. He saw Jude pacing in front of the fallen trash can, then felt the sun beating down on his head.

"Hello," Aggie said cheerfully, greeting John.

John's eyes were on Randy.

"Listen, I've been thinking about you a lot since we had coffee the other night." Aggie was oblivious to John's preoccupation. "How're you doing? Have you been able to start writing again yet? You said you hadn't done anything in a while."

Randy crushed his cigarette on the sidewalk, staring at Aggie. The interest she had expressed in John's writing and her concern for him seemed completely unfeigned.

John turned to her and laughed brusquely. "What are you talking about, *write?* Shit, that's over. Everything is. Look where I am."

"But, John," Aggie protested, "it takes time."

Leonard entered the conversation, impatient. "That's self-pity, John. You've got to avoid that."

"Yeah," Haircut threw in, "get off the pity pot."

"Pity pot?" John snarled. "Christ, the jargon you all use! It's charming, almost as good as this fucking heat."

Sighing, Leonard spoke to Haircut, his tone measured: "I suppose it's time to go in."

Haircut scowled at John, then replied, "You're right."

Ignoring Leonard and Haircut, John looked at Randy and, his voice much softer, asked, "So what brings you here?"

John's face had relaxed, so that he appeared almost kind. Randy didn't know what to say.

"Well?" John sounded pensive. "Tell me, what's been going on?"

Taking in John's countenance, his thoughtful expression, Randy recalled the way Graham had been that night as he'd browsed through the photo album, wistful. Then he remembered what had occurred between them afterward. He brushed the side of his thigh with the palm of his hand, mumbling, "Some...something happened." Glancing past John, he saw the handsome man walking up the church steps. He sucked in his breath.

"Nothing to do with Fey and Stella, I hope." John's voice was abrasive once more. "Christ, I never want to see those sick queens again. They're impossible if you're not bombed."

Before Randy could respond, Aggie spoke up, addressing John: "Are you coming in? It's going to be crowded. We have to get seats."

Grimacing, Haircut said, "Come on, Aggie, you know John likes to sit alone."

Ralph touched Randy's arm, his smile lecherous, his enormous nose reflecting sunlight. "Let's go. It's about to start."

Seeing the purplish lesion near Ralph's nose, Randy looked away. In the distance, he saw a thin man with a can approaching the church. He was very young, in his early twenties, Randy surmised, and was moving slowly. Nowhere's safe, Randy thought. What's the point? He turned toward the church and saw the handsome man disappearing through the front door. There was a faint rapping in his chest. He noticed Jude bolting up the steps. Haircut grabbed his arm. "We better hurry. We don't want to have to sit in the back."

"Ok…okay." Randy glanced through the open doorway, searching for the handsome man, but couldn't see him. He felt Haircut pulling at his arm and started to move.

In a trance, he followed the others up the steps.

They took a slow, creaky elevator to a large room on the third floor. The room was hot and crowded, with dozens of men and a few women swarming around a long table holding two big coffee pots and four plates of cookies. Others were seated in the many folding chairs that faced a smaller table at the front of the room, in the center, an armchair behind it. Randy saw the handsome man sitting there.

"Who's that?" he whispered to Haircut. Everyone else had gone to get coffee.

Haircut grinned. "Oh, that's Garth. Beautiful, no? And his sobriety's flawless. He's qualifying today."

"Qualifying?"

"Yeah, you know, he's the speaker."

Randy kept his eyes on Garth. "But what does he do? I mean, it's…it's like I've seen him before."

"You probably have." Haircut's grin expanded. "He used to be one of the biggest models around. Then he got sober and realized what shit it all was."

"Really?" Randy found this hard to believe. He tried to remember if he'd ever seen Garth in an ad.

"Yeah," Haircut went on, "Aggie knows him real well. She's got this house upstate where she spends a lot of weekends. He's stayed with her there a bunch of times."

At the mention of Aggie's name, Randy became aware of her

standing in a corner near Garth, talking with John. Their conversation was animated: Both were speaking at the same time.

Noticing them, too, Haircut exclaimed, "Jeez, I don't what Aggie sees in that creep. I mean, *him?*" He shook his head. "I guess she's trying to help him. Or maybe she wants everyone to like her. A lot of rich women are like that."

Randy stared at Haircut. "Huh?"

"It's true, they are. But then Aggie's special. I think she just enjoys being nice to people. You should see her with her girlfriend Susan. She's this ex-junkie Aggie met a few years ago. She lives up at Aggie's house in the country, stays there all the time. She's had a pretty hard life, but Aggie takes good care of her."

"Oh, yeah?" Randy wanted to ask more questions about Garth, but felt overwhelmed by everything happening around him. He saw the muscular woman with the liter of Diet Coke seated in the front row, one of the men she had been conversing with outside next to her. Their heads close together, they were studying a thin blue book the woman was holding, its title, *Twelve Steps and Twelve Traditions,* written in large letters on the cover.

Jude sat behind them, upright in her chair. The shabby man Randy had seen on the steps was near her. He was no longer crying, but was talking to himself.

In the fourth row, Randy noticed the young man with the cane easing past three men toward a chair in the middle. All three stood and tried to help him. Declining their assistance, the man shook his head weakly.

As Randy watched him make his way toward a seat, his movements painfully slow, he thought he could feel the heat of the room expand and close in on him. There was a tall fan at the front to Garth's left, but its effect on the room's temperature was minimal. The man with the cane sat, appearing exhausted, as if the effort of finding a seat had drained him. Randy's head started to throb. He wiped his brow, wanting to flee.

Haircut yanked at his sleeve. "Let's sit down. Leonard's saved us some seats. It's too bad we came in so late. They're in the back."

Randy followed him to the back row. There was a set of keys on one of the chairs. "Whose are these?" he asked.

Haircut smiled, leaning over to pick them up. "Why, Leonard's. That's how we save seats around here."

"But couldn't…couldn't someone steal them?"

Haircut wrinkled his brow and gaped at Randy. "That wouldn't happen. Not *here*. Never. Come on, relax."

Randy sat in the chair where the key's had been, Haircut to his left. As Randy sat, he saw John leaving Aggie and rushing toward him, followed by Ralph, who had been standing by the coffee table. John reached him first and took the empty seat to Randy's right. Angry, Ralph skulked away and stood near a group of men at the back.

John spoke to Randy, grinning: "Ready to be brainwashed?"

Randy didn't know what to say. He stared at two posters on the wall behind the table where Garth was sitting. One read "The Twelve Steps," the other "The Twelve Traditions"—just like that book those people were reading, he thought.

A short woman with long, stringy hair and bad teeth strolled up and grabbed a bell from Garth's table. She shook it above her head, flicking her wrist with a strenuous enthusiasm. As the bell pealed, stragglers by the coffee table hurried to claim their seats, Leonard among them. He sat on Haircut's left.

"Be prepared for some real crap," John remarked to Randy.

"Shhh!" Haircut hissed.

The woman at the front spoke: "My name is Veronica, and I'm an alcoholic." Her voice was loud and cheerful.

"Hi, Veronica," the crowd answered in unison.

Turning toward Randy, John giggled. Randy sank into his seat.

"Welcome to Third Avenue Clean and Sober," Veronica continued, smiling at the crowd.

John again turned to Randy. "'Boy Pussy' is more like it. That's what everyone calls this meeting. If you can't get laid here, you can't get laid anywhere."

"Come on," Haircut muttered, piqued.

"Third Avenue is a special interest group for gay men and lesbians," Veronica explained, "but everyone is welcome. We meet once a week, at five every Saturday, and encourage the discussion of drugs as well as alcohol."

Randy glanced up at Garth, who was fidgeting, his eyes half-closed. He looked nervous. Clenching his jaw, Randy tried to imagine himself at that table, having to speak to all these people. He couldn't; he'd rather die.

"Roxanne will now read the preamble," Veronica announced. She nodded toward the first row, at the woman holding the Diet Coke.

"Oh, God," John remarked, "it's dotty Roxie!"

Earnestly solemn, Roxanne cleared her throat, then held up a small card and read from it, her voice booming huskily: "Alcoholics Anonymous is a fellowship of men and women who share their experience, strength, and hope with each other that they may solve their common problem and help others to recover from alcoholism."

John laughed. "Ugly, isn't she?" he whispered to Randy. "Can you imagine what she looked like as a man?"

Haircut overheard this. "Shut up, okay?"

John only laughed harder.

Embarrassed, Randy sank further into his seat, his eyes on Roxanne. Her greasy blond hair, its black roots visible, fell in ringlets around her face, highlighting deep pockmarks—distinct despite her heavy makeup—and her muscular frame, which looked absurd beneath her frilly, flowered blouse. This absurdity was augmented by the way she clasped the liter of Diet Coke to her breast, and Randy almost started to giggle. He stopped himself and looked at Garth.

"The only requirement for membership is a desire to stop drinking," Roxanne went on. "There are no dues or fees for AA membership; we are self-supporting through our own contributions."

Garth was sitting absolutely still now, no longer fidgeting, staring ahead, his hands clasped in front of him. He seemed to have calmed down. Randy gazed at him. The words that Roxanne read faded away. He couldn't remember if he'd seen Garth before, and if so, where, when. He was achingly handsome, in the way that Dennis Crawley must have been, his hair thick, falling over his brow, his skin tanned and glowing, his face luminous. The only flaw in his beauty was the thin scar that ran across his left cheek. Randy wondered how this had happened. He stared at his eyes. They were striking, enormous and brown, magnetic. Warmth emanated from them toward the audience. Randy was sure he could feel it flowing through him, in his veins.

Garth shifted in his seat and turned his head. A ray of sunlight shining in through an overhead window fell directly on him, so that it appeared to encircle his face, accenting his placid expression, giving him, Randy felt, an almost-miraculous radiance. Garth's eyes scanned the audience, then, suddenly, met Randy's gaze, just as they had done outside. Randy flushed. The posters on the wall behind Garth's head seemed to flicker in the light. They stared at each other. Stunned, Randy realized what it was about Garth that had struck him: With his tanned skin and penetrating eyes, he looked almost exactly like Mark Randall, an older Mark, wiser and mature, a Mark who was nearly perfect.

Haircut leaned toward Randy and whispered, "Veronica's gonna introduce the speaker now."

Randy pulled his eyes from Garth. Roxanne had finished reading the preamble, and Veronica was addressing the room.

"And now, to share his experience, strength, and hope with us, please welcome Garth of this group." Veronica's tone was lively, even passionate. The audience applauded wildly.

Looking at Garth, Randy didn't budge.

"My name is Garth, and I'm a grateful, recovering alcoholic," he began in a deep, lustrous voice, one that made Randy quiver.

"Hi, Garth," the room replied. Randy allowed himself to smile.

At first Garth talked about his childhood in the Midwest, using some words that, initially, Randy only partly understood. "My family was normal," he said with a grin, his teeth sparkling in the light. "Normal white trash and normally dysfunctional." Randy wondered what he meant. Everyone else in the room seemed to know; they all laughed.

He had two brothers and three sisters, and a father who drank much of the time. His mother died when he was three. "I never really knew her." As he said this, his voice was almost inaudible. "I just have this dim memory of her rubbing Vicks on my chest."

Randy felt a tightening in his gut. He focused on the wall behind Garth, on the poster listing the Twelve Steps, and read the first one:

"We admitted we were powerless over alcohol, that our lives had become unmanageable." He looked back at Garth. His words seemed to pierce his skull.

His father frequently beat him and—Garth learned this from one of his brothers when he was much older—molested his sisters regularly. Unhappy, Garth kept to himself, reading, living in fantasies, imagining what things would be like when he was an adult. But he didn't have much hope that anything would improve.

"For as long as I can remember I thought that I was different, that I didn't belong in this world," he said. "And I always knew that I liked men." His voice was calm. Randy felt as if he were being enveloped by him. "Of course, I was afraid to admit this or do anything about it when I was young. It made me feel like a freak."

Many in the audience nodded knowingly.

"When I was fourteen I met this guy Jim, much older than me, in his forties, I guess, someone who'd just started at the plant where my dad worked. Jim took an interest in me, and we began doing things together, going to movies, bowling, things like that. My dad didn't mind; it kept me out of his hair."

Randy's stomach fluttered. He stared at Garth, frightened by his words.

"I liked Jim a lot. He was smart; I thought he knew everything, that he understood me. When I was with him, he let me drink. Actually, I had my first drink with him. It was great. I hated the taste, but I loved the feeling it gave me. When I was drunk, I didn't feel so different anymore. It was like, for the first time, I could relax. It seemed like I belonged."

Randy felt just then as if he had gone back in time, as if he were twelve again. He tried to picture Garth at Mark's age, to imagine him sitting on a chair in the sun, bare-chested and smoking a cigarette.

"Jim rented a cabin in the woods outside of town, and at least once a week we'd go out there, hang out drinking. That cabin became really special for me. It was a place where I could escape from everything I'd known at home." He stopped. Staring in front of him, at the faces in the room, he lowered his voice and said, "One night while I was there I got totally wasted and passed out. When I woke up, Jim was on top of me."

Randy edged forward. The room seemed to disappear.

"The world changed for me after that night." Garth glanced down, then up again. "Jim and I became lovers. Secret ones."

Randy's head throbbed painfully. He felt as if the space between him and Garth had vanished. It was as if they were one.

"I was frightened by the sex at first, pretty freaked, but I learned to like it. Life at home didn't matter anymore; Jim was everything for me. But he was only around for one more year. After that, he lost his job and went on a bender. One day, without telling me, he just moved. I had no idea where he'd gone. I was devastated. I felt betrayed and began drinking a lot more, every day, taking drugs, pot and acid, staying home as little as possible. I started hanging out in the men's room at the local bus station, hustling. When I was sixteen, I ran away to New York."

The heat of the room felt excruciating to Randy. Garth's face became blurry, and his words sounded fragmented. Even so, Randy understood everything.

He went on to describe his life in New York, beginning with his year as a prostitute. He explained how he had found a "sugar daddy," Trenton, who was an agent for models. Trenton helped him get modeling jobs, and his career took off. He made more money than he had ever thought possible, went to all the best clubs, knew famous, important people, had hundreds of lovers, most one-night stands. Despite his success, he felt empty. He turned to drugs and alcohol as often as he could—particularly after the sweetness started claiming many of his friends.

"I guess my bottom began when Trenton died," Garth said. Randy could see that he was trembling. He thought of Jake, about Graham and Dennis. Then, with a shock, he thought about himself.

"I'd never really loved him, but I'd always known that he was there. I'd relied on him for everything. I didn't think I had anything to live for. I mean, I'd found out that I was positive anyway."

Randy squirmed.

"I suppose I wanted to die. I drank all the time, missed photo shoots, lost jobs, and got involved with this coke dealer Dean." Garth glanced to his left, then again to the front, his eyes livid. When he spoke, his tone was angry. "He was a creep, a total bastard,

completely fucked up, but handsome, incredibly sexy. I was mes-
merized by him. He treated me like shit, lied, cheated on me.
Sometimes he beat me. I didn't care. I thought he was all I had left.
Nothing mattered."

Randy leaned back. The welts on his sides rubbed against his
chair. He shot up, his spine rigid.

Garth took a swift, deep breath. Then, his voice much softer:
"One afternoon I woke up, hungover as usual. I didn't know where
Dean was. We didn't live together, but I was sure he'd been with me
the night before. There was dried blood on my cheek. I tried to
remember what had happened, but couldn't. I never did find out.
That wasn't unusual; I blacked out all the time back then. I lay there
all day, waiting for Dean. I thought he'd show up, but he never did.
It seemed like my life was over. If I'd had a gun, I think I would have
used it, killed myself. I decided that I'd do it in the morning, get a
gun or some pills."

Garth took a sip from the soda he was holding, again trembling.
Randy was trembling himself. He thought that Garth was about to cry.

But he didn't. A few seconds later, he spoke, slowly, even more
softly, his voice strained: "Late that night something happened,
something I still find hard to believe. It was a miracle, I know. Just
as I was about to fall asleep, I saw this bright, white light. Then I
heard a voice saying, 'You don't have to live like this anymore.' I realize now that it was my Higher Power. I didn't at the time, though. I
just knew—I don't know how, but I did—I just knew that it was
over. I surrendered." He took another sip from his soda, then
clasped the can tightly. "I came to AA the next day."

No one in the room seemed to breathe. Randy sat still, staring at
Garth's huge brown eyes. They appeared electric, as if something
were burning beneath them. Garth looked across the room and
smiled briefly. Randy was certain that he was smiling at him.

"You know," Garth said, his tone brightening, "we alcoholics are
resilient. I really think that being born one is a gift. Hitting a bottom, suffering as we did and living through it, has given us the
strength to move on to a higher plane, to have a spiritual life. I survived my childhood, my father, Jim, everything that came
afterwards, all those years of being half awake. I'm surviving being

positive today. We've all survived something, horrible things, things that were done to us and things that we did to ourselves. We're strong; we've handled stuff that might have killed anyone else. It's incredible what we can do now that we're sober and have put our pasts behind us."

The room seemed to be spinning. Randy no longer heard Garth's words. Minutes passed. He thought about his life, seeing Jake, Graham, Mr. Hewitt, his father. I survived, he told himself, just like Garth.

Then he became aware of the audience's applause; apparently Garth had finished. Everything appeared misty, the room, the faces in it. He couldn't see Garth. Instead, for a second, he thought he saw Mark Randall sitting at that table. He started shaking. The heat of the room seemed to draw him in, cover him. This wasn't unpleasant. He sensed an exhilarating freedom within himself. He felt like a child. His throat constricted. Tears ran down his cheeks. He realized he was sobbing.

As the applause ended, he felt someone take his hand and squeeze it. He glanced to his left. Through his tears, he saw that it was Haircut and that he was smiling at him. Embarrassed, he pulled his hand away, raised it to his eyes, and ran it across his face. He clenched a fist. Still shaking, he managed to stop his tears. He hated being this way, didn't want anyone to see him. He didn't want to feel anything.

"Are you okay?" Haircut murmured, concerned.

"Uh-huh. Sure." Randy felt his muscles grow taut. He wiped the last of his tears from his eyes, then turned from Haircut and saw Aggie, also in the back row. She was talking to the man beside her. Ralph was standing behind them. Seeing Randy, he grinned and winked. Randy looked away toward Roxanne, who was clutching the thin blue book she'd been reading, her eyes closed. He noticed Jude, steely-eyed, and near her, the shabby man from the church steps, muttering to himself.

His eyes returned to Garth. Veronica was standing in front of him, speaking to the room. "Are there any AA-related announcements?" she asked.

A good-looking man in his thirties stood and said that there was an AA dance that night at the Gay Community Center. Tickets were ten dollars at the door.

Randy concentrated on Garth, thinking about what he'd said, all the things that had happened to him, still astounded by his resemblance to Mark, by his story, by how similar parts of it were to his own—although Garth had been successful. And he was positive. Shivering, Randy thought of Graham and what they'd done. He wondered if he were positive himself.

The heat in the room began to feel even more oppressive. The fan at the front whirred futilely. He forced himself to listen to Veronica, who was speaking again. This time she wanted to know if there were any visitors from out of town or anyone new to this meeting in the room. A man from San Francisco introduced himself. When he was finished, Veronica asked if anyone present was celebrating an anniversary in AA. Nine people raised their hands. An older man named Steve had twenty-eight years, a woman sitting behind him three.

The last celebrant was Roxanne.

"My name is Roxanne, and I'm a *very* grateful recovering alcoholic." An immense grin spread across her huge face. "This coming Tuesday, God willing, I'll have twelve years."

The audience applauded, many whooping and whistling.

"Jesus," John muttered in Randy's ear, "they've put up with her for *that* long?"

Randy tried to laugh, but couldn't. His eyes flitted across the room, settling on the young man he'd seen earlier walking with the cane. He appeared frail, completely helpless. Randy wondered if Garth would ever be like that, if he himself would become that way, too. He looked toward the front, twitching. He didn't want to think about this; he couldn't see the point.

"Is there anyone here counting days?" Veronica asked. A dozen people waved their hands in the air.

She called on a freckled, balding man sitting in the first row. "I... I'm Tom," he said tremulously, "and...and I guess I'm an alcoholic. I've got thirty-two days."

"Hi, Tom," the audience responded, applauding with enthusiasm.

Haircut tapped Randy's shoulder. "Come on, raise your hand. You've got one day."

Randy shuddered. "No. No, I can't."

Haircut laughed. "Well, maybe later."

Randy stared at the floor.

When everyone who was counting days had been called on, Veronica spoke: "The format for this meeting is that we share until six. I'll now turn the room back to Garth."

Haircut leaned over. "Garth gets to pick them," he told Randy. "You know, the people who share."

"Share?" Randy glanced up. Half of the people in the room had raised their hands.

"Yeah, listen."

The first person Garth called on was Jude, who had been waving her arm wildly above her head. "I'm Jude, and I'm a fucking alcoholic." Her spiky red hair bristled under the room's harsh light. "I'm not grateful. Shit, I'm just a pissed-off bitch in recovery."

A few people sitting near her tittered nervously.

"I'm sick of these fucking meetings. I fucking hate them. The only time *I'm* grateful is when I'm getting fucked or painting my cunt."

The audience giggled, then, collectively, roared with laughter.

"She's too much," John snickered. "God, I love her. She almost makes coming here worthwhile."

Randy grasped the sides of his chair. These people are loony, he thought, completely whacked. But then there's Garth. He gazed at him. Garth was staring away from Jude, evidently not paying attention to her. Randy wondered what he was thinking, how long he'd been in AA, why he bothered to stay, being positive and all. Garth turned his head and caught Randy's gaze. Randy looked down.

Others shared after Jude. One was a distraught, frazzled man in his late twenties, who told of the difficulties he was having writing a Fourth Step. Randy didn't know what he was talking about. A woman standing in the back talked about her sponsor, who, she complained, had become too controlling. A man in a coat and tie spoke for more than five minutes about problems at his law firm. Randy stopped listening. He decided that he'd had enough; he wanted to leave.

The last person to share was the young man with the cane. "My name is Peter, and I'm an alcoholic." His voice was alarmingly weak.

Alert once more, Randy sat frozen, studying Peter's face, noting how drawn it was, how pale it appeared. He looked dead.

"Like Jude, I'm not grateful today." Peter's pitch became more forceful. There was a pronounced tremor in his voice. "Not at all. My...my..." He stared straight ahead, rocking back and forth. Suddenly he burst into tears. Moving quickly, the man on his right placed a hand on his shoulder and whispered something in his ear. Sobbing, Peter cried, "Leave me alone! My lover died ten days ago. Christ! He was buried last weekend." He continued to sob, but said nothing more.

The room was silent. "I'm sorry," Garth murmured, a palpable sadness in his tone. "Believe me, I am."

Randy felt a violent pounding in his chest. His eyes darted from Garth to Peter, then back to Garth.

No one said anything. Randy closed his eyes. He felt as if the room's heat were gripping him, yet he was freezing, shaking. He thought he was going to cry again. He opened his eyes. Garth was glancing in Peter's direction. His gaze was gentle and kind. He understands, Randy thought, he knows. But *what* does he know?

It was now six o'clock. Everyone stood and joined hands. Garth led them in a prayer.

"God," he began as the others in the room followed. His voice seemed to Randy to have become a slow drawl, each word that he spoke separate from the others. "Grant me the serenity..."

Randy focused on this word. It sounded foreign, sad. He stared at Garth, remembering that summer in Canada, Mark Randall. He wondered if he'd been happy then, if he'd been at all serene. Maybe that last morning, when he'd talked with Mark at the gas station. Maybe just for those minutes. But never since.

"...to accept the things I cannot change, the courage to change the things I can..."

He felt Haircut and John's hands linked with his. A warm draft blew past him. Momentarily sleepy, he yawned, then, just as abruptly, jerked his head up, wide awake.

Garth's eyes were shut, his head tilted down. There was a faint smile on his face. "....and the wisdom to know the difference."

Just then he felt the freedom he'd sensed before, at the end of Garth's talk. He almost laughed.

"Keep coming back," the crowd chanted. They swung their linked hands, raising them slightly, then brought them down. "It works if you work it."

He did start to laugh now, but held it in. He wanted to keep what he felt to himself.

The audience applauded. The meeting was over.

Randy stood by his chair, holding onto it, giddy.

"I'll be back in a flash," Haircut said to him. He and Leonard went to the coffee table, John as well.

The whole audience seemed to Randy to be moving in different directions, to be talking at the same time. He felt as if he were at a party or a bar. Besides himself, only Jude appeared to be alone. She sat stiffly in her seat, glaring toward the poster listing the Twelve Steps.

Aggie was speaking with Ralph, Roxanne conversing with one of the men she'd been with outside. Garth was surrounded, but he was ignoring everyone else and listening to Peter, who, though no longer crying, was still upset.

Haircut and Leonard returned from the coffee table. They stood next to Randy, one on each side.

"What did you think?" Leonard asked him.

Randy felt embarrassed by this question. "It…it was okay."

"Okay?" Haircut chuckled. "Come on, you know it got to you. I could see it."

John came back, a cup of coffee in his hand. Aggie and Ralph were close behind him.

"So," John laughed, speaking to Randy, "are you ready to do your Fourth Step yet?"

Haircut and Leonard frowned.

Before Randy could reply, Ralph and Aggie arrived. Ralph stood in front of Randy, his expression coy. "How's the chicky now that he's lost his AA virginity? Want to go out for some coffee?"

"I…" Looking past Ralph, Randy saw that Peter, a bit less distraught, was leaving the room and that Garth was heading toward them. His heart throbbed.

Aggie noticed this as well. "Oh, look, here comes Garth. Great. I didn't get a chance to talk to him outside. Wasn't he fabulous?"

"Wonderful," Leonard agreed. "One of the best. A real power of example."

"Flawless," Haircut chimed in. "Really the answer."

Garth joined their group, a grin on his face. "Hey, girl," he said to Aggie. "I saw you out front earlier, but I was too nervous to speak to anyone. I get pretty spaced before I qualify." He kissed her on the cheek and nodded at the others. Then he turned to Randy. His smile broadened.

Randy blushed and looked downward, stopping at Garth's hips.

"You were superb." Ralph took hold of Garth's arm. "Absolutely riveting."

"Honestly, you were," Aggie exclaimed.

"Thanks. Thanks a lot." Garth kept his eyes on Randy.

Randy looked up, seeing once more how brown Garth's eyes were, how warm they seemed. He blushed even more.

"And who are you?" Garth asked him. His voice was low. "I don't think I've seen you before."

"I...I..." Randy couldn't speak. He was sure that his face was crimson.

"He's new," Haircut explained. "This is his first meeting."

"Really?" Garth studied Randy, thoughtful. Then, under his breath: "I guess I knew."

John Stanley, who had been standing slightly to the side, seemed annoyed by this remark. "Exactly *how* did you know?"

Garth ignored him. Still gazing at Randy, he touched his arm and, speaking softly, said, "Congratulations. I know how hard it is." He squeezed his arm lightly before releasing it.

Randy stared at Garth, already missing his touch. His eyes seemed the gentlest he'd ever seen, yet they radiated a dizzying strength. He's safe, Randy thought; he has to be. He understands.

"So are you going out for coffee?" Aggie asked Garth. "We were thinking about Veselka's."

Turning from Randy, Garth answered her, regret apparent in his inflection: "I'm sorry, I can't. I've got to work. They've put me on the night shift." He immediately returned to Randy and, smiling, said,

"I'm a waiter at Flora's. You know, that restaurant on West 4th Street. It's my sober job."

"Oh, yeah?" Randy lowered his eyes, then quickly raised them.

"Come in and see me, any night. Or maybe we can go out for coffee sometime, after a meeting."

Standing absolutely still, Randy gazed back at him, unexpectedly moved—by his words, his voice, by the empathy he'd heard there, that he saw in his eyes. He felt a sense of joy come over him. It seemed to settle in his soul.

"So, Randy," Haircut asked, "do you want to come with us?"

Randy glanced toward them. "Well..." he began. He looked from Haircut to Leonard, then to Aggie and Ralph, finally toward John, who had backed off from the group. Everyone else was staring expectantly at Randy. Garth's not going to be with them, he thought. Feeling shy, he sensed the joy he'd experienced evaporating. He wanted to go home, go to bed, be alone, find that joy again and savor it. "I...I can't," he said.

"But fellowship's important," Haircut protested. "You can't isolate anymore. Not if you want to stay sober."

"Let him be." Leonard's tone was even. "He'll come round."

"Let's at least find him a sponsor while he's here."

Interrupting them, Garth said, "Look, I'll be seeing you all. I was supposed to be at work fifteen minutes ago."

Aggie spoke to him brightly: "Gee, I'm sorry you have to go. But don't forget, it's my anniversary in a month. I'm expecting you at my house in the country." She looked at the others. "All of you, actually. We'll have a party." Speaking to Randy, she smiled: "You'll come, too, of course. I love entertaining newcomers."

Randy grinned back at her. He could feel his joy returning.

Garth pulled a card from his shirt pocket and slipped it into Randy's hand. "Here's my number. Call me, okay? Anytime, please." His eyes rested on Randy a second longer. Then, with a smile, he turned and left the room.

Randy and the others left shortly thereafter. Outside, Randy felt as if he were floating. It was dark now, the moon was full, and there was a breeze in the air, a gentle, warm one. He took long breaths of the fresh air, oblivious to the chatter of his new friends. He barely registered the few other people from the meeting who remained in front of the church—Roxanne, standing with two men; Jude, pacing by the steps, eyeing a trash can—and didn't notice John Stanley as he moved to the side, then hurried off. Randy was anxious to be by himself; he wanted to think about Garth.

"Listen," Haircut said as Randy departed for home, "you've gotta get a sponsor. And start raising your hand. At least give your day count. It's important to acknowledge your sobriety."

"Sure, yeah, I will," Randy answered, though he hadn't paid close attention to him. He was clutching Garth's card, trying to fathom everything he felt.

As he drifted toward his apartment, his pace deliberately slow, he held on to an image he'd retained of Garth, sitting at that table, bathed in sunlight. Randy sensed a glow within himself; it seemed to be spilling out from his core. He knew that he was smiling—and that he wasn't high at all.

His glow became dimmer as he proceeded east. A cloud passed in front of the moon. He reached Avenue A and saw a familiar panhandler on the corner. Across the street, he was startled to see Peter from the meeting, his cane in his hand, creeping past Tompkins Square Park. Randy watched him for a moment, then rushed on. The glow he'd felt began fading more rapidly. By the time he entered his apartment and found Jake smoking a joint in the living room, it was practically gone.

XXII

Randy didn't want to get a sponsor or share his day count. He thought it sufficient that he went to at least one meeting a day, that he "kept coming back," as they said in the program. "You're crazy," Haircut told him when Randy refused to take these suggestions, and Randy suspected he was correct. He felt unbalanced—depressed and unsettled one day, flighty or manic the next—and slept poorly, but was too anxious to feel tired. "It'll get better," Leonard said.

"Take it one day at a time." Advice such as this infuriated Randy. He wanted to protest, but never did.

More than two weeks passed. He kept going to meetings, although the qualifications he heard there blurred together; none had the impact of the first. He was surprised that he continued to go and that he didn't drink or get high, didn't even want to very often. "The desire's been lifted," Leonard offered. Whatever, Randy thought. He wasn't sure why he'd bothered with any of this. Yet the meetings did seem to quell a fear he sensed at the back of his mind. Then, too, there was that glow he'd experienced after the first meeting. But he had not been aware of any glow since.

Jake was a problem, withdrawn and then belligerent, frequently stoned and glued to the television set. "Jesus," he'd said that evening when Randy returned from his first meeting, "I hope you got *that* out of your system. Maybe things'll get back to normal here now." They didn't. Actually, Randy rarely saw Jake: He spent his days away from the apartment, at meetings or, afterward, at coffee shops, which, timorously at first but at the urging of Leonard and Haircut, he'd started to frequent with his program friends. Sometimes, between meetings, he wandered the streets alone. He'd decided that he wanted to avoid Jake as much as possible. He hoped that, eventually, things between them would improve, that a period apart might salvage their relationship. To think otherwise made him nervous.

Haircut gave him a white pamphlet called a meeting book, and he discovered there were hundreds of meetings held all over the city, day and night, each with a name he found peculiar: Free and Clear, Living Sober, Just for Today, things like that. Many were open discussions, where anyone, even those not in the program, could go. Some, step meetings, concentrated on the study of the Twelve Steps. Randy was bored by these; he wasn't interested in the program's philosophy. He preferred the gay meetings, where, though still tense, he felt more at ease. He heard little of what was said, but saw familiar faces in these rooms: Haircut, of course, and Leonard, John Stanley, too, and Aggie, Ralph, Roxanne, Peter, Veronica, Jude, plus dozens more whom he had come to recognize. He found their familiarity comforting. And he liked some of them, especially Aggie, who smiled at him whenever she saw him. But the face he most wanted to see was nowhere in sight: Garth seemed to have disappeared.

The yearning that Garth had provoked in him remained acute as the days passed. It was particularly evident at three or four in the morning, on those nights—those many nights—when he could not sleep or, if he did, when he awoke with a start, his heart racing. Hoping to calm himself, he'd picture Garth as he remembered him, flooded by sunlight, warmth apparent in his eyes. He held onto this image as tightly as he could. Half awake, he imagined it floating before him in the dark. If he slept, it was prominent in his dreams. He never recalled how.

He kept Garth's card tucked away in a drawer, and considered calling him or visiting him at the restaurant, Flora's, where he worked. He did neither; he was too shy. He did walk by Flora's several times, stopping to look in the window, but on each occasion could not see Garth. The last time this happened, he remembered that Garth had said he was positive, then felt his stomach knotting. He rushed away and did not go back.

He worried inordinately about Garth's health after this, but was reluctant to mention his fears to his friends. Yet his speculations continued to prey on him. By the middle of his third week in the program, he could stand it no longer. That Wednesday evening, while at Veselka's, he braced his nerve and turned to Aggie, who was sitting beside him.

"Where...where's Garth been?" he asked her. "I mean, I haven't seen him in a while."

Aggie shook her head and sighed. "Oh, the poor dear. He's working his sweet little buns off, doing two shifts a day."

"Yeah?" Randy drew on his cigarette, immensely relieved. But he still couldn't understand why he'd never seen Garth at Flora's. He decided Garth had been busy, in the kitchen or something.

Haircut, Leonard, and John Stanley were seated across from them, John having tagged along at Aggie's insistence and to Haircut and Leonard's dismay. All were intrigued by Randy's inquiry, Haircut and Leonard leaning toward him as John, brooding, backed off.

"Yeah, he's got all these debts from his old life," Haircut said.

"He's been going crazy trying to pay them off. I guess he's doing an eighth and ninth."

Randy knew by now that Haircut was referring to the eighth and ninth steps. That's where they apologize to their friends for all the shit they've done, he thought, something like that. "Making amends," they called it. He supposed Garth considered paying his debts an amends. The whole idea seemed nutty to him.

"He shouldn't neglect his program," Leonard observed gravely. "It's not good if he's missing meetings. He should go to DA."

"DA?" Randy had never heard of this. He raised his cigarette to his lips.

"Debtor's Anonymous," Haircut explained, grinning. "You know what they say: Coming into AA opens doors—to other Twelve-Step programs anyway."

Everyone except Randy and John laughed. Randy was preoccupied, thinking about Garth.

"Christ," John muttered, shaking his head, "don't you people ever quit? Why don't you just give the Twelve Steps a rest?"

Irked, Leonard opened his mouth, but said nothing.

"So what's this about Garth?" John asked Randy. He sounded edgy. "What's so fascinating about *him?*"

Randy gripped his coffee cup and took a quick puff on his cigarette.

"Yeah," Haircut exclaimed, "you do seem *awfully* interested." He giggled, squeezing Leonard's arm. "Just remember: No relationships the first year. Don't be like me."

Smiling, Aggie broke in. "Well, Garth'll be at my party," she informed them. There was a lilt in her voice. "You know, for my sixth anniversary, on the fifteenth of May, in a couple of weeks. That's a Saturday, so don't forget: We're all going to the country."

Randy *had* forgotten about this; so much had happened since she'd mentioned it before. Hearing it now, he beamed at her. The rest of their conversation flew past him.

As soon as they finished their coffee, he hurried west to Flora's, alone. When he got there, he was thrilled to see Garth through the window, smiling at his customers while waiting on tables. Randy watched him for five minutes, taking in once more his tanned skin and bright eyes. That night at home, he slept soundly for the first time in weeks.

The next few days were good ones for him, the best he could recall since his first meeting. His sleep was less fitful, and he would awake refreshed. He saw that the weather was beautiful, then realized it had been this way for over a week, sunny and warm but never humid, the most glorious spring in years, everyone agreed. More relaxed, he found himself becoming attentive at meetings. Garth's been through this, he thought; he's listened to the same sort of things. Although he'd been in the program for nearly twenty days, only now did the concepts elucidated there actually begin to sink in.

AA was a simple program for complex people, he heard, people who had been born with a progressive, chronic disease, alcoholism, a compulsion to drink and drug that could only be described as insane. This wasn't their fault, of course, but the progression of their disease had caused them to destroy their lives in various ways. Before coming to AA, some had what was referred to as a "low bottom" and lost everything: their lovers, their jobs, their homes, the respect of their friends and families. Others, seemingly more fortunate, had "high bottoms" and retained what the low bottoms had lost; the surface of their lives still looked good. Even so, they shared with the low bottoms a spiritual malaise, an emptiness inside that ate away at their cores.

The only treatment for this disease was AA, a spiritual program for what was, in essence, a sickness of the soul. By following AA's suggestions—going to meetings daily, finding a sponsor, sharing, working the Steps, engaging in prayer and meditation—alcoholics would have a spiritual awakening and could thus begin to recover, become serene and truly sober, not merely dry. The resultant transformations in them were miraculous, enabling them to be, as AA's literature read, "happy, joyous, and free."

Randy assimilated all of this, listening to the qualifications, hearing what people shared—although he still never shared himself.

At a meeting one night he bought what was called the Big Book, a thick blue volume entitled, simply enough, *Alcoholics Anonymous*. He took it home and read some of the stories in it, stories from the

1930s about alcoholics—stockbrokers, doctors, housewives—who had recovered in AA. He thought these stories old-fashioned, yet they gripped him. He especially liked one about a woman who drank as she did her laundry, while her husband was at work. After reading of how she reached her bottom and about her subsequent recovery, he heard Jake snoring beside him in bed. He wanted to hit him. Restraining himself, he looked around the room, away from Jake—at the clothing on the floor and at the graying walls—mulling over his life.

He was going to be thirty-three in two months. This shocked him; he hadn't really grasped it until recently, since he'd come into the program. He wondered where his life had gone, how he'd gotten to this point, living with someone who, he had to admit, disgusted him. A lot of people he'd heard speaking in AA seemed to have done so much by his age. They had good jobs; many were very successful. Randy wasn't even working, and he had no skills. This was frightening; the money that Graham had sent him the last time was nearly depleted. He didn't want to, couldn't somehow, go back to his clients, yet he had to do something. Jake would see to that. He wished he were someone else, someone successful and famous, or rich like Aggie, someone like Graham and Dennis.

Or Garth.

He looked down and saw Jake, his right arm flung across his head, his mouth hanging open. He's all I've got, Randy thought, and that's going, too. He recalled his sessions with Graham, regretting that there would be no more of them—until he remembered everything they'd done. His stomach reeled. Nothing matters, he told himself. I'm going to get sick. I'm going to die.

He bolted up, throwing his legs over the side of the bed, wanting a drink. He clenched his jaw. The urge receded. He decided he needed to leave the apartment, but didn't know where to go. It was too late for another meeting. And he couldn't visit Sylvia, or Fey and Stella. He hadn't seen any of them in weeks, though they called often. He'd put them off; his friends in the program had told him to avoid "people, places, and things" from his old life.

He thought about these AA friends of his. Most appeared happy with their lives, content in their sobriety. Haircut was overflowing with the new things he'd learned. Leonard, though dogmatic about AA and a little pompous, apparently had achieved some sort of serenity. And Aggie, Randy suspected, approached the program as she did both her life in the city and her weekends in the country with her girlfriend: calmly, shielded by money.

He then thought of John Stanley. Sobriety didn't appear to agree with him at all. He was bitter all the time these days, rancorous and sarcastic. Randy felt much less drawn to him than he had when they'd first met; he found his dark moods unsettling. "Self-pity" Leonard called John's customary humor, but Randy was sure it was something else, exactly what he wasn't certain. Whatever it was, it was obvious that drugs and alcohol had helped hide it before.

He recalled an exchange he'd had with John shortly after leaving a meeting with him one night. John was silent as they walked, occasionally glancing at Randy from the corner of an eye. Just before they parted, he gazed at him again, still silent, clearly melancholy. Then, speaking faintly, he said, "You're so lucky."

Randy shrank back; he couldn't believe what he'd heard. He looked at John and, incredulous, asked, "What do you mean?"

John's melancholy expression disappeared, and he smiled thinly. "You heard me. You're the luckiest fucker around."

Randy lowered his eyes to the sidewalk, embarrassed. "But...but why?"

John produced a short, barbed laugh. "Because you're young. Young and gorgeous. You're every faggot's dream. Enjoy it while you can. It won't last." He stopped, then, melancholy once more, added, "You know, don't you, that it's long gone for *me?*"

Randy was haunted by what John had said that night, even now, more than a week after the conversation had occurred. He didn't want to become like John, ever. Yet things seemed so hopeless much of the time. "You've gotta work the program," Haircut had told him. "Just work it and surrender." Leonard spoke of prayer constantly. "Get down on your knees, and turn it over to God," he'd said. Randy found this idea strange. He couldn't remember having prayed, even as a child. His father had always laughed at religion.

Beside him, Jake coughed, then exhaled, producing a particularly grating snore.

Randy jumped out of bed and glanced down at Jake, taking rapid breaths. Moving impulsively, he fell to his knees and clasped his hands in front of him. He was afraid Jake would awake and see him. And he didn't really know how to pray. He closed his eyes and thought about Garth, then tried to form words, but could find nothing to say. Help me, he thought.

The next day he was awakened late in the morning by a messenger delivering an envelope from Graham. He wondered if the plea he'd made the night before could be considered a prayer. If it had been one, it seemed to have had an effect: The envelope contained a check for one thousand dollars. While easing his financial concerns, this delivery only made him feel worse, since the envelope included no note. He stared at Graham's handwriting on the envelope, noting that it was almost illegible. He ran his hands across his thighs, nauseous. He contemplated going back to bed, but Jake was still asleep. He went to a meeting instead.

The first familiar face he saw was Peter's, ghostly pale and horribly thin. Randy couldn't take his eyes off him. He wondered if Graham had gotten sicker since he'd seen him. Then he worried about what the future held for himself. He wished Garth were in the room, so he could talk to him.

The speaker was Roxanne. He didn't hear her, was scarcely conscious of the meeting until the shares started in the last half hour. He listened to the voices around him, but could make no sense of them. His nausea grew worse.

Near the end of the meeting, he became aware of Peter sharing, sobbing as he had done before. "I'm going to die," he cried. "Soon."

Quaking, Randy listened, hearing Peter tell of the treatments he'd been receiving from his doctor. They weren't working; he was getting worse. "Sometimes I think dying would be a relief."

When Peter was finished, Randy sat still, quaking even more. Suddenly and unexpectedly, he felt an urge to raise his hand. He wavered. A dozen hands were raised, vying for Roxanne's attention. Who's going to notice? he thought. He lifted his arm slightly, half-heartedly. Roxanne looked around the room, at the raised hands. To Randy's shock, she called on him.

He couldn't talk at first; he only gazed at Roxanne, frozen. He finally opened his mouth, and was surprised to hear words emerge. "I…I'm Randy," he said, very softly, "and I'm…I'm an alcoholic."

"Hi, Randy," the others in the room answered.

He was silent, dropping his eyes to the floor. He took a deep breath. "I…I don't know why I raised my hand. I mean, I don't know what to say. It's just that I…I'm…Shit, I'm scared."

He stopped. His heart was pounding. The audience waited patiently, but he said nothing else.

By now it was time for the meeting to end. Everyone stood and linked hands for the closing prayer. Randy wished he could evaporate.

Afterward he saw Leonard trudging toward him from the back of the room, his steps heavy and purposeful. Evidently he had been standing there throughout the meeting. Randy hadn't noticed him until then.

"I think you've got a problem with self-esteem," Leonard said. He stared at Randy with a disconcerting intensity and nodded significantly. "Yes, I'm sure you do."

Randy focused on Leonard's thick neck, then peered past him toward a group of men standing beside the coffee table.

"I've got a suggestion for you," Leonard continued somberly. "Later, when you get home, just look in the mirror and say to yourself, 'I love you.'"

"Oh, yeah?" Randy muttered. He was sorry now that he had shared at all. "Really?"

"Oh, yes, try it. You'll see."

Randy left the meeting immediately, anxious to get away, astounded by Leonard's suggestion. Yet once he was home, he could not get it out of his head. Jake was in the living room watching TV. Randy walked past him without saying a word.

He went to the bathroom. There was a mirror on the medicine cabinet above the sink. He glanced up at it, then quickly downward. Leonard's full of shit, he thought. He glanced up again, seeing a face in the mirror, that of a young man, brown hair falling across his brow, his skin clear, his eyes alert but fearful. He was very handsome, just the way Dennis had been in the pictures Randy had seen, like Mark Randall, too, and like Garth. That's me, Randy told himself.

He leaned toward the mirror and gazed at his reflection, at his eyes, which now seemed, somehow, less frightened. He almost wanted to press his lips against the glass. Instead he looked at his image and, speaking distinctly, said to it, "I love you."

"Jesus Christ! What the fuck are you up to now?"

Randy quickly pulled back from the mirror. Jake was standing behind him, at the doorway.

"Is this some more of your AA crap?" Jake growled. "Shit, that's all you think about anymore."

Randy moved forward, glaring at Jake, then saw that his eyes were red and that he was swaying unsteadily. Fucking pothead, he thought.

Jake lurched over to Randy and grabbed him around the waist. "Come on, sweetheart, get over it. I mean, we haven't even fucked or anything in weeks."

Randy pushed at Jake's shoulders and shoved him off, rushing past him, out of the bathroom to the bedroom. "And we aren't going to do it now either!"

Jake followed him. "Shit, what's happened to m'baby?" His tone was much softer, and his voice was cracking. "I want him back."

Randy turned around. He could see an almost-childlike wistfulness in Jake's eyes, pathetic but appealing. I don't want to lose *that*, he thought.

Jake approached Randy and took hold of his hand, stroking it. "Let's just get high and take an afternoon nap, okay?" He smiled meaningfully.

Randy recalled the pills he'd stolen from Graham. The bottle was in his bureau drawer. He had meant to throw them out ten days ago, when he'd realized they were still there. Leonard and Haircut had suggested at the time that he do this, but he never had. He thought of taking one now; he could make up with Jake and forget about everything.

Jake squeezed his hand. "Please sweetheart." He smiled once more, revealing a large silver cap on a tooth at the back of his mouth.

Randy then remembered Garth; he'd be seeing him very soon. Jake's hand felt cold pressed against his, cold yet sweaty. Frowning, Randy pulled away from him, trying to disregard his fading smile, the disappointment and anger evident in his eyes.

"Well, fuck you then!" Jake snapped. "You and your fucking AA prigs!" He pivoted around and left the room.

Rooted to the spot, Randy felt numb. He heard the front door slam. A faint sadness came over him. He grabbed a cigarette from the pack in his shirt pocket. For an instant he considered going after Jake; maybe he'd try and placate him. He decided that he wouldn't bother. He had a new life now. Jake was just a fuck, a pig and a shit. On top of that, he wasn't sober.

A few days before the weekend of Aggie's anniversary, the weather changed, turning insufferably humid overnight. Summer appeared to have arrived early. Overwhelmed by the heat, Randy felt his emotions fluctuating wildly, almost as much as they had during his first two weeks in the program. On one hand, he was excited, eager to see Garth. But the situation with Jake was distressing. The silence that existed between them and the hostility he sensed underneath this felt sharper, more pronounced every day. Any thought of the future terrified him. He scarcely slept. He clung to what he heard at meetings and tried to follow suggestions, to share and pray, but found that he couldn't. Garth seemed to be his only salvation.

"Don't worry so much," Haircut said to him that Thursday at Veselka's, after he'd asked Randy about Jake, and Randy had told him how bad things were. "Jeez, we'll be at Aggie's in a couple of days. Her place is flawless. She's got horses, and a pool. And her girlfriend Susan's a fabulous cook. She taught herself how when she gave up junk."

"Really?" Randy had never met Susan, and he couldn't imagine what she was like, couldn't understand how anyone who had once been a junkie stayed in the country all the time.

"Yeah," Haircut continued, "it's gonna be great. You'll see. Anyway..." He smiled puckishly. "Garth'll be there. You'll forget all about Jake then."

Randy puffed on his cigarette. "Yeah. Yeah, sure, okay." He wanted to change the subject. But he knew that Haircut was right: He shouldn't let Jake get to him. He just wished it wasn't so hot, that things with Jake would get better—and that Garth was with him today.

The plan was to meet at ten Saturday morning by the clock at Grand Central Station, the five of them, Randy, Haircut, Leonard, John, and Ralph. They would spend the day in the country and leave that evening. Garth was going to Aggie's on Friday afternoon, Randy was told; he was taking three days off from work and staying until Sunday. Aggie wanted to use that time to talk with him on her own.

When Randy went to bed shortly after midnight on Friday, Jake was out. Great, Randy thought, he won't hassle me about where I'm going when I leave in the morning. He managed to sleep, and awoke just before nine. The television in the next room was blasting a children's cartoon, and he could smell pot. He rose and dressed, then walked through the living room toward the kitchen. He wanted to fix a cup of coffee before he left.

Jake was in an armchair in front of the television set, smoking a joint. He glanced up when he heard Randy enter. His eyes were glazed.

"So m'baby's up." Jake's inflection was harsh.

Randy continued walking.

Jake watched him, guarded. Then, abruptly, he mumbled, "You know, sweetheart, don't you, that it's over?"

Randy froze. He was afraid to turn around. *"What?"*

Jake chuckled weakly. "You heard me. I said it's over. Fucking finished. Dead, kaput."

Randy swirled toward him. "What the fuck are you talking about?"

Jake had a dim smile on his face. His eyes were now half shut. "Us, sweetheart, us. We're finished."

Randy thought that he couldn't breathe. The room was sweltering, the air heavy and humid. "I don't have time for your shit," he cried. "You're just fucking stoned." He hurried to the kitchen.

"I don't know what we're going to do," Jake continued, his voice becoming distant, regretful. He seemed not to have heard Randy or to notice that he had moved on. "You'll have to find another place, I guess. We'll do something."

Standing by the kitchen sink, Randy scooped a teaspoon of instant coffee into a cup, his hand trembling.

"I tried," Jake went on. His words were slurred. "Jesus, I tried. But you just…" He sighed.

Randy realized he hadn't put any water on to boil. He looked at his watch; it was after nine. He threw the teaspoon down, then flew from the kitchen toward the front door.

Jake rose unsteadily when he saw Randy rush by. "Sit down, sweetheart. We've gotta talk."

"Later," Randy shouted back at him. He hurtled out of the apartment to the stairs.

Outside, the air was foul, oppressively smoggy, the sky overcast with thin clouds. A radio blared across the street, the noise horrendous. A car sped by, and Randy had an urge to throw himself in front of it. He stood still. I'm fucking nuts, he thought. Shaking, he hailed a cab.

He was relieved to see that Grand Central was half empty and that all of his friends had arrived. Everyone except John carried at least one shopping bag. The station felt like an oven to Randy, and he was soaking wet.

"Just gotten out of the shower?" Ralph ran his fingers through his thin blond hair and winked at Randy.

John looked at Ralph, fuming, then stuffed his hands in his pockets and turned away.

"Come on," Haircut said. "We better hurry. The train leaves in ten minutes. Leonard's bought us all tickets. Let's go."

On the train, Randy sat by the window, Ralph on his right, the others across from them, Haircut and Leonard close to each other, their legs pressed together, John perched at the edge of his seat by the aisle. Gazing outside, Randy stared at the tenements they passed, at the graffiti-covered walls of abandoned buildings, at the heaps of garbage in vacant lots. He knew that he should feel excited; this was the first time he'd left the city since he'd visited a client in Connecticut over a year ago. More important, he was about to see Garth. But the sky was so dismal and gray.

And then there was Jake.

Ralph leaned toward him. "What's the matter?" he asked, squeezing Randy's leg. "Under the weather?"

Turning from the window, Randy focused on the lesion near Ralph's large nose, then, quickly, on his eyes. At first he thought he could see a clear empathy there and, for a second, felt like confiding in him, about Jake, about Graham, even about his fear of getting sick. But when he took in Ralph's full face, he saw that he was displaying only his usual leer. He lowered his head.

"Well?" Ralph again squeezed Randy's leg.

Randy felt blood pounding through his veins. He could not look at Ralph. "I...I...My lover and I had a fight. Earlier, just before I left." He glanced up. John, who had been subdued all morning, was smiling faintly.

Haircut frowned. "I'm not surprised. Jake's a prick. What do you expect from a user? You'd be better off without him."

"Yes," Leonard agreed. He peered at Randy, his eyes milky and solemn. "You'll get over it. Just remember: Feelings aren't facts."

No longer smiling, John shook his head, muttering, "Shit, enough of the program crap! Is everyone supposed to be fucking cheerful all the time?" He shut his eyes as if to sleep.

Randy gripped the arms of his seat and shifted his eyes back to the window. They had left the city and were speeding by suburban streets. The lawns of the houses they passed were brilliantly green, and he could see children on swings and riding bicycles. He looked at the sky and was surprised to discover that the clouds were clearing and that the sun was coming out. He recalled Garth. His heart fluttered.

Impervious to the sounds of the train's other passengers, to the prattle of Haircut, Leonard, and Ralph, he continued to stare out the window. Gradually, the suburbs disappeared. He saw tilled fields and blossoming trees, and realized they had reached the country. The sun shone brightly now, directly on him. He smiled. Jake can go to hell, he thought; I"m fine by myself.

Aggie met them at the station, standing alone by a red Ford station wagon. It was just before one. The temperature seemed to Randy at least ten degrees cooler than it had in the city, and he felt a soft breeze in the air. Buoyant, he searched the parking lot for Garth.

As if reading his mind, Aggie chirped, "Garth's back at the house, with Susan and the guys."

Leonard grinned. "The *brood*," he murmured dryly, amused.

"Brood?" Randy was confused. "Guys?"

Ralph laughed. "Aggie's got a whole menagerie out there. Eight dogs, four horses, half a dozen cats. And ducks, too."

"Yeah?" Randy followed the others into the car.

"Yeah." Aggie smiled. "They sure keep Susan and me busy." She started the car and pulled out from her parking space.

Her house, she informed them, was twenty miles from the station. As she drove—Ralph, John, and Randy in the back, Haircut and Leonard squeezed together in the front beside her—Randy studied the passing scenery, enthralled. He saws acres of verdant fields, horses grazing, and long, shadowy driveways, mansions visible in the distance. Jake and the city seemed far away.

Animated, Haircut pointed toward an immense, red-bricked house at the top of a hill, overlooking a particularly impressive estate. "Don't the Rockefellers live there?" he gushed.

"Oh, God," John muttered. He was sitting between Randy and Ralph, and had been silent since they'd left the station. "Where did you get *that* information."

"Actually," Aggie piped in, "they did live there at one time. But that was years ago. I'm not sure who owns it now."

Randy gazed at the estate as they whizzed past it, trying to imagine what it was like inside.

They turned onto a pebbly driveway at the outskirts of a town called Lincolnville and, proceeding carefully, drove over it.

"Well, everyone, we're here," Aggie said blissfully, but Randy did not hear her. He was too distracted by the view around him, struck by the trees flanking the drive, by their thick green foliage, the sunlight dappling through the branches, by the butterflies flitting near the ground. It felt to him as if he had not seen anything like this in years.

They rounded a corner and arrived at a large wooden house nestled in a sunny grove. Green hills rose prominently along the skyline beyond it. The house was old and in some disrepair, its whiteness faded yet dazzling in the sunshine. A pretty woman in her early twenties, tall and with long, dark-blond hair, stood in front of it. She was dressed in blue shorts and a bright red T-shirt, and was surrounded by an assortment of huge baying dogs.

Randy examined her through the car's window. That's Susan, he told himself; she used to be a junkie. This seemed strange to him; she appeared so wholesome, her face incandescent, her hair flying across her ruddy cheeks. He supposed she'd changed a lot since she'd given up smack.

Aggie stopped the car, and everyone hopped out. All the dogs ran to Aggie, barking, tails wagging. Susan smiled at them—shyly, Randy noticed. He looked toward the house, then took a long breath. Behind Susan, standing on the porch, he saw Garth. He was bare-chested and leaning against a pillar, his right arm raised, the hair in his armpit conspicuous. Randy felt naked and wanted to rush to him.

Garth lowered his arm and hurried down the steps toward them, a wide grin on his face. Randy gazed at his skin as he moved. His chest was muscled and tanned, his nipples large and dark. He felt himself getting an erection.

"Down, kids, down," Aggie laughed, talking to the dogs, who were all jumping up on her, pawing at her legs and chest.

Garth arrived, his teeth gleaming. "Hey," he said to the group, then glanced at Randy.

Susan also approached them, slowly.

Pulling away from the dogs, Aggie threw an arm around Susan and kissed her on the cheek. "This is Susan, Randy. I guess the rest of you know her." Smiling at Susan, affectionate, she said, "What's up, hon?"

"Well, the food's about ready." Susan smiled back, touching Aggie's hand. "Garth's been helping me out. You just have to make the salad."

"So what are we waiting for?" Haircut cried.

They all headed toward the house, followed by the dogs.

Garth fell into place beside Randy. "How've you been?" he asked, his voice deep and eager. "I've been thinking about you." He paused, uncertain. "That is…well, I've been wondering how you've been getting along. You know, in the program."

Randy stared at the muscles of Garth's shoulders, at his brown skin, at the streaks of hair curling out from under his arms. "It's…I'm okay," he said. "I mean, I've been going to a lot of meetings. All the time, every day."

"That's good. I wish I could say the same."

Randy could see that Garth was gazing at him—intently, he felt.

"Yeah, I...I haven't seen you around. I..." Just then he observed John walking several feet to their left, watching them. He was unable to say anything else.

They entered the house through the kitchen, followed by the dogs. Randy saw a long table at the back of the room, cluttered with dishes, bowls, potato peels, and egg shells. More dishes were piled in a sink, and a tall plastic bag full of garbage was propped against a wall. Cats appeared to be everywhere, reminding Randy of Sylvia's apartment. Two were on the table, staring at Aggie's guests, four others at her feet, rubbing their heads against her legs and hissing at the dogs.

Randy wasn't sure why, but he found this disorder comforting. Sunlight poured through the windows, making the room extremely bright, highlighting four small paintings, colorful portraits of dogs, which were framed and hanging on the walls. He could smell something cooking, something delicious, and realized he was starving, that he hadn't eaten since the previous afternoon.

"I see you're as domestic as usual," Leonard drawled, speaking to Aggie, amused, his eyes roaming the room.

Hearing this, Susan flushed, then scurried to the table, shooed the cats away, and started clearing the dishes.

"Oh, I know, I know," Aggie giggled, "it's a mess. And I haven't painted the house yet either. I'm a slob."

"You said it, my dear," Ralph answered with a smile.

Grinning, Aggie walked to the refrigerator and opened its door. "Why don't you quit complaining and make yourself useful? You can help with the salad."

Garth rushed to her side. "Here, I'll do it."

Haircut grabbed Randy's arm. "Come on, let me show you the living room."

Randy was staring at Garth. "Well, I . . ." He was reluctant to leave.

"Come on."

"Yeah, all right." Glancing at Garth again, Randy allowed Haircut to pull him through the doorway. Two golden retrievers followed them.

The living room was spacious and, in striking contrast to the kitchen, luxuriously appointed, carpeted with a thick Oriental rug and full of expensive-looking antiques. Randy thought of Mr.

Hewitt. Yet while Mr. Hewitt's house had been immaculate, almost like a museum, this room seemed lived-in, homey. Sweaters and jackets had been thrown across two high-backed mahogany chairs, and paperback novels, newspapers, and magazines were scattered across a wide marble table and on the floor. He saw four more portraits of dogs on the wall, slightly larger ones, and photographs in silver frames displayed next to porcelain figures on a shelf to his left. Many of the photos were of an older, well-dressed, obviously prosperous couple—Aggie's parents, Randy supposed—but quite a few were of Aggie and Susan, smiling, their arms around each other. Randy felt jealous. He wished he could be like that, could have some of this, too.

"Can you believe all this shit?" Haircut exclaimed. "Jeez, Aggie's loaded."

One of the dogs leapt onto an armchair, wagging his tail.

"Yeah," Randy answered, "she's sure lucky."

They returned to the kitchen and found Aggie and Garth working together at the dining table, peeling onions and chopping tomatoes, several dogs asleep at their feet, three cats watching them from a windowsill. Susan was doing the dishes, while John, silent, stood by one of the windows, staring out onto a garden. Following his gaze, Randy saw a line of ducks waddling together past a distant oak tree.

"Where's Leonard?" Haircut asked Aggie, looking past her toward a window.

"Oh, he and Ralph are taking a walk outside."

"Well, I'm going, too."

"Sure, be my guest. But don't go far. We're going to eat soon."

"Don't worry. I'll round 'em up." Haircut turned to Randy. "You wanna come with me?"

His eyes on Garth, Randy shook his head.

"Okay. So I'll see you in a minute then." Haircut ran out the door.

Once Haircut had gone, Randy didn't know what to say or do. For a moment it seemed very strange being here, in the country, away from Jake. Still standing, he thought of helping Aggie and Garth, or maybe Susan, but wasn't sure how.

Garth looked up and smiled at him. "Are you okay? Not bored or anything, are you? Come on, sit down."

Randy tried to smile back, but felt awkward. "Oh, okay. Thanks." He sat in a chair near Garth, glancing at the scar on his left cheek, then at his bare skin. Turning quickly toward a window, he allowed the sun that was floating in to wash over his face.

John bolted to the door and hurried outside.

"So what do you think of my mausoleum?" Aggie asked Randy.

"Huh?" Randy stared at her, not comprehending.

"All that crap I've got in the living room." Smiling, Aggie threw some chopped tomatoes into the salad bowl sitting on the table before her. "None of that stuff means a thing to me. I just got it from my parents when they died. I had to put it *somewhere*." She picked up a large wooden fork and tossed the salad, then, stopping, pointed at a portrait of a dog hanging on the wall behind her. "The only things in there I really care about are Susan's dog paintings. The rest of it's all…I don't know, garbage, I guess."

Finishing the dishes, Susan spoke up self-consciously: "Oh, come on, Aggie, my stuff's just silly."

"Don't be modest, hon. Everyone loves your paintings. Leonard bought three of them."

"Yeah, but I'm no artist. Not really."

Garth laughed and said, "Aggie's right, Susan. Your paintings *are* wonderful. Besides, even if they weren't…well, she'd still like them." He paused, then, his voice lower, added, "She's in love."

Susan turned to him, blushing. Randy felt himself blushing as well.

"You both are," Garth went on. "That's one of the reasons it's so great being with the two of you, seeing you together. It's like what we were talking about last night: Love's the important thing, those connections we manage to make. I've realized that, really just seen it since I've come into the program. With all the shit we have to put up with, it's a miracle we can connect at all. It makes everything else worthwhile, though, doesn't it? It's…" He stopped, glancing toward Randy.

Randy met his gaze, then looked at the floor.

Embarrassed, Garth pushed back his chair and stood. "Never mind.

We don't want to get into *that* again. I think everything's about ready. Let's eat."

"Yes, let's!" Aggie grabbed the salad bowl and stood, too.

"I'll get the stuff in the oven," Garth cried.

Susan gathered plates from the cupboard above the sink.

Oblivious to the activity around him, Randy remained immobile, his eyes following Garth, fixed on the line of light hair rising from beneath the waist of his pants toward his navel. A minute later, seeing that everyone else was loaded down with plates and food and ready to leave, he quickly rose and, overcome, went with Garth, Aggie, and Susan out the door.

They ate on a patio near the swimming pool, Aggie, Susan, Garth, and John on one side of the table, Randy, Haircut, Leonard, and Ralph on the other. The dogs stayed close to them throughout the meal.

Susan and Garth had cooked a sumptuous feast of broiled chicken, mashed potatoes, fresh peas, and homemade biscuits. Randy found everything delicious, the best food he could remember having eaten in a while. It seemed a complement to the surroundings, the warm sunshine gleaming down, the clear water in the pool. He said little, content to listen to the voices laughing around him while watching Garth.

Like Randy, Susan was silent most of the time, but she looked radiant, sitting next to Aggie, smiling frequently. Only John was morose. He was mute as he had been for much of the day, not focusing on the group, although he occasionally eyed Randy surreptitiously. Randy barely noticed this. He was too caught up in the luminosity he sensed in the balmy afternoon air, a magic he attributed to Garth.

A pleasant lethargy settled over them once they'd finished eating. Randy heard a rooster crowing, its sound distant, then a bird singing in one of the trees. He looked across the table and saw Susan smiling at him.

"Aggie tells me you're just coming into the program," she said gently.

"Yeah." Randy cleared his throat, feeling awkward. "Yeah, I am."

"It's hard, isn't it?" Susan was staring directly at him, no longer smiling but appearing very sympathetic. "I had a horrible time when I came in. I was a mess."

"Really?" Randy liked her voice, its softness; it drew him to her, made him want to talk.

"I don't think I ever could have stuck with it if Aggie hadn't been around. She saved my life, I know it."

"Oh, yeah?" Randy glanced to Susan's right. Aggie was laughing with Garth. Randy let his eyes linger on Garth's sinewy arms. Looking back at Susan, he studied her frank, open face. He wondered what she'd gone through when she was a junkie, if she'd met Aggie in the program, what they were like when they were alone with each other. He glanced at Garth once more, then again at Susan. "Did you...did you and Aggie meet...?"

At that moment, Leonard spoke, addressing the table. "Maybe we should have our own little meeting," he suggested, patting his stomach and pushing away his plate. "It's Aggie's anniversary, after all."

John grimaced, then snapped, "Let's not!"—the first words he had spoken since the meal commenced.

"Jeez!" Haircut frowned. "Why don't you just relax? We've at least gotta give Aggie her presents."

"Yes!" Ralph agreed. He jumped up.

Leonard stood as well. "Let's go get them."

"Oh, guys, you shouldn't have," Aggie protested, although it was clear from her tone that she was touched.

Susan leaned toward her, whispering, "You deserve it," then kissed her on the cheek.

Ralph spoke to Randy: "How about you, chicky? You got her something, didn't you?"

"Well, I..." Randy looked away.

Haircut pulled at Ralph's arm. "Come on, hurry. I can't wait for her to see what we bought."

"All right, all right," Ralph replied.

Ralph, Haircut, and Leonard scrambled to the house.

Randy watched them leave, his embarrassment excruciating. He'd forgotten to buy something for Aggie. He recalled the shopping bags the others had been carrying on the train and realized those must have contained gifts. He sank into his chair. He felt like a fool.

Aggie and Susan talked to each other as John, gloomy, wandered toward the trees on the pool's far side, at the deep end.

Garth rose and came to Randy, then, a bit hesitant, sat next to him, smiling. "Everything okay?"

Randy flinched. Being this close to Garth made his embarrassment worse. He glanced toward the pool and at the trees surrounding it. Sunlight streamed through the branches. The light's reflection in the water made him dizzy. I don't deserve any of this, he thought.

"Say, what's wrong?" Garth's voice was kind. "What's going on? I mean, you've been so quiet all day."

"I...I..." Randy's eyes came back to Garth. He focused on the brown skin of his chest, wanting to touch it. "I didn't get Aggie anything," he muttered rapidly. "I forgot."

"Oh, so that's it!" Garth laughed. "Neither did I. Or John either from the looks of it. Listen, do you really think Aggie cares about *that?* She can buy herself anything she wants. She's just happy you're here."

"Yeah?" Randy gazed at Garth's face. He found what he'd said hard to believe. Garth must have given Aggie something earlier, he told himself. And no one expects anything from John. He still felt guilty. Even so, there'd been something he'd heard in Garth's tone, he wasn't sure what it was, but it made him feel better. He started to smile. Looking over Garth's shoulder, he observed John standing by the edge of the pool, staring at them. He lowered his eyes to his legs.

Haircut, Leonard, and Ralph returned.

"Here you are, doll." Haircut presented Aggie with a brightly wrapped package.

"Oh, guys, guys," Aggie cried. Then she opened her gifts.

Leonard had bought her a best-selling novel and tickets to an upcoming AA event, a fund-raising dinner held once a year. Haircut gave her two recently updated editions of some program literature, Ralph a print depicting three cocker spaniels. Aggie appeared moved by everything she received. Randy thought she was going to cry, and felt guilty once more.

As if sensing this, Garth smiled at him. "Come on, don't. Please."

A breeze blew past Randy. The sun caressed his arms and face. Warmth suffused him. He smiled back.

Susan stood. "I think I'll take a dip," she murmured to Aggie, then peeled off her shirt and shorts. She was wearing a one-piece black swimsuit underneath.

Randy watched her walk to the side of the pool. She paused at the rim. He thought she looked incredibly beautiful standing there in the sunshine, her legs long and tanned, her face ebullient. She leaned toward the water, her arms extended in front of her, then dove in. The ripples she created were speckled with light.

The dogs, who had fallen asleep under a tree, awoke and ran to the pool, barking.

"Come on, kids," Aggie laughed at them. "Stop, *please.*"

Ralph stretched his arms above his head and yawned. "Oooh, it's gotten so hot. It's making me sleepy. I think I'll risk a little sun." He unbuttoned his shirt and removed it.

Randy turned, then saw that Ralph's chest was emaciated and covered with lesions, much larger than the ones on his face. Woozy, he stood. The heat of the sun burned the back of his neck. He couldn't stay still. "I…I think I'll take a walk," he mumbled to Garth. He hurried toward the other side of the pool.

John was standing by a potted plant, staring at the trees. Seeing Randy, he walked up to him. "Hi," he said. His pitch was unsteady, uncharacteristically so.

His head pounding, Randy didn't hear him. He was thinking about his apartment, wishing he were there in bed. He wondered what Jake was doing. He wanted a drink.

"So," John continued, sarcasm now evident in his inflection, "are you having fun yet?"

"Uh-huh. Yeah, sure." Randy glanced back at Garth. He was watching them.

"Well, *good,*" John chortled. He hesitated, then abruptly, his tone again faltering, said, "Shit, I'm being a bitch, aren't I?"

"What?" Randy looked at him. His voice sounded strange, sad. I never should have left the city, Randy thought; being away's too weird.

"I don't mean to be, you know. It's just that I was thinking…well, I mean, do you suppose...could you ever...?" John shook his head. Suddenly angry, talking to himself, he muttered, "Christ, I'm too old!" Randy's eyes flew to Garth. He had risen from his chair and was approaching them.

"That *is* what you think, isn't it?" John was trembling.

Garth arrived. "Hey," he said to Randy, "what about that walk? Do you mind if I join you?"

John rushed away.

Randy glanced toward the others sitting at the table in the distance. Haircut and Ralph were staring at him, giggling. "I...I..." he stammered to Garth. "I don't know, I..."

"Come on." Garth touched Randy's hand. "I'll show you the stable. Aggie's got these beautiful horses. They've won a lot of prizes. You really should see them while you're here."

Randy's hand tingled. He looked at Garth's chest. It glistened in the sunlight. He heard himself speaking, ardently: "Yeah. Okay, sure."

"Let's go then, before it's too late."

They crossed a path that led through the trees and strolled toward a hill.

Randy wasn't sure what to say as they walked. He felt overwhelmed by everything: the heat of the sun, the luxuriant grounds near Aggie's house, by being in the country at all. But mostly it was Garth's closeness that subsumed him, his brown skin and warm eyes, his smile. Randy couldn't believe that he was with him.

Garth was the first to speak. "It's nice being alone," he remarked as they started to climb a small hill. "When I'm at a party these days...well, after a while I need a break." He chuckled. "I guess I'm just not as social as Aggie is."

"Oh, yeah?" Randy glanced at Garth's biceps, seeing a small mole on his skin. He didn't know why, but he was glad it was there.

They continued in silence, climbing the hill, then Garth said, "John acted sort of upset back there. I hope I didn't interrupt anything."

"No. No, that's okay." Randy let his eyes return to Garth's arm.

"It must be hard for him. You know, getting sober. I suppose it is for you, too. It is for most newcomers. I remember feeling pretty pissed myself. It was like I'd lost my best friend." Garth turned toward Randy, smiling. "You don't act angry, though. That doesn't seem like your problem. You *are* kind of shy, but I like that. It suits you."

Randy's face felt hot. He gazed in front of him. They had reached the top of the hill, and he could see the stable beneath them, far away, at the end of a long field. The ground looked incredibly green.

"Susan's shy, too, you know," Garth went on. "But then you probably noticed that."

They began their descent. Randy didn't say a word.

"She really hates being in the city, around thousands of people, says it reminds her of her days as a junkie. That's why she stays up here all the time."

Randy started to speak: "But does...doesn't she...?"

Garth looked at him, grinning. "Yeah?"

"Well, doesn't she ever get lonely?" As soon as he said this, Randy was afraid he'd sounded stupid. He bit on his lip.

"Oh, no." Garth's grin broadened. "Susan likes her space. She says it keeps her centered. And there're meetings in town. She's got friends."

"Really?" Randy stared at the green field stretched out beneath them, then tried to imagine what it was like being Susan, living here. He pictured himself at Aggie's house, with Garth, and glanced at him. Garth smiled back.

At the bottom of the hill, they started across the field, their pace slow. The sun beat down on them, yet the heat, tempered by a light breeze, did not feel oppressive to Randy now. He could see tiny beads of sweat on Garth's chest. For a second, he wanted to take his own shirt off, take off everything, run across the field naked.

"So tell me about yourself," Garth asked him. "I mean, you learned everything there is to know about me when you heard me qualify." He laughed. "It's only fair that I should know something, too."

Fragments from Garth's talk flashed through Randy's head: his seduction by his father's friend, the relationships he'd had, his lover's death. Then he recalled that Garth was positive and stared at him, seeing, briefly, Mark Randall.

"Don't be shy." Garth leaned toward Randy. "I won't bite."

"There's...there's nothing much to tell."

"But everyone's got a story. Come on."

Garth appeared completely placid, not at all threatening. Randy wanted to trust him, was almost sure he could. He wanted to tell him about Mr. Hewitt, about everything that had ever happened to him. Their stories were so similar; talking to him in this way might be a relief. He opened his mouth. "Well, I…"

The wind stirred, carrying with it strains of soft music, a classical piece. It sounded like it was coming from the stable. Randy listened. Delicate chords seemed to wrap themselves around him. Then, rejoining the breeze, they drifted away.

Randy felt as if he were drifting, too. "What…what was that?"

"That's Bach." Garth smiled. "Bach. She's playing them Bach."

Randy looked at him, mystified.

"The horses," Garth explained, detecting his confusion. "Aggie plays music for her horses. She thinks it soothes them. She's got CDs programmed to play for hours. Today it's Bach. Come on, we're almost there. You'll see."

Although the stable was still quite distant, Garth started to run across the field toward it. Randy followed, running as well.

Both were out of breath when they got there. As they entered, Garth laughed. "This is it," he said, catching his breath.

Panting, Randy looked around. Sunshine flooded in through a large rounded window high above, down onto a dusty tiled floor. Stalls were on both sides of him, horses in each, one brown, two black, and a palomino. A CD player was on a table near the entrance. He found the music coming from it dazzling, the high notes of the harpsichord breathtaking. There was a heavy scent in the air, a pleasant mixture of hay and dung. Specks of dust danced before him; it almost seemed as if he were floating with them.

The palomino neighed as Garth walked to it. "Hey, girl," he said. He took hold of the horse's head and hugged it. "You hungry?" He looked back at Randy. "Come here. You've gotta meet Jessie."

Randy approached Garth and the mare. As he arrived, Jessie swiveled her head toward him and nuzzled his shoulder. Surprised, he backed off.

Garth laughed. "Come on. There's no need to be scared. She's just being friendly."

Randy inched up to Jessie and raised a hand to pet her, grazing the skin on Garth's arm. He blushed, then, cautious, touched Jessie's neck. She moved her nose to his hand.

"See," Garth said, "she likes you."

Randy felt Jessie's breath on his palm. He stroked her neck, feeling her smooth coat, glancing at Garth, who was grinning at him. Randy thought he looked more handsome than ever; his skin was dotted with sunlight, highlighting the line of fine hair rising to his navel. He seemed vibrant and totally alive. Randy wanted to throw his arms around him. But he didn't. Garth's dying, he told himself, abruptly. He's dying, and so am I.

"We should come out here riding sometime," Garth said. "Have you ever done that?"

"No, I...I don't think so." Randy focused on Garth's chest. He saw a few light hairs on his skin, just above his heart.

"Neither had I until I met Aggie. It's great. I've gotten so that I can do it bareback."

Randy thought of the conversation they'd had on the way over here, when Garth had asked him about his life. He wanted to talk to him now, really talk to him, tell him things he'd never been able to say to anyone. He was certain he could.

A bird fluttered in the rafters above them, near a corner of the roof.

"Let me show you the other horses," Garth offered. "Maybe we'll pick one out for you."

They moved to the stall next to Jessie's. A black mare was inside.

"This is Lily," Garth told Randy. He caressed Lily's neck. "She's Susan's favorite."

"Oh, yeah?" Randy glanced at the mare, then at Garth. A wind instrument played on the CD. He felt the music seep to his depths. He stared at Garth's face, again seeing Mark. He felt as if he were about to cry. He looked down at the muscles in Garth's arm, wanting to touch them, needing to speak. The bird in the rafters flapped its wings. "Garth..." he said. Hearing Garth's name on his lips sounded strange, a little frightening.

"Uh-huh?" Garth smiled. Then, as he gazed at Randy, his expression changed, becoming serious, concerned. "What's the matter? Is something wrong?"

"No. No, nothing." Randy spoke rapidly. "But...I mean, you know...when I heard you qualify a few weeks ago..."

"Yes?" Garth inclined toward him and touched his arm, fleetingly, then pulled back.

"That is, when we were talking back there on the field..." Randy was convinced he could feel the heat of Garth's skin shooting toward him. He stared at his eyes. They seemed gentle. "Well, there were some things I wanted to tell you then."

"Really?" Garth studied Randy, thoughtful. "Go ahead. I want to hear."

Randy felt blood rushing to his head. He wasn't sure now that he could say anything. He heard the bird fluttering. Lily shook her head and neighed. Grabbing a cigarette from the pack in his shirt pocket, he managed to say, tentatively, "You remember that guy you were talking about when you qualified? The one you saw when you were a kid?"

Garth narrowed his eyes. "Jim?" There was a hint of incredulity, an edge of contempt in his tone.

"Yeah. Yeah, him." Randy lit his cigarette, shaking. He took two long drags. As he exhaled, words rushed out: "Well, I knew someone like that, too. His name was Mr. Hewitt. I saw him for years, from the time I was ten. And there were other things you said that day. I mean, in your qualification. You've done a lot of things I've done. I've got this lover, Jake. He's a complete shit. And I used to give massages. You know, sex stuff, for money. Then I met this guy Graham. He's really famous. But he's sick. And we did things...we did things that..." Randy took another drag on his cigarette. His stomach was reeling, and his throat felt tight. Breathing was difficult, if not impossible. He took in Garth's eyes, the warmth he saw there, an almost-shattering empathy. He glanced downward, then up again. Garth's eyes were fixed on him, steadfast and tender. Randy concentrated on the hair falling across his brow, on his tanned skin. "Shit, you're just like Mark," he muttered, quickly and indistinctly. He dropped his cigarette onto the floor and ground it out with the heel of his shoe. Shaking even more, he gasped, "And you're going to die, too." He burst into tears.

Garth stood still, alarmed. Then, moving rapidly, he threw his arms around Randy and pulled him forward, to him. "What's wrong?" he asked, his voiced strained yet palpably sympathetic. "Randy, what's wrong? Has it really been that bad?"

Randy let his face sink into Garth's chest. His sobs grew stronger, and he gripped Garth's back.

"What can I do?" Garth held Randy tightly. "I'm sorry. God, I'm sorry!"

Randy felt his tears mingling with the light sweat on Garth's skin. He pressed his face against his neck, clutching him.

"Let it go," Garth whispered. "Just let it go."

Tears streamed down Randy's face, blurring his vision. He started to feel self-conscious. What am I doing? he wondered; I don't want Garth to see me like this.

"Come on," Garth said, "tell me about it."

Clenching his teeth, Randy tried to make his tears stop and was partially successful. His face was still pressed against Garth's neck, and he became aware of the suppleness of Garth's skin, of his musky, fresh scent. He realized he was getting an erection, and felt more embarrassed. He lowered an arm from Garth's back.

Garth held onto him. "Let it out. You can do it."

Randy pushed his face into Garth's skin. He was completely erect now, and still shaking. He waited, mortified yet excited, unsure what to do or say. Impulsively, precipitately, he moved his free hand up to Garth's groin and raised his head. He kissed Garth on the lips.

Startled, Garth backed off, but only slightly. Randy took hold of Garth's hips and drew him nearer. He could feel Garth's muscles growing taut. He lowered his right hand and fondled Garth's groin. Garth began to relax, then became erect himself. Randy kissed him again. This time Garth kissed him back.

Randy pushed his tongue into Garth's mouth, grasping at his groin and unzipping his pants. Garth ran his hands under Randy's shirt, across his back. Randy found Garth's penis and grabbed it.

Shuddering, Garth pulled away. "Wait," he mumbled. "Wait, this isn't right. Not now, not yet."

Randy held onto Garth's penis, stroking it, ignoring his words. He fell to his knees and started to take the penis in his mouth.

Garth wrenched himself from Randy. "No," he said, more forcefully this time, but gently as well. "It's too soon."

Randy released Garth's penis, staring at him—at his penis, still erect, extending out from his pants; at his tanned, smooth chest; at his flushed face. His expression was disturbed, a little frightened. Randy thought he looked angry and lowered his eyes. He remained on his knees, wishing he could sink beneath the tiled floor into the ground, vanish forever. Garth spoke, saying only, "I'm sorry," then touching Randy's arm.

This contact with Garth shocked Randy, and he jumped to his feet, jarred by Garth's mild tone, the understanding and kindness he'd heard there. He twisted around, away from Garth, and ran from the stable.

Outside, he was stunned by the sunlight; its glare was a terrifying contrast to the dimness inside. The air felt sickeningly humid, even worse than it had in the city. He stood in front of the stable, not knowing where to go. Then he heard Garth hurry out through the stable's doorway, and he began to run.

"Wait!" Garth called, running after him.

Randy ran across the field, past clusters of trees toward a hill. He forgot where he was and why he was here. Garth was close behind him, shouting his name, but Randy was only vaguely aware of this. He felt a breeze blow past him, and heard in it the sound of the harpsichord floating from the stable. He ran faster, and his legs grew weak, but he propelled himself forward. Finally, just before he came to the hill, he could continue no longer. Gasping, he collapsed under a tree, then lay on his stomach, pushing his palms against his face. He started to sob.

Garth caught up and lay down beside him, placing his head on Randy's shoulder and clasping his arms. "Randy, please, stop! I didn't want to hurt you. That's the last thing in the world I wanted to do. Please!"

The sound of Garth's voice drew Randy back, and he took a long breath, one racked with sobs. "Fuck!" he screamed. "It's fucking unfair! Fucking everything!" He rolled to his side.

"Randy!" Garth grasped Randy's shoulders. "Please, Randy!"

Randy heard an urgency in Garth's voice and felt his tears begin
to subside. Garth moved his arms around Randy's chest.

Choking, Randy tried to speak: "I...I'm sorry, I..."

"Yes?" Garth brushed his lips against Randy's neck.

"I...I just wanted you to love me." As he said this, Randy started
to cry again.

Garth turned Randy toward him and ran a finger over the tears on
his face. "But, Randy..." He caressed his cheek. "I've been infatuat-
ed since we met. Shit, you're so beautiful. That's not what got to me,
though. What really did it was when I saw how shy you were at the
meeting. I don't know why, but it did." He lowered a hand to Randy's
arm and let it rest there. "I've been thinking about you ever since."

Randy looked up, probing Garth through his tears. He couldn't
believe what he'd heard. "Well, why...?" He glanced at Garth's
groin, then at his face. "Back there, why didn't...I mean, don't you
want to fuck me?"

Garth produced a slight smile, but was silent at first. He only
drew Randy nearer, stroking his hair. When he spoke, his voice was
tender—unbearably so, Randy felt: "I want us to know each other
before we do anything. And you're just getting sober. I don't want to
take any chances. You know, of hurting you. You've been hurt
enough already."

Randy gripped Garth's sides. He could see on his face a distinct
sadness, a pain that seemed to pierce his own core. He felt, dimly,
something inside himself open up; he wasn't certain what it was.
"How...how can you tell?"

"It's so clear! Even before you said anything—you know, about
that man you saw as a kid, about all the stuff you've done—well, I
think I knew." Garth ran a strand of Randy's hair through his fingers
and gazed at him, his eyes penetrating, warm. "I mean, I've been
there myself."

Just then Randy sensed the opening within him being filled, by
that glow, much stronger than it had ever been. It was deep inside. He
wanted to move closer to Garth, as close as possible, actually become
him if he could, shake off his own skin forever. He tried to find words
to express what he felt, but found this difficult. He drew a leg up

between Garth's thighs and gripped his hips. He wanted to tell Garth that he loved him. Instead he asked, "So why can't we fuck?"

"Come on, Randy!" Garth smiled once more, again faintly.

"Wait, okay? It'll happen. It's just..."

Randy glanced over Garth's shoulder and saw that the sun was lower in the sky. It was getting late. He clung to Garth's hips. "*Please.*" No longer smiling, Garth stared at the hill before him. "You know that I'm positive," he said evenly.

Randy felt his body getting tense. "We...we can be safe."

Garth peered into the distance, at the late afternoon sun, visible behind a tree. "It's more than that. It's not that simple."

Randy pressed his head against Garth's arm. "But why?"

"Well..." Garth looked directly at him. "Something could happen. Anytime. I mean, I had these tests a couple of weeks ago. You know, at my doctor's. He didn't like what he saw."

Randy was afraid to move. Garth's skin felt cold against his cheek. It seemed to him that the sun had fallen further behind the tree. The countryside appeared obliterated by shadows, drained of all color. He shivered.

"Don't you see?" There was a tremor in Garth's voice. "I don't want to drag you into all that."

Randy pictured Graham as he had been the last time they were together, emaciated, skeletal. Practically dead, Randy said to himself; it's happening to him, and it happened to Dennis, and it'll happen to Garth now, too. Closing his eyes, he thought, And me?

"You understand, don't you?" Garth spoke slowly.

Randy opened his eyes, then studied Garth's smooth, brown skin. He couldn't imagine him becoming like Graham. He seemed too vital, too *present*. He focused on the thin scar on his left cheek. "But nothing's going to happen," he cried quickly. "You'll be okay. I just want to be with you."

Garth lay quietly for nearly a minute, gazing at Randy, reflective. At last he cupped a hand under Randy's chin, lifted his face toward him, and murmured, "Shit, you've got the most beautiful eyes!" He continued gazing at him, somber yet affectionate, then finally smiled. "Maybe you're right," he said, brightening. "Maybe things'll work out. There's a lot of stuff they can do these days."

Randy could hardly breathe. "Yeah?"

"Uh-huh." Garth wavered. A trace of uncertainty flickered across his face. But then, smiling again, he exclaimed, "Yes, we've got time. I'm *sure* we've got time."

The sound of the harpsichord drifted toward them from the stable. Garth glanced at the sky, evidently noting for the first time the sun's position. "Wow, it's late. We better get back. Susan and I have to give Aggie this cake we made." He rose.

Randy remained on the ground, his eyes on Garth. "Do...do we have to go?"

Garth leaned over and clasped Randy's hand. "Yeah. I mean, it's Aggie's anniversary and everything. But listen, I'm going to be taking some more time off from work soon. I can do it in a couple of weeks, I think. I've been working way too hard. If you like, we can meet then."

Randy allowed Garth to pull him up. He stood next to him. "Where?"

Garth grinned. "Why, at a meeting. We'll talk in a few days, figure out when. We can go out for dinner afterwards."

Randy began to smile. "That'd be great."

"So come on, cheer up." Garth paused for an instant. Then, in a swift, spontaneous motion, he drew Randy to him and kissed him on the lips, lingering there for just a moment. Flushed, he started to release him, but stopped. "God, you're sweet," he said, growing redder.

Randy stayed in Garth's arms a second longer.

"We better hurry," Garth whispered in his ear.

Randy let Garth take his hand and lead him, glowing, up the hill, then back to the house.

The rest of the day felt anticlimactic to Randy, more like a dream. He paid no attention to Haircut and Ralph when they giggled on seeing him and Garth return, nor to John Stanley as he lurked by the pool, eyeing them. He ate little of Aggie's cake; he wasn't hungry. It was enough for him to observe Aggie and Susan sitting together laughing; to imagine himself living here with Garth; to watch the sun as it set, its rays shining on Garth's skin.

He grew more alert when they prepared to leave, then became

faintly depressed, knowing that Garth was staying behind to spend another night with Aggie and Susan.

"You'll call me, won't you?" Garth asked Randy at the door. "You've still got my card?"

Randy nodded.

"Or I'll call you. I'm going to be pretty busy this week, but if I've got a free minute, I will. What's your number?"

Smiling, reassured, Randy gave it to him.

He settled into a reverie on the train, gazing out the window at the darkness, ignoring his friends. They were quiet much of the time anyway. Haircut and Leonard spoke to each other only occasionally, always softly. Ralph fell asleep. John was sullen throughout the trip, not looking at Randy, enervated.

The heat of Grand Central Station was intense, yanking Randy back to full consciousness. He couldn't wait to get home and go to bed.

"Bye, Randy," Haircut shouted to him as he and Leonard wandered off toward the subway. They were going to Leonard's apartment uptown. Ralph winked at Randy, then followed them. John left in the opposite direction, not saying a word.

Randy took a cab home. The blare of the traffic was as oppressive as the heat.

His apartment was empty and in its usual disarray, Jake's clothes tossed about, dozens of dishes in the sink. The white walls appeared dingy and dank, sodden with the night's humidity.

He found a note from Jake on the kitchen table. "Sweetheart," it read. "Sorry about this morning. I guess I overreacted. You'll forgive me, won't you? Did you see the invitation to Graham's book party? That should be something, right? We'll make a night of it. Love, J."

Randy held onto the note, exhausted, staring at a blue cotton shirt, one of Jake's, which was flung across a plastic chair near the table. Nothing's changed, he told himself; nothing matters. He longed for bed, but first read Jake's note one more time.

He was struck by the reference to Graham; he didn't know what Jake was talking about. He glanced down at the table and saw an opened envelope, his name on the mailing label, printed neatly in computer type. He picked it up. The invitation was inside.

Tremulous, he read it: "Henry Reimer & Sons request the pleasure

329

of your company at a gathering to celebrate the publication of Graham Mason's new novel, *After Death*. Thursday, June 10. Cocktails from six to nine." An address was given at the bottom, that of the Florence Cruikshank Gallery in Soho, a space Randy had heard Adrian Peterson speak of.

Images of Graham flashed before him, images of him naked, his ribs protuberant under the skin of his shriveled chest, fucking Randy, whipping him. He became more aware of the humidity in the air; it felt intolerable. Sweating copiously, he hurried from the kitchen, undressed, and sank into bed.

Despite his fatigue, he found it difficult to fall asleep; visions of Graham kept intruding on his thoughts, eradicating any sense of tranquility. He coiled his legs up and tried to remember the prayer he'd heard in the program, the one about serenity. The words eluded him.

He wrapped his arms across his chest and curled up more tightly, pressing his eyelids together, then attempted to relive everything that had happened to him that day, to revive his recollections of Garth. Slowly any impression of Graham receded. Slipping into sleep, he felt himself going back to that green field, to the tree near that hill, to Garth, bare-chested and tanned, lying next to him, holding him, saying, *Yes, we've got time. I'm sure we've got time.*

XXIII

Randy wasn't surprised by Jake's enthusiastic response to Graham's invitation. Graham was famous, and this was the first book he'd written in well over a decade. His party promised to be glamorous, full of celebrities, an event. Randy himself would have been eager to go just a few weeks before. But now he had no intention of doing so. For one thing, he was certain his friends in the program wouldn't approve; undoubtedly the party would be full of the "people, places, and things" they warned him against. Randy didn't plan to mention the invitation to any of them; he didn't need their advice. The very idea of his going there was terrifying. He never wanted to see Graham again.

"What do you mean you're not gonna go?" Jake asked him the

afternoon after Randy's trip to Aggie's. They were both in the living room, Jake having only recently returned, high on cocaine, from an all-night party. "Are you nuts? Do you think we get an invitation like this every day? Think about who's gonna be there."

"I don't want to talk about it," Randy answered, turning away. He had no patience with Jake's badgering; it was bad enough being back. "I guess you just want to fuck us up again," Jake snapped. He lit a joint.

Randy headed for the door.

"Little shit," Jake muttered, then switched on the TV.

Randy rushed from the apartment, an unlit cigarette clenched between his teeth. At the bottom of the stairs, he looked at his watch; it was after three. A vagrant was asleep under the stairwell. Apparently he had slipped into the building on the sly. Randy hurried past him.

Once outside, he glanced around. Everything appeared much too familiar. A pile of rubbish spilled out from a trash can at the corner. A group of teenaged boys stood by the curb, one carrying a radio blasting a song by Janet Jackson. The heat was just as overwhelming as it had been the day before. Randy could not stay still. He lit the cigarette clenched in his mouth, then started west, swiftly, in the direction of Flora's.

He walked for an hour, haphazardly, going in circles, his chest heaving, taking nothing in. When he reached Sixth Avenue, he lingered at 4th Street, three blocks from the restaurant, but did not venture further. Instead, he stared at the harried pedestrians who passed him; they looked as miserable as he felt himself. He observed a group of men near a coffee shop, selling bags of pot. Aggie's house seemed a million miles away. Garth's still there, he thought. He decided Garth wouldn't want to see him even if he had come back, that he'd probably be too busy. He noticed a church across the street and remembered there was an AA meeting held there around this hour every day. He attended it, but saw no one he knew. He didn't listen to the speaker or to anyone who shared. When it was over, he returned to his apartment and went to bed.

He dreamed he was with Garth, in Graham's bed. Photographs of Dennis and Mark were on a table beside them. Garth was fucking him. As Garth ejaculated, he laughed coarsely. Randy stared at his face; it had become Graham's, pale and gaunt, ghostly. Randy clutched at the sheets, grasping dirt. He glanced up and saw a hill, near it a cluster of trees. Specks of earth fell on top of him. It was then he knew that they were lying in a grave.

In the days that followed—hot, humid days filled with meetings that felt somnolent to Randy; with indolent hours spent in coffee shops; with lengthy, uncomfortable silences between him and Jake—the party at Aggie's seemed like some fantasy he'd had, his time alone with Garth an hallucination. He had vivid memories of Aggie and Susan, of their house and their pool; of that lush, green hill; and, most of all, of Garth's brown skin, of what had occurred between them. But he could not trust the veracity of his recollections; they were too remote from the life he'd always known, his years with Jake. Garth was almost too nice, he felt, so different from anyone he'd ever met. Although Garth had said that he reciprocated Randy's infatuation, Randy could not believe what he'd heard. He was sure he could never rely on anything.

Only Haircut, Leonard, and Ralph's discussion of Aggie's party assured him that at least some of what he remembered was real.

"Did you see the Tiffany lamp Aggie had in the kitchen?" Haircut inquired animatedly one evening at Veselka's, three days after their return. He was sitting at a table next to Leonard, across from Randy and Ralph. Aggie was still away, having decided to spend a week alone with Susan.

"Oh, yes." Leonard smiled, then wiped the icing of the chocolate cake he was eating from his thick lips.

"I betcha Randy didn't," Ralph giggled. "He was too busy with Garth."

"Yeah, right." Haircut turned to Randy, giggling himself. "So tell me," he asked him, "what *did* go on in that stable?"

Leonard laughed then, too, though less effusively than Haircut and Ralph.

"Not...nothing much," Randy stammered. "We just looked at the horses."

"Sure," Haircut gibed. "Come on, you were gone for more than an hour!"

Ralph and Leonard laughed more boisterously.

Unable to respond, Randy stopped listening to them. We were at Aggie's all right, he told himself; it wasn't a dream. But his friends hadn't been around when he'd talked with Garth. What had happened then had been wonderful—magical, actually—yet it felt bewildering now, more unreal than everything else that had occurred that day.

He considered his time with Garth while lying in bed that night, disregarding Jake as he snored beside him. He couldn't understand how he had said some of the things that he had, telling Garth about Jake, about Mr. Hewitt, about the massages he used to give, saying that he wanted the two of them to be together. He never talked like that, never said what he felt. He had cried, too—and made a pass at Garth! Recalling *that* was excruciating. And all the while Garth had looked so much like Mark.

This was particularly disorienting. But if he thought about it long enough, seeing Garth as he had appeared, melded with Mark, brought on traces of that glow. He couldn't fathom this, nor the vague connection he sensed in his memories of that day, a connection to his past, one that went far beyond Garth's resemblance to Mark. It felt like the solution to a puzzle he hadn't known existed, a fragile, tenuous link that could slip away as quickly as any passing glow. He found this connection frightening.

Then, too, Garth was dying; his doctor hadn't liked what he'd seen. He was going to disappear, like Dennis, like Graham—like Mark. Garth had been wrong when he'd told Randy they had time. That was as fanciful as Randy's musings about Aggie and Susan's life together, his wish that he and Garth could be like that. The sweetness had gotten there first. Things would never get better—though it was hard to accept this.

"M'baby," Jake whispered in his sleep, throwing an arm across Randy's thigh. Randy shot up. The clock on the bedside table told him it was four in the morning. He vacillated, then, abruptly, leapt out of bed and dashed to the chest of drawers by the far wall. Garth's card was inside. He grabbed it and took it with him to the telephone in the living room. He picked up the receiver, staring at the card, hesitant. At last, his hand shaking, he dialed Garth's number.

After three rings, he heard a recorded message, Garth's gentle voice: "Hi, this is Garth. I can't take your call right now, but if you leave a message, I'll call you back as soon as I can. Thanks a lot. Talk to you later." Then a beep.

Randy tossed the receiver onto the cradle. It's the middle of the night, he said to himself; Garth's not there. Trembling, he thought, Maybe he's dead. He sped to his room.

Jake was still snoring heavily. This sound, its familiarity, suddenly felt comforting to Randy, solid and secure. He clasped Jake's sides, hoping to sleep, but couldn't. He kept seeing Garth, bare-chested as he'd been, but emaciated, shriveled like Graham. He tightened his grip on Jake.

He remained in bed all morning, never quite sleeping. At eleven Jake stirred and, erect, pressed his groin against Randy. Randy grabbed his penis.

"Sweetheart?" Jake mumbled, drowsy, surprised. Half asleep, he rolled on top of Randy.

Randy let Jake fuck him, but was barely aware of it.

When Jake was finished, he lit a cigarette, then smiled at Randy and said, "So, are m'baby and I gonna go to Graham's party?"

Randy drew away from him and rose from the bed.

"Jesus, sweetheart," Jake cried, angry yet hurt, "are you gonna be like that again?"

Randy did not respond. He went to the bathroom and took a shower, then watched TV with Jake for a few hours. Jake smoked a joint, occasionally glancing at Randy, discreetly. Randy wanted to talk with him, but could think of nothing to say.

At six he left the apartment to attend a meeting.

He tried not to dwell on Garth or on anything about that day at Aggie's, yet whenever the telephone rang, he jumped up to answer it. It was never Garth. He did his best not to feel disappointed; he didn't want to feel anything. Although Garth had told him to call, the idea of his doing so or of visiting Garth at the restaurant was intimidating. Garth was just being nice to me, Randy thought, that's all it was. Often he was convinced that Garth was sick or dead. He then forced himself to think of something else.

He still went to meetings; they kept him busy. And he didn't want to drink or get high, didn't want to go back to what he'd known. But attempting to comprehend what was said in the rooms was more difficult than it had ever been. As he questioned, then denied his memories of what had happened with Garth and the hopes he'd had for the two of them, he began to feel that he could never believe what the program taught. It's all a load of shit, he told himself; I don't even know what a spiritual awakening is. What's the point of working the steps? Everything's going to end anyway. Nothing he heard in AA corresponded with anything he'd been exposed to before. It was frustrating trying to understand it.

"Look," Haircut said to him one night, noting his obvious confusion, "you really gotta get a sponsor. Remember, a slip is just a drink away."

"Yeah, yeah," Randy muttered, provoked, then was silent. Why can't people in the program mind their own business? he thought.

That night and on subsequent evenings, rather than go out with friends after meetings, he went home. He decided he was tired of hanging out in coffee shops, that he had better things to do. His impressions of the program grew hazier every day.

He did manage to take in an announcement made at one of the meetings he attended: Peter, the young man with the cane, had died a few days before. When Randy heard this, he shuddered, then rose from his chair and fled.

He was aware, too, of John Stanley's behavior at meetings. He avoided Randy and kept to himself, sitting alone and leaving after the closing prayer. Randy recalled their conversation at Aggie's party and felt guilty, but didn't know how to react, how to approach John, what to say.

As his difficulties with the program persisted, he focused more closely on what was happening at home. He couldn't imagine what he and Jake would do without Graham's checks, which, surprisingly and disconcertingly, but to Randy's relief, came regularly every week, at least a thousand dollars each time. He never deposited these in the bank; that seemed too much of a hassle. Instead, he went to a nearby check-cashing store. He gave money to Jake if he asked for it; he thought this easier than arguing. And, he felt, he had to let Jake know they weren't broke. He didn't want to be nagged about going back to work. He wanted to avoid *that* for as long as possible, maybe find something else to do.

Jake was usually around the apartment, watching television and smoking pot. Although they said little to each other, Randy sensed Jake's eyes on him even when Jake appeared to be concentrating on the TV. He worried that Jake was angry with him because he didn't want to go to Graham's book party. At times, he thought Jake might have regrets about what was happening to them. He did himself.

He didn't want to let his life with Jake slip away. The possibility of a relationship with Garth seemed remote, unlikely in the best of circumstances, considering how different Garth was from the others Randy had been with, doomed now by Garth's health. And, despite the checks he received, it was obvious that Graham would be dead soon and that what they'd had was over. He was frightened by the thought of a solitary future, of being alone to face what he was convinced lay in store for him. Even so, the present situation with Jake was intolerable. Maybe I *should* go to Graham's party, he thought; maybe that'd help. He wished he'd met Garth when he was younger, and wondered what things would have been like if the sweetness had never appeared. But he knew it was useless to think in this way. As things stood—unless through some improbable turn of events he and Garth did get together—Jake was all that he had.

Nearly two weeks after his return from the country, on a Monday evening, he went to a meeting on East 10th Street and, halfway through the qualification, noticed Aggie entering the room. It was the first time he'd seen her since he'd been at her house. She waved at him, grinning, and he waved back, his memories of that day flooding through him. They felt at that moment very real.

Aggie came to him when the meeting was over. "Hey, Randy," she said, greeting him with a smile. "We really missed you after you left. Susan and Garth kept talking about how great you are."

"Yeah?" Randy felt himself smiling back. He gazed at her open face, into her bright eyes.

"Yeah, I'm so glad you all could come up. It really made Susan and me happy." Aggie's eyes shone, and she winked at him. "Garth, too." Randy glanced at his shoes, then at Aggie again. "How...how is he?"

"I'm sure he's fine. But I haven't spoken to him since he left my place."

"No?" Randy gripped the pockets of his pants. "Why not?"

Aggie laughed. "Oh, I don't know. I've been pretty busy. He has been, too, I think. You know, with all those shifts he's been doing. He left my house for the city early Sunday afternoon, said he was tired and wanted to rest up for work." Her smile became impish. "I'm surprised *you* haven't talked to him since then. The two of you *did* seem to hit it off. He told me he was going to have dinner with you the next time he was free."

"Yeah." Randy tightened his grip on his pockets. "Yeah, I guess so."

"You *guess* so?" Aggie's smile grew larger. "Well, Garth seemed pretty definite about it to me."

"Really?" There was something about Aggie's manner, her calm perhaps, that made Randy want to trust her.

"What, you don't believe me?" Aggie almost laughed again. But then, studying Randy, she stopped herself and became serious. "Why, you really don't, do you?"

Randy flushed. "He...he's got all this stuff to do."

"Yes, but still..." Smiling, Aggie spoke gently: "Listen, I *know* he wants to see you. He told me so."

"Yeah?"

"Oh, yes! He said he likes you *a lot*."

Randy stared over Aggie's shoulder at the doorway, embarrassed, wanting to get away.

"Why can't you believe that?" Aggie's expression was sympathetic. A flicker of understanding crossed her face, and she touched his arm. "Is it that you're scared?"

"What?" Randy pulled back, away from her, more desperate to leave.

"I can understand that. I was pretty scared myself when Susan and I first got together."

"But you..." Impressions from his day at Aggie's flashed through Randy's mind: the long, pebbly driveway; Susan in the pool; the stable; the horses; then, the strongest image of all, a bare-chested Garth. Everything he remembered felt distant to him, and yet—as he listened to what Aggie said and stared into her clear eyes—tangible, frustratingly so, just beyond his grasp. "But you and Susan..." He couldn't continue. Aggie's rich, he thought; she can have anything she wants.

"No 'buts.'" Aggie touched his arm once more. "If I've learned anything since I've gotten sober, since I've met Susan, it's that you've got to grab any chance for happiness that you can, whatever you're lucky enough to find, just grab it and—well, you know, surrender."

Recoiling, Randy blurted, "Garth never called me."

Aggie laughed. "So? He *is* busy. And he's probably feeling shy, too, just like you. He does want to hear from you, though. Call him yourself. After all, it works both ways."

"I tried. He wasn't home." Randy wished he could change the subject, but felt compelled to go on.

"Try again. You'll reach him. Honestly, you will. Trust me."

"But what...?"

"Yes?"

"What if he...?" Randy attempted to swallow. Then, his voice muffled: "What if he's sick?"

"What's that?" Aggie looked away from Randy, startled, then back at him. "Come on, you can't think like that." There was a slight, uneasy edge to her tone. "Garth takes good care of himself. He'll be fine. Don't let...don't let *that* get in your way."

Randy glanced toward the doorway. Garth said we'd meet in two weeks, he thought; it's been almost that long now. I could be hearing from him at any time. Returning to Aggie, faltering, he mumbled, "Listen, I've gotta go."

"Really? Are you sure?" Aggie sounded both surprised and disappointed. "I mean, this is the first time I've had a chance to speak with you alone. I thought the two of us could have coffee." She grinned. "I want to see to it that you're straight about Garth."

Randy considered staying; he was moved by the affection he heard in Aggie's voice and by the seemingly genuine disappointment she'd expressed. But he felt shy. And he didn't want to risk missing Garth's call, the one he was now certain he'd receive.

"Can…can we make it in a few days? There's something I've gotta do at home."

"What about Friday? We can hook up at that meeting on Charles Street, the one that starts at eight, at that church there."

"Okay, sure." Randy started to turn away.

"So I'll see you then. But first, come here." Aggie took hold of Randy's arm before he could depart and drew him to her, kissing him on the cheek. "That's from Susan," she said as she released him. "She really wants you to visit us again."

Randy couldn't look at her; he was too embarrassed. "I…I will. That's real nice of you."

"I'll see you Friday, okay? And don't forget: Call Garth."

"Yeah. Yeah, right. Thanks a lot." Randy hurried outside.

The rush of emotions stirred up in Randy by his conversation with Aggie was overpowering. He couldn't understand how he had been such a fool, how he could have doubted what had occurred at her house, doubted Garth. He realized that he should have been exhilarated by everything that had happened to him in the country, and yet he'd been depressed ever since, immobilized by his fears. Aggie was right, he decided; he had to seize the opportunity, "grab it," as she'd said, take this chance at happiness. Garth *was* going to call. And he wouldn't get sick. They'd get together. Things would work out.

After leaving Aggie at the meeting, he ran back to his apartment. But though he stayed near the telephone until he went to bed at three, Garth didn't call that night nor during the next two days. Randy couldn't quite find the nerve to make a call himself. It hasn't been two weeks, he thought; there's time. Then, as the days passed and he still heard nothing, his old doubts and fears resurfaced. He was sure something was wrong.

His fears were redoubled by the continuing tensions he experienced whenever he was alone with Jake, by Jake's sullen moods, by the nearly constant silence between them. Randy found it difficult to stay at home for more than a few hours at a time.

What he saw outside seemed no better. New York was in the grip of a wretched heat wave, one that showed no signs of relenting.

Everyone on the street appeared to be in a foul humor, their faces strained, their tempers short. Randy witnessed arguments wherever he went, outbursts amongst the drug dealers who worked in front of his building, between taxi drivers and their passengers, shopkeepers and their customers. The normal din of the city, the blasting radios and honking horns, sounded worse than usual, and Aggie's house seemed more distant than ever. His day with Garth felt like an anomaly, an aberration—until he remembered what Aggie had said, that Garth liked him, liked him a *lot,* that he really wanted to see him. Then a vestige of hope returned.

Still, Garth didn't call, and Randy was left to himself: at the apartment with Jake; at the meetings he attended, dutifully, numbly; or, much of the time, meandering alone through the Village.

On Wednesday night he ran into Haircut at a meeting, and Haircut convinced him to go out for coffee. "You've been isolating a lot lately," he told Randy. "That's no good. You know what they say: Being by yourself's like being with your own worst enemy."

Randy went to Veselka's with Haircut and Leonard, but regretted having done this the moment they got there.

"So what step are you on now?" Leonard asked him, appearing, Randy thought, extraordinarily jowly. Leonard raised a forkful of cherry pie to his lips. "Have you gotten to the third yet? You know, are you learning to turn it over?" He glanced meaningfully in Haircut's direction, then back at Randy, swallowing his pie, smiling slyly. "But, of course, you need a sponsor for that, don't you?"

Haircut sighed. "Randy just doesn't want to listen. He won't take any of our suggestions."

Randy left after half an hour, restless and bored, irritated by their persistence. Such proselytizing in the midst of casual social situations—such "fellowship," as the program called it—no longer seemed enough. He wanted something else, wanted what he'd felt in the country, something that went beyond any mouthing of slogans or AA philosophy, something more immediate and concrete.

More than anything, beneath his apprehensions, he wanted Garth.

The following afternoon, Randy and Jake were sitting in the living room, silently watching a talk show on TV. Jake looked contentious, his furtive glances at Randy displaying a definite edge of hostility. Randy stared defiantly at the television screen, but couldn't concentrate. Jake's presence felt horribly oppressive.

After an hour of this, Jake abruptly jumped up and exclaimed, "Christ, I can't take this shit anymore!"

Randy glared at him. "So go!"

"Yeah, right." Jake turned sharply, then stomped from the room and out the front door.

Randy tried to remain calm, to focus on the TV and forget about everything else. He was unable to. We're finished, he thought; it can't go on. He went to bed.

He slept for hours, dreamlessly, until Jake returned drunk at one in the morning and crawled into bed beside him, sobbing.

"M'baby!" Jake wailed. "Baby, baby, what's happening to us?"

Randy's shock at this display of emotion on Jake's part, at what Jake had just said, quashed most of the anger he'd felt on being awakened. He waited a moment, then rolled over, facing Jake.

"I don't want it to end!" Jake cried. "Fuck, sweetheart, don't let it end! They're all shits out there. I need you."

Despite a lingering trace of anger, Randy was touched, unexpectedly so, drawn to Jake's pain. He moved closer to him. Tentative, he asked, "Where…where'd you go? What's the matter?"

"Oh, never mind, sweetheart!" Jake thrust a hand onto Randy's groin. "Please, never mind! Let's just make up and forget all the shit that's gone down."

Randy felt Jake's hand on his penis and started to get an erection.

Jake drew him nearer, stroking him. "That's m'baby. Oh, yes, m'baby's here."

Randy moved his hands up Jake's thighs, to his fleshy sides. As he did this, he thought of Garth, remembered his tight body. He pulled back slightly.

"Come on, sweetheart." Jake lowered a hand between Randy's legs. "We did it the other day. We can do it again now." He pushed a finger into Randy, against his sphincter.

Pulling further back, quickly, Randy shook his head. His erection wilted. "Why don't we just talk, okay?"

Jake emitted a sudden, harsh laugh, drew his finger from Randy, and rolled away from him. "Yeah, right," he mumbled. He lay on his side, his back to Randy. Then, with another harsh laugh, his words slurred, he said, "I guess you're like all the others. Shit, you won't even go to Graham's party with me. I guess you think I'm too old."

"What's that?" Randy recalled John Stanley in the country, bitter by the pool. "What do you mean?"

"All those fucks at the bars. They just want some young twinkie." Jake's tone was plaintive, and this jarred Randy. It was so similar to the way John had sounded.

"Just wait," Jake continued, angrier. "You're getting up there yourself. See what it's like when you're not a hot young thing anymore. Christ, it sucks! You'll see."

Randy felt his stomach churning. He didn't know how to react or what to say. Jake must've gotten rejected at some bar, he thought. This didn't surprise him: Jake was over forty. He wanted to laugh, but couldn't. Jake's words alarmed him; they echoed too closely some of his own concerns about the future, the ones that had come up since he'd started going to AA. He slid closer to Jake, then, impulsively, draped his arms across his chest and placed his head on his back.

The instant Randy did this, Jake twisted around and clasped Randy's shoulders. He pushed him onto the mattress, lay on top of him, and rubbed his groin against his stomach. "Come on, sweetheart, let's fuck, okay? I don't give a shit about those creeps."

Randy's stomach churned more violently. Sitting up, he shoved at Jake's shoulders.

Drunk as he was, Jake offered no resistance. He fell off Randy, back onto the bed. "Fucking faggot," he muttered, curling onto his side.

"Why don't you just go the fuck back out and pick up some little shit, whatever you can fucking get?" Randy screamed, then lay down, veering to the edge of the bed, far from Jake.

"Fuck you!" Jake hissed. He switched off the light. "Let's see what you say when you're older." He lay motionless, not looking at Randy, silent until, gasping, he moaned, "Shit, what the fuck's going on with us anyway?"

Shortly thereafter Jake started snoring. Randy remained awake, his eyes wide open. The heat in the room seemed to smother him.

He fell asleep an hour later, but his rest was fitful.

*

When he awoke at ten, Jake was gone. Although Randy had been in bed for more than fifteen hours, he felt exhausted. He knew that altercations such as the one he'd had with Jake the night before had occurred between them many, many times, and it seemed to him now that they would fight many more times, in similar ways, year after year, until both he and Jake were dead. He felt as if the room's heat had sunk to his guts and settled there. He didn't know what to do. Time was passing. He was getting older. His life seemed hopeless.

Then, suddenly, he recalled Aggie, her soft voice, what she'd told him: Garth liked him. *A lot.* He wanted him to call.

He bounded up and sat on the side of the bed. Everything he saw—the clock on the bedside table, Jake's clothes on the floor, the dreary white walls—appeared markedly defined, so vivid and clear that, somehow, it all looked repulsive. What the fuck have I been thinking? he asked himself. He'd been an idiot. He couldn't let his fears get in his way any longer. There wasn't time for that. If he didn't act, he'd be back where he'd been, stifled by Jake, giving massages, waiting—for what? The sweetness? The end? He had to trust what Aggie had said, trust something for a change.

But what if Garth...? he wondered. He stopped himself. Enough of that shit! he thought. It's now or never.

He thrust himself from the bed and ran to the chest of drawers, retrieving Garth's card, then hurried to the living room, picked up the phone, and, not hesitating at all, dialed Garth's number. He reached the answering machine. He hung up when he heard the recording, leaving no message, and clutched the arms of his chair, certain it was too early for Garth to be at work. He found his pack of Merits, lit a cigarette, and took several long drags. Then he realized it was Friday and remembered he was supposed to meet Aggie that night. Aggie must have spoken to Garth by *now,* he decided; she has to know *something.*

He spent a restless day in front of the television set, jittery, paying no attention to the programs, filled with a hope he couldn't trust. He tried to banish all his fears, and was relieved that Jake didn't return. At 7:30 he went to the meeting, half an hour early.

343

He sat in a seat near the back, perched on its edge, watching people arrive. Aggie was not one of them.

When Ralph came in at five before eight, Randy dashed to him and, panting, asked, "Have you seen Aggie?"

"Good lord, chicky," Ralph exclaimed with a laugh, "you're positively frantic!"

"I was supposed to meet her here tonight." Randy's words gushed out, nearly incomprehensible. "We were gonna have coffee."

"Well, no, I haven't seen her in a while, not since that day at her house." Leering, Ralph ran his fingertips across Randy's arm and chuckled. "Don't worry. You can go out with me instead."

Randy scanned the room, but still couldn't see Aggie, only John Stanley traipsing in. John stopped in his tracks and stared at Randy, then headed for the back.

Randy stayed for the entire meeting, Ralph sitting next to him, but Aggie never showed up. Randy didn't hear anything that was said. As soon as the meeting was over, he rose and turned toward the door.

Ralph pulled at his arm. "Hey, chicky, what's the hurry? I thought we were going out for coffee."

Randy saw John leaving through the doorway. He looked back at Ralph. "I can't. I've gotta make a call." A brief pause. Then, desperate: "Listen, do you have Aggie's number?"

"Not with me, but..." Ralph formed a lecherous grin. "It's at my apartment. Why don't we go there?"

Randy found it almost impossible to say anything. "No. No, that's okay." Without uttering another word, he rushed outside.

John was standing in front of the church. Randy scurried past him. "Randy?" John called out.

John's voice barely registered with Randy. He started across the street.

"Randy, can we talk?" John sounded both wistful and apologetic.

"Later, okay?" Randy shouted, moving east.

At his apartment, he found Jake stretched out on the couch in the living room, reeking of alcohol and sleeping. Heedless of him, Randy went to the phone and dialed Garth's number. Garth wasn't home. He then tried Haircut, but he wasn't there either. Randy left a message: "Listen, you gotta call me when you get back. I need

Aggie's number. It's real important." He hung up and waited for the phone to ring, ignoring Jake's heavy snores, attempting to dismiss a growing certainty, a gnawing sense that he'd been right all along: Garth was doomed—and he was, too.

Soon he couldn't wait any longer. He leapt to his feet and flew out the door.

He ran west, all the way to Flora's. Once there, he stared through the restaurant's window. It was crowded inside, with many waiters scooting between the packed tables. Randy couldn't see Garth. With great trepidation, he walked in.

The buzz of conversation in the restaurant was discordantly intense. Randy wanted to race back to the street. He froze by the reception desk, studying the dining area: the young, well-dressed diners; the potted palms by the white, columned walls; the smiling, eager waiters.

A tall man in his early thirties wearing a crisp white shirt and tight blue pants approached him. He was handsome and muscular, with jet-black hair and slightly pockmarked olive skin. Randy assumed he was the head waiter.

Eyeing Randy suspiciously, the man sneered. "May I help you?" His words were clipped, the disdain in his tone only flimsily disguised. "Do you have a reservation?"

"I…I'm looking for Garth." Randy glanced past him toward a festive group of men and women sitting at a large round table in the dining area, several bottles of champagne conspicuous in front of them.

"Garth?" The man pronounced the name with contempt. "He's not here."

"No?" Randy kept his eyes on the group at the table. A slim, tow-headed woman in a red, low-cut evening dress lifted her glass and rose unsteadily, obviously intoxicated. She appeared to be offering a toast.

"He hasn't been around in a while." The man scowled, then added skeptically, "He *said* he caught some bug. Well, it's been more than ten days. He'd better come back soon if he wants to keep his job. As you can see, we're extremely busy."

Still focused on the woman in the evening dress, Randy grabbed a pack of cigarettes from his shirt pocket. His throat felt as if it were contracting.

The man gaped at Randy. "There's no smoking in *here!*" he snapped. "At any rate, I assume you're not dining with us, so I'll have to ask you to leave."

Randy looked back at him, not having understood. "What?"

The man smiled stiffly. "I said piss off," he murmured, just under his breath.

Randy hurried out to the street. The noise of the traffic shocked him. His heart was palpitating as he hailed a cab.

Jake was awake when he got home, in bed, under the covers.

"Hey, sweetheart," he muttered wanly, looking drowsy and uncharacteristically contrite. "How's m'baby?"

Randy slumped into a chair in a far corner.

Jake frowned, apparently hurt. He said nothing else at first. Then, his voice uncertain: "Haircut called."

Randy glanced at him. "Haircut?"

"Yeah, he said something about some woman's number you wanted. You better call him. I didn't take it down."

Randy bolted up.

"Look, sweetheart, about last night…"

"Not now!" Randy answered, rushing away.

He ran to the phone in the living room, hoping Haircut could allay his fears, but anticipating the worst. He grabbed the receiver and dialed Haircut's number.

Haircut caught the agitation in Randy's voice immediately. "Jeez, why're you so nervous? So Aggie didn't show up, big deal. She can be pretty flaky sometimes."

Randy ground out the cigarette he was smoking and lit another one. "Look, do you have her number or not?"

"Yeah, yeah, sure. Criminy, calm down. Here in the city? Or are you gonna try her in the country?"

"Both!"

The instant he'd finished talking with Haircut, Randy dialed Aggie's city number. He reached her answering machine and left a message: "Aggie, this is Randy. Call me, *please!*"

He then phoned Aggie's house in the country. There was no answer. He grew more terrified; he knew Susan was usually home. He dialed the number again and let it ring for more than two minutes. There still was no answer. He considered the possibility that Susan might be at a meeting, and checked his watch. It was nearly midnight—too late for any meeting up there, he was sure.

Clinging to a glimmer of hope, he started dialing the number a third time, then stopped, grasping the receiver, staring at the apartment's barren walls, recalling the head waiter at Flora's, his haughty, brusque manner, what he'd said about Garth; Jake as he was that night, sheepish, possibly apologetic, sluggish and high; Graham, sickly and pale, slowly dying. A familiar sense of lethargy descended on him, a numbness, a chill. What'd I expect? he asked himself. Why'd I even bother? He felt as if he'd known from the beginning how things would turn out; his life had always been this way. Garth was going to die. Randy would be left to continue as before, until he died as well. Nothing would ever change.

He hung up the phone and stood still, rigid. Then he wandered to the bedroom. Jake had fallen asleep and was snoring. Randy lay beside him, careful not to touch him. He concentrated on Jake's breathing, tried to think of nothing else. It's over, he thought. He never should have allowed himself any hope. Garth's death, some disaster, had always been inevitable. Realizing this almost felt comforting.

He bent his legs toward his chest and slid closer to Jake, listening to him snore, attempting to ignore his tears. It's over, he thought one more time. Then, as he drifted off: That cunt Aggie lied.

He didn't think he was shocked by the announcement he heard at the meeting he attended the next day, that five o'clock meeting on Third Avenue and 5th Street, the one he'd gone to the very first time he'd come to AA. It seemed to him that he'd been expecting it forever.

"Are there any AA-related announcements?" Veronica asked, and Roxanne raised her hand. Even before she opened her mouth, Randy thought he knew what she was going to say.

"Garth S., a member of this group, is in Cabrini Hospital." Roxanne's voice was low. "I know he'd like to hear from any of you, so please see me after the meeting if you'd like some more information."

The moment she finished speaking, Randy rose from his seat, left the room, hurried home, and went to bed.

He slept for hours, a deep, heavy sleep, deathlike. Only once was he aware of anything outside of himself, when he sensed Jake standing above him and thought he heard him say, "Shit, sweetheart, don't get like this again. Don't fuck us up. We need each other. What else've we got?" Afterward he wasn't sure this had happened; it felt like a dream.

Nothing came through to him fully until nine that night, when Jake crept to the bedroom, leaned over the bed, and, cautious, tapped Randy's shoulder.

"Someone called Aggie's on the phone," he said warily.

"I don't want to talk to anyone!" Randy cried. He turned onto his side.

"Come on, sweetheart, she says it's important."

"Fuck her," Randy mumbled, sitting up. Half asleep, he crawled from the bed and to the living room, then picked up the phone.

"Oh, Randy, I'm so sorry! About yesterday, not showing up and everything. It's just that so much has happened." A strong emotion was evident in Aggie's inflection. "I turned my phone off last night. I had to sleep, I was exhausted. And I didn't have your number. I had to get it from Leonard, and I...I didn't know how...I didn't know what to say."

Randy heard a catch in her throat and surmised from this that she was on the verge of tears. "Yeah. Right."

"You do know about Garth, don't you?"

"They announced it at a meeting this afternoon." Randy clenched a fist. He wanted a cigarette, but had left his pack in the bedroom.

"It's pneumonia." Aggie's words spilled out, merged together. "It happened so suddenly, a couple of days after you all were up at my house. He...I...I guess he was run down."

Randy noticed that Jake had come into the living room and turned on the TV. He tightened his grip on the receiver.

"He didn't even let me know he was sick until the other day, didn't tell them at work how bad it was or anything." Aggie was choking. "He said he didn't want people to worry."

"Is he...?" Randy gazed at the television screen. A commercial was playing, an advertisement for American Express. A handsome couple, casually dressed but clearly affluent, were dining on a patio overlooking the sea. "I mean, he..."

"Yes?" Aggie asked, choking even more.

"He's going to die, isn't he?"

Aggie began crying softly. "Oh, don't say that, please!" She drew in her breath and managed to stop. "He looked a little better today. Susan came down from the country on Thursday. We've been with him most of the time since then. We're going again tomorrow. You can come with us if you'd like."

Randy thought of Haircut at the hospital, the anger and frustration he'd displayed there, then, shivering, pictured the lesions on Ralph's skin.

"Let me know. We're going around eleven. Garth really wants to see you." Aggie paused. "He's going to get well," she quickly added. "You've got to believe me, he will."

Randy stared at Jake, slouched on a chair in front of the television set, smoking a joint. He moved his eyes back to the screen. The commercial was over, and a crime drama was on. Two men were shouting. One had a gun.

"Randy?" Aggie's pitch grew higher. "Randy, are you there?"

Randy didn't answer.

"Listen, Randy, are you all right?"

Randy continued gazing at the TV. "Yeah. Yeah, I guess so." He watched as the two men on the screen fought, grappling with each other. The gun the one was carrying fell to the ground.

"I'll phone you in the morning, okay? You can let me know then if you want to come."

"Uh-huh." Randy realized Jake was watching him. He looked high, yet seemed concerned.

"I'll call at ten."

Avoiding Jake's eyes, Randy inspected the television screen. For a second he saw nothing. "Right."

"Try not to worry."

"No." Although he was not looking at Jake, Randy was sure that his eyes were still on him. He glanced downward.

"I'll talk to you later."

Randy looked up. "Wait," he said to Aggie, his tone becoming harsh. "Listen..."

"What, sweetie?" Aggie spoke gently.

"Why did you...?"

"Yes?"

"Why'd you tell me...?" Randy saw Jake gazing in his direction. Furious, he asked, "Why'd you lead me on? Why'd you tell me that things would work out? Shit, you said that Garth'd be okay."

"Oh, Randy!" Aggie started to cry again. "Please, Randy, don't!"

"Fuck you!" Randy screamed. "You and all your AA shits! You can all go to hell!" Quivering, he slammed the phone down onto the receiver.

Jake lurched to his feet. "Jesus, sweetheart, what's going on? What's the matter?"

Randy stood still, his breath uneven. The heat in the room overpowered him. Everything appeared hazy. He raised a hand toward his eyes and felt tears on his cheeks.

Jake approached him. "Are you all right? Who's this Aggie woman you were talking to?"

Randy sat still.

Jake moved closer. "Well?"

Randy wiped his eyes and tried to focus on Jake. Everything was still indistinct. He opened his mouth. "A...a friend. A friend of mine's going to die."

"What that?" Jake stopped moving, peering at Randy, blankly. His expression slowly softened, and he murmured, "Gee, I'm sorry."

Randy gazed past Jake.

Jake hurried to Randy and threw his arms around him, pulling him forward to his chest. "God, sweetheart, that's a real drag." He patted Randy's back, then hugged him. "But fuck, shit happens, you know. You should try and forget about it, relax. Why don't you just come over here with me and sit down?"

Randy felt Jake's hands on his shoulders.

"Come on."

He let Jake lead him to a chair in front of the television set, and he sat there.

Jake sat next to him. "That's right, sweetheart." He took hold of Randy's right hand and caressed it. "Just relax."

Randy stared at the TV. One of the men who had been fighting lay dead on the ground. A pool of blood surrounded him.

Jake stroked Randy's hand, his eyes on the TV, silent. Then he turned to Randy and spoke: "I guess things haven't been too good with us lately, have they, sweetheart?" His voice was subdued, almost tender.

Randy did not reply.

Jake produced a weak smile. "Come on. M'baby can be more cheerful than that. We don't want to give up, do we?" He played with Randy's fingers. "Let's try and work things out, okay? We should do stuff together, fun things, like we used to do." His smile became wider. "We can start by going to Graham's party. That's coming up real soon."

Randy allowed his hand to rest in Jake's, but paid no attention to him. He tried to concentrate on the television screen. Just for an instant, he recalled Garth, lying with him on the hill. He pushed that image away and focused more closely on the TV.

"What about it? Shall we go?"

Randy studied the screen, the pool of blood, shot from an overhead angle. It was brilliantly red. Jake ran a finger across his palm. This is it, Randy thought. He tried to accept that.

"Well, what do you say?"

Looking past the television screen, Randy realized he was nodding, though only slightly. "Yeah. Yeah, I'll go," he answered. His intonation was flat. He thought it clear what he could expect now— just as he was sure that it would all end soon.

Grinning, Jake squeezed Randy's hand. "That's m'baby. That's m'baby, all right."

Randy winced.

"Shit, sweetheart," Jake went on, nearly laughing. "I mean, *shit.* I just know we're gonna be fine."

XXIV

Once he'd given in to Jake's appeal and agreed to go to Graham's party, Randy felt he could not turn back. He was convinced that his fate had been sealed, not only by Garth's illness, but also, somehow, by everything that had happened to him for as long as he could remember. He had strange, unsettling dreams—of Mr. Hewitt, of that trip to Canada, of Garth buried there on a hill—and found it frightening to sleep, yet he could do little else. He stayed close to home as much as possible. It was all he could trust.

Aggie phoned often, but he refused to speak with her or with any of his other friends who called, Haircut, Leonard, and Ralph. He let Jake answer the phone and, if alone, did his best not to pick it up. He had stopped going to meetings after he'd heard the announcement about Garth and, though he still didn't drink or get high, thought about doing so. He clung to a distant hope that if he remained sober, then, in some way, Garth would get well. But most of the time he was certain this would never happen, and he tried not to think about Garth at all. Garth's destiny, he felt, was cast in stone, as preordained as his own.

This feeling was reenforced by a telephone conversation he had with Haircut, the only one he'd had with anyone in days. It occurred on the Wednesday after Aggie's call about Garth, when, Jake being out, Randy inadvertently, thoughtlessly, picked up the phone as it rang.

There was nothing unusual about what Haircut said at first. He was full of the sort of admonitions Randy had anticipated: Randy *had* to go to meetings. He needed to share and get a sponsor. His sobriety was fragile and dependent on his working the steps. Randy was about to hang up. Then Haircut mentioned Garth.

"You really should visit him, you know." Haircut's voice was low, accusatory. "It's not just pneumonia. They've found a lot of other things wrong with him, some sort of virus in his brain. I don't think he's got much time."

The air in the room was suffocatingly humid. Gazing in front of him, seeing little, Randy found his pack of cigarettes in his shirt pocket and lit one.

"He looks *awful*," Haircut continued, his inflection now shaky. "He's lost so much weight. And he's gotta breathe through this tube. I couldn't believe it." He wavered, then, his voice softer, added, "When I was with him at the hospital, I kept seeing myself in his place."

Randy did not know what to say. He dropped the phone onto its cradle and, trembling, went to bed.

That night Jake wanted to have sex. Though less than eager, Randy complied, putting up with Jake as he fondled him roughly.

He thought he had no choice, and believed this would help him forget what Haircut had said. But as Jake thrust his penis into him, he grew more and more listless, just as he'd been the last time they'd done this, a few nights before, just as he was whenever he and Jake had any sort of contact these days.

Once they were finished, Jake talked about Graham's party. "So what are you gonna wear?" he asked, smiling. "It's gotta be something special. This is gonna be an event."

Saying nothing, Randy stared at a large water stain on the wall to the left of the bed.

"Shit, sweetheart!" Jake sat up. "Get it together! His party's a week from tomorrow."

Randy rolled over, coiling his legs toward him. "Later, okay?"

"Well, all right." Jake's voice became more subdued. Ever since he and Randy had reconciled, he'd been less critical of Randy and seemed anxious to avoid another argument, almost as anxious to avoid one as Randy was. "But don't forget…" He pinched Randy's buttocks, chortling. "Me and m'baby have gotta get our outfits together."

He turned out the light, and they both fell asleep.

The next day they were awakened at noon when the postman delivered a registered letter from the brokerage house handling Graham's account. It contained a check for $1,500.00 and a note from the broker's assistant. Groggy, Randy read it in bed, under the covers, Jake sitting beside him, reading over his shoulder:

Dear Randy Somners: Our records indicate that you have been receiving a regular stipend from Graham Mason as payment for editorial assistance rendered during the past few months. Due to Mr. Mason's recent poor health and at the request of his lawyer, this letter serves notice that your assistance is no longer required and that with the enclosed check your payments will cease. Best regards, Marcia Robertson

"Fuck," Jake cried once he'd finished reading, "what are we gonna do? You've gotta go back to work."

Randy threw the letter onto the bedside table, lay down, and shut his eyes.

"Come on, sweetheart, we can't ignore this. Christ, we don't want to end up on the street."

"Not now!" Randy turned away from him.

Reluctant, Jake rose from the bed. "I guess we can wait a week or so. You might even meet someone at Graham's party." He looked down at Randy, shaking his head. "But, shit, if you don't...well then, we've gotta *hustle*." He left the room.

Once he had gone, Randy lay still, trying to disregard the oppressive heat, to sleep. He didn't think he cared what he did. If he had to go to Graham's party, go back to work, give massages, whatever, it didn't matter. None of this would last forever. Nothing ever had before.

A week passed. The heat wave that had endured for weeks continued, growing worse every day. Randy stayed in bed more often than not, depressed but making do. Any dreams he had were vague, and he only dimly recalled them when he awoke, so he ignored them. He hoped his life was returning to normal. It seemed to be. He just had to get through Graham's party. He dreaded going there, but reminded himself that it would be over soon.

On the afternoon of the party, he was awakened at one when Jake jumped from their bed and snatched his clothes from the floor. Half asleep, Randy watched him dress.

Jake was animated. "I'm gonna go shopping," he chirped as he zipped his pants. "Why doesn't m'baby come with me, get out of the house for a change? We can buy something new to wear at the party tonight. You want to look hot, don't you?"

Randy pulled the covers to his chin. "I want to stay here, okay?"

"Come on, sweetheart!" Jake moved to the bed and sat next to him. "You've been moping around here a lot lately. It's summer outside and everything. M'baby's gotta have some fun." He lowered a hand to Randy's waist and caressed him.

Squirming, Randy murmured, "I'm tired."

Jake sighed. "If you say so." He patted Randy's arm, then stood and walked to the chest of drawers across from them. "I'll just take some of our money with me, all right?" He opened the top drawer. "Maybe I'll buy m'baby a little present."

Randy watched him take a handful of bills from the drawer and pocket it. He looked away.

Jake turned toward the door. "I'll see you soon, sweetheart."

"Yeah. Yeah, see you." Randy didn't budge.

Jake studied him, puzzled. For a second he appeared worried. "Okay," he said at last, then hurried out.

As soon as he'd gone, Randy dozed off.

He dreamed he was lying with Garth in a grave, a deep pit on a hillside in Canada. It was dark inside, save for a shaft of light shining down through an endless tunnel, coming from the sun in the sky high above. Garth was dead, stiff and still, naked, his body tanned and smooth, his penis large, encircled by thick black pubic hair. Randy could feel heat surging from him. He snuggled against his side, into his warmth, embracing him, playing with his penis.

Just then, far above him, he heard a voice, Graham's, shouting, "You're monsters, all monsters, all of you!" He looked up. In the distance, near the sky, Mr. Hewitt stood on a patch of grass under a tree. He was peering down the long tunnel, staring at them and laughing. Terrified, Randy snuggled closer to Garth. As he did, Garth moved, ever so slightly, placing an arm around Randy's back and pulling him into his hot skin. Absorbing Garth's warmth, Randy felt secure and completely alive.

He awoke with a start. A key was turning in the front door. He glanced at the clock on the table beside him; it was past five-thirty. A radio was blasting outside. The heat in the room was intense.

"Sweetheart?" Jake called from the entryway.

Randy was shaking. He felt frightened and very sad, peculiar. He wanted a drink.

Jake entered the bedroom, carrying three shopping bags and looking excited. "Wait'll you see what I bought m'baby!"

Sweating, Randy sat up slowly. The radio outside was playing a jingle, a commercial for a bank.

Jake dropped the bags onto the floor, then, a gleeful smile on his face, reached into one of them and pulled out a striped, short-sleeved shirt. He tossed it to Randy.

Randy made no effort to catch it, and it landed beside him on the bed.

"I found that at The Gap," Jake said, clearly pleased. "I thought it'd look good on you. I mean, you haven't bought anything new for yourself in a while."

Moving sluggishly, Randy picked up the shirt. It had blue and green stripes zigzagging diagonally across a bright red background, and was extremely small, too small for him to wear, he could see. It looked as if it had been made for a child.

Jake grinned. "Pretty cool, right?"

Randy clutched the shirt. "Yeah. Thanks."

Jake grabbed two of the bags from the floor. "Let me show you what I got for myself. I'll be right back. I'm gonna go put them on. We've gotta hurry, it's late. Don't peek now. I want it to be a surprise." He headed for the bathroom.

Randy stayed on the bed, still holding the shirt. The radio outside was playing a disco tune from the seventies, one he remembered having listened to years before at Mike's. It had an infectious beat, yet he was sure that he caught a hint of melancholy just beneath the song's upbeat tempo. It made him think of everything he'd missed, the world Graham and Dennis had known. Garth had known some of it, too, he remembered. He shivered, recalling his dream. He wanted to cry. He tossed the shirt to his side and lay down.

Jake returned. He had changed into a pair of black-leather pants and a thin beige shirt. Both were too tight. His stomach pushed against the waist of his pants, threatening to unclasp them.

"Well?" Jake turned to his right and displayed his new clothes. "What do you think?"

Randy closed his eyes. He didn't want to move, go anywhere, do anything. He saw no reason to.

Jake wrinkled his brow. "You're not going back to sleep again, are you? Fuck, it's almost six. That's when the party starts."

Randy lay quietly, still.

Angry, Jake approached the bed. "Come on, get dressed, okay?"

Randy kept his eyes shut. "Do...do I have to go?"

Jake's voice grew higher: "What's that?" He sat next to Randy. "What do you mean 'do I have to go?'"

"I don't think I can."

Jake gazed at Randy, more amazed now than angry. He placed a hand on Randy's shoulder, pouting. "Jesus, you can't do this to me. We've been planning this for weeks. I've let you stay in bed all the time lately. Get up just this once."

Randy squeezed his eyelids more tightly together. He heard the disco music outside, and his dream came back to him. He remembered how he'd felt next to Garth, in that grave. Garth had been dead, but he'd been warm. His warmth had been soothing. It seemed to Randy that he'd become a part of Garth then, that he'd been safe. He pushed his groin into the sheets, thinking of Garth's hot, tanned skin.

"Come on," Jake pleaded. "Maybe you should take one of those pills you got from Graham. They're still some left, you know. I saw them in your drawer earlier. You've gotta do *something*. I mean, I bought m'baby a new shirt and everything."

Randy opened his eyes. Heat seemed to be pressing in on him. It felt comforting, like it was meant to be near him, would always be if he let it. It made him feel secure. He edged his way up, sitting next to Jake. "It's too small," he said.

"What is, sweetheart?" Although Jake had not understood Randy, he sounded relieved, as if he could tell that Randy was giving in.

"The shirt. It's a kid's shirt."

Jake glanced at the shirt, lying beside them on the bed. "Shit, you're right, it *is* too small. That was pretty dumb of me, wasn't it?" He chuckled.

"I don't have to wear it, do I?" Randy stood. Dizzy, he closed his eyes. He pictured Garth in the grave, snuggled against his side, recalled how they'd been, enfolded in heat. He began to feel that way now.

Jake rose and walked to Randy, then wrapped his arms around him and kissed the nape of his neck. "M'baby can wear anything he wants. Just hurry, *please*. We're gonna be late." He tweaked one of Randy's nipples.

Randy drew away from him and started toward the chest of drawers. The warmth in the air seemed to follow him.

"Come on, hurry," Jake exclaimed.

In a daze, Randy dressed.

They hailed a cab and drove to the Florence Cruikshank Gallery on the east side of West Broadway, a block north of Canal Street, speeding over streets sparkling under the glare of the early evening sun. Randy sat in his seat, resting the back of his head against the cushion, lulled by the music he heard coming from portable radios that seemed to be everywhere, spewing myriad sounds, salsa, soft rock, and disco.

"Wow, sweetheart, I'm pretty sure this is the hottest day yet, don't you think?" Jake asked.

Randy did not answer. He felt pleasantly warm. Nothing seemed real.

The cab stopped in front of the gallery, and they got out. It was ten minutes before seven. A breeze blew past Randy, startling him. For the first time since he'd left his apartment, he realized where he was and what he was doing. Alert now, he looked through the gallery's window at the huge crowd inside, everyone, it seemed, fashionably attired, some formally, in jackets and ties or in light summer dresses, but most more casually, completely in black or in colorful shirts that dazzled him. He had tossed on the first things he'd found, an old green T-shirt and a pair of faded jeans. He felt self-conscious and frightened.

"Let's go," Jake said impatiently. "What're you waiting for?"

Randy felt another, cooler breeze. He looked through the window once more, chilly.

"Come on, sweetheart."

Randy vacillated.

"Hurry up!"

"Ok...okay." Tentative, Randy followed Jake to the door. As they stepped inside, a burst of frigid air hit him directly in the face.

Jake laughed. "Thank God for air-conditioning, right?"

Randy stared at the throng of people massed in front of him, hundreds of them, all, it appeared, chattering and drinking. The clamor of voices and rock music was overpowering. He felt as if icy air were crawling under his clothes and into his skin. He wanted to run back outside.

"Christ, what a scene!" Jake's voice was barely discernible above the noise. He shoved into the crowd and moved toward a bar at the far end of the immense room.

Staying close to Jake, Randy found it difficult to focus on anything. Bodies pushed against him, flesh that seemed chilled. He saw large canvases on the pristine white walls, garish portraits of pop stars. Somehow these paintings looked familiar to him. Everything else became a blur, a fusion of colors, a babble of voices, all hideous. He was freezing, and longed for the heat he'd felt outside. He wished he were home in bed, asleep and dreaming.

As they forced their way through the mob toward the bar, he heard a barbed voice, coming, he could see, from a man standing next to a thin blond woman in a bright red mini-dress. "There's something wrong with her cunt tonight," he was saying to her. His tone was amused and haughty, and he had a pronounced English accent. "That's why she's not here."

The speaker was handsome, with thick dark hair and large hazel eyes, and was wearing a light linen jacket, well-cut and loose fitting, ocean-blue with a thin collar. Randy wasn't sure how or from where, but he thought he recognized him.

Jake stopped precipitately and looked to his right. It was evident from his expression that something had upset him. Randy stopped, too. At first he could not imagine what had provoked Jake. Then, in a nearby corner, he noticed Adrian Peterson, sipping from a wine glass and talking with an older man.

"Shit!" Jake muttered, red-faced. "What the fuck is *he* doing here?"

Adrian appeared much more prosperous than he had, his hair impeccably coiffed, greased and slicked back. It was obvious that it had been styled only recently. He was dressed in black silk slacks and an expensive-looking shirt patterned with prints of tropical fish and coral. His companion—Harold Lynch, Randy assumed—was wearing a greenish-gray jacket, tortoiseshell glasses prominent in its breast pocket, and gray tailored pants. He was inspecting Adrian benignly. Both were smiling.

"Let's go!" Jake snarled. "I don't want them to see us. There're too many other people here, practically everyone important in town. Who cares about those shits?" He resumed his trek toward the bar.

Randy started to follow. Then, directly behind him, he heard a voice calling, "Why, I know you!" He swirled around. The Englishman who had been speaking before was hurrying toward him.

"Remember me?" he drawled once he had reached Randy. "That loo at The Scrotum?"

Randy blanched, realizing this was Oliver. He looked toward the gallery's window, now quite distant from him. The sun was slightly lower than it had been, but still shining brightly. The street appeared warm and inviting. He wondered if he could sneak out of here, get away from Oliver and everything else, go home.

"Well, well," Oliver said. He was grinning puckishly and had a glass of white wine in his hand. "It's been a while, hasn't it?"

Randy kept his eyes on the window.

"We do seem to hook up at these vile events, don't we? I'm surprised I didn't see you at the Whitney last week, at the 'Fierce Women' opening." Oliver shuddered. "That was a horror show. But I'm sure you heard about it."

Randy shifted his eyes to Oliver, then stared at him blankly, saying nothing.

Oliver disregarded Randy's silence. "So are you bored yet?" he asked. He took a sip of wine. "These things are always so ghastly."

Randy turned his head and saw Jake in the midst of the crowd, near the bar. He looked back at Oliver. His handsome face seemed odious, cruel. I sucked him off, Randy thought. He lowered his eyes, stopping at Oliver's shirt. It was black, with long sleeves and a flowerlike, open-cut weave. Traces of skin showed through the slits in the material, skin that was pasty, almost colorless, not at all like Garth's.

Oliver was still grinning at him. "Maybe we can find a way to amuse ourselves," he said. There was an insinuating, mischievous inflection in his tone. "I believe there's a loo around here somewhere."

Randy looked further down and saw Oliver's shoes, navy loafers, seemingly new. He was not wearing socks. There were thin blue veins running across his pale ankles. Randy felt a draft of cold air. He wanted to stamp on Oliver's shoes, crush his feet.

A man's voice, piercingly shrill, rang out above the din of the crowd: "Oliver!"

Randy looked up. Dakota Montoya and Denise Lamour were coming toward them.

Responding to Dakota's greeting, Oliver nodded at him. "Oh, God," he mumbled to Randy, "those two ghouls!"

Dakota ran to Oliver and kissed him on the cheek. Denise caught up and stood next to Dakota, expressionless. Although she was only an inch taller than he was, she was very fat and overwhelmed his tiny frame.

"So!" Dakota pulled away from Oliver. "How are things?" He glanced toward Randy, then leered at Oliver and remarked, "A lecherous cunt as usual, I see." He glanced at Randy once more, his gaze steady and faintly flirtatious. He did not seem to recognize him. Returning to Oliver, he asked, "Any sign of Mr. Mason? You don't suppose he's kicked, do you? Just in time for his big night?"

Oliver smiled. "Now *that* would be droll."

Denise spoke for the first time, dryly: "Don't worry, babe, he'll be here. He's good for a few more weeks."

Randy wanted to dash for the door, to the heat outside, but was sure he couldn't. He looked behind him and, through the dense crowd, saw Jake ordering a drink at the bar. He wondered how he could make his way over there. He then saw Adrian and Harold Lynch, near the bar now, too, engrossed in conversation. Even from this distance, he could tell they were avoiding Jake.

His eyes wandered back to Denise. Repelled yet fascinated, he lingered on her fat arms and face; her ebony skin and copper-red lips; her long, electric-orange hair; the huge red glasses resting on the bridge of her shiny round nose; her enormous chest; her bulk. She was wearing a filmy silver blouse and a sheer black skirt that fell down to her thick ankles; her shoes were black suede, open-toed with pointed heels, her toenails aquamarine.

Randy then looked at Dakota, pockmarked, short, and homely, disheveled in a ragged blue sweater and scruffy black jeans, puffing on a cigarette and scowling. Another monster, Randy thought; they're all fucking monsters.

Oliver was laughing. "You *are* a bitch, darling," he said to Denise. "Still, I love your new things. So much better than that 'Fierce Women' crap you foisted on us at the Whitney."

Peering up at the wall, Randy saw a golden-hued representation of Nancy Sinatra, nude save for a pair of high-heeled boots, cracking a whip across the back of her father, who was also naked, his body shriveled and thin, his wrinkled skin lined with bleeding welts, his stumpy penis erect. Randy surmised that Denise's work was being shown here, then recalled Denise's portrait of Madonna at Graham's; *that* was why these paintings looked familiar to him.

On the other side of the room, he noticed a tall, shirtless black man in skin-tight, brown-suede pants propelling his way through the crowd. Stunned, Randy recognized him as Calvin, from The Scrotum, the one who'd beaten Haircut. It felt at that moment as if the air-conditioning had been adjusted and that the air had become even colder. He pulled his pack of Merits from his shirt pocket and, shivering, lit a cigarette.

Dakota noticed Calvin, too. Smirking, he pointed at him. "I've had that one," he said to Oliver. *"Twice."*

Oliver gazed at Calvin, then, a smile on his face, turned back to Dakota. "And?" he asked, titillated.

"Huge," Dakota answered. "Absolutely humongous."

Denise eyed Calvin with distaste. "Gutter lowlife," she muttered. "Nigger trash. You faggots are shameless."

Randy glanced behind him. Jake was rushing from the bar, Adrian and Harold ordering drinks there. Randy was certain that Jake was trying to get away from them. He inched back from the group he was with, veering in Jake's direction, then stopped, staring toward the gallery's window. The sun was lower, but it was not twilight yet. He was sure it was still very hot. He wanted to be outside, soaking in the sun, or in bed, snug and warm, drifting off forever.

A tall, imposing woman in her forties, raven-haired and wearing a bold red business suit, was making her way through the horde of people in the room, waving at Oliver, Dakota, and Denise. She moved with a determined, purposeful gait, thrusting herself between groups of revelers, all of whom appeared to give way to her will.

"Oh, look," Dakota whispered to Denise and Oliver, "it's that cunt Suzanne."

"Graham's publisher, right?" Denise asked.

"Yes. Now be nice to her."

Suzanne joined the group, her face fixed in an expansive smile, one that seemed blatantly artificial to Randy.

"Hey, guys," she said briskly. Her eyes darted from Dakota to Denise, then to Oliver, finally to Randy, remaining on him briefly, as if she were trying to place him. Apparently unable to and no longer interested, she returned to the others. "So glad you're here." "Yes," Dakota answered, his tone mellifluous. "We were just talking about you." "Oh, *really?*" Suzanne leaned toward him. Her smile vanished. "And what were you saying?"

Seeing that everyone else was preoccupied, Randy moved further back, until he was completely apart from the group, several yards away. As he did this, Jake arrived, out of breath, holding a glass of wine.

"That fucking hustler didn't say fucking anything to me," he growled at Randy. "What a pretentious shit!"

Randy was watching Suzanne, who was studying Dakota as he spoke, her eyes sharp and attentive. He couldn't hear what Dakota was saying.

"Adrian always was a scumbag," Jake went on. "I don't know what I ever saw in that fuck." He gulped his wine, then squeezed Randy's arm. "Well, screw him! Is m'baby having fun? I saw you talking with Dakota Montoya and Denise Lamour a minute ago. Let's go back and talk to them some more, okay? I haven't seen those two in a long time."

Randy glanced past Suzanne toward a distant corner and saw Calvin with a middle-aged man wearing a kilt. An Abba song was playing, the music's volume high. Randy's skull was pounding. He ground his cigarette on the floor, then looked down at the drink in Jake's hand. He wanted one, too. "I...I...Shit, I can't talk to them anymore," he said.

"What's that?" Jake seemed confounded.

"I hate them. They're monsters."

"Come on, what're you saying?" Jake laughed nervously. "I mean, sweetheart, they're famous. You'll never get anywhere with that attitude."

Randy continued to stare at Jake's glass of wine. "I don't care. I want to go home."

Jake appeared dismayed. Then he became angry. "Fuck, no! We're gonna stay here. I want to have fun. Besides, you know you've gotta try and meet someone tonight."

Randy lifted his head. "What?"

"You heard me: Meet someone. You've got to. Shit, Graham's finished. We're almost broke."

"Oh. Oh, yeah," Randy mumbled. The air felt frosty. "Right." Turning from Jake, he looked around the gallery: at Oliver and the others, huddled together and giggling; at a smiling, unctuous Calvin, chatting ardently with the man in the kilt; at Adrian and Harold, laughing at the bar and holding hands; at the hundreds of people in the room, all, it seemed, cackling above the Abba song. He found the sound of their voices unbearable and looked toward the window, at the fading sunlight. He wanted to become a part of the sun's dying rays, take its heat into his lungs, make it stay inside. He glanced around the room once more. Everyone appeared grotesque, deformed, ill-defined. He turned back to Jake, at first saying nothing. Then, his voice quavering, he asked, "Why bother?"

"What's that?" Jake sounded bewildered. "What'd you say?"

"Why bother doing anything? Shit, what's the point? Nothing's going to change. We're never gonna get anywhere. Who'd want to anyway?"

"What the fuck are you talking about?" Jake was angry again. "You're not making sense."

Randy drew his pack of Merits from his shirt pocket and lit a cigarette. "Yeah," he muttered. His tone was resigned. "You're right. What the hell? Never mind." He lowered his eyes toward the floor.

Jake sighed, looking away. Suddenly excited, he lifted an arm and pointed across the room. "Jesus, sweetheart, there's Jackson Reeves."

Randy raised his eyes. The name was familiar. Then he remembered: It was because of Jackson that he knew Graham; Jackson was the client who had given Graham Randy's name.

"Yeah, it's him all right," Jake continued, still pointing. "You know, that choreographer. You saw him once a long time ago."

Randy stared in the direction Jake was indicating. A balding, thin man in a white cotton shirt and black linen pants stood alone near a portrait of Eartha Kitt in a straightjacket, his eyes glued to a young blond man six feet away from him. The balding man was indeed Jackson Reeves, Randy realized, although the memories he had retained of him were faint. Jackson was just one of the many men he had been with, each barely distinguishable from the other. And it had been a while since they had seen each other, Jackson being from the South and rarely in the city, almost a year, since well before Randy had met Graham.

"We should go over and talk to him," Jake suggested. "Maybe you and him could set something up."

Randy felt currents of cold air streaming across his arm. He turned toward the window. The sunlight was much dimmer. Looking at Jake, he asked, "Do I really have to talk to him now?"

Smiling, Jake spoke softly: "Sure, sweetheart, why not? When else are you gonna have a chance? Shit, I'll be with you." He touched Randy's hand. "Come on, let's go." He started walking in Jackson's direction.

Hesitating, Randy let his eyes return to the window. Although it was only just twilight, it seemed to him to be growing darker rapidly. He didn't know why, but just then he wondered if Garth had died yet.

Jake was a few feet away by now. He stopped and looked back at Randy. "What's the problem? Aren't you coming?"

"Uh-huh, sure." Randy's mind was on Garth.

"Well, hurry up then." Jake continued toward Jackson.

Moving distractedly, Randy followed him, walking past Oliver and his friends.

Oliver grabbed Randy's arm as he passed, grinning at him. "Oh, there you are. Suzanne and I were just talking about you."

Randy lurched to a halt. "What's that?" Oliver's words had not registered. He noticed Dakota giving him a sidelong glance, his expression somewhat different from what it had been, probing, more coy.

A thin smile on her face, Suzanne peered at Randy. "I was asking Oliver if I might have seen you last week at the Whitney. You know, at that lesbian thing, 'Ferocious Dykes,' or whatever it was called."

"'Fierce Women,'" Denise murmured, correcting her.

"Well, yes." Suzanne frowned, then returned to Randy. "You were there, weren't you? In drag, perhaps?"

Oliver chuckled. "I doubt it. But then he would look rather tasty in a dress."

Suzanne narrowed her eyes, not listening to Oliver. "So were you there?" she asked Randy once more.

Randy couldn't look at Suzanne; he found her voice cutting, didn't know what she expected of him. He gazed over her shoulder. "I…"

"Wait," Dakota said to Randy, breaking in. "I just realized something. I mean, I think I know you from somewhere." He turned to Denise. "We do know him, don't we, cookie? Didn't we meet him at some party a few months ago?"

Transparently bored, Denise stared at him. "I don't know what you're talking about."

"Yes, you do!" Dakota was emphatic. "He's that trick of Graham's. You know, the whore, that masseur."

Denise studied Randy. A trace of recognition crossed her face. "Of course!" She giggled. "He was the one who got humped by that chicken hawk when he was a kid."

"That's right," Dakota laughed.

Oliver smiled. "I see." He looked at Randy. "So you were an early bloomer."

Shivering, even colder, Randy bit down on his lip and crushed out the cigarette he was smoking, then lit another one, his eyes darting toward the bar. A tall woman with limp brown hair, wearing an old blue frock and black sneakers, was getting a drink. Randy clenched his jaw, recognizing her as Melissa Livingstone.

"I'm not quite sure what you two are talking about," Suzanne said to Denise and Dakota, "but I presume you're talking about sexual abuse. That used to be a very hot topic at Reimer. We did quite well with some of our abuse titles." She spoke to Randy: "Tell me, were you…?" She paused, her face assuming an expression of exaggerated sympathy. Then, her words clipped and perfunctory, she asked, "Were you actually sexually abused when you were young?"

Randy barely heard her. He was thinking about Melissa's act, remembering how she'd whipped herself on that stage, talked about some man she'd been with as a child, her stepfather. He felt as if the party at The Scrotum had happened decades before, yet knew it had been only five or six months since that night. Still, a lot had gone on during that time: the "story" he'd written, all the shit with Graham, those evenings at Fey's, hanging out with Sylvia, joining AA. And meeting Garth. He pivoted to the right and saw Jake in the distance, talking with Jackson Reeves, then came back to his circle, regarding Dakota and Denise, recalling how they'd joked about Mr. Hewitt when he'd met them, just as they'd done tonight. Suddenly it seemed he was at The Scrotum again, that nothing had changed, that he'd be here, exactly as he was, for the rest of his life, that what he'd done with Mr. Hewitt *had* been a joke, the way Dakota and Denise made it out to be, that his whole life had been one. He looked toward the window and saw that it was darker. For a second the remaining light seemed to vanish, and the sky appeared pitch-black. Frightened, he glanced at Suzanne. She was staring at him, apparently waiting for a response. This intimidated him, and he tried to call up Garth's face, but couldn't. He had almost forgotten what he looked like. He focused on Suzanne's suit, which appeared brazenly red, fiery. He couldn't see anything else in the room and didn't want to. He found it all too horrible. If that night at The Scrotum was the beginning, he thought, then this is the end.

"Well," Suzanne asked him, an impatient edge creeping into her tone, "are you...? Damn, what do they call it?" She raised a hand to her chin, pensive. Then, brightly: "Oh, yes: Are you a survivor?"

At that moment Dakota spoke up excitedly, interrupting her: "My God, look who's here!"

Randy swerved to his left. Graham, in a wheelchair, was entering the gallery, pushed through the entryway by a large woman in a nurse's uniform. All conversation in the room stopped. An old song by the Police was playing, its sound deafening. Randy felt swept up in it. The room appeared blurred, obscured by smoke, then infested with blackness.

Almost everyone in the gallery started to applaud.

"An ovation for a dying queen," Oliver whispered to Dakota.

Coming back, Randy tried to grasp what he saw. If in the past Graham had been thin, painfully emaciated, this evening he looked scarcely present. He was partially covered by a thick blue blanket, only his head and the shoulders of his black dinner jacket visible above the wool, and was staring abstractedly in front of him, as if taking little in. His face had no color whatsoever, and his skin seemed like an extension of his bones. Propped in his wheelchair, he appeared frozen there, dead.

"Christ," Dakota muttered, "he looks like shit."

"Yes, it's a tragedy," Suzanne said blithely.

Denise shrugged. "Yeah, but what can you do?"

A flood of remembrances swept over Randy, memories of the stories Graham had related to him, tales of the sixties and seventies, of a younger Graham and of Dennis, of a time Randy had missed, when people had been free. He absorbed the room, the applauding crowd, full of effusive, painted faces, of fervent, jarringly false smiles that did nothing to conceal from him the viciousness he intuited in the chilly air, nothing to help him forget the void he sensed within himself. He glanced at Oliver, at Denise and Dakota, at Suzanne, then returned to Graham, rigid and pale in his wheelchair, besieged by admirers. He wondered what had happened, how the time that Graham had loved had come to this, to this packed, freezing room overflowing with sycophants and poseurs, if things back then had, in fact, been any better than they were today, if life ever had been worth living, or if, perhaps, Graham's tales weren't as fanciful as Randy's recollections of his time with Garth seemed now.

"Listen," Dakota said, speaking to Suzanne, his eyes on Graham, "something just occurred to me."

Her interest piqued, Suzanne leaned toward him. "And what's that?"

Dakota looked at her, a half-grin on his face. "I think you've got an excellent marketing opportunity here."

"Yes?" Suzanne's eyes were wide open. "How so?"

"Well, you see," Dakota explained, motioning toward Graham, "this isn't just Graham's first book in a decade, you know."

Suzanne arched her brow, appearing even more alert, crafty.

"Oh, no." Observing Graham, frail and wan, being wheeled toward the bar, Dakota smiled. "No, my dear, it's also his last."

Suzanne smiled back at him with obvious approval. "So you thought of that, too? I have to admit it's crossed my mind." She placed a hand on her chin, surveying Dakota. Her smile broadened. "Smart. *Very* smart. Smart, smart, smart."

Dakota beamed. "Yes, I thought so."

Randy heard the Police's song, floating in the air: "Living from day to day/Is there somewhere we can hide?"

"We should talk," Suzanne said to Dakota. "I can see you have some interesting ideas. Are you on-line?"

"Not yet." Dakota sounded zealous. "But I'm getting a modem soon."

"Good." Suzanne reached into a pocket of her suit. "Good, good." She drew out a business card and handed it to him. "Call me, okay? We can have lunch. But now I *must* talk to Graham."

"Denise and I are going to talk to him later," Dakota offered, "after the commotion's died down."

"Fine. So I'll see you." Smiling at the others, Suzanne turned to leave.

Randy looked behind him. Graham was by the bar, inert in his wheelchair, surrounded by dozens of people. His nurse was passing him a glass of wine. Randy stood still, transfixed. It seemed clear that Graham would be dead soon. He wanted to learn what lay behind his impassive eyes, and wondered if there was something he knew, something intangible, maybe something about those old days. This was the last chance he'd have to talk with him, he was certain of that; he couldn't allow himself to be afraid. He hesitated, drawn to Graham yet frightened by the thought of approaching him. At last, guardedly, he started toward the bar.

"Hey," Oliver called after him, "where're you going?"

Ignoring Oliver, Randy pushed through the thickening mob, hearing a prattle of voices buzzing around him and the Police's song. Bodies pressed into him; he felt as if he were being smothered. He stopped, searching for the gallery's window. The crowd was so dense he couldn't see it. He moved toward the bar once more, faster now.

Aware of almost nothing, he bumped into Adrian, who, with Harold Lynch, was heading toward the entryway.

"Excuse *me!*" Adrian appeared taken aback. Then he laughed. "Fancy running into *you* here."

Randy wanted to move on, but felt he couldn't. Looking away from Adrian, he stared at Harold's long, red face. He seemed flustered and irritated. Flustered himself, Randy turned back to

Adrian, focusing on his shirt. There was a print of a conch displayed just above its left breast pocket.

"I saw your boyfriend earlier," Adrian said with a grin. "I must say, Randy, he's looking sort of chunky these days. His body's gotten so weird."

Randy glanced toward the spot where he'd seen Jake earlier. He was still there, talking with Jackson Reeves. His leather pants had slipped a bit down his hips, and his shirttail had risen.

"I guess you're treating him well," Adrian went on. "Very good." He chuckled. "You should be glad, though, that he wasn't at the Whitney last week, at that 'Fierce Women' opening. He never would have passed muster there."

Randy's eyes flew from Jake, and he glared at Adrian. Fucking queen, he thought.

"Let's get out of here," Harold mumbled to Adrian, annoyed. "We're going to be late."

Adrian smiled at him, then took hold of his hand. "Sure. Sorry about that." He looked at Randy. "Well, bye, bye now. We've gotta run. Me and Harold have to meet one of his clients at Lutéce."

Harold started toward the entryway.

Following him, Adrian turned his head and, sneering at Randy, cried, "Have a good life!"

He and Harold disappeared.

Randy remained where he was, staring through a gap in the crowd at the gallery's window. The darkness outside seemed complete now, horrific. He felt as if it were deep within him, in his blood. Turning from the window, he noticed the group he'd been with, Oliver, Dakota, and Denise. Suzanne was gone, but Melissa Livingstone had joined them. Her hands were flung in front of her, gesticulating wildly. Oliver was laughing, Denise and Dakota stone-faced. Randy looked away from them and pushed through the throng.

It was difficult to reach the bar; the mob around Graham was nearly impenetrable, full of people vying for his attention. Randy saw Suzanne at the front, talking demonstratively to Graham, with much determination. Graham's eyes, cold and dead, peered past her through the crowd, off in Randy's direction. He seemed totally listless, barely alive. Then a trace of life flickered across his face, and he smiled, directly at Randy. Randy was stunned. It seemed as if Graham had been waiting for him.

He crept forward, feeling as if Graham were pulling him nearer, that the crowd was parting, that nothing could stand in his way. Trembling, he reached the front and stood before Graham and Suzanne, noting how Graham's eyes were bloodshot and how he reeked of alcohol, still sensing the tug he'd felt, yet profoundly upset. Graham looked even sicker, thinner, and weaker than he had from a distance.

Graham sipped his wine, no longer smiling, again listless. His eyes remained on Randy.

Suzanne paid no heed to Randy's arrival. "We know you're not quite up to a book tour," she was saying to Graham, "but maybe we could arrange a little something with some talk shows."

Graham winced. Turning sharply, he glowered at Suzanne, then moved his eyes back to Randy. His nurse stood behind him, stiffly composed, ignoring Suzanne's words and, it seemed, everything else in the room.

Unnerved by Graham's scrutiny and by his enfeebled appearance, Randy looked down at the bottles of wine on the bar. They were reflecting the gallery's overhead lights, glowing. He looked up.

Graham winked at him.

"Do you think you could manage it?" Suzanne asked Graham, her voice cheerfully pert. "'Good Morning, America,' something like that? It would help us a lot." She stared at his wheelchair, then scanned his gaunt body. "I think you'd make quite an impression."

Graham's face turned red. With an abrupt, furious motion, he twisted his head toward her. "What the fuck are you talking about, you miserable bitch?" He spoke cuttingly, his words slurred yet distinct. "What the fuck do you know about *anything?*"

Suzanne pulled back, alarmed. "Why...what...? I mean, I...I didn't...God, you're demented!"

Behind them, Randy heard a woman scream, "It's my world, too! This is my fucking space!" He spun around. Melissa Livingstone was standing to the side of Oliver, Dakota, and Denise. She had ripped off her blue frock, thrown it on the ground, and, wearing only black sneakers and a pair of frilly pink panties, raised her arms above her head. Innumerable welts were visible on her chest, back, and legs.

"Yeah, this is my fucking space!" she cried. "All those mother-fuckers can eat shit!"

The crowd in the room, more hushed now, moved forward, forming a large circle around Melissa and watching her perform. Many murmured appreciatively, others giggled with delight.

Recovering from Graham's outburst, Suzanne peered at Melissa with marked uneasiness. *"Downtown,"* she muttered, and looked at her watch.

Graham, pointedly disregarding Suzanne, kept his eyes on Melissa for just a moment, then, turning to Randy, smiled and said, "Oh, yes."

Randy whirled back to him.

"Oh, yes," Graham said once more, still smiling. "See." He gestured toward Melissa. "Didn't I tell you everything had turned to shit? I'm not going to miss it at all."

"Motherfuckers!" Melissa screamed. She pushed her hands down the waist of her panties. "Bastards!"

Randy felt as if he were fading. There was something he sensed in Graham, something he could see on his ashen face, something that made him recall, strangely, the warmth he'd felt outside and in the dream he'd had that afternoon, a link with the past, with Dennis and, stranger still, more powerfully than anything else, with Garth. He remembered all the things he and Graham had done, what had occurred between them that last time in particular. None of this frightened him anymore. For some reason, seeing Graham now, he felt safe.

"They can all wallow in their shit," Graham mumbled. His voice grew weaker. "It's what they deserve."

The warmth had to be deep inside, though, Randy told himself, the way it had been in that dream, like it had been in the country, like it had been with Garth. It was so cold in here.

Graham took a slug of wine, then started to cough. He couldn't stop.

His nurse, her composure shattered, leaned over him, extremely concerned. "Oh, Mr. Mason, please! Don't you think you've had enough?"

Drawn back, terrified by Graham's fit, Randy looked behind him. Jake and Jackson Reeves were pushing through the mob surrounding Melissa, coming toward him.

Graham coughed much harder, wheezing. His face turned beet-red. "Come on," his nurse said frantically, speaking to Randy and Suzanne, "give him some room. He needs to breathe."

"Yes. Yes, yes, of course." Suzanne glanced at her watch. "It's time for me to go anyway. I'm late for dinner." She hurried toward the gallery's entrance.

Randy slipped away to the opposite end of the bar, then, his heart racing, watched as the nurse, crouched on her knees, attended Graham, desperately checking his pulse. Graham was no longer coughing, but his wheezing sounded worse, more alarming. His head was thrown back against his wheelchair, and his eyes were shut. At least a dozen of his friends, who had been standing nearby waiting to speak with him, hovered over him now, all appearing apprehensive.

"You've fucked me up long enough!" Melissa screamed in the background, striking her bare chest with her fists. The crowd around her roared with approval.

"So where's the whip?" a man near the front shouted at her.

"Fuck off!" Melissa struck her chest once more. Apparently she had forgotten to bring one.

Jake and Jackson showed up and stood beside Randy, both smiling and intoxicated. They seemed unmindful of the pandemonium around them.

"Hey, sweetheart," Jake cried, greeting Randy. "You remember Jackson Reeves, don't you?"

A lecherous grin on his face, Jackson touched Randy's right hand and limply fondled it. Randy moved away from him.

"It's been much too long, hasn't it?" Jackson said. "I'm going to be in the city for a few more weeks. My company's on tour. We can make up for lost time." He studied Randy, then, nonplussed, added, "Goodness, you're looking older."

Randy recoiled, moving further away.

Disturbed, Jake said, "Nah, it's just the light in here. Come on, let me get you a drink."

Randy glanced toward the bar, at a waiter pouring white wine into clear, shiny glasses that were glittering under the gallery's lights, then off toward Graham. He was slumped back in his wheelchair, his nurse near him, many of his friends still there as well. His eyes were open now, and he was breathing laboriously. All the blood seemed to have drained from his face.

Angling away, Randy looked toward the front window. It's black as hell out there, he thought. He swerved back to Jake, who, two glasses of wine in his hands, was passing one to Jackson and keeping the other for himself.

"Jackson and I thought maybe you and him could get together this weekend," Jake said to Randy.

Jackson weighed Jake's words. "Yes, but I…"

Jake leaned toward him. "What's that?" His voice was unsteady.

Jackson formed a weak smile. "Well, you know I like them young."

Jake chuckled. "Jesus, Jackson, you don't want to break any laws, do you?" He sounded nervous. "I mean, Randy's just a kid."

Randy's eyes returned to the darkness.

"Those cunts have had it their way for too long!" Melissa screamed.

Randy reeled his head around. The crowd watching Melissa's act had thinned out, many having dispersed to other parts of the gallery. To the right of Melissa, against a wall, he noticed Calvin necking with the man in the kilt. Oliver stood near them. Seeing Randy, he raised a hand, beckoning him to come over.

"I suppose you're right," Jackson said to Jake. "Besides…" He stopped, then, looking at Randy, remarked, "Jake tells me you're full service now."

Randy couldn't look at Jackson, could not take in what he'd said. He didn't want to talk to him, didn't want to be here; he wanted to be with Garth. He glanced at the bar.

Speaking to Randy and Jackson, Jake asked, "So are you two gonna get together or what?"

At the other end of the bar, Randy heard the nurse talking to one of Graham's friends: "I'd better get him home. I think this has all been too much for him."

Turning, Randy saw her start to wheel Graham across the floor. Graham's head had fallen to the side, and his eyes were shut again. Proceeding rapidly toward the entryway, two of Graham's friends beside her, the nurse pushed the wheelchair past Dakota and Denise, who had moved away from the crowd surrounding Melissa and were standing alone, chatting.

"Graham! Graham!" Dakota called when he saw them pass. "Graham, where are you going?"

The nurse and Graham's friends continued walking. Graham's eyes remained closed.

"Hey, sweetheart, did you hear me?" Jake said to Randy.

Randy looked at him, then at the glasses of wine on the bar. He felt himself inch toward them.

"Well?" Jake asked.

Randy's eyes shot back to Jake. "Leave me the fuck alone, why don't you?" he cried. He stared past Jake, searching for Graham in the crowd, but could not see him. In one quick movement he veered to the bar, grasped a glass, and raised it to his lips, swallowing the wine in one gulp. He placed the empty glass on the bar and picked up another one, then returned to Jake and Jackson.

"Jesus, sweetheart, what's got into you?"

Jackson stood by Jake's side, silent and edgy.

Randy felt the wine careening to his depths. It was the warmth he'd been longing for. The gallery seemed to become brighter; he wanted to absorb its light. He thought the room had vanished, and could see nothing. Then, for just an instant, he saw Garth on the hill.

They stayed for another hour, long after Jackson—perplexed by Randy's behavior, increasingly tense—had gone; long after Dakota, Denise, and Oliver had left as well. Randy remained close to Jake, avoiding anyone else in the room, his eyes on the window, waiting to get away. He tried not to drink too much, just enough to mellow him out. It had been weeks since he'd had any alcohol, and he found it went straight to his head. But it helped take some of the edge off.

Jake was less cautious, grabbing glass after glass of wine from the bar. He appeared entranced by everyone he saw, although the people he attempted to speak with were indifferent to him. Despite

Randy's pleas, he insisted on staying until after nine-thirty, when the gallery was nearly empty.

Back on the street, it was clear from Jake's unsteady bearing just how drunk he was. He was in a good mood.

"Oh, sweetheart," he exulted, "I'm so glad m'baby decided to have a little drink with me in there, that we're together again. Shit, isn't life great?"

Randy felt the warm air engulf him, an immense relief from the gallery's chill. He remembered his dream, being in that grave with Garth, and felt high, pleasantly so, yet also, just beneath this, distinctly melancholy. He nodded back at Jake.

Jake was weaving. He threw an arm across Randy's shoulders. Consumed by the warmth and by his vision of Garth, Randy moved closer to him.

They bought a large can of beer at a delicatessen and shared it during the cab ride home. When they reached their apartment building, Randy felt more intoxicated.

Inside, Jake tossed off his clothes and fell into bed. Randy undressed, too, and lay next to him, then became erect. He snuggled closer.

"Fuck me," he whispered. "Please, fuck me." He took hold of Jake's penis, thinking of Garth.

Moving clumsily, Jake grabbed Randy around the waist and laughed. "Oh, baby, baby, I think m'baby was a hit tonight."

Randy pushed his groin into Jake and bit his neck. He didn't want to hear anything he said; he just wanted to dissolve into his skin, into its heat, into that dream.

"Really, I think Jackson likes you. He'll probably call tomorrow." Jake giggled, rolling away from Randy. "M'baby did sort of scare him for a minute, though, didn't he? Jesus, sweetheart, you can be such a nut sometimes."

Randy threw his arms around Jake's chest and pulled himself into his back, moving a hand down to Jake's penis, wanting it inside, splitting him apart, to feel semen streaming through him, carrying him to Garth. He suspected he'd be carried there soon enough. But he needed to be certain that he was.

Jake rolled further away. "I'm so tired, sweetheart."

"Come on, fuck me!" Just to make sure, Randy thought, just to be... He smiled. Just to be safe.

Jake was already half asleep. "Oh, sweetheart, sweetheart," he mumbled, then passed out.

Still erect, Randy listened to him snore. He knew he'd never sleep, not now. There was something that he felt he needed to do, although he wasn't certain what it was. He sat up, glancing down at Jake's gaping mouth, then at the clock by the bed. It was ten-thirty. He rose, walked to the window, and stared out at the blackness, recalling Graham's gaunt face and dead eyes, feeling, somehow, as if he were a part of Graham, desperate to become more so. He could not stay still. He wanted another drink.

Then he remembered the pills he'd stolen. He wavered, wondering whether he really wanted to get into *that* tonight. He decided that he did, that if he got high enough, he could figure things out, he'd know what to do.

He hurried to the chest of drawers, pulled out the pill bottle, and swallowed three dexedrine, found his clothes on the floor and dressed. He sat on a chair, waiting for the pills to take effect, thinking about the book party, about what a nightmare it had been, then about Garth.

Ten minutes later the telephone rang.

Garth! he thought, and ran to it.

"Randy?" The voice on the other end sounded tentative and uneasy.

Randy saw a pack of cigarettes beside the phone. The voice was familiar, yet seemed totally strange.

"Randy, it's John, John Stanley. I...I'm sorry I called so late."

Randy gripped the phone, then took a cigarette from the pack and struck a match. He thought he could feel a hint of the dexedrine. "I can't talk, John. Not now. I've gotta do something." He was sweating.

"It'll only take a minute." John's tone was more even. "It's just that I haven't seen you in a while, at meetings or anything, and I... I've been thinking a lot about things."

"What do you mean?" Randy was shocked; John sounded much gentler than he usually did, than he ever had.

"You know, about my life, what I've done, what's been going on lately, and…well, I want to apologize for the way I acted at Aggie's."

"Apologize?"

John laughed nervously. "I guess Leonard and the others would say I'm trying to make an amends. And you know what, they'd be right, that *is* what I'm trying to do." A brief pause. Then, softly: "Believe me, I'm really sorry."

"Wha…what for?" Randy nearly hung up. John's apology embarrassed him. It was so unlike John. He wondered if the program was having an effect on him, if it was possible to change. He couldn't believe that, didn't want to think about it.

"I expected too much from you." John stopped, faltering. "I mean, I thought you could…I don't know, fill some sort of gap, help it all make sense. I should have known that you were as confused as me."

Randy was certain he could feel the dexedrine now, much stronger this time. He wanted to run outside, into the heat. "Look, John, I'm really busy."

"You see a lot of crap in the rooms." John seemed not to have heard Randy. "It's all we've got, though. I mean, I never want to go back to being the way I was before…before I got sober."

"Yeah. Yeah, sure, I know, but I…" Randy dragged on his cigarette and glanced toward the doorway. "Look, I've gotta go."

"Oh, yeah?" John hesitated. Then, sounding worried, he asked, "Listen, Randy, are you all right? Is everything okay?"

Randy threw the phone down and ran out the door.

He was deeply agitated by John's call, and his agitation only grew worse when he noticed Sylvia standing at the bottom of the stairs.

She appeared agitated as well. "Oh, Randy," she cried when she saw him, "Despair's gone. Hugh threw her out."

Randy stared back at her. He found what she'd said incomprehensible.

"That bastard got totally fucked up," she continued, distraught. "He said he couldn't take my cats any longer, that he hated Despair. He…he just picked her up, threw her out the door, then left, and…" She glanced at the stairwell, sniffling, becoming more discomposed. "Shit, where is she? God, I hope she didn't get outside." She burst into tears.

Randy flew toward the doorway, more agitated than ever. "I…I've gotta go, I'm late. But…but I'll be back later, I'll help you find her."

Sylvia looked under the stairwell. "Baby, where are you?" she called, sobbing.

Randy rushed out.

The street appeared darker than he'd ever imagined it could be, the street lights dim and scary. They reminded him of hulking black trees, and seemed threatening. He drifted west, through dense, humid air, not sure where he was going or what he had to do, becoming more and more agitated, terrified.

Near 4th Street and Second Avenue he saw bright lights and a large crowd. Relieved by the bustle, the light and the distraction, he hurried there.

A film crew was shooting a night scene, one that took place by an apartment building on the northwest corner. Long trailers were parked near the curb, and sodium lights had been set up around the building's doorway, illuminating half of the block. At least a hundred people were watching.

Randy heard a fat woman at the back of the crowd speaking to an older woman standing beside her. "I can't believe it, Ruth," she said, thrilled. "Who'd of ever thought that Demi Moore'd be here on 4th Street?"

"Come on," her friend replied, "Demi's not here. Those all're just extras."

The first woman shook her head. "You never know."

No longer frightened, excited instead, Randy looked toward the front of the crowd at the film set, searching for Demi Moore. He had seen her in a film a few months before, a romantic comedy he'd attended with Sylvia. He couldn't find her; all he could see were the film's technicians and five women extras, each of them dressed in a miniskirt and a sequined halter top.

Several yards to his right, he heard a clear, piping voice: "Demi's gotta be around here somewhere, sugar. I mean, we've been here for almost two hours already. I've *gotta* meet her. I was meant to."

Randy turned and saw Fey speaking to Stella. Neither noticed him; both were gawking at the film set.

Fey continued talking: "Demi's one of the biggest stars around these days. You know that, don't you, Stella? Not a big as Kim was, of course, but then who is?"

"Shhh!" Stella hissed at him. "Demi'll hear you."

Randy wanted to laugh. He was astonished at how glad he was to see them, by how comfortably familiar they appeared, Fey in his tight old jeans and a filthy pink blouse, Stella in a blue Barbie T-shirt. He felt a rush from the dexedrine—he could definitely feel it now—and did laugh, out loud. The two women he'd heard speaking before stared at him. He kept his eyes on Fey and Stella.

"Maybe Demi'll give us a part," Fey was saying. "Maybe they're looking for some old-time glamour queens."

A teenaged boy walked by carrying a radio that was playing a song Randy recognized, its tune plaintive, its beat pronounced: "Oooh, baby, I want you, I need you, I want you so bad."

"Could you keep it down back there?" one of the film's technicians shouted at the boy.

The boy moved on, his pace erratic. It was apparent that he was stoned and that he had not absorbed this command. Drawn to the music coming from his radio, surprisingly touched by it, Randy started to follow him.

"Yeah, sugar, this could be our big break," he heard Fey say to Stella as he left. He decided he'd visit them again someday.

He followed the music for more than three blocks, strolling in time to the song's beat, swept up in its rueful mood and by the dexedrine cascading through him. The tune, sweetly melancholy, stayed with him even after the boy entered an apartment building just off Broadway. The notes seemed to carry him west.

He walked crosstown on 4th Street. Everything he saw, the buildings and people he passed, the cars speeding by, appeared hazy in the heat, unformed. He felt distant from it all, as if he were part of the thick, still air, of the warmth surrounding him, of the clear sky, of its crescent moon. He remembered all the times he'd traversed this same route while going to Graham's, then reminded himself that Graham would be dead soon. Garth would be, too. They'd go where Dennis had gone, to a world unlike any Randy had ever known.

Near Sheridan Square he tried to find a café he had frequented in the days before he'd met Graham, one of the ones where he used to sit for hours, imagining what the lives of the people he'd observed there had been like, impossibly glamorous, he'd felt then, so unlike his own. He hadn't visited this café in a while, since he'd started to see that world through Graham's eyes, learned what it had become. The café was gone. In its place was a new restaurant, La Vida, one that appeared expensively trendy, like Flora's, where Garth had worked. Flora's was only a few blocks away, he recalled. He almost started to cry.

A man and woman in their twenties, well-dressed and attractive, stood in front of La Vida, attempting to hail a cab. The man was drunk, the woman angry.

"It was the coke," she snapped at him as a cab pulled up. "That fucking coke!"

Reeling, the man fell into the cab. The woman followed him, slamming the door.

Randy watched them drive off, abruptly, unexpectedly furious. Monsters, he thought, fucking monsters. Shaking, he lit a cigarette, for a moment not sure where he was. He managed to reorient himself: Graham's apartment was just two blocks from here. He felt very alone. He wanted to visit Graham, but realized this was now impossible. He waited for nearly two minutes, uncertain. Then, suddenly decisive, he started west on Christopher Street. He knew what he could do.

He walked past bars and all-night delicatessens, noticing how few people were on the street at this hour, convinced that years before there had been many more, but that most of them were dead. He imagined himself as Dennis, cruising the bars and the street, and wondered if Dennis and Garth had ever met, if they'd had sex. This seemed a possibility. He smiled. The thought appealed to him.

At the end of Christopher he arrived at a wide, busy highway and crossed it at a light. There was a promenade on the other side, many piers jutting out from it toward the Hudson River. He debated which one to explore, staring at the pier in front of him. Roughly two dozen men were pacing its length, and he felt it too crowded. He needed space; he wanted to breathe.

He walked a few blocks north, passing pier after pier, taking in the hot, tranquil air, feeling one with it and with the night.

At 14th Street he came to a pier that looked deserted. Music ebbed out from far away, from close to the river, he could tell, an old disco tune sung by a woman with a sad, alto voice: "The love we had is getting weaker. Tell me what went wrong." He started down the pier toward the song.

He saw no one as he walked, not a soul, yet the music grew louder: "I've been waiting so long, waiting for it to return." He knew there were people nearby.

He found them at the end of the pier, two men necking on a bench, a large radio on the ground beside them. To their left, at the pier's edge, by the river, a tall, dark-haired, shirtless boy danced alone, swaying to the music, his tanned skin lit by the street lamps positioned near the water.

"My life feels like it's ending," the woman sang. The sound of a calliope was prominent behind her. "The time I had with you is gone."

Randy stared at the boy, enthralled by his sensuous motions. Dazed, he realized he'd seen him before, on his way to Graham's that last time, dancing beside a telephone booth. He started moving toward him.

The boy saw Randy approach and, swaying ever more sensuously, smiled at him.

The music continued in the background: "We can get it back, I know we can."

Randy drew nearer, and the boy undulated forward, stopping a few inches in front of him. Saying nothing, he smiled and swayed. Then, referring to the music, seductive, he asked, "So do you like Violet? Miss Violet Winter? The Queen of Disco?"

The cadence of his voice was soft and rhythmical; Randy thought it sounded melodious, like a part of the song. He didn't want to respond, to risk breaking the mood. He stood still, absolutely certain what was about to happen, what he needed to do.

"There'll never be another Violet." The boy raised an arm and scratched his back, slipping toward Randy. "Everything from those days is gone."

Randy stared at the black hair in his armpit, then at his bronzed chest. He was not surprised when he saw a small purplish lesion just below his left nipple. "Yeah," he answered. "Yeah, you're right, it's all over."

The boy came closer and pulled Randy to him, wrapping his arms around him and kissing his neck. Feeling the boy's warm, sweaty skin, catching his sweet scent, Randy pressed his crotch into him, then glanced over his shoulder at the two men on the bench. They were still necking, oblivious to everything else. He wondered if they'd just met or if they were lovers. He decided the latter was the case, that they'd been together for years and years, happily so. He couldn't imagine what that would be like. Garth's face came to him, his features blurred. He focused on the music: "We can get it back! We can, I know we can!"

The boy moved his lips up to Randy's ear. "They were nasty in those days," he whispered. "Down and nasty."

Just then, with a startling clarity, Randy pictured the AA meeting on Third Avenue, Garth at the front, sunlight streaming across the room. He wondered if there was a meeting going on somewhere now, but decided it was too late for one. It wasn't meant to be.

"Yeah, nasty," the boy whispered again. "They were nasty then. We can get nasty, too."

Randy dropped his eyes to the lesion on the boy's chest and let them rest there, aware of the night's heat, of a warm breeze blowing past him, carrying him off, it seemed, over the pier, east to the street, back to Graham's apartment, to Graham and Dennis. He wanted to join them. "Nasty?" he asked the boy, looking up. The street lamps shimmered, resembling for a moment the trees he remembered from Canada.

"Uh-huh." The boy caressed the denim on Randy's pants, directly above his penis. *"Nasty."*

Randy felt the boy's hand on his crotch and became erect. Another warm breeze stirred, and he sensed himself being carried off once more, this time to Flora's, to Garth. He lowered his right hand, unzipped the boy's pants, and took hold of his penis. Raising his eyes, he probed the boy's grinning face, saying nothing, smiling back at him.

Then he spoke, his voice very low: "Okay."

The boy slid one of his hands between Randy's legs. "What's that?"

"I said 'okay.'" Randy's voice was now louder and much clearer. The resolve he heard in his tone amazed him. He glanced toward the shimmering street lamps, then gazed at the boy's bare chest. His smile grew wider. "Sure." He tightened his grasp on the boy's penis. It was erect. "Yeah, let's get nasty."

Also from Akashic Books:

The Fuck-Up by Arthur Nersesian
274 pages, trade paperback
ISBN: 1-888451-03-3
PRICE: $13
"The charm and grit of Nersesian's voice is immediately enveloping, as the down-and-out but oddly up narrator of his terrific novel, *The Fuck-Up*, slinks through Alphabet City and guttural utterances of love."

—*The Village Voice*

Once There Was a Village by Yuri Kapralov
163 pages, trade paperback
ISBN: 1-888451-05-X
PRICE: $12
"This was the era which saw the 'invasion' of hippies and junkies and swarms of runaway boys and girls who became prey to pimps, tactical police and East Village violence.... In this personal memoir of his experiences, Kapralov relives the squalor and hazards of community life along Seventh Street between Avenues B and C. The street riots of 1966, the break-up of his own stormy marriage, poignant or amusing but always memorably etched stories of the Slavs, Russians, Puerto Ricans, blacks and artists young and old who were his neighbors, his own breakdown–all of it makes a 'shtetl' experience that conjures up something of Gorki and Chagall."

—*Publisher's Weekly*

These books are available at local bookstores or by mail order. Send a check or money order to:

AKASHIC BOOKS
PO BOX 1456
NEW YORK, NY 10009
(Prices include shipping. Outside the US, add $3 to each book ordered.)

Henry Flesh dropped out of Yale in the sixties and moved to Manhattan, where he became immersed in speed and in the vibrant downtown culture. Since then, among other things, he has performed in theater troupes off-off-Broadway, while cavorting at such fabled venues as Max's Kansas City. He spent a great deal of time abroad, including sojourns in London during the height of the glam rock era in the seventies, and in Morocco and Crete. Mr. Flesh currently lives in New York City's East Village, and works as a book and magazine editor. He has just completed a novel about the end of the world.